THE SHADOWS BEYOND

TJ ROSE

CONTENTS

Introduction	VII
Epigraph	IX
1. Cinn	1
2. Julien	11
3. Cinn	16
4. Julien	27
5. Cinn	39
6. Julien	63
7. Cinn	74
8. Cinn	86
9. Julien	96
10. Julien	111
11. Cinn	123
12. Cinn	140
13. Cinn	157
14. Julien	173
15. Julien	189
16. Julien	196

17. Cinn . . . 204

18. Cinn . . . 213

19. Cinn . . . 230

20. Julien . . . 233

21. Cinn . . . 241

22. Cinn . . . 250

23. Cinn . . . 261

24. Julien . . . 270

25. Julien . . . 282

26. Cinn . . . 295

27. Julien . . . 303

28. Julien . . . 311

29. Cinn . . . 315

30. Julien . . . 329

31. Julien . . . 339

32. Cinn . . . 345

33. Julien . . . 347

34. Cinn . . . 355

35. Julien . . . 358

36. Cinn . . . 362

37. Julien . . . 364

38. Cinn . . . 374

Fullpage image . . . 380

Continue the Adventure...   381

Acknowledgements   382

Also by TJ Rose   383

About the Author   385

Welcome! The Shadows Beyond is part one in the Shadow and Light duology, an urban fantasy MM romance.

Before you proceed into the world of Auri, please take heed of the following content warnings:

- explicit adult content

- one usage of period-appropriate homophobic language

- alcohol & substance abuse (side characters)

- historic child abuse

- smoking

- grieving for deceased family members

- drowning, mention of trauma

This book is written in British English.

There is a crack, a crack in everything
That's how the light gets in

- Leonard Cohen, Anthem

One

CINN

*T*hud, thud. Thud, thud.

Cinn's head pulsated with pain that did nothing to help the disorienting fog enveloping his mind.

His bleariness cleared, and an oval-shaped window came into focus. Outside was only darkness. Darkness and…

He blinked.

Holy fuck, was he on an *aeroplane*?

A large intake of breath was his last before his throat tightened. His heart kicked into overdrive, as a sickening wave of vertigo struck him.

Think think think.

He squeezed his eyes closed. His limited oxygen supply had him gasping for air.

After four shaky breaths, he forced some level of coherent thought back into his brain.

Why are you, Cinn Saunders, someone who's never left England before, and has a crippling fear of flying, thousands of miles high in a tin can?

He pried his eyes open to find this wasn't any old tin can—it had to be a private jet, if the lack of other passengers, aside from a woman sleeping opposite him, was anything to go by. Any crew remained to be seen. *Oh God, please let there be a crew. Don't tell me she left this thing on autopilot and then took a nap.*

The jet featured comfy cream sofa-seats and polished metal tables. The table in front of him housed an ice bucket with an open champagne bottle poking out of it—wherever they were travelling, they were going there in luxury. With trembling hands, he reached down to unzip his rucksack, placed by his feet. His headphones were clearly visible at the top. *Thank God.*

He'd packed the bag earlier today... *Why?*

Cinn rubbed his pounding head, which his panic-fuelled adrenaline was intensifying. Was too much alcohol to blame for it? No. This felt different. Hazier. His brain worked overtime trying to piece together the tatters of his fragmented memory.

His most overwhelming sensation: guilt.

After that? Fear.

It hit him like a punch to the gut—a visceral reaction so deep, he pressed his fist to his mouth.

It was meant to be a simple job. Return to Rosewood Parlour, the restaurant where he was undertaking a culinary training programme, in the early hours of the morning, to let two of Heino Richter's henchmen in. Escort them into the manager's office. Open the safe. Close his eyes, and pretend it wasn't happening.

It would have all gone to plan if only Cinn had controlled his stress levels. Why, oh why, did he not think to bring his Walkman with him? Maybe then he could have used his music to stop his episode. After the safe's door had clicked open, by his own hand, he'd watched as Ronnie and Spiky scooped fistful after fistful of the last few evenings' takings into their duffle bags. That was when it got too much—when the vision of their head chef, Benny, had popped into his head, shaking his head with so much *disappointment* in his eyes.

Only a few hours before the robbery, Cinn had been with Benny—and Sarah, their newest dishwasher—in the side alley adjacent to the restaurant, taking a two-minute smoke break. Benny had told one of his hilarious stories in his thick Irish accent, while Sarah threw her head back in laughter, and Cinn leant against the wall looking between them both, thinking, *this is alright.*

So when the reality of robbing his own restaurant, the place he'd grown to love over the last couple of months, had hit, so did the panic attack.

And they never ended well.

This one—this visit to *the dark place* as he'd named it in his childhood—had ended in particular disaster. Namely, the death of Heino's two men, in addition to the two police officers who'd burst through the door at precisely the wrong moment.

Four dead bodies.

That's what the two detectives had said again and again, in the interview room, after his arrest.

As if he didn't know. As if he hadn't *seen it.*

The dead female police officer had possessed the same chestnut curls as his mother. He'd fixated on them, sprayed out above her expressionless face and her lifeless body.

After an eternity in a holding cell, they'd then left him waiting in an interview room to stew for hours, the cool metal chair and the bleak walls his only company. Well, and his court-issued attorney. They'd barely said a word to each other since he'd refused to engage with the tired-looking, middle-aged woman. Although what could he possibly say? How could he explain the unexplainable?

Well, the truth is, I accidentally fell into the dark place and then brought back some sort of hell-demon-beast thing, which laughed like a manic clown, picked up Ronnie's knife and slaughtered everyone else in the room while I just screamed and screamed.

Nope. Wasn't going to fly.

The two detectives eventually arrived, in similar dark-navy suits, two pigs in a sty, sliding into the room with their badges flashing.

"Interview of Cinnamon Saunders, commencing at seventeen zero five on November third, nineteen ninety-five…"

He knew the drill already. After all, he'd done this all once before.

He'd answered, 'no comment' to every question in a row for several hours, despite their mounting frustration. They slid photograph after photograph in front of him, stills from the security cameras. Cinn had touched an image of himself on the floor, his hands clutching either side of his head. He still possessed the faintest lingering of the familiar headache that had struck him like a sledge-hammer, a thousand invisible needles jabbing at the very core of his consciousness.

"And this," one of the detectives had said, "is where it gets interesting."

Interesting. This was the word used to describe the moment Cinn's life—his small but precious life that he'd built from the rubble all for himself—fell apart. *Interesting.*

Another glossy piece of paper had been pushed towards him. This time, a printout of pure white. A photograph of nothing. The poor detectives, and apparently their team of technology specialists, were baffled by the CCTV printouts. They knew it wasn't Cinn's doing, of course. They wanted to know how Heino Richter had managed to tamper with it.

"You know, Cinnamon, we're trying to help you here. We know you were forced to take Ronnie and Samuel into Rosewood yesterday. We know Heino Richter set all this up. Tell us your side of the story, give us something on Richter, and we can—"

"No comment," Cinn spat. Any information he gave on Richter would have immediate repercussions for Tyler. The man he'd done all this for.

It was at that point *she'd* arrived. The woman currently sleeping opposite him.

She'd stormed into the room like she owned it, dressed in her stark white suit, her heels creating a loud *clickety clack*. Her gaze drifted over Cinn to magnetise towards the two detectives, unblinking. "Gentlemen," she said, voice like honey. "This room is now mine. As is your guest here."

One detective's face reddened as he stood up, wagging a thick finger. "Miss, you're interrupting a criminal investigation. On what authority—"

They were silenced by the flash of a badge Cinn was too far away to read.

An outraged, "You can't just—"

The woman raised her hand, blue eyes frosting. "I've had five hours sleep in the last forty-eight hours, three cups of coffee, and just reduced your receptionist to tears. I'm on a roll. Don't push your luck."

With a glance at each other, the two men scooped up the photographs, turned off the recording system, and filed out of the door, slamming it shut behind them.

"You too, Mrs. Thompson."

His attorney had blinked, looking baffled. Cinn prepared for her to protest—surely she didn't want to leave him all alone with no representation?—but the woman only gave him a weak, confused smile before leaving the room. She was an even more useless attorney than the one he was assigned when he was convicted at sixteen.

The woman in white took the seat opposite him. She smiled a too-white smile. "Cinnamon, isn't it?"

He'd cringed, feeling his face pull into the scowl it made whenever he heard his full name. There were many things he'd never forgive his mother for, and his name was one of them. "Just Cinn."

"Just Cinn. Nice to meet you. I think you'll want to come with me."

What happened after that was a whirlwind.

They'd taken a rental car from the police station to his house. She'd said he would need a few things. That they were going somewhere. Luckily, his flatmates were all out. He'd grabbed some clothes... his Walkman, as many cassettes as would fit in the remaining rucksack space...

They'd gotten back in the car. *Why, oh why, had he got back in that damned car?*

On the drive out of the city, she'd answered everything he asked before that with elusive and vague responses.

He'd given up attempting to talk to her, and pulled his headphones over his head, cranking the volume up until his eardrums were being shredded by Pixie's *Doolittle* beats. Reciting the nonsense lyrics of the opening track to himself must have calmed him down, because he eventually fell asleep.

When he awoke, they were at some sort of fancy airfield place—glossy jets lined up like toys in a neat row on a concrete field.

His memories got even fuzzier.

Seeing the jet, and screaming at the woman that there was no way he was going anywhere with her, no way he was *flying* in an *aeroplane*.

The woman offering him a bottle of pills from her pocket.

Screaming at her some more, saying that there was no way in hell he was taking anything.

And then... darkness.

The bitch must have drugged him, after all.

His anger brought him back to full alertness, and Cinn's eyes darted around the jet, taking stock of his options while trying not to think about the fact he was flying thousands of feet above the Earth in a metal bird that could explode or crash at any moment.

Cinn glared at the sleeping woman. Light wrinkles made her certainly past fifty, yet her dark, glossy grey hair was cut into the box-fringe style often seen on women thirty years her junior, hovering above thick-rimmed black glasses. An unfinished glass of champagne sat on the table between them. Cinn leaned forward and flicked the glass over, spilling the liquid all over her lap.

Oops. Turbulence.

Her eyes snapped open as she muttered various curse words while wiping her white linen trousers with her sleeves.

"Morning," Cinn said with a perfectly straight face.

The woman glared, lips pursed, blue eyes icy.

Cinn countered with a foul look of his own. "I told you not to drug me."

A razor-sharp smile. "I didn't."

Their staring contest continued until Cinn grew bored. He didn't need games. He needed answers.

"I need to go back to London," he snapped. "As soon as we land. My friend is in danger."

"The same 'friend' who forced you to allow Heino Richter access to burgle your restaurant, destroying your career prospects and your life?"

Her words stunned Cinn into silence.

"He didn't force me," he eventually got out. "I offered." It was true. When Tyler had appeared at his doorstep, black and blue, eyes so swollen he could barely recognise him, Cinn promised him he'd sort it out.

Because that was what he did.

Tyler fucked up. Cinn sorted it.

Just this time. One last time. How many times had he promised himself that?

"What I don't understand," said the woman, genuine curiosity peppering her voice. "Is how Richter thought there would be enough in your little restaurant's safe to cover Tyler's debt."

Cinn flinched backwards, his head colliding with the seat. "How... How do you know all of this?"

The woman smiled again, adding more fuel to the inferno of anger quickly building within Cinn.

"It was just meant to be a start," he said. "The first of a few jobs I'd help Richter with. And then Tyler would be free of him for good. He agreed not to let Tyler deal for him again if I got him the money. Fuck knows what's going to happen to Tyler now, if Ricther hasn't got the cash. That's why I need to go back. Even if I'm in a cell, I can call people—"

"You'll be able to call people when we land. We're not going to the middle of the jungle."

Cinn turned to look out of the window, which he'd avoided so far, needing to break eye contact with the infuriating woman. The dizzying expanse of clouds and sky sent an immediate wave of nausea through him.

Rage boiled up, pulsating through every vein. He'd been taken from London, drugged, and then forced into enduring one of his worst nightmares—flying.

Cinn jumped to his feet, snarling, "You still haven't told me where we're going or why you've kidnapped me!"

The woman tucked a long grey strand of hair behind her ear. "Sit down."

"Fuck off!"

"Sit down, and I'll answer your questions in a civilised manner. Or continue to act like a delinquent child, and you'll quickly find yourself back in a cell, in the company of actual killers. I promise you, you'll be of very little use to Tyler there."

Cinn kicked the side of his opulently cushioned seat, his foot connecting with the metal to send shooting pains up his leg.

"Fuuuuuuuck!" he screamed at the ceiling of the jet. He couldn't face looking at the woman for a second longer.

Cinn clenched his fists, feeling the bite of his nails against his palm. This wasn't good. If he didn't calm down, and soon, he might have another episode. And who knew what that would look like when he was a thousand miles high in the sky. Although, surely there weren't many ghosts up here...

"I imagine it was that unchecked temper of yours that landed you in juvenile prison seven years ago."

The woman was trying to wind him up. And it was working. "Who even are you? How do you know everything about me?"

She remained infuriatingly calm. "Sit. Down."

Cinn gritted his teeth so hard he could taste the metallic tang of his frustration. It took every inch of self-control he possessed to force himself back down into his chair.

"There," said the woman, and Cinn hated giving in to her so much that it physically hurt him. "Now we can talk as adults."

"Fucking *talk* then, lady. Who are you, where are we going, and why the fuck are we going there?"

He braced, prepared for more games, but to his surprise, she leaned back, poured herself another drink from the ice bucket on the floor, and started talking.

"Eleanor Sinclair. Most call me Madame Sinclair. We're currently en route to Valais in Switzerland. I work as a small cog in a large organisation that I'll get to later. My boss, Viktor Sturmhart, has had people keeping tabs on you for a little while now. Most of them stemming from hospital and police reports from years ago. And some psych records."

Cinn internally grimaced, remembering that brief stint in juvie where he'd tried to convince a therapist that 'ghosts are real' as she'd phrased it. They certainly hadn't seen eye to eye on that one.

"When you were arrested, we were faxed copies of every file. Not long after, I was on this very jet, coming to get you. Don't you feel special now?"

Cinn could only blink. Was it possible she... *knew?* She... *believed him?*

"And the reason you want me is....?"

"We believe that you have a rare ability, Cinnamon. *Very* rare. We want to help you. And we want to make sure nobody else gets hurt."

He flinched. "Don't call me that. And what happened at Rosewood... that wasn't my fault."

It was. It was *all* his fault. There had been close calls before, sure. But four deaths? They'd stay with him forever. Maybe even in more than one sense...

"This is exactly why you need to be at the Institute. I can only imagine how much you want to learn how to control yourself, Cinn. To master your skill. We can help you with that."

Was this manipulation on a master level, or was the previously feisty woman's motherly tone genuine?

"The Institute? What's that?"

"The Aurelia Arcanum Institute of Esoteric Sciences is known as the European hub for government, research, and further education for... people like you. And me. It's a multifaceted institution with many sub-sections focusing on different spheres of activity." She paused, scrutinising him. "That all means it's a large collection of groups working together."

"I'm not stupid," he spat. "You don't need to dumb it down."

His head swam. Esoteric sciences? Multifaceted institution? A horrible thought struck him—what if they wanted to experiment on him? Cut open his brain, see what was wrong with it?

Something buzzed. Madame Sinclair pointed upwards, red nail polish gleaming. "Oh look, the seatbelt light."

Cinn grimaced. This was going to be a bumpy ride.

Two

JULIEN

I t was five minutes past midnight when Julien reached the campus. *Witching hour.*

Shadows cast by the branches of centuries-old trees stretched like ghostly fingers across the cobblestone paths, while the ancient spires of St. Caelum's pierced the starlit sky. The downpour had reduced to a heavy drizzle now, and so the hush of the night was broken only by Julien's footsteps as he crossed the lamplit courtyard to reach his destination.

As arranged, Julien found Darcy and Elliot waiting for him beneath the majestic portico of Aurelia Library, its towering columns framing the entrance. *Three cloaked figures meeting under moonlight. Fitting.*

He nodded to them both, impressed that Elliot wasn't late. Although he did look like he'd just rolled out of bed—his dark blond curls looked particularly untamed as he waved at Julien. Darcy, however, seemed as fresh and as sprightly as when he'd seen her that morning.

"Midnight dreary." Darcy pulled down her damp hood. "Ready?" She gestured to the closed, very much locked, door.

Upon Darcy's delicate touch, the ornate, heavy oak swung open with a grandeur befitting the secrets and knowledge held within.

Julien wolf-whistled. "You weren't lying then. And you're sure our presence won't be detected? Because if we're caught..." He shuddered. That would be an awkward conversation indeed.

"Positive. Grace assured me she tripped all the security systems at the end of her shift. We're safe."

The library looked markedly different, being vacant and unlit. Some light seeped in from the oversized windows, and feeble rays of moonlight glinted off elaborate chandeliers. Treading lightly on the polished wooden floor, Julien trailed after Darcy, who led them through the labyrinthine expanse of towering mahogany shelves to their destination—the room they favoured most out of the library's collection of small study spaces.

Elliot clicked the door behind them while Julien headed straight for the unlit fireplace, its mantle adorned with the faces of two stone lions, jaws wide. Bending down, Julien blew hard on the stone-cold coal, once. Flames burst into life.

Warm orange tones lit up the cramped, cosy space—walls lined with rich, aged, leather-bound tomes, and plush armchairs beckoning them into their embrace. Julien's gaze lingered on an especially ancient-looking Morris chair in the corner. If he tried hard enough, he could almost see past echoes of Béatrice sitting in it, her feet tucked up as she turned the pages of her current read at lightning speed.

There was no time for Julien to linger with his sad thoughts tonight—they were on a mission.

"We're lucky I could make it today. Did you hear about the latest umbraphage attack in Toronto?" Elliot asked. "Half of the gendarmerie were dispatched. I'm surprised I wasn't sent too."

"How could we not have heard? It was all Auri could talk about today." Darcy sighed, tucking one long auburn lock behind her ear. "An umbraphage attack following the worst hurricane in decades. It's certainly given the Arcane Purifiers some fuel for their fire."

Elliot's face twisted at the mention of the AP, and so Julien cleared his throat, not wanting the distraction of the controversial topic. "Well Darcy? Did you get it?"

She flashed that smile she reserved for moments of superiority. "Darling, does a star twinkle in the midnight sky? Do Hamlet's soliloquies contain a hint of introspection? Is Bordeaux not the most superior wine—"

Elliot threw a plump cushion at her, something Julien would have done himself if he'd been closer to one.

From her shoulder bag, Darcy removed a planchette: a small, heart-shaped wooden piece, worn by time and use. Its smooth, curved side featured a raised pattern resembling a compass, while on the reverse, two wheels lay opposite a hole to hold a pen.

Julien stared down at the nineteenth-century automatic writing device, not bothering to hide his scepticism. It looked simply antediluvian.

"Are you joking, Darce?" Elliot picked it up. "This piece of plankwood?"

Darcy smacked his arm and grabbed the instrument off him. "Stop that! I had to *borrow* it from Old Figgins's personal collection, and it needs to return in one piece."

"You really think we'll have more success with this than a ouija board?" Elliot inserted his finger into the hole and whizzed it along the table, laughing. "It looks more like a skateboard for mice."

"Let's get on with it," Julien hissed, and carefully removed a piece of blank paper from his satchel. He placed it on the wooden table alongside a blue ballpoint pen.

"You have to be joking." Elliot, aghast, glared at the pen as if it had personally offended him. "She's hardly going to use that to communicate with us. She'd rather die. It's *blue* for one."

"Well, it's lucky for her that she's already dead then," Darcy snapped, before catching herself and glancing at Julien. "Sorry, Julien. I wasn't thinking."

Julien waved his hand. "Elliot's right." Rummaging around in his bag, he procured a sketching pencil. "This will have to do." He placed it in the hole near the edge of the planchette.

Darcy began to prepare the space in earnest: candles lit, lavender burnt, clear quartz placed. All a load of meaningless nonsense, of course, but Julien indulged her. As she chanted undecipherable phrases under her breath, Elliot brought out his pot of aethraven ink and drew a repeated pattern of runes on the floor, encircling the table: Lumistel, Quertarum, Eldraith, Lumistel, Quertarum, Eldraith. Béatrice would have been proud of the handiwork.

From its place under his shirt, Julien slipped Béatrice's locket over his head, to lay it on the table reverently. The locket, adorned with a celestial array of moons and stars, was once her most cherished item, and now it was his. Even more so as he'd had to steal it back from the authorities after her death.

The trio each placed their fingers upon the planchette. The other two had as much confidence in this working as he did, but their expressions still bore traces of apprehension. And of hope.

"Béatrice Eléonore Montaigne, *éclaire notre chemin*. We're here for you. We're ready to listen. Come to us. Talk to us, *ma soeur adorée*." Julien cringed at himself. "We need you," he added, his traitorous voice cracking ever so slightly.

As they focused on the planchette, their fingers poised to guide its movement, a rising tension mounted in the room. Yet the wooden piece remained stubbornly still. Their desperation and grief failed to stir any supernatural response.

The minutes stretched. The fire softly murmured. The wind whispered. But the planchette remained motionless.

With her free hand, Darcy gripped Julien's arm. "I'm sorry, Julien."

Julien swallowed down the disappointment and frustration that threatened to explode out of him. "Well, we had to try. For her."

"We'll get straight back to the elixir tomorrow," said Elliot. "I think we're so close to cracking the dose."

Darcy scoffed. "Close? You almost died last time. In fact, you *were* dead for ninety seconds."

"*Oui*, and it's the closest we've come."

With a scowl, Darcy spoke, in that annoying, firm voice she used whenever she decided she was in charge. "No. You are never again taking Mortalisfade. Ever."

With a sudden burst of intensity, the fire crackled, tiny bright fire-motes bursting out of it, glowing like stardust. Then it spat a smoking piece of yellowed parchment, to fall on an aged shaggy rug. A few lines of looping cursive ran across it.

Julien was the first to grab the note, warm to the touch. He read it, read it again, and looked up to say, "She's got him. She's bringing him here."

Three

CINN

C inn spent the entire aeroplane landing squeezing his eyes shut, trying not to think about the fact that he was still a million miles high, about to crash land in a fiery inferno. The awful pressure tormenting his eardrums didn't *pop* until the very end. He clenched his armrest throughout the last few nerve-racking seconds before the jet hit the ground with a bump.

"I'm never flying again," he ground out.

Another lady, dressed in a smart uniform, appeared and ushered them out of the door and down the boarding stairs. Glancing around, Cinn could only guess they were at another private airfield.

He'd never left England before. Switzerland seemed very similar so far. The same soft hues of pink and orange marking dawn, the sun's gentle rays stretching across an otherwise blue sky.

"So... this is Switzerland?" he asked Madame Sinclair, who was trailing behind him as he crossed the concrete runway. Two attendants carried their bags: his duffle and her large suitcase.

"Indeed."

"But you're not Swiss."

"No. I'm American, but I've lived in Europe for so long, I consider myself a citizen of the world, rather than one nationality."

Cinn rolled his eyes. "And the other people at the Institute..."

"Are from all sorts of places. Mostly Europe. Lots from England. I'm going to introduce you to three people I trust. They're Scottish, American, and French."

Cinn snorted. *Did they walk into a bar?*

"They'll help orient you and get you anything you need."

Would one of them help him get home? Unlikely. He was on his own, just like he always was.

Cinn had a million more questions, but Madame Sinclair directed him towards the back of a sleek black taxi, while she took the front passenger seat. After she reeled off an address in another language, she poured over a notebook, leaving Cinn to sulk in the back. He slipped on his headphones and plugged them into his Walkman.

For the first half an hour, he attempted to take mental notes on which roads they were travelling, but the few signs he saw were hard to pronounce and even harder to remember.

Large dual carriageways eventually turned into winding roads, which turned into small streets—quaint, detached and terraced homes with neat rows of chimneys and windows.

The car slowed, pulling up onto the pavement. After payment was exchanged, the taxi driver handed Madame Sinclair a set of keys.

"We've got you a little maisonette. All to yourself."

"Huh?"

"These are the keys to your new home. Number five. It's sparsely furnished, but it should do for now."

Keys... a *house*... a home all to himself? It was more than he could have ever hoped to dream of.

Shame it was in Switzerland, and he'd be back in London by tomorrow night.

He reached out to grab the keys, the metal cool to the touch.

"I would come in with you, but I've got urgent business to attend to. I imagine you'll want to relax and sleep properly, anyway. Someone will ring ahead to let you know when you'll be taken to the Institute."

"It isn't here?" he asked, then winced. *Obviously, it's not on this road, Cinn.*

"It's a short drive away. We're currently in the town of Talwacht, where lots of us live. You'll like it here."

Cinn scanned the sleepy row of houses, unsure why she would think that. He climbed out of the car.

"Oh, and Cinn?" Madame Sinclair had rolled down her window. "Don't do anything stupid."

The car roared to life and was at the end of the road before Cinn opened his mouth to reply.

He jogged to the front door, desperate to stretch his legs after sitting for so long in the holding cell, aeroplane and car. Once he was inside, he dumped his bag onto a wooden floor and stood still for a moment. The last lingering residual pressure from the plane thumped silence into his ears and he became acutely aware of the sound of his own breath, his own heartbeat. He'd never lived alone, and he didn't want to, either. It must be incredibly lonely.

Even though he wasn't staying, Cinn allowed himself a short tour of the homely house. One bedroom, a double bed claiming most of the floor space. A bathroom with an actual bath. When had he last taken a bath? Back when he was living with his first set of foster parents? A small living room, with a sofa and a tiny television. A dining table big enough for two. A modest sized kitchen, with a loaf of bread and a foil-wrapped block of real butter waiting for him. As he wolfed down two slices, he inspected the kitchen further to find ample cupboard space and a decent stove. Shame he wouldn't be able to use it.

He glanced at the front door. The longer he lingered here, the more tempting it became to stay. To go to this mysterious institute where someone might be able to finally help him, after all these years. Or cut open his brain. Who could say? If he was so special, why had they waited until now to track him down? He didn't trust them as far as he could spit.

But what if...

No. Tyler needed him, and that sealed the deal. He had to get back to London. Lay low until he figured out if he was still a wanted man or not.

Then a last glance at the plush sofa sent a wave of exhaustion cascading down upon him. He blinked, his eyes remaining shut for a fraction too long. He'd 'slept' on the plane, if you could call that drug-induced coma sleep. Before that, he'd only had twenty minutes here and there in the holding cells at the police station. Every inch of his body cried out for rest.

So what would be the harm in a quick nap? Surely he'd be more likely to get home safely if he was fully alert and functional.

He half stumbled towards the sofa, to sink deep within its embrace, letting the darkness of sleep drag him under.

He awoke to far less natural light streaming in through the window. Cinn groaned, pushing his head back into the cushion. It was twilight—he'd slept all day.

Wiping a hand over his face, he peeled himself off the sofa. After one last lingering look around the room, he forced himself towards the front door. His time here was up. He wasn't meant for here, not meant for a life living in a house with a bath and a fancy stove. And if that crazy woman thought for one second he'd do what he was told, she had another thing coming.

Patting his pockets, Cinn stock-checked. In addition to the clothes and cassettes in his bag, he had one lighter, five mints, and zero money. What currency did they even use in Switzerland, anyway?

Well, you've done far more with far less.

He set about rooting through the sparsely furnished apartment for anything worth anything—he'd beg, barter, and steal his way home if he had to.

Cinn briefly contemplated stuffing the wall clock into his bag—it had silver edging and looked vaguely antique—before deciding against it, and leaving empty-handed.

Not a single other soul could be seen on the street, but Cinn crept along the shadows, regardless. He knew exactly what he had to do: find a main road, hitch-hike to the train station, and lock himself in a toilet cubicle at the first sign of a ticket inspector. Simple.

He inserted his *Blunted on Reality* cassette into his Walkman, thinking the title of the Fugees's album apt for his situation, put on his headphones, and walked.

And walked.

And walked some more.

God, what he'd do for a cigarette right now.

Or a map. But mostly a cigarette.

After over an hour of walking through silent residential streets, stomach empty and fingers starting to freeze, the first slivers of regret started to form. Surely this escape plan would have been easier in the daylight of tomorrow?

The clouds parted, and he tried to orientate himself using the moon. He spun until he was fairly sure he was facing west, the direction they'd landed in earlier. A thick layer of trees greeted him, a narrow winding path cutting through what appeared to be a grove. He stared into the darkness, supposing he could use his lighter as a torch, if it really came to that.

He tugged his headphones off his head, wrapping everything up neatly to put back in his bag. This was murder territory.

Indeed, the feeling of being watched pounced upon him as soon as he stepped into the dark thicket. Twice he spun around to check if the footsteps behind him were real or a product of paranoia. When the path widened, he picked up his pace, eager to find civilisation, even if it was just another housing estate.

He squinted through the darkness. The path opened out into a small, grassy clearing. And across it... was that an exit he could see between two brick walls, dimly illuminated by two sconces?

Shadows that had previously hugged the wall moved, blocking his view of the gate. Three silent figures—a woman and two taller men.

Clearly, they weren't hanging out here for fun, but Cinn decided to press on and ignore them completely. He avoided eye contact, ducked his head, and tried to weave around to the left of them.

"Hey," said one of the men, in a European accent Cinn couldn't quite place. Tall, with blond hair falling in curated waves around a pale face. An annoyingly symmetrical face. "Where are you going?" He grabbed Cinn's wrist.

Surprise froze Cinn still.

The auburn-haired girl beside him tutted. "That's not how you greet someone, Julien," she said, a subtle Scottish twang to her voice. The second man—a darker, lean-looking fellow with a lion's mane of corkscrew-tight dark blond curls—laughed.

"None of your business. Unless you want to give me a lift to the train station, let go of my arm." Cinn wrenched his limb free of the vice-like grip, rubbing it to soothe the bruise.

"You're not allowed to leave," the guy stated, in a manner that seemed so matter-of-fact, so absolutely true, Cinn laughed. The asshole was starting to remind him of a spoiled prince, with his pretty face and entitled attitude.

"Watch me."

"I mean it," the guy continued. Was that a trace of panic in his voice? Of fear? "You're under strict instructions to stay within the boundary of this town. Take one more step, and we'll have to restrain you by force." He flashed Cinn a predatory smile.

Who were these people? Madame Sinclair's guard dogs? Cinn almost stopped then, almost gave up. Then he heard the words clear as day, as if Tyler was right there, whispering in his ear: *Don't give them an inch, Cinn.*

He was going to wipe the smile off of that infuriatingly perfect face if it was the last thing he did.

Cinn went to kick the man's right knee, but he easily slid to the side. Changing tactics, Cinn lunged for the guy's coat, planning to hold the cuff while he punched him in the face. To Cinn's immense displeasure, his opponent had the audacity to laugh as he jumped back to dodge Cinn's attack, then hooked his leg around Cinn's ankle, sending him sprawling to the ground.

Damn.

The pretty boy could fight.

Cinn groaned, then blinked up at branches stretching across the night sky, a lattice of dark criss-crossing the stars. Something was painfully digging into his back.

Off to the side, the girl made a soft squeaking sound—of protest?—but there was no time to look that way. His attacker was aiming another foot at the soft part of his stomach.

Get up.

With energy he didn't truly have, Cinn forced himself to leap up and throw himself at him, figuring a surprise attack was the only weapon available. He dove at the guy, ramming into his side to grab a fistful of his thick blond hair. Cinn pulled at it, hard, snapping his head backwards—perhaps he could make himself perfectly clear if only the dickhead would listen for a moment.

Unbelievably, the fucker *smiled*, revealing two perfectly symmetrical dimples. "Oh darling, how did you know I was into that?"

Cinn released him, shoved him with all the force he could muster, and followed it up with a punch that ended up connecting with his collarbone.

Before he could do anything else, a fist flew towards his face, hitting him square in the jaw. Cinn stumbled left, stunned. A gunshot-like ringing burst through his eardrums. Reaching new levels of fury, he launched himself at the man again, aimless this time, only intending to knock him to the ground.

Yet his opponent didn't fall as expected—beneath the man's slender frame was a surprising amount of strength.

"Just listen for one second," he hissed, fisting Cinn's shirt.

"Fuck you." Cinn promptly spat in his face. He'd learnt *that* particular trick on his very first day in prison.

His attacker was horrified—disturbed even, going by his expression—and released Cinn to wipe the saliva off his cheek with the sleeve of his black trench coat.

Cinn readied his right hook, but before he could enact what would surely be the final blow, strong arms wound their way around his neck. While he'd been so focused on the blond demon, his mate had crept behind him, got him in a headlock. *Perfect.*

"Get off me, you prick," Cinn growled, reaching for the switchblade he always kept in the left pocket of his jeans—to find it missing, long since confiscated by the police.

"Oh, stop it, the three of you!" snapped the woman. "Does everything need to descend into violence?" Closing the space between them, she leant forward, uncurling a gloved palm to reveal white powder.

Upon seeing it, the two men leapt away, one to each side, but for Cinn it was too late—one gigantic breath, and the woman had blown the mass of ultrafine crystallised particles directly into his face.

Cinn coughed, spluttered, spat. The substance had entered his mouth, throat, nose, eyes.

Years of taking absolutely nothing, and now drugged twice in twenty-fours hours.

"I'm guessing this isn't the fun sort of powder?" Cinn wheezed, feeling his stomach start to clench, and his muscles begin to seize. "What t-th..." His tongue, fat and heavy in his slack jaw, refused to move any further.

"It's Frostbite," the demon princeling said. "Don't bother fighting it," he added with a smirk Cinn itched to punch off his face. "It'll only make it worse."

Pure fear gripped Cinn. Rarely before had he felt as powerless as he did standing there, rooted to the spot, only able to blink. A rush of adrenaline coursed through him as his pulse spiked. With desperation, he attempted to force words out—he needed to warn them what might happen if they continued to put him under stress—but he only produced a strangled half cry.

The girl sighed and moved towards Cinn. Her alabaster skin revealed a sea of light freckles. "It was just to immobilise you until you calm down. Here, I'm going to give you a fifth of the antidote dose. It should be enough to let you talk, and to stop you shitting yourself."

The two others snickered. Cinn, paralysed and powerless, could only watch as she placed a tiny chunk of a red pellet on his tongue. It fizzed as it dissolved.

She used her gloved hand to brush the remnants of the powder from his face onto the ground.

Cinn's tongue came back to life somewhat, allowing him to spit out, "Naff off!"

The girl stepped back.

Stretching out his jaw, he continued, "What the fuck is my leaving to you lot, anyway? You working for that Sinclair woman? Who are you?"

"Introductions were actually on the agenda, but you derailed it," the blond drawled, rubbing at his cheek as if Cinn's germs might still remain there.

The girl rolled her eyes with an exasperated shake of her head. "Julien, you're the one that took this right off the tracks. All you had to do was say 'hello, nice to meet you', but no, instead you jump straight to threats. No wonder you spooked him."

The other bloke, crazy-curls dude, laughed. "You're acting surprised, Darcy." Was that an American accent Cinn detected? These three were certainly an eclectic mix.

She spun to face the man. "And thanks *so much* for your support, Elliot. I thought we both agreed that not attacking the person who we're supposed to be responsible for, supposed to be *asking for help* from, was the more sensible idea."

"Hey, you only told me not to channel in front of him, not to not attack him."

"It was implied!"

Elliot shrugged. "The back and forth was getting old."

Cinn flicked his eyes between the odd trio, unable to fully move his head still. Just what had he stumbled into? And what did they need his help with?

The girl—Darcy—smiled at him, the way you might smile at a toddler you wanted to placate. "How about this? I give you the rest of the antidote, and then we all go back to mine for a nice mug of tea." Her wide green eyes pierced him with her gaze.

After a moment's thought, Cinn eventually made a noise of assent. It was late now, and he barely knew where he was. Once he'd convinced the group he was going to be of no use to them whatsoever, perhaps he could use *them* somehow. Darcy wore a sparkling jewelled necklace over her expensive-looking jumper—maybe there would be more shiny things to swipe on his way out.

Four

JULIEN

The short walk to Darcy's cottage, nestled in a quiet spot near the edge of town, was awkwardly silent. Darcy led the way with Julien and Elliot trailing closely behind Cinnamon, essentially caging him with their bodies, blocking any further escape attempts.

Julien expelled a deep breath. The previous half an hour had been a close call, far too close for comfort. Shortly after Eleanor Sinclair had called to update him, the fire in Darcy's living room had crackled, spitting out another smoking parchment piece that demanded the three of them hurry to the gate at the edge of the green—Eleanor citing information from 'her sources' that Cinn was on the move, and had entered the grove.

If they'd arrived five minutes later, they might have lost him. He could only imagine the fury on Eleanor's face if they'd let him slip through their fingers. Likely she would have tracemotes on the newcomer before the day was over, lest he go wandering.

She'd whirlwinded into his apartment the day before last to announce she was flying to England to collect someone she needed his help with. The details were vague: a man, a year or two younger than him. A criminal record. And most importantly: *a shadowslipper*.

"He's... not exactly Auri material, is he?" Elliot whispered, his lips twitching into a snide smile. "What exactly is he wearing?"

Julien's eyes raked over the guy's baggy clothes that hid every inch of the smooth, olive skin he'd brushed up against during their fight. The grey woollen beanie that he wore, tugged down low on his head, was fraying slightly at the seams.

Non, this man was definitely not his type. But there was certainly something about him...

Probably just the adrenaline from the fight talking.

When they were brawling earlier, Julien's eye kept magnetising to the small silver bar that adorned his right eyebrow. The temptation to pull it had been strong, but Julien didn't want to *really* piss him off. Not when he needed him so badly.

"Maybe his style is all the rage in London these days," he replied.

"Can you imagine what your father would say if you started dressing like that?" Elliot continued to snicker to himself, but Julien gave him no response. Elliot would often bring Julien's father up, and Julien would shut down the conversation instantly, yet it never deterred Elliot.

Cinnamon's head snapped back towards them at Elliot's laughter, but they were saved by the distraction of Darcy announcing, "Home sweet home!" Good job, too—Julien did not want a repeat of the fight from earlier, in which his shorter opponent had certainly held his own.

The fire was down to its dying embers by the time they settled in the living room of Darcy's small cottage, and Julien set to work reviving it—one long, hard breath, and the heatmote-infused grate did its job. He stared at the blazing inferno, half expecting immediate instructions to burst out of the now-present flames. Instead, the telephone rang.

Darcy was closest. After the caller had spoken for a moment, she replied smoothly, "Of course." She placed the phone on the wall hook. "Eleanor is on her way."

"I bet she is." Elliot grinned and looked at Cinnamon like he was a rabbit about to be devoured by a wolf.

"How are you feeling, Cinnamon?" Darcy guided him to the seat closest to the fire—the cosy emerald armchair that Julien usually took for himself. "The heat should help with the last lingering effects of the Frostbite."

"My name's Cinn," he replied, sitting on the very edge of the chair and fiddling with the lining of his beanie. "Nobody calls me Cinnamon."

"Someone must have, at least once," Elliot sniped, earning him a whack on the head from Darcy, which Julien approved of—they now needed 'Cinn' on side, if they were going to enlist his help.

"So Cinn," he started, consciously using his most charming smile—the smile that nobody could say no to. This should have been his approach from the start, but he'd let the panic of almost losing access to him take hold. Julien sat down cross-legged in front of the fire, beaming up at Cinn, maintaining strong eye contact. The wary-looking man's deep golden-brown eyes held a surprising amount of warmth, despite the scowl he wore on his face. *How much prettier would he be with a smile?*

"Yes?" Cinn snapped, glaring at him now. Julien had gotten distracted. Very distracted.

"We understand that this must be very confusing for you," said Darcy, clearly deciding Julien wasn't up to the task of placating their captive. "I'm sure Eleanor wasn't the most forthcoming. But she's coming here now, and we can go through everything else you want to know."

The teapot whistled on Darcy's stove and she left the room, beckoning Elliot with her.

Cinn eyed Julien warily, as if he expected a sudden attack now they were alone. "Are you Swiss? Or what?" he abruptly asked.

"French," Julien said, deliberately rolling his '*r*'. "My homeland is the City of Lights," he continued, exaggerating his accent in that seductive way that often had people melting in front of him.

Cinn didn't look impressed. Strange.

"Who the hell even is Madame Sinclair, anyway? Does she run this place? The *Institute* or whatever?"

Julien barked a laugh. Eleanor would have loved to hear that. "Not exactly. I suppose you could say she's... middle management. I primarily know her as a friend of the family, but our paths cross here from time to time."

"Does she often fly across the world to personally kidnap people?"

"Only the very special ones." Julien used the opportunity to bat his eyelashes ever so subtly, but Cinn was unaffected, staring back with a deadpan expression.

With saucers clinking, Darcy and Elliot carried in two trays laden with teacups and dark chocolate cookies. Setting hers down on the round coffee table with a flourish, she announced, "Ma just sent me this new chai blend from India." Darcy thrust a cup into Cinn's hand before falling onto the sofa beside Elliot, turning on the bronze torchiere beside her. "They just spent a month there and stockpiled twelve different types of tea before returning to Scotland."

Julien eyed Cinn discreetly as he lifted the mug to his lips. Cinn took the smallest ever sip, his face pinching when he swallowed. Then he leaned past Julien to swipe a biscuit, with a lunge so quick that it almost cracked a joke.

Cinn devoured most of the cookie with a single large bite. "Is there... black pepper in these?"

Darcy's hands clapped together as her eyes sparkled. "To enhance the richness of the chocolate! You bake?"

"Not exactly. I cook. I'm a chef. In training, anyway. Well, *was* in training." Cinn's eyes dropped to the well-worn blue rug.

"Well, you can help me in the kitchen anytime. These two Neanderthals can't tell a paring knife from a pastry brush."

Elliot snorted out a spray of tea as Cinn's head snapped up to glare at Darcy.

"I'm not staying."

Julien shuffled forward an inch. "Cinn—"

A knock at the door had Cinn flinching backwards, panicked eyes flashing towards it. For the first time, a trace of fear could be detected on his face. "What is she going to do to me?"

Darcy stood, but before she took a step, Eleanor burst into the room, heels thundering on the wooden floorboards. "Evening," she said calmly, her gaze landing straight on Cinn. "Mr. Saunders. I hear you went on a little walk." She hung her long black coat on the wooden coatrack.

Elliot shuffled along on the sofa to make space for her while Darcy sprung up, wringing her hands together. "Madame Sinclair, can I get you anything?"

"Something stronger than that should suffice." Eleanor nodded at the tea, sending Darcy scurrying off. Julien had never understood Darcy's unease around Eleanor, but then, he'd grown up attending dinner parties with the formidable woman since he was five.

"Look," started Cinn, sitting forward. "Unless you plan to produce some sort of legal documentation that says you can keep me here—"

Eleanor held up her hand. "We have just saved you from a life behind bars, Cinnamon Saunders. If I were you, I'd be grovelling at my feet. And if I were you, I'd be hesitant to go back to the outside world until I knew I wasn't going to be responsible for any more deaths."

Cinn recoiled, face horrified, as he slumped back into himself, but Eleanor smiled. She'd said the magic words, and she knew it.

"Now, now," she said, as she accepted the half glass of brandy Darcy offered her. "There's no need for that. I promise you that this is the best place for you. We can help you. Train you. Besides, as moteblessed, you need to be with your own people."

Cinn shook his head. "What?"

"Moteblessed. It's the overarching name our community gives to those of us able to channel motes of any kind. Some of us have a narrow range of motes we can influence. Some, like Elliot here, have trained their mind and body to withstand a great range and quantity of motepower, particularly elemental-based motes. He's one of Auri's finest up-coming members of our gendarmerie."

Pride practically seeped from Elliot's pores, and Julien laughed, which helped to squash down the tiny prickle of jealousy that he couldn't help but feel whenever Elliot's channelling abilities were complimented.

In disbelief, Cinn stared at Elliot, opening his mouth as if to question what Eleanor said. Elliot smirked, wiggled his eyebrows, then proceeded to raise every drop of tea out of his mug to form a swirling ball of brown liquid between his hands. A gasp came from Cinn, followed by a string of expletives. His mouth fell slack as his thick eyelashes rapidly blinked at the floating tea, which was now being expertly manipulated back into the teapot through the spout.

"Elliot! That's unhygienic!" snapped Darcy.

With a soft laugh, Eleanor swirled her brandy. "Darcy is also able to manipulate a wide variety of motes, and is researching the synthesization of them into compounds. Julien, on the other hand, specialises in how we can utilise them within technology. These are just three examples of professions or areas of study in our moteblessed community. And then we have you. Stop shaking your head at me, Cinn. You utilise shadowmotes when you have your... experiences. You just never knew it."

Julien stared at the mixture of shock, bewilderment and... relief?... that warred on Cinn's face. What must it have been like, growing up moteblessed and not having the faintest clue what that entailed? Confusing, certainly. Lonely even, maybe. What had Cinn thought was happening when he had his 'experiences'?

"So... you're telling me that it's their fault? These *shadowmotes*? Can I stop them? Can I fix myself?"

Cinn sounded like a broken man on the edge of desperation, and a soft noise burst out of Julien before he could stop it, but it was Elliot who beat him to say, "Being moteblessed is a privilege that most could only dream of. Why would you want to stop it?"

"Mate, did you miss the part where I murdered four people?" Cinn snarled.

Darcy looked to him with wide, sympathetic eyes. "That wasn't you though, if what Madame Eleanor told us is correct. You just... accidentally brought back a psychotic-murderer spirit or something. Right?"

"Same result."

"She's right, Cinn," said Eleanor. "There's no blame for you to shoulder. However, now you need to learn how to make sure it doesn't happen again."

The firelight danced in Cinn's eyes as he considered her words. "Fine," he eventually spat through gritted teeth. "But I can leave as soon as I've learnt to control it? These shadowmotes or whatever? I'll be free to go? And my record wiped clean?"

"We can discuss all of that in due course. Although, this isn't something you're going to learn overnight. These three have been practising motecraft since they were children, and they still have a lot to learn."

"Hey," said Julien. "Where are these unfounded accusations coming from?"

Eleanor continued, "From tomorrow, you'll start private sessions with a colleague of mine. Albert Noir."

"Does he have the same problem as me?" Cinn asked.

Eleanor caught Julien's eye in the most subtle of glances. A cue to bite his tongue lest he reply out of turn—Eleanor was running this show.

"No," she said smoothly, withholding the very noteworthy fact that nobody had the same talent as Cinn. Well, nobody still alive to tell the tale, anyway. "But he's a highly competent scholar and will take good care of you."

"If you can suffer through his bad jokes," said Elliot, and Darcy glared at him. She had a fondness for the old man that Julien and Elliot did not share. "And his morning breath."

Abruptly, Eleanor stood up. "I could only step away for a short time. Cinn, see to it that I don't have to pay you any more unscheduled visits. My time is precious and I don't like wasting it. Julien, walk me out, please."

Without a backward glance, she marched towards the door, forcing Julien to surge up to follow her. Once they'd left the cottage into the frigid night air, she beckoned him down the path to the gate.

"What is it?" Julien was already annoyed at having to leave the warm fire.

"I'm sure this is obvious, Julien, but do not start dragging him into your little project anytime soon."

Seething, Julien clenched and unclenched his fists. "You're the one who told me all about him. You've practically delivered him to our doorstep."

"So you can keep a constant eye on him between the three of you," she hissed. "You know exactly why he's actually here, and why that's so important. You know damn well it's not to play mouthpiece for your sister, as sad as her death was."

"But—" Julien stopped himself from pouting like a toddler. Pushed down his anger. Smiled sweetly. *Play the game.*

"There's nobody here that Viktor Sturmhart and I trust more than you to make sure the boy stays put, keeps his head down, and doesn't get interfered with by the wrong people. He's a baby, Julien. He knows nothing about this world. A newborn cub. If you try to get him to run before he can walk..."

Inside, a maelstrom of fury threatened to burst out of Julien. *What about Béatrice? How have you just forgotten all about her, just like Père? You promised to help.*

"And how is the internal review of Béatrice's death going?" Julien asked, voice level.

"We're still going through things, Julien. However, the general consensus is still that it was an accident. A tragic accident."

Lies!

Eleanor moved towards him, to rest a hand on his shoulder and squeeze it in a rare moment of affection. He resisted the impulse to shrug it off. "Still? It's been three months."

"Exactly, Julien. It might be time to—"

"I'm going back inside. You should know I'm not babysitting your ward. I'm sure Darcy will be happy to, and I'll stop Elliot from tormenting him, but I'm too busy with work to ferry him around and entertain him."

He knew he'd gone too far when Eleanor's tone turned icy cold. "Julien, have some compassion for once in your life. And if you really can't do that, then listen to this: your direct orders from Viktor Sturmhart, in addition to *your father*, are to ensure no harm comes to Cinnamon Saunders. Keep him here, and out of trouble. You know the stakes that are at play here. Do not fuck this up. Especially with your application to MEET about to be reviewed."

Pressing his tongue to the roof of his mouth, Julien nodded. He'd play along if that's what it took. "I'll keep an eye on him, but he hardly seems like the hardened criminal you described."

"I told you that he spent a year in juvenile prison as a teenager, not that he was a common thug."

Julien shrugged. "Just saying, I doubt he'll be a flight risk now."

With a parting nod, Eleanor slid into her car, and Julien stomped all the way back to the front door. Laughter burst out of the living room entrance. Startled by the sudden change in dynamic, Julien paused.

"Then we'll take you to this bar we love," said Darcy.

"Darcy loves it. We just tolerate it," Elliot sniped.

He'd been gone all of five minutes and they were already making weekend plans?

He rounded the corner, lifting his coat from the rack. "I'll drive you home, Cinn."

"But it's not on your way." Elliot stared at Julien intently, but Julien only stared back, daring him to make a scene.

Cinn gave an uncomfortable squirm in the armchair, glancing between the pair of them.

With loud clinks, Darcy gathered three empty teacups onto a tray—Cinn had finished his chai after all. "You're going home? Fantastic news. I figured you'd demand to crash on my sofa again. You've used it more than your own bed this month."

Julien would often suffer through the occasional stab of a loose spring rather than face another night alone in his penthouse suite. Béatrice's bedroom was opposite Darcy's, but he couldn't ever quite bring himself to sleep in her bed. Just being in her room was bad enough. He knew this well—they'd many times attempted to summon her to the space, figuring it to be a familiar, special place.

"Let's go," Julien said pointedly to Cinn, who finally jumped up, mumbled goodbyes to the other two, and followed him outside to where his car was parked, next to Elliot's motorcycle.

He tried not to laugh when Cinn made to get into the driver's side before muttering something about stupid European cars.

Once Cinn clicked his seatbelt, he ran his hand over the dashboard of Julien's Mazda Eunos 800. He'd bought it on impulse last year after a particularly draining visit home. It was jet black, like his mood at the time.

"Nice ride," Cinn said.

"Do you drive?"

"Nah. Never have. Don't really need to in my part of London."

Great. It looked like Cinn really would be reliant on them to ferry him around.

"*Oui*, your public transport really is... something," said Julien, wrinkling his nose at the memory of the one time he'd attempted to board an overcrowded bus. Thank goodness for the black cabs.

"You've been to London?"

Julien glanced at him. "*Oui*, of course. I grew up in Paris. It's just a stone's throw away."

"I've never been to Paris." A wistful edge coloured Cinn's voice. "It looks so nice in the movies."

"Most of it's a cesspool. My father and his wife live there though, so I go back, every now and again." *Not as little as I'd like.*

"Are they... *moteblessed*? Your parents?"

A laugh bubbled out of him before he could contain it. Of course, Cinn would have no idea who his father was. "*Oui*. It usually tends to be genetic. It's likely one of your parents was."

Cinn fell quiet for a moment. Julien glanced at him. What had Eleanor said about his upbringing? *Shit-show of a childhood. Foster system since age thirteen. School dropout.*

"Is this you?" Julien asked, as he pulled up outside the address Eleanor had given him on the phone that afternoon. The institute owned twenty percent of the property around town, so why on earth had they stuck Cinn so far out? Wouldn't it have been better to keep him close to the centre?

Cinn squinted through the darkness. "I guess it is."

A small pause stretched. Cinn didn't look delighted at being dropped off to be all alone in a strange new house, and Julien had a sudden urge to invite himself in. Then Julien reminded himself that Cinn was a normal, functioning adult, unlike himself. "I'm presuming Eleanor wants me to take you to Auri tomorrow. I've got a lecture to catch at midday, so I'll pick you up at ten."

Cinn grabbed the door handle, then froze, turning his head to look Julien directly in the eye. "You said you needed my help. Earlier, when you used that stuff on me."

Oui, I did. Yes, I do. I really, really do.

"Did I?"

Cinn's piercing gaze was unrelenting. Eleanor's clear orders from earlier warred with the image of his dead sister's body.

Naturally, it was an unfair contest.

"There is something I have in mind. But it can wait." *A day or two.*

Cinn ran his fingers through the messy dark hair that poked out of the front of his hat, seeming poised to say more, but eventually, he just slid out of the car. "Cheers for the ride," he mumbled, before walking up his path, head down.

Julien stared at Cinn's door long after he'd closed it. Cinn was a puzzle. An intriguing puzzle. And there was nothing Julien liked more than a good puzzle.

Five

CINN

C inn stared out the window, coat on, hands in pockets. The morning sunlight brightened the red-brick roofs of his neighbours' houses. After waking up at the crack of dawn, he'd been ready and waiting for his lift to 'the Institute' for some time now.

This had been, without doubt, the most certifiably insane forty-eight hours of his life. If he rewound time to only three days prior, he'd still be sleeping, ready for his night shift at Rosewood Parlour. *Rosewood Parlour.* He'd only started there a few months ago, but already felt more at home there than any other place he'd worked. He'd grafted so hard to earn Benny's respect and Sarah's friendship, all for nothing.

What did his colleagues think had happened to him? Did they think he was a murderer, or had Eleanor's people covered the whole thing up? At the very least, they probably knew that he'd attempted to rob the safe. Shame prickled its way across his skin at the image of Benny's frowning face when he turned up to work the next day to a crime scene.

He'd need to let his flatmates know he wouldn't be home for a while, that they should sublet his room. What would they do with all his stuff? He'd had to leave so many music cassettes behind...

And thinking of money—how was he supposed to get any? The details of what shape his life would take were hazy, but he definitely wasn't expecting a regular wage slip to be delivered into his hand. He'd have to be prepared to be skint. Like usual.

Most importantly, Tyler. *Tyler, Tyler, Tyler.* Every time his face had forced its way into the forefront of his mind over the last two days, Cinn alternated between wanting to cry and wanting to punch something.

Before he'd slept yesterday, he used the telephone—once he figured out how to make international calls—to call every memorised number that could possibly help him get into contact with Tyler, or at least verify his whereabouts. For all he knew, Richter's men had deposited Tyler's dead body in the River Thames by now.

His biggest hope was pinned on their old friend Bradley, who often let Tyler stay with him. He hadn't picked up yet.

Three beeps of a horn distracted him from spiralling panic.

Pulling his beanie on, he locked the front door and jogged down the drive to Julien's car, the shiny black metal impeccably spotless.

He'd expected to only have to put up with Julien, so it threw him to see the other two in the car. Although Darcy was a nice enough girl, he'd also have to deal with the twat with all the hair.

And sure enough, Elliot scowled at him from the passenger seat.

Cinn slid into the back and blinked in disbelief at Darcy. Clutched in her hand was a mug of tea. Not a travel cup, but a chunky yellow round mug. In a car.

She smiled before taking a sip. "Don't mind me. Maz drives so smoothly I don't spill a drop."

"You mean, *I* drive Maz so smoothly with my impeccable skills, even on these godawful country roads, that you don't spill a drop." Julien peered at Darcy in the rearview mirror, then his gaze flashed across to meet Cinn's.

"Yes, Julien, it's one hundred percent your unrivalled driving ability, and not at all down to the mote-infused metal plating all over Maz's insides."

"I'm glad we're in agreement, then."

And with that, Julien pushed the car into first, and they were off.

With the conversation hitting a lull, Cinn's gaze latched itself onto the thing taking up the most space in the car—Elliot's hair.

"You'll catch flies if you're not careful." Elliot twisted around to face him, his eyes thin slits.

Cinn closed his evidently gawking mouth. "Sorry. Your hair..." He gestured to it lamely.

A roll of the eyes. "Irish mother. Venezuelan father. Quirky as fuck gene mix."

"Don't mind him." Julien reached over to ruffle the corkscrew curls in question, then pushed Elliot back into his seat. "He loves the attention, really."

The three soon fell into easy banter and inside jokes, and so Cinn stared out the window, attempting not to listen. He was fairly successful at it too, until a soft, hushed tone from Elliot caught his ear.

"Today's the date."

And even softer from Julien, "I know it is."

And then, from Darcy, a shout. "What's that, Julien?"

Again, Julien's eyes flicked to Cinn's for a fleeting moment. "Just that it's the *fifth of November,* Darcy."

"Oh! Of course it is." Darcy's eyes widened. "Not that we can actually do anything with that information. As we've no idea what she was on about."

"Who?" asked Cinn. "What's special about today?"

No reply, only eyes firmly fixated ahead of them. *Shock.* Cinn turned to stare out of the window again. They'd driven a fair way out from the town now and had only passed fields and sheep for miles. Cinn fixated on the adorable, fuzzy creatures, wanting to stop to run his hands through their wool. London couldn't have seemed further away.

Then they drove over a hill, and he saw it—what could only be the Institute. A collection of buildings sitting in a valley, an array of stonework and turrets and towers jam-packed together.

"The Aurelia Arcanum Institute of Esoteric Sciences," announced Darcy dramatically, wiggling her fingers into jazz hands.

Cinn stared at it, almost mumbling something about the long, stupid name before catching himself.

"Us folks tend to call her Auri," said Julien. "The Swiss locals think we're down here torturing lab rats and generating artificial electrical discharges."

Cinn risked being seen as stupid; Eleanor Sinclair had been through all this yesterday. Yet he had to ask, "But what... actually happens? What is it?"

Darcy's face whipped towards him. "Auri? A collection of various departments all united in a shared space. It's essentially a campus. The European hub for people like us."

"Moteblessed? Like you guys?"

"Like *you*, Cinn."

Darcy reached for his hand and squeezed.

Julien drove them into a small car park. Several other cars pulled up beside them, and to their right, two buses unloaded numerous passengers onto a cobbled pavement.

Three steps onto the campus, Cinn paused to absorb the majestic sprawl of this so-called 'Aurelia Arcanum Institute of Esoteric Sciences', where every monument and building seemed to reach for the heavens with an air of scholarly grace. Towering spires, adorned with curious golden symbols, punctuated the skyline, casting intricate shadows on manicured lawns. Beyond their current road, stone facades weathered by the passage of time enclosed a quaint courtyard between buildings.

With each new thing his eyes latched onto, his sense of awe grew and grew. He reached out into nothingness, running his hand through empty space. It seemed to Cinn even the very air crackled with unseen energy. Unseen power.

"I feel like I've... travelled to another world," murmured Cinn, eventually. University had never been on the cards for him, but the grandeur of the buildings and the buzz of the people as they raced between buildings was what he imagined Oxford or Cambridge must be like.

You do not belong here.

Julien was studying him closely. Was that a hint of amusement on his lips? "Auri tends to have that effect on people. And, also, quite literally, some people have been transported here. Using the Displacement Baths."

Darcy shook her head. "Julien, it's far too soon to fry his brain with transdimensional travel."

"I'm not on shift today, only training, so I should be good to go by four. You still going to that lecture, Julien?" asked Elliot. "By that famous motetech guy?"

Julien huffed and raised an eyebrow. "Honestly, Elliot, you're the only person I've met that doesn't know his name. Doctor Valerius Weaver is a world-renowned—"

"Yeah, yeah."

Cinn coughed to remind them of his existence.

"I'll walk you to Noir's office, Cinn." Julien gestured to a nearby path.

Elliot made to go with them, but Darcy dragged him off with a promise to find them later.

And so Cinn was alone with Julien again. Julien and his damn dimples.

His eyes slid sideways.

Why did the infuriatingly self-assured guy have to have that permanent just-stepped-out-of-a-glossy-magazine look? One of those annoying bright pink ones with boy bands on the cover. With his flawless skin and long blond glossy waves, he'd easily blend in with one. And those cheekbones. They framed his flinty grey eyes in such a way that added an intensity to every expression.

Cinn fell back a step to scowl at the back of his head. He wasn't usually one to admire beauty in others. Rather, he picked his friends for their strengths. Their banter. Their loyalty.

Stupid rich-prick princeling, messing with his brain with his pretty face. Pretty *punchable* face.

They continued to stroll across the bustling campus, Cinn trailing a step behind, silent as Julien listed building names he couldn't keep track of and what departments they housed.

"Noir's office is at the top of one of the Nexus Towers. The Ivory Tower." Julien pointed at two symmetrical towers rising majestically from the ground, their sleek obsidian facades gleaming in the sunlight, accentuated by veins of silver marble coursing through their structure. A delicate wrought-iron bridge spanned the expanse between them, joining the two towers part way up.

When they got to the entrance of the leftmost tower, a grand pair of glass doors awaiting them, Julien stopped. "It's alright if I leave you here, right? I want to try to grab the speaker before the lecture begins." He then started describing how to reach the office, but Cinn's brain retained absolutely nothing, short-circuited by the sudden shock of being left alone in this overwhelming place to fend for himself. "Got that? You'll be okay, *oui*?" Julien stared at him. Was he daring Cinn to beg him to walk him right to Albert Noir's office door?

Cinn smiled. "Sure." *Abso-fucking-lutely.*

"I'll be at the Cerulean Auditorium for the lecture, but I'll come find you after."

Will you though? How will you find me?

"Gotcha." Cinn spun away from Julien, and with all the confidence he could muster, marched through the glass doors. Why was his heart racing and his throat constricting? He was a grown twenty-something man, for fuck's sake. Not a child on their first day of school.

A spacious lobby greeted him. Hurried feet pounded on the ceramic tiled floor. *Why is everyone in such a goddamn rush around here?*

Eyeing the numerous staircases and hallways, his fate was decided. He'd have to ask someone.

The first passer-by he tried to speak to completely ignored him, but in their defence, Cinn had practically whispered his 'excuse me'. Heat burning his cheeks, he pressed himself against the wall to regroup. Why was this so hard? Abruptly, he remembered the liberation he'd felt when Tyler had become his voice for him, back in the early days of juvie when he was painfully shy and scared. That was many years ago, though. Cinn didn't rely on anyone anymore. He was stronger now. Fearless.

"EXCUSE ME," he shouted at some poor lady, who promptly spilled her coffee all over her clipboard. "Sorry. I'm looking for Albert Noir's office."

She peered at him, unimpressed. "You're in the wrong tower. You need Ebony Tower. Take the lift up to the bridge and cross over. He's floor seventeen, I think."

Cinn tamped down a rush of anger. Why on earth had Julien walked him to the entrance of the wrong tower?

The woman pointed him in the direction of the lifts, and Cinn joined a fast-moving queue. Peering past the crowd, his heart sank. These weren't your mother's elevators.

A tight line of four sleek, translucent tubes awaited him. He watched as, one by one, people entered them alone or in pairs, neutral expressions on their faces as if they whizzed vertically up at the speed of light in these tubes every day. Well, they probably did.

"How do I make it work?" he asked the person behind him when it was seconds away from his turn.

A guy around his age frowned at him. "Huh? What?" The look of panic on Cinn's face must have clued the stranger in to his situation, because he continued, "Stand still and hold the floor number in your mind. It helps to close your eyes, your first time."

"Which floor is the bridge on?"

"Twelve. Don't worry, you'll be fine. It's fun." The guy smiled—a handsome, kind smile—and Cinn had the embarrassing urge to ask him to go with him. Alas, before Cinn could, he pushed Cinn towards an empty tube, alone.

One shaky step later, shock engulfed Cinn as he discovered that within the tube, all sound faded away. A vacuum. It was just him and his unsteady, frantic breathing.

Twelve.

Twelve.

Twelve?

Twelve!

Oh fuck. He'd forgotten about the closing-his-eyes part.

The slices of toast he'd wolfed down earlier threatened to make a reappearance as he ascended rapidly upwards, propelled by air. Floors one to eleven flickered by him like he was looking through a zoetrope toy.

And then, he was there, at floor twelve, floating in mid-air. The curved glass door slid into itself, and Cinn stepped from the weightless vacuum onto a solid carpeted floor.

Smoothing down his clothes, he attempted to casually walk towards the bridge like he hadn't just flown up a tube.

When he reached the bridge, Cinn found it to be a step too far.

"It's just... floating! Unsupported!" he screeched, at a man dressed in a very smart suit.

The man gave him a wide berth and strode onto the the bridge.

Clinging to the metal railings, Cinn dashed across the glass surface with haste, eyes fixed firmly in front of him. What was the purpose of the bridge's design? A pointless display of power?

Another tube trip, and a short walk up a spiral staircase later, Cinn had done it—he'd found Noir's office. He raised his hand to knock, mouth drying, when the door swung open.

"Come in," said a voice, not from near the door, but from the other side of the room.

Cinn entered. The moderately sized office was cramped, made claustrophobic by large amounts of clutter, and walls lined by bookcases that seemed to sag under the weight of heavy tomes.

Albert Noir seemed required to fulfil the promise made by his surname. Standing with a slight hunch, he was dressed entirely in black, complete with a wool scarf. Wild tendrils of grey hair, sticking out at crazy angles, framed a head more wrinkles than face. Bushy eyebrows knitted together as he, in turn, scrutinised Cinn.

"So you're him? Our new shadowslipper?"

Without being asked, Cinn sat down at Noir's cluttered desk. A peculiar rattling sound seemed to be coming from within it. "I've never heard that word."

"The literature gives us a few different names for it, using the word shadowrealm to describe the place where you go, coined from shadowmotes, of course."

"Yesterday they said I was moteblessed."

At that, Noir made an exasperated sound, lowering himself down in the chair opposite to say, "Always hated that name, myself. Too religious. As if we're chosen by some god." He snorted, then ran his hand through a scraggly beard. A silver pipe lay in front of Noir, which he picked up and stuffed with a substance from a nearby tin. Cinn waited for him to light it with a lighter, or a match, or *something*, but Noir just pinched the bowl with two fingers until it produced thin wisps of smoke. He took a long pull on it, painfully reminding Cinn he was on day three without a single cigarette.

"I would have guessed that magic would make people more religious."

It was the wrong thing to say. Noir's crinkly eyes narrowed into slits as he pressed his fingers together. "This isn't *magic* boy. There are no tricks here. This institute is one of science."

The Aurelia Arcanum Institute of Esoteric Sciences.

It was in the name, to be fair.

Cinn waited for him to continue, lest he say the wrong thing again.

"So. They've given you to me, hm? I suppose I am best placed for the position." He peered at Cinn over his half-moon spectacles. Cinn kept very still, forcing his chin up and his gaze steady. The old man seemed to be deep in thought for several moments, before finally saying, "So, how are you?"

"How... am I?" Cinn blinked.

"Yes. How are you? A few days ago you watched a spirit from another realm tear four people apart. You were then almost incarcerated for life, before being whisked away across the continent by a mysterious authority, and told that you haven't been raving mad your whole life, you simply possess an almost unheard of mote-related ability, that the Institute desires to utilise so badly, they'll do anything to keep you here. So, Cinn. I'll ask again. How are you?"

Something inside Cinn cracked, just a little. His mouth hung open, a few strangled syllables forcing their way out before he mumbled, "Not great."

"Excellent. Honesty is an important part of emotional regulation. If we're going to work closely, Cinn, which is necessary for what I need to teach you, you need to keep being honest with me. In return, I'll pay the same respect to you."

The sack of weights that had been dragging Cinn down lifted from him slightly. He sank back into the chair. "All I've wanted since Eleanor took me is for someone to explain to me what this"—he waved his hand around—"is all about. Can you explain it to me from the beginning? In a way that I'll understand. None of this *esoteric sciences* crap."

A spark ignited in Noir's eye as he sat up straight, pulling a thin circular stone slab out from a drawer and placing it on top of the papers on his desk. "Do you remember the Calamities of Nineteen Sixty-Five?"

"Sir, I'm twenty-three."

"Yes, yes, but you've heard of them, surely?"

Of course he had. Though he understood the seismic impact of them only in the way those who hadn't lived through them could. He'd seen the handful of grainy videos. Studied the key dates in the few history classes he'd turned up for. A relentless series of back-to-back disasters had rocked the world. Tornados. Droughts. Tsunamis. Volcanic activity. They'd caused sizeable dents in population, and sent economies haywire.

"What do they have to do with anything?"

"You asked me to start at the beginning, and they *were* the beginning. The discovery of motes came very shortly after the final calamity—the eruption of Mount Pelée. Although most argue they likely emerged—" Noir shook his head, muttering to himself before continuing. "We'll be here all day if I go off on tangents. What you need to know is that after the Calamities, a handful of scientists began studying groups of people who started reporting unusual abilities."

"Surely the news would have gotten wind of all this, if some people could suddenly shoot laser beams out of their eyes or whatever."

Noir's mouth twitched. "I must note that particular skill has never been recorded. But Cinn, you underestimate the power of fear. Have you ever disclosed your ability to anyone? Outside of the psychiatrist you spoke to at Feltham?"

The word *ability* still felt wrong in association with his affliction. "Yes," he replied. "Just one other person." He remembered that night well. It was a couple of months into his prison sentence and he'd been wrapped in Tyler's arms after a particularly bad trip. Tyler was sure he'd taken pills from the sketchy geezer in the cell opposite them. He'd spent three hours trying to convince him otherwise. He'd fully expected Tyler to laugh at him, or call him insane. When Tyler had grabbed his chin, looked him in the eye and whispered, 'I believe you,' every molecule of his being melted in relief.

"Exactly. Those few people who walked around shouting about it or showing off were swiftly *dealt with,* the outcome varying by the country they lived in. Some were killed for witchcraft, and elsewhere, lots were sent to research facilities. Eventually, a committee was set up to study those affected. And the eventual discovery..."

Noir tapped the slab of rock three times. Radiant light beamed out from it, though the source wasn't evident—it seemed to come from the circular stone itself. Within the bright beams, tiny specks of *something* floated. Darted about in random directions. Vibrated, even.

Mesmerised, Cinn reached for them, his eyes flicking to Noir's for permission. He nodded, so Cinn's fingers threaded through the air, trying fruitlessly to catch the strange dust-like specks that were clearly... alive? "Are these... motes?"

"Yes. These are lumenmotes. This particular stone device attracts them. Anyone can activate the tablet, see?" Noir tapped it three times, and the light faded.

"You don't have to be moteblessed?"

"It depends on the motetech, but for this one, no. In a few hours, those stone columns you saw lining our paths will activate and emit light until dawn."

"Saves on your electric bill, I guess."

Noir snorted. "You have quite the sense of humour, young man. But, back to our conversation. What next, what next?" He looked quite lost for a moment, and Cinn shifted in his chair until finally he declared, "The discovery of motes changed everything." To which Cinn fought back an eye roll. "At first, we were just passive observers of motes. We studied them relentlessly, documenting their many forms, and theorising about their sudden appearance and the nature of their existence. Then, as time went on, we began to wield them. With enough innate skill and practice, we learned we could synthesise them, infuse them into material, bend them to our will." Noir's voice reached a dramatic cadence as he gesticulated wildly. *The man belongs on a stage.*

Reaching out carefully, Cinn tapped the stone tablet himself, wanting to study the lumenmotes again, to settle his reeling mind. "How does this all relate to my condition, though? These light ones are the first motes I've ever seen."

"Are they?" Noir peered at him and waited. Relit his pipe and gave another deep pull.

"Yes." But his irritated reply didn't rattle Noir, who continued to stare. Cinn watched the little light flecks dance in the brightness created by the stone. Something about the way they moved reminded him of something. "No..." he said slowly, as if waking up from a dream.

"Go on."

"I have seen them before," he whispered. "In the dark place."

"When you've shadowslipped?"

"The ones there aren't as... bright and friendly. I think I thought they were bits of floating ash or something. To be honest, whenever I end up there, I'm solely focused on getting back to reality as quickly as possible. But they do move in the same drifty way."

"This reminds me," said Noir, ruffling around in his drawer again. "We're going to spend a lot of sessions together unpicking the specifics of your ability, but until you've mastered it, there's something I can give you which should largely reduce the amount of unwanted slips into the shadowrealm." He presented Cinn with a long thin rectangular object, made of smooth, shiny golden metal. "Any wrist will do."

Confused but too tired to question, Cinn offered his left arm. To his surprise, Noir bent the solid-looking metal around his wrist, joining the band with an audible *click*. "Blimey," he muttered, lurching his hand back to touch the bangle for himself. It was rock solid, with no sign of any clasp. It seemed to have shaped itself to Cinn's skinny wrist, because it wouldn't slide off his hand. The seamless metal band was alarmingly warm, and something in it hummed with energy.

"How do I get it off?" he snapped at Noir. He'd been slowly warming to the eccentric fellow, but his lack of consent for this permanent adornment to his body had pissed him off.

"Relax," Noir said, offering Cinn his pipe. He refused—God only knew what the codger was smoking. "Hold the band in your hand for a few moments. Let it know that you want to remove it. It will expand, and come off easily."

"*Let it know?*" Cinn repeated, but Noir had already moved on to sliding him a stack of books. *Big* books. Heavy books. Books Cinn wouldn't have a hope in hell of reading.

His heart rate shot through the roof.

"I'm not really the best read—"

An alarm blared, piercingly loud. Not the sound of ringing metal. Not the electronic beeping of the fire alarms of his schooldays. It was the most peculiar screeching sound that seemed to be coming from everywhere and nowhere at once.

Noir, panic written all over his face, bolted out of his chair with alarming haste.

"What is it?" Cinn asked as Noir pulled on his coat.

"Evacuation order. Now. Follow me and stay close."

A moment later, Cinn was sprinting down the tower's spiral staircase, chasing after Noir, surprisingly nimble for one of his age. When they reached a corridor with the tube-like elevators, Noir grabbed the collar of his coat and thrust him into it with him, pulling Cinn's body close against his. Cinn closed his eyes, but his stomach still dropped out of his body as they plummeted to the bottom level at disturbing speed.

All around the lobby, others were also evacuating—hurrying to the doors, gripped by a grim panic that Cinn couldn't help but internalise himself.

This was not an everyday event.

"Noir!" someone shouted. "The Cerulean Auditorium is under attack. All hands on deck."

Cinn stuck to Noir like glue as the old man tore across the campus, alongside hundreds of others. Vaguely, he understood that his particular hands would not be at all useful in whatever 'attack' was taking place, but he had no idea of where else to go. So, he followed.

It didn't take long to trace the smoke in the sky all the way to the source.

And what a sight it was.

The building, composed of massive slabs of azure-blue bricks, was dome shaped and several stories tall. At least, it *had* been, because a large portion of it was cracking, slipping, crumbling to the ground with almighty crashes. Just visible through the increasingly thick smoke were three black circular shapes hovering in the sky. They were ebony-black, yet they hurt to look at, like bright light.

Though he took several stumbling steps backwards, dozens of people streamed past him, jostling Cinn in their rush to get closer to the auditorium.

The Cerulean Auditorium.

Where Julien had gone to watch that guest lecturer he was so excited about. Was he still inside the building? Cinn shouldn't care about that rude asshole, especially after he'd abandoned him earlier. That he did infuriated him greatly—his inability not to care about others had always been his most vulnerable point.

Noir had left him, or he'd left Noir. Either way, he was now alone in the crowd of frightened watchers.

An abrupt shrieking sound had his eyes magnetising back upwards, to the black voids. To his horror, bursts of red light launched out of them, streaming like fireworks. Fireworks that burst into flames. Not the warm orange glow of a fireplace but wickedly dark flames. Crimson-red flames. Scarlet-red flames. Blood-red flames. Hungry flames.

Within a heartbeat, the unnatural-hued flames coiled and danced like malevolent spirits desperate for destruction as they engulfed the entire building.

Cinn pressed his fist to his mouth in a silent scream. How many people was he watching die?

The first telltale signs of Cinn losing himself to the dark place—of Cinn *shadowslipping*—began. Sweaty palms. Heart racing impossibly fast. The sensation that he was floating, untethered to this world. He fell to his knees just as the metal on his wrist began to burn. A hiss of pain escaped him as he inspected the bangle. There was no visible injury to his skin. The metal cooled and with it, the symptoms of his affliction.

Strong hands pulled him roughly to his feet. "Cinn! We've been worried about you! Are you okay?"

Cinn turned to find Darcy's concerned eyes piercing his. "I'm fine. But isn't that where Julien..." He gestured to the burning inferno.

Her lips pressed into a grimace, then her eyes widened as she shouted, "Elliot!"

In three strides, Elliot crossed the thick crowd, throwing his arms around Darcy and squeezing her to him. "I just got here. About to go ask what I can do. Is Julien still in there?" His voice cracked on Julien's name, and the primal fear etched onto Elliot's face was echoed on Darcy's. "Stay here. I'm going inside to find him."

"Don't be stupid!" Darcy shrieked, gripping Elliot's arm. She looked to Cinn, as if he would be any use in this crisis. There was no way he would be able to restrain Elliot, the man was built like a brick wall. "That could be suicide. Let them—"

Elliot brought his hands up to cup her face. "It's *Julien*, Darce. *Julien*. We can't lose anyone else. I don't know what I'd do if—"

"Luckily, we don't need to find out."

Three heads snapped towards the French accent.

"Oh!" cried Darcy, launching herself at Julien with such velocity that Cinn flinched backwards.

Elliot appeared to be holding himself back from also throwing himself at Julien. He settled for grabbing the hand that wasn't rubbing Darcy's back.

Relief coursed through Cinn's veins, and he couldn't help but smile at the three friends. Their obvious devotion to each other tugged on his heartstrings, causing a surge of unexpected homesickness.

"Alright?"

It took several seconds for Cinn to clock that Julien was talking to him. He nodded in response, turning back to the auditorium. The chaos was now organised—security guard-like figures pushed the crowds back, and a line of people dressed in dark uniforms stood next to the building, palms raised. Although the thick smoke obscured his view, it appeared they were trying to extinguish the flames using massive balls of swirling water.

"Those officers are our gendarmerie."

Transfixed, Cinn stared, unblinking. It was like he'd stepped into a movie. A movie with black holes in the sky and superheroes and *magic*.

The surrounding air crackled with a malevolent energy. With a bright flash, the grass to the left of them burst into the same red flames, only for a passing moment, the fire vanishing to leave a smoking, charred symbol on the ground. Shocked gasps circulated through the crowd as people began to point in various directions—several other patches were appearing, burnt into the ground, spaced out across the lawn.

Cinn took one cautious step towards the closest one. The symbol was a twisted amalgamation of jagged lines and intersecting circles, its chaotic design defying any sense of order or symmetry. A central circle was marred by sharp lines slashing through it, like a blade cutting through reality itself. Radiating outward, smaller circles intersected with the main form, resembling ripples of disruption originating from a pebble dropped into a pond. The words to explain why eluded Cinn, but it was an unsettling sight.

"It's the mark of the Arcane Purifiers," Elliot hissed. "They must have been targeting today's speaker, Julien. Your guy, Valerius Weaver. Else they would have attacked the Solstice Atrium, or St. Caelum's. It makes sense, given Weaver's outspokenness about furthering motetech."

Darcy shook her head, face crumpled in disbelief.

"I guess the cold war finally heated up," said Julien. He raised his arm—a patch of his black wool trench coat had been roughly burned off, the edges surrounding the scorched area curling slightly. "Quite literally. At least they seem to have put out those flames, though."

What remained of the burned structure smouldered, but Julien was correct—no red flames lingered. Orders were now being shouted for everyone to go home.

"Wait here while I check if they need me," Elliot shouted over his shoulder as he sprinted towards the gendarmerie.

"*November the fifth.* This isn't a coincidence," Darcy said to Julien. "You know what this means."

Before he could be left yet again in the dark, Cinn looked at Darcy expectantly to ask, "What isn't a coincidence?"

Of course, she deferred to Prince Julien, apparent leader and keeper of all information. When Julien said nothing, Cinn turned and stomped off—admittedly vaguely—towards where he hoped the car was, to sulk by himself. If they wanted privacy to talk about their oh-so-secret things, they could have it.

Swimming against the crowd, who were clearly ignoring the request to bugger off, Cinn pushed his way through and wandered the streets until he found the small car park, nestled in a small dip. Julien's ridiculously shiny black car, 'Maz'—he rolled his eyes—was easy to spot, even in the fading light.

He leaned against the car door for a while, wondering if smearing fingerprints on Julien's windows would be appropriate revenge. Before he could enact his plan, the three musketeers arrived. Julien remotely unlocked the door, and Elliot made for the passenger side.

"Wait," Julien said, and Elliot froze. "Let Cinn sit in the front."

A look crossed Elliot's face, so dark that Cinn braced for some sort of outburst. But after a beat, Elliot moved out of Cinn's way.

It wasn't until they'd cleared the queue out of the car park that Julien said, "We're more than happy to tell you everything, Cinn. It just wasn't the right time or place back there."

Why did Cinn get the feeling he was parroting a script written by Darcy?

"So, start talking then. What's the big deal with today's date?"

Julien expelled a heavy breath, lightly drumming the wheel. "Before we get to that, you should first know that a few months ago, my younger sister, Béatrice, died."

Cinn's head snapped towards Julien before he could tamp down his abrupt reaction. Julien's expression was tightly controlled, but Cinn caught the swallow of his throat.

"I'm... very sorry for your loss."

"The official line is that it was a tragic accident. However, we believe she was murdered."

Out of the windscreen, the last drops of sunlight fell behind the hill. It took with it the last remnants of Cinn's energy—because these three were about to be sorely disappointed. "Is this what you meant when you said you needed my help? Because, if so, you should know that I'm not a telephone to the dead. Not by a long stretch."

A hand squeezed his arm. "Of course we know that, Cinn," said Darcy from the back seat. "And we would completely respect your decision not to help us. We understand that shadowslipping is probably very traumatic for you, and wouldn't want to cause you any stress."

Something in her tone suggested some of what she said was aimed at Julien.

"I don't have much—okay, *any*—control over it," said Cinn quietly. "I've never done it on purpose before and I've certainly not tried to *find* anyone there." The idea was laughable.

"We have some knowledge of what we could try, with your full permission," Darcy said softly.

These idiots did know that four people died last time he shadowslipped, right? "I can't risk bringing anything... *anyone*... back. It's only happened a handful of times over the years, but last time..."

Darcy squeezed his arm again. "I believe our method will be completely—*relatively*—safe, Cinn. However, the choice is entirely yours."

"And you're here to learn, aren't you?" said Elliot. Nothing was inherently wrong with what he said, but it prickled Cinn's skin, nevertheless.

"Yes, Elliot, but not from experimenting with our every whim," Darcy hissed.

"Everything we've tried so far from your book of tricks has got us nowhere."

"That still doesn't mean we can demand he do this for us, with very little in it for him!"

An idea struck Cinn. A solution to at least one of his problems. "I'll do it. Well, try to, or whatever."

"What?" Julien glanced at him, eyes wide, and his voice had a slight shake when he continued, "You will?"

An uneasy feeling choked Cinn, and his next words tasted bitter in his throat. "In exchange for payment. I need cash. Not for me. For my mate. Tyler. He's in trouble. I was trying to get him out of it by agreeing to let my restaurant be robbed. Then that obviously fell flat on its face, so Richter's gang will still be after him. And I'm just—" He cut himself off, gesturing widely to the beautiful Swiss countryside, and the fancy car he was being driven in. All the way to his new *house*. God, if Tyler could see him right now...

"Oh Cinn, if you'd have just told us yesterday—"

"Done," said Julien, a degree too loudly. "Deal."

"But I haven't even told you how much."

Julien's mouth quirked and Cinn took it as a sign that the number wasn't going to be an issue. *Nice to be him.*

"Get the details to me and I'll prepare the transfer paperwork for the bank."

Fuck. Did Tyler even have a bank account? And how long would it all take?

However, Cinn didn't have a chance to worry further before Julien ploughed on. "So. Your next question. The date."

Cinn nodded. "The fifth of November." After a pause he continued, "Remember, remember, the fifth of November, gunpowder, treason and plot."

Then he realised he was in a car full of foreigners. Well, Darcy was Scottish, but...

Darcy gasped. "I didn't even make the connection! I haven't been home for bonfire night in so long."

"What?" snapped Elliot. "I don't get it. Is it a nursery rhyme?"

"Some dude called Guy Fawkes tried to blow up our parliament because he was pissed at them," said Cinn. "They probably deserved it."

"That... about summarises it," said Darcy. "He was then hung for treason."

Julien whistled. "So, what you're saying is... they chose this date for their first violent act as a... what? Nod to the rebels of past times? A sign that they mean business?"

"I mean, it could be just a weird coincidence."

"What's the deal with the 'Arcane Purifiers' anyway?" said Cinn. "What the heck are they doing blowing up buildings?"

"They think it's necessary action, for the good of mankind and the planet." Darcy.

"They're zealots." Elliot.

Cinn looked to Julien.

"It's a complicated matter," he said at last.

Elliot laughed. "Don't let daddy dearest hear you describe it as that. I think he'd have some choice words for you."

"I don't want to bore you to death, Cinn, but essentially the Arcane Purifiers are concerned—with good reason—about the damage mote-craft inflicts on our planet."

Cinn shook his head. "Huh? What does it do?"

"None of it has ever been proven," snapped Elliot.

"Oh, come off it!" said Darcy. "Don't bury your head in the sand."

"Enough," shouted Julien. "It's already been a day and a half without ending it with us rehashing this shit again."

"This shit might be what got Béatrice killed!"

Cinn's eyes darted between Julien and Elliot. Uncomfortable and confused didn't even begin to describe his current state of awkwardness. "Why do you say that?"

Darcy leapt in. "We found today's date circled in her diary. Many times, in red pen. She'd scribbled *'Jour J?'* over it."

"D-Day," Julien translated.

Cinn tensed at his own words when he asked, "So... was your sister like... involved in the Arcane Purifier group?"

"*Non*. No way. She wouldn't have kept that from me. She was clearly... investigating them or something. Recording evidence."

Cinn couldn't help but glance at the other two in the rear-view mirror. They weren't as convinced.

Darcy caught his eye and leaned forwards. "It's important to know, Cinn, that until today, they've never hurt anybody. They've been all words, no action. Just lots of meetings with Auri's consortium, in addition to public speaking. Evidently, though, AP decided that political lobbying wasn't getting them anywhere. The consortium is more than happy to bury their heads in the sand and ignore them. And to be fair, just last week there was a massive earthquake in Egypt. The country is often cited as having the world's lowest seismic risk. They recorded a seven on the Richter scale, and half a city was destroyed."

"Because of motes?!"

Elliot made a sound like he was about to jump in, but stopped himself.

"It's a complicated debate," said Julien.

Cinn openly glared at him. "I'm not stupid."

"He's not saying that, Cinn. But he's right."

Darcy's strained tone seemed to close the conversation, and the rest of the car journey passed in contemplative silence. Well, he presumed it was silent—he'd plugged in his headphones. Finally Julien pulled up at his house, with a promise to pick him up tomorrow.

"I imagine anything scheduled for tomorrow at Auri will be cancelled, while they sort this shit out. Shall I pick you up at noon, and we can reconvene at Darcy's cottage? Perhaps attempt to reach Béatrice?" Julien's intense gaze burned into him. "If you think you're up to it? Darcy has done lots of research into shadowslipping and she thinks she can create an environment where nothing can be brought back through when you return."

The prospect of willingly entering the dark place scared him. *Petrified* him, even. Living in fear of entering it had been a constant torment his entire life. But now he was here, it was finally time to learn to control it. He could enter his next session with Noir armed with more information and skill than he currently possessed.

And so, Cinn nodded. "I'm happy to try. But Tyler gets the money either way, right?"

"Of course," Julien said smoothly.

He watched their car drive away from his doorstep, half glad to be rid of the odd trio, yet half reluctant to be alone again. The three of them were the closest thing he had to friends in this brave new world, although he wouldn't trust Elliot as far as he could throw him. And probably not Julien, either. His list of allies was going well then.

He dragged an armchair over to the wall telephone. It was time to phone Bradley's number again and hopefully track down Tyler. If he was still alive.

Six

JULIEN

It was ten a.m.

Ten a.m. and Julien had already eaten breakfast, read the weekly Auri-produced newspaper, completed a three-kilometre run, showered, tinkered with the translation device prototype he was developing for fun, practised his German verbs so he could test said device, and drunk two cups of coffee.

Julien rolled his neck. Still two more hours to kill. That was fine. He could do two more hours.

Next, he would work. Slipping on his reading glasses, he reached for the papers on his coffee table.

His phone rang, vibrating his side table and hurting his ears with its loud shrill. One glance at the caller ID sent two fingers straight to his temple. After a deep breath, he picked it up and held it a few inches away from his ear.

"*Père.*" If his father picked up the note of annoyance already in his voice, he didn't mention it.

From his first line of rapid, angry French, it was clear he had called to rant. "Three people deceased, and over fifty injured, and my own son doesn't find it within himself to call and assure me of his well-being?"

"You could have called *me* last night, *Père.*" Fifty people injured? The newspaper had said thirty. His father always did have more information than everyone else, however.

"I should not have to chase after reassurance. I expect the courtesy of my offspring to prioritise familial duty and ensure his parent is spared the inconvenience of concern. It's basic decency, something I thought I had instilled, but evidently, the appreciation of such matters..."

Julien held the phone away from his ear and hummed a low note. "Julien? *Julien?*"

"I'm sorry. Do you want to have an actual conversation now?"

His father emitted an exasperated huff. "I suppose my energy is best spent on the terrorists who claimed the lives of three of our own last night. All of my sources indicate that none of these *Arcane Purifiers* had the audacity to reveal themselves at the scene of the crime and take responsibility for their actions?"

"Correct, *Père*, none of them were walking around with a giant sign on their backs that said 'I did it'. Not that I saw anyway."

"Well, they've truly outdone themselves this time. There's no conceivable way the consortium will close their eyes to this. Shooting themselves in the foot is an understatement. If this is their idea of promoting their cause, they've just orchestrated their own downfall."

The temptation to openly support the Purifiers just to piss off his father was strong, but Julien resisted.

"Anyway, shifting our focus to other matters, Eleanor relayed the news that she has successfully secured the proven shadowslipper from London and placed him under your guardianship."

"That would be correct."

"And? What is your assessment? Do you believe his skills are sufficiently honed to be a valuable asset against the umbraphages?"

Not even in the slightest, but getting him to communicate with Béatrice is a much higher priority for me, as it should be for you, dear Père.

"My role is only to make sure he stays put in Talwacht," said Julien. "I'm sure Eleanor will be given all the information you want."

"Right, right. How did your MEET application fare in the end?" Before Julien could reply, he continued, "And how is the charming Darcy Beaumont? Now, there's a blossoming young woman destined for success. I crossed paths with her father a few weeks ago, and he regaled me with tales of her accomplishments."

"I bet he did."

"Will you bring her to my birthday soiree again?"

The mention of his father's annual party sent a visceral shiver down his spine. Every muscle in his body tensed as Julien glanced at his wall calendar. The event was marked with a small illustration of a penis with a jewelled crown on it.

"I was actually planning on bringing someone else home for your birthday party weekend."

He grimaced at his own words, surprised by them. He knew why he'd said it—bringing someone else along to act as armour between himself and his father would make the experience ten times better. Now he'd have to follow through, however.

A beanie-hat-shaped possibility floated through his mind.

His father hummed. "Truly? Someone you're courting? We would be delighted to extend our hospitality to her. Carrie in particular is dying to dote on a daughter-in-law."

Julien's mouth parted in the silent scream he frequently made at any mention of his father's second wife acting like his mother.

"Regardless, the delightful Darcy Beaumont is more than welcome as well. I've already extended an invitation to her family."

"I have to go now."

"Yes, yes, I'm sure you're very busy. See you soon."

And with that, his father hung up on him.

Julien flung the receiver across his coffee table, then watched the cord rebound it back towards him. His hands tore through his hair in frustration. That had been one of their more pleasant phone calls, yet it had still reduced him to this.

The unpublished article he was required to review, a proposal for mote-powered steam engines for cargo ships, still sat on his table expectantly, but Julien pushed it away.

There was only one thing he could do to placate himself when he was in this mood. Julien walked over to his piano, sat down, and soothed himself with the jazz-infused melodies of Miles Davis.

Although it was tempting to knock on Cinn's door to glimpse the interior of his house, it was cold, and the door was far. Three short beeps of Maz's horn and Cinn emerged seconds later, traipsing down his path while still pulling on his coat.

After Cinn left them yesterday, Elliot had launched into a spiel about not trusting him, not liking him, and then—surprisingly—started questioning their entire plan of getting Cinn involved in their quest to contact Béatrice. Julien had stayed silent—a useful strategy when dealing with Elliot's outbursts—but his words planted seeds of doubt in his mind. Should they really be messing around with shadowslipping? The practice was largely unknown, and Cinn obviously had no idea what he was doing.

Cinn slid into the car, closing Maz's door gently behind him, earning him a point.

"Planning to tune all of us out today?" Julien asked, nodding at the chunky headphones around his neck.

Cinn snorted. "Only if you're annoying. But music helps me control my episodes. Well, it can help stop them. And I know that's the opposite of what we're doing today, but..." He shrugged.

"If you're into music, why don't you put something on?" Julien gestured to the radio's scan and seek function as Maz's engine purred to life to drive them out of Cinn's quiet street.

Cinn flicked through the channels, bypassing anything German, French, or Italian until he hit something English. Julien glanced over to see his face light up. The vocals were a bit too squeaky for his liking, and the bass too loud, but Cinn was soon bobbing along and mouthing along with the lyrics. Most of the words seemed to be 'hello', aside from some notion of the singer's demands to be entertained.

Julien certainly wasn't. Well, not by the song, anyway.

Cinn must have seen something in his expression, as he said, "Don't you like Nirvana?"

"Who?"

With a shake of his head, Cinn went back to enjoying the music, tapping his foot along to the beat. Several headache-inducing songs later, they arrived at Darcy's cottage. Cinn would never again be allowed control of the radio.

A white picket fence enclosed Darcy's overgrown front garden. It was getting harder and harder to battle your way through it to reach her door.

"Darcy's not in, so we need the spare key." Julien grinned mischievously and pointed to an ornate, antique-looking lantern hanging by the door. "I invented this for her."

As Cinn raised an eyebrow in question, Julien tapped a hidden sigil on the lantern, causing it to flicker with a gentle glow. Moments later, there was a bright blue burst of light within the lantern's glass enclosure. Julien unlatched one panel and it swung open to reveal the spare key waiting for them, a few remaining blue sparks—veilmotes—still fading out.

Julien motioned for Cinn to retrieve the key, at which point Cinn may have mumbled something about key safes being perfectly adequate, which Julien may have ignored.

Once they'd closed the door behind them, Cinn hovered, wrapping his coat around him like he didn't want it to be taken away from him. "Where are the other two?"

"Elliot exists in the magical world of Elliot-time, where nobody else's schedules are important. Darcy said she had to run out to get something."

Julien ushered Cinn into the kitchen. He poked around in Darcy's cupboards, looking for any breakfast tea to offer Cinn, who hadn't enjoyed his chai experience last time. However, he couldn't make head nor tail of Darcy's stock, arranged in mismatched jars with undecipherable codes scribbled on them.

Cinn, meanwhile, paced up and down the kitchen, hands in jean pockets, radiating discomfort. Just when Julien was going to ask what the matter was, he burst out with, "Do you have any smokes? I tried to find a shop last night, but I was too knackered. But I got an envelope with a few hundred francs in it through my letterbox, from Madame Sinclair's assistant. So I can pay you."

"Don't be ridiculous."

Julien didn't really smoke much—albeit occasionally in social situations with a glass of red wine—but he knew exactly where Darcy's supply was. He opened the bronze tin in her bottom drawer and took out the packet of Gitanes. "These okay? They're what we all used to smoke in Paris."

Removing two, he gestured for Cinn to follow him into Darcy's tiny back garden. The warm hues of the last wave of autumn foliage blanketed the ground. A black iron bench, that ivy was attempting to claim for itself, lay at the far side of it. Once seated, Julien passed Cinn a cigarette. "These might be a tiny bit stale."

He took it gratefully. "I usually smoke roll-ups."

"Really? They've always looked rather inconvenient to me. Too many elements to obtain to make them."

Cinn raised his eyebrows, his piercing glinting in the light. "They're cheap though." He lit his cigarette from the lighter Julien flicked on and offered him. When he took his first deep drag, his eyes rolled back in euphoria before closing completely, and Julien had to suppress a laugh.

For a short time, the pair sat in peaceful silence. Julien lit his own cigarette before leaning back into the bench, listening to the sound of the wind and the distant twittering of birds.

"I thought it was just you that came from Paris," Cinn said at last.

Caught off guard at his sudden interest, Julien took a second before replying. "I was the only one born there. I first met Elliot when I was twelve, at this international summer camp for moteblessed teenagers. And yes, it was as awful as it sounded," he said, laughing at the grimace on Cinn's face. "Then we attended La Sorbonne together in Paris. We met Darcy there. Béatrice joined the university the year after me, and then, *voilà*." A nostalgic collage of images of the four of them lounging around in Paris's parks and cafés during the summer breaks distracted him from saying more.

"Okay…" Cinn said slowly. He tipped his chin back and blew a series of impressive smoke rings into the air, to watch them disappear. "So it was a coincidence that you and Elliot found another *moteblessed* friend there, or…?"

Julien laughed. Cinn knew so little about his tiny corner of society. "*Non*, definitely not. There are a handful of universities across Europe that tend to attract groups of moteblessed students. There's a slightly different admission pathway, admittedly. But we all studied alongside 'normal' students and completed what is equivalent to your master's degree, alongside some extra-curricular, invite-only classes."

Julien winked at him. Cinn returned a weak smile that didn't meet his eyes, before his gaze wandered and he twirled a strand of hair poking out of his beanie. Were the intricacies of Julien's world overwhelming him?

Well, it was Cinn's world too now, so the quicker he was up to speed, the better.

Cinn finished his cigarette and flicked the butt into an ashtray on the ground. Julien offered him the end of his—he'd found the first few puffs more than enough—and Cinn quickly accepted it before asking, voice strained, "So what did you study then, at your fancy university?"

"Engineering and art."

Cinn snorted. "Do they go together?"

"They do indeed, actually."

After popping a mint into his mouth, then offering another one to Julien, Cinn kicked the ground with the heel of his boot and looked at his shoes. "Anyway. I have a bank account for you. If it's still alright to transfer that money."

"Certainly," said Julien. "Have you got all the details?"

Cinn rummaged around in his back pocket to produce a small slip of crumpled paper. "This is actually my mate Bradley's bank account. Tyler is staying with him."

"And how much am I transferring him, exactly?"

At this, Cinn did look up to meet his eye, steadying himself, and Julien found himself instantly lost in the depths of his determined gaze. He couldn't deny it: there was something about Cinn's face that entranced him. Perhaps it was the fusion of two elements in Cinn's countenance: boyish innocence paired with a quiet maturity that seemed to surpass his years.

"Ten thousand. Pounds. Or whatever that is in francs, or however it works." An angry red flush dotted Cinn's cheeks and his jaw clenched.

Julien almost laughed at the display. He constructed his best deep-in-thought face. "Hmm. I will see what I can do. Move some things around and such."

In actuality, the amount was no bother to him whatsoever. He'd expected it to be triple that, at least, if this Tyler fellow was that deep in trouble.

"It needs to be soon," Cinn said, frowning deeply, and Julien felt a sliver of remorse for toying with him. An oddly large sliver.

"I promise I'll sort it all out by the end of the day." Then Julien watched Cinn closely as he continued, "Your boyfriend is very lucky to have you."

Cinn's body tensed, a deep frown etching into his forehead. "What makes you call him that?"

"Something in the way you say his name."

Cinn's gaze returned to the ground. He pulled his beanie lower down over his head. "He's not my boyfriend. Not anymore, at least." Emotion clouded his voice.

Julien basked in the glory of being right. Of course, he was rarely wrong when it came to these things.

"We haven't been together in a long, long time. I—" Cinn cut himself off, eyeing Julien warily.

Julien remained expectantly silent, his sole focus on Cinn.

"I... told him I couldn't be with him until he got himself clean. And five years later, here we still are."

"Really? I'd have imagined you'd have been quite the incentive."

Julien's attempt at flirtation crashed and burned, evident by the way Cinn's frosty face shot him a glare that could rival an arctic chill. "It doesn't work like that. You can love someone with everything you've got, every last inch of you, and it can still not be enough. Sometimes it's not something they can control." The atmosphere around them shifted, an awkward tension taking hold. "Don't judge someone without even meeting them, alright? Tyler's had it tough. Way worse than me."

Julien threw up his hands, conceding with a theatrical gesture of surrender, although he harboured a subtle disagreement about self-control—years of practising self-discipline in various ways wouldn't let him. "Absolutely," he replied in his best honeyed voice. And then, to rectify the situation. "I'll say it again. Your *Tyler* is very lucky to have a friend like you. Even from a thousand miles away, you're still desperately trying to help."

Cinn shrugged. "He'd do the same for me."

Julien wasn't convinced. "Anyway, you don't need to worry so much about homophobia and such when you're at Auri, but be more wary about what you say or do in town. Those folks aren't quite as accepting."

Cinn's eyebrow quirked up. "Don't worry, I'm not planning on shagging anyone in the middle of the town square."

Julien threw back his head and laughed, enjoying the way his whole body shook. It had been a while since he'd laughed this hard. Without breaking eye contact, he said, "Exhibitionism not your style? Shame. You'd be quite the sight."

Cinn's light-olive cheeks were already rosy, but now they *burned*.

So fun to play with. Too fun.

Julien waited for Cinn to look away, to ease his embarrassment. But he didn't. He didn't smile, only stared back at Julien. Was he waiting for him to make the next move? Waiting for him to break eye contact first? Well, if he was playing that game, he was in for a surprise. Julien easily—lazily even—gazed into Cinn's gorgeously golden eyes, framed by thick, dark lashes.

One eyelash had shed and nestled itself in the crinkle of Cinn's right eye.

"Don't move," Julien whispered, as his thumb ghosted upwards across Cinn's cheek to catch the lash. He allowed his knuckle to brush over Cinn's eyebrow bar before sweeping the lash onto the back of his hand. He raised it to Cinn's lips. "Make a wish."

And still with that unbreakable eye contact, Cinn blew, his full lips pressing together in a manner surely, *surely*, deliberately sensual.

"What are you doing?" Came a gruff voice.

Cinn recoiled from Julien, pushing himself into the corner of the bench as Elliot stormed into the garden, leaving the kitchen door swinging wide open.

Julien sighed. Why could he never have nice things without a price? "Smoking. Want one?"

"No thanks. I thought we were here to try to reach Béatrice." Elliot's unsmiling gaze settled on Cinn, and did not waver.

"We are. You were late."

Elliot could read every slight nuance of Julien's expressions, and so he communicated a crystal clear: *Why the hell are you making a scene? Pull yourself together.*

Because she was an angel sent from heaven, Darcy materialised in the doorway, shouting, "How many times have I told you not to leave this door open? Well? Are you coming in? I've got everything we need."

Seven

CINN

Now that it was time to begin, the panic set in.

If someone had told Cinn just a week ago that he'd sign up to deliberately fall into *the dark place,* the place he lived in fear of most days of his life, he'd have laughed in utter disbelief.

The shadowrealm.

It had a proper name now. It was a real place. It wasn't all a figment of his imagination.

Although, the handful of times something—or *someone*—had returned with him had proven that to him before.

The very first time it had happened, that he'd *shadowslipped,* was his thirteenth birthday. Two weeks after 'the river incident'. He'd been trying to wake his mum up from where she'd fallen asleep on the sofa. He could still see it now: her pale face partially obscured by greasy hair, hand outstretched towards the empty wine bottle on the floor.

She'd promised him pancakes.

Pancakes from that diner down the road. They'd never been able to afford them before, but she'd promised him because it was his *birthday*.

So he'd shook her. Gently at first, then violently.

The more he shook her, and the more she failed to wake up, the more unsteady his breaths became, until he was sure he was about to suffocate.

The light in the room faded, even though it was the middle of the day, and then, all of a sudden, he wasn't in his living room at all.

Cinn only very briefly slipped into the shadowrealm, that first time. He'd found himself in a kitchen, a similar shape to their own. It even had the same sink and the same cream cabinets. He met an old man there. A rather nice old man. He'd given Cinn his newspaper, and Cinn read it, even though it was twenty years out of date and there were lots of complicated words he didn't even attempt to read. He sat at the old man's breakfast table with him until he decided he should probably try to get home, which is when he jumped off the stool, fell through the man's kitchen floor, and promptly awoke in his own flat.

If only all his trips had been that peaceful.

He already knew that today's certainly wouldn't be.

Cinn followed Julien through the cottage, halting when Julien paused outside of a door.

"Hold on."

Julien slipped inside the room, and returned with a framed photograph, a double portrait. Cinn's focus shot straight to a younger-looking Julien. In the photo, his mouth was open in a wide grin, white teeth gleaming as he beamed at the photographer. His arm was slung around a girl with the exact same shade of blonde hair as his own—albeit slightly curlier. She was pretty. *Béatrice* was pretty.

"It will help to hold her image in your mind."

Cinn nodded and gently took the photo from Julien. The Julien he saw before him today was so starkly different from the Julien in the picture, and he couldn't help but pity him. Though he was fairly sure Julien would *not* want that.

"And what exactly am I asking her if I see her?" *Yo Béatrice, you involved in any terrorism plots lately?*

Julien hesitated. "Darcy says you should just focus on making contact today. Seeing if you can actually find her there." He clamped his lips together.

In the dining room, Darcy instructed Cinn to lie on the empty, dark wooden table, as if it were a makeshift operating theatre. He did so, feeling foolish, like a spectacle on a stage. After a moment spent staring up at the dark beams of the cottage's ceiling, he sat up to find the others not focused on him at all—they were rushing about, lighting candles in an efficient, practiced manner.

"But what will the candles do?" Cinn asked.

"Oh, those are just for atmosphere," Darcy replied, wiggling her fingers in the air.

Cinn resisted palming his face.

"But this isn't," she added brightly, waving something in his face. "This is aged white bark from a paper birch tree. Over a hundred years old."

Cinn frowned at the gleaming white material. "Seems unlikely."

"It's infused with luminaquartz. We're going to use it to link Béatrice's magnet item to your body." She broke off a small chunk of bark and ground it with a mortar and pestle.

"So... after we begin, will the shadowmotes suddenly appear?" Cinn was dubious.

Darcy flicked through a thick leather-bound tome. "I don't think you'll see the shadowmotes until after you slip. Also, in order to prevent you bringing anything back with you, Cinn, we're going to draw on your body with some special ink. Usually we'd draw a protective circle around you on the floor, but my research suggests this will be even safer. Do you mind removing the top half of your clothes?"

Cinn stared at her. "You're joking. What the fuck is this freaky, culty, ritual shit?"

Julien snorted, but Elliot scowled at Cinn, practically snarling, "Just trust her. She knows what she's doing."

Grumbling, Cinn shimmied out of his hoodie and T-shirt. Although he wasn't shy about showing his body, he couldn't remember the last time anyone had seen his naked torso, and he had to fight not to cover it with his arms. Already he could feel Julien's burning gaze cataloguing the tattoos usually hidden under his baggy clothes. He prayed the colour of his cheeks wasn't betraying him.

The last thing that remained was his new protective gold band. It would have to come off—the whole point of it was to stop him slipping. Noir had said for him to 'tell' the metal circle to release itself. Cinn sighed and gripped the shiny object tightly, enclosing it with his other hand. He focused all of his energy into imagining the metal was pliable under his touch. He imagined it thinning, widening enough to slip it off his wrist. The electric tingle dancing under his fingers told him it was working. When he pulled his hand away, the bangle was ever-so-slightly larger, and slipped off him with ease. He placed it next to himself, feeling slightly smug.

Darcy turned to Elliot. "Have you got the aethraven ink? One of you two can copy out the symbols, though. You know what my drawing is like. I'll end up removing his liver or something."

Elliot produced a small jar of thick black liquid and a thin artist's paintbrush.

"I better do it." Julien's hands shot out, snatching both items from Elliot.

Elliot opened his mouth—to protest?—and then crossed his arms, stepping back from the table with a sulky pout. "You were happy to let me do it on the floor in the library," he mumbled.

"That was because we were playing with toys. This is serious business."

Julien certainly had a *serious business* look about him as he eyed Cinn's exposed skin, which prickled under his gaze. Julien propped the book Darcy passed him on the table and studied it for a moment. He pressed one cool hand to Cinn's bare skin as his other dipped the brush into the ink jar, then made feather-light, deliberate strokes, brushing intricate patterns onto him that he couldn't comprehend. Perhaps he'd have fared better decoding the symbols if he wasn't finding Julien's proximity, Julien's touch, and the orangey scent of Julien's hair so overwhelming that it was frying his senses, just like that moment on the garden bench earlier.

He closed his eyes, but that just made every sensation even more powerful, including the feel of Julien's fingers pulling his skin taut—was he deliberately kneading Cinn's muscles with his fingertips, or was Cinn imagining it?

Each wet stroke of the brush sent a shiver down Cinn's spine, the cool ink tingling against his skin, leaving behind a trail of heat in its wake. Just when it was getting to the point where he was biting back inappropriate sounds, Julien announced he was finished.

"We're going to use this treasured item of Béatrice's as a 'magnet item' to help draw her to you." From his pocket, Julien produced a silver locket—the oval type that often housed pictures inside—engraved with moons and stars. "She wore this every day." He turned the locket around to reveal the other side was charred and blistered, once smooth metal now warped and blackened. "Until the day she died."

Cinn flinched as Julien placed the cool metal onto his stomach, in the centre of the inkwork circle he'd created, looking Cinn dead in the eye as he did. Cinn swallowed, unsure of why this simple action was eliciting such an intense reaction from his body—so much so that he had the sudden urge to promise Julien he'd keep the locket safe for him.

Darcy held the mortar with the powdered luminaquartz in it, then spat in it.

Cinn let slip a sound of disgust. "Is that going on my body?"

"Preferably, yes."

"Did you have to use spit?"

"Apparently, yes."

Cinn sighed. "Just get on with it, then."

The ink already felt strange, his body being so exposed even stranger, so what was Darcy's spit added to the mix? Cinn just wanted this entire ordeal over as quickly as possible now. He was already fantasising about stepping into his new bathtub in his fancy bathroom later.

Darcy rubbed the paste into the middle of the inked ring, then coated the locket with it before pressing it firmly into his flesh. The chain link tickled his belly button.

"I've prepared a compound for you, to stimulate your body into slipping." Presenting a small circular tin containing fine, light brown crystals, Darcy continued, "It's a bit like an adrenaline shot, but you'll feel the effects slightly slower."

Cinn eyed the dubious powder, remembering the Frostbite she'd used against him the other day.

"It's this, or we stress your body in other ways. We could try electric shocks, or—"

"No, no, this is fine," Cinn said quickly. "As long as it's medicinal."

A pause. "Sure." Darcy offered him the tin. "Rub a fair bit on your gums."

The taste was vile, reminiscent of burnt copper and bitter herbs. The urge to grimace was strong when the synthetic compound sent a tingling sensation through his mouth, alike to tiny sparks dancing on his tongue.

For a moment, nothing happened. Then he felt the *thump, thump, thump* of his heartbeat steadily increasing.

The cool ink on his skin prickled.

Suddenly, he was slipping.

First went his hearing—replaced by a low buzzing.

Next went his vision, as the world faded at its edges.

Finally, the sensation of falling.

Falling....

Backwards

Backwards

Backw—

This trip was markedly different from Cinn's other episodes of shadowslipping.

For a start, this was the first time he'd deliberately slipped, the first time he was entering the space for a *purpose*.

Usually Cinn would arrive screaming, heart pounding, body shaking, eyes darting wildly around to see where he'd ended up this time and who he had the pleasure of meeting.

Although each experience had been slightly different, nothing had ever been so visually striking as where he found himself on this occasion.

Often, his surroundings took on a warped version of his current reality—or, a version of reality that the host spirit had lived in—but this time, Cinn found himself in a city. A distorted city that lay in ruins, a surreal tapestry of chaos painted in shades of ominous red. Colossal skyscrapers, larger than he'd ever seen, stood like twisted sentinels, their jagged silhouettes etched against the blood-red sky.

Bizarre crimson vines snaked like arteries of some massive creature across broken buildings and crumbling asphalt. They were all over everything, as far as his eye could see, the red tendrils coiled around structures, thorns pulsating with something, some *energy* Cinn somehow understood to be... malevolent. The very ground seemed to writhe with their presence. It was like Cinn had stepped into one of the sci-fi horror movies that he'd watched in his childhood—but hopefully his trip would end more happily than *Alien*.

Choosing a direction at random—it was hard to see far into the distance, everything being obscured by a thick, ashen mist—Cinn walked, eyeing the fractured and uneven tarmac that shook under each step.

Twice he had to stop to calm his beating heart. *You're safe. They've got you.* But did they? Should he really be so trusting of three random strangers, especially as one or two of them were proven assholes?

He pressed on regardless.

Strange shadows danced along the cracked surface.

Buildings leaned at odd angles, defying the laws of physics, their windows casting sinister glows.

Whispers echoed through the broken alleys.

Then a sudden compulsion struck him, and Cinn looked up, past the towering skyscrapers, into the hazy red mist that coated the sky.

He wished he hadn't.

The moon! It was... broken. *Shattered.*

Fractured pieces of the orb hung suspended beyond hazy crimson mist.

A celestial mosaic of destruction.

Each shard emitted an eerie glow, casting beams that painted the city below in crimson shadows.

Every molecule in Cinn's body froze as he stared at the moon, the jagged edges of the broken lunar puzzle taunting him.

Something floated past his vision. Something tiny, something dark.

A *shadowmote!* Shadowmotes in fact—several more blinked into existence.

How could they appear to be made of pure darkness, but still emanate light? He reached for one, and held in a breath as the shadowmote moved towards his hand, landing on it like a butterfly. Like it was attracted to him. How had he never noticed them before? *Because you were too busy having a panic attack and screaming at the spirits to get away from you.*

Another shadowmote drifted nearby, and he reached out for that one too. As soon as his hand reached its field of orbit, it floated over to join its friend.

Cinn collected three, four, six, ten. "Hello there," he whispered. Could they hear him? Were they sentient? Would Darcy or Noir know?

As if in answer, they vibrated before flying off his hand and fading away.

He took a few steps onto the crumbling asphalt, moving towards the nearest red-ivy-covered wall.

That's when he felt it. The presence.

A subtle shift in the air sent icy shivers down Cinn's spine, an intangible whisper of evil that curled around him like a phantom breeze. Unseen eyes seemed to pierce through the red mist, and an ominous weight settled in the pit of his stomach, the unspoken promise of something that lurked just beyond the frayed edges of his perception.

A ghost of a breath hit the back of his neck.

He ran.

Sprinting through the disorienting landscape, Cinn's footsteps pounded against the shattered ground of the once-city. His pulse raced in tandem with his hurried strides, the ghostly breath lingering on his neck hauntingly, urging him forward.

Turn around.

Face it.

See what you're up against.

But it was Tyler's, *don't give them an inch, Cinn,* echoing through his mind that gave him the final push.

He turned.

An amorphous black mass, a shapeless void that seemed to defy the very essence of form, hovered a distance away from him. No discernible features adorned its shadowy surface, only an indistinct darkness that absorbed the surrounding red glow, rendering it an abyssal silhouette.

Cinn's breathing became a series of choked, ragged gasps as the creature moved closer and closer towards him. It moved with an unsettling fluidity, tendrils of inky darkness extending and retracting in a grotesque dance. The air seemed to congeal in its presence, and as it drew nearer, an oppressive coldness enveloped Cinn.

Hisssssssssssssss

Then everything fell apart. Literally—the ground below Cinn started to give way, its already precarious form shaking and throwing up thick dust. Cinn's gaze darted around, his eyes landing on shadowmotes floating nearby, watching the scene.

"Help me!" he screamed at them, and they zipped closer, but then stopped.

He gasped, glaring at them like that would help.

Then one shadowmote in particular caught his eye. It was *looking* at him. And Cinn *felt* it as if it were a part of himself. He pulled it towards him, and miraculously, the other motes followed, as if magnetised together. The ground gave another almighty shudder. On instinct, he flung the motes towards the increasingly large splits in the tarmac.

The shadowmotes multiplied. First dividing into two, then four, then eight, each emitting their dark glow.

Soon there were hundreds, thousands even, all heading to the same place—the splintering earth that was surely about to collapse any second. For a moment the ground reminded Cinn of a piece of pottery that had been broken and then glued back together, for the motes had filled the cracks with a glowing seal.

Hisssssssssssssss

He'd been so focused on the disintegrating ground, he'd almost forgotten about the monster. If it touched him, would he bring it back to his reality, just like he had done only a few nights ago? At least that had been recognisable as a ghost. A murderous ghost, true. This… *thing*, however? He couldn't risk bringing it back with him, no matter Darcy's promises that it couldn't happen.

Glancing around for more shadowmotes to draw on, he found the air now empty of them. Had he used up his finite supply? As the creature's inky tendrils lurched towards him, he stumbled backwards, tripping over something and falling to the ground, hand flying up in a futile attempt to protect himself from the creature.

A repulsive amalgamation of decay and sulphur hit his nostrils.

Hisssssssssssss

There was nobody to hear Cinn's primal scream, but he unleashed it anyway as the black mass changed shape to become a voracious void, a hungry maw desperate for its prey.

A flash of light to his right.

The bright—oh-so-blissfully *bright*—light grew and grew to the point of blinding him, forcing Cinn to close his watering eyes. Was this 'the light'?

Well, if this was it, it had been... something.

A warm hand wrapped around his and squeezed.

His eyes opened slowly to reveal the absence of the monster, and the blurred outline of a woman with a shade of blonde hair instantly recognisable. She even had her brother's grey eyes.

"Béatrice?" Cinn practically screeched.

Blinking to clear his vision, he scanned the length of her body, clothed in a sparkling -silver sequined dress. This, and a silver headpiece, created the sense she was in some sort of costume. No visible injuries jumped out at him. The spirits he saw when he shadowslipped sometimes had obvious ailments, but Béatrice's body, although pale, looked unharmed.

"Béatrice?" he asked again, slowly.

Her grip on his hand tightened, and she opened her mouth as if attempting to speak, but only silence filled the air. Frustrated, she repeated the futile effort, widening her mouth until Cinn glimpsed her tonsils, mimicking a soundless scream.

"It's okay!" Cinn grabbed her shoulders to calm her down, but as he did so, his fingers sank deep into her, her flesh turned to putty in his hands.

Darkness enveloped him.

Eight

CINN

"Cinn!"

"Béatrice!" he screamed, reaching into the empty air. The golden bangle was back on his left wrist. Three concerned, shocked faces stared at him with wide eyes, expressions grim.

Darcy pushed him back down onto the table. "Christ! You're okay. You're back with us. Now lie still, Cinn."

"Did you find her? Did you see her?"

"Julien, give him a second!"

He'd made it back. He was back, and he was alive, and that *thing* hadn't followed him.

However, something was wrong. Very wrong.

"My skin... my skin is burning," Cinn croaked, rubbing his hands over the black marks etched into his chest and stomach with that strange black ink.

Darcy gasped, knocking his hands out of the way. "It's reacting badly to the aethraven. Cinn, I swear it was fine up until now. Elliot, get hot water, pronto. Julien, run to my bathroom cabinet and bring the entire box down here. Go!"

Cinn's skin crawled like a thousand fire ants were gnawing on him at once.

"Why did you put the bangle back on me?" he said, to distract himself.

"You were writhing and screaming. Elliot had to hold you down. Then Julien made the call to bring you back."

Elliot had likely enjoyed that experience. Would Cinn find giant bruises on his arms later?

Footsteps pounded on creaky floorboards, then both Julien and Elliot were back. Within moments, Darcy was pouring and rubbing various substances all over him, and the burning ceased.

Cinn moaned in relief, rubbing his face. His body ached like he'd just run a marathon.

"Well? What happened?" asked Elliot, and Cinn wanted to punch him.

Sitting upright, Cinn swung his legs over the edge of the table. A demand for another cigarette first danced on the tip of his tongue, but Julien's desperate, hopeful face made him crack.

In as much detail as his energy level would allow, he described the whole absurd tale. When he got to the bit where Béatrice's skin had seemed to melt in his hands before he awoke, he'd glanced at Julien, expecting to see disappointment, or even despair.

Instead, he saw only calculation.

Swiping it from the table, Julien held up Béatrice's locket, swinging it like a pendulum. "What if we tried using an even stronger magnet item? That book you lent me has given me an idea for next time."

"There will be no *next time*, Julien," Darcy flatly declared. "Just look at him!"

"But he saw her!" said Elliot. "Surely it's worth another shot."

Cinn looked to Julien, who was staring at his half-naked, shivering form, skin red and raw from both Darcy's scrubbing and the ink. He ran his hand through his hair before stepping towards the table with pursed lips. "It's up to Cinn."

"The hell it is!" snapped Darcy.

At the same time as Cinn said, "I'm fine. I'm okay to try again. Not immediately, though."

Darcy's head whipped towards him. "Cinn, you know Julien will get that money to your friend now regardless, right? I personally assure you it *will* get transferred."

"I know that. I know he'll send it," he told her, and he believed it. "But I still want to try again. Today was the first time I've been in the dark place—*shadowrealm* or whatever—and felt a tiny bit of control. I could... do stuff there. Control the shadowmotes. They... they listened to me. I think I want to see what else I can do. I know Noir is going to help me, but the extra practice won't hurt. Especially if it's purposeful, like finding your friend. Though mostly, I don't want to be scared of it anymore. I'm done with that. So if you promise that it's safe, that I won't bring anything back with me, I can try again for you."

The three of them stared at him, mouths hanging open at his grand speech. To be fair, he'd stunned himself, with the length of time he'd held the floor.

"That's all well and good, Cinn, but this... abnormal creature thing you described has me worried." Darcy's eyes flicked between the other two. "Could it be...?"

Frowning, Elliot pursed his lips and ran a hand through his shaggy mane of hair. "What did you say, Cinn? Shapeless black masses that turn into inky, octopus-like, giant-mouth things? That's definitely not far off..."

"The form they take here could be different to there, anyway." Darcy's voice dropped to almost a whisper.

Cinn had been, yet again, left in the dark, and so snapped loudly, "What are you all on about now?"

Darcy hesitated, made a sound, but stopped when Julien raised his hand and gave her a tiny shake of his head.

Cinn's entire body shook as he clenched both fists. "You must be joking? After what I just did for you?"

"He's right, Julien."

"It's only that Eleanor wanted to explain everything to you herself personally, Cinn, in due course. About why you're here." Julien shifted uncomfortably, folding his arms. Could there be a hint of genuine sympathy in his eyes?

Throwing his hands up, Cinn shot daggers at each of them. "What do you mean, 'why I'm here'? I'm *here* because I accidentally brought back a ghost that killed four people."

An uneasy silence settled over the room.

Three pairs of eyes looked anywhere but Cinn's.

"Not... exactly," said Julien at last.

Cold ice threaded through Cinn's veins so fast, he jerked backwards.

"Let's go sit by the fire," Darcy suggested. On autopilot, he pulled on his clothes, then let himself be guided into the living room. Soon, roaring flames were heating his cheeks as he sprawled on the rug.

"Obviously," Darcy began, glancing at the other two. "Auri would have rescued you from the prison system, regardless. Well... they might have, I'd like to think, but there's actually another specific reason they've brought you here."

"The reason you were personally escorted all the way here by Madame Eleanor Sinclair," said Elliot, snickering. "Not just anyone would get that honour."

Darcy and Elliot were taking the lead, but for some reason, it was Julien who Cinn wanted to hear from. Sitting with him on the rug, Julien faced the fireplace, hands outstretched, and Cinn stared at him until he turned.

Julien sighed, a frown line crinkling his forehead. "The consortium has high hopes that you will be a useful tool in our fight against the increasing number of umbraphages, a near-constant and very deadly threat we're finding incredibly tough to manage. The amount of moteblessed we've lost fighting them..."

"Umbrawhat? And who's *we*?"

"The world."

A stunned silence.

"It's practically becoming an epidemic. Almost every few weeks now, another one appears. Sometimes following a natural disaster, but not always. The Arcane Purifiers have been claiming that they're linked."

"And I will help, how?" Cinn said, voice flat. "I'm not sure I like the phrase 'useful tool', to be honest."

Julien winced. "Sorry. I meant *helpful asset*. The consortium is convinced the umbraphages originate from the shadowrealm. Which you may now have just proved. As the only person able to channel shadow-motes—"

"The *only*? Surely not!"

Julien's eyebrows shot sky-high. He rested a hand on Cinn's knee before saying, "I figured Noir told you. Cinn, you're the only confirmed shadowslipper currently alive today."

Julien, Darcy, and Elliot froze stone-still, awaiting his reaction.

When Cinn threw back his head and laughed—laughed so hard his whole body shook as his breath came out in little snorts—they still continued to stare, albeit with a dash of concern on their faces.

"Of course I am." Because this was his life, and it always had to be as difficult as possible. Cinn's gaze drifted over to the window. "Why... is it dark outside?!"

Darcy crinkled her eyebrows. "It's seven p.m., Cinn."

"What?! How many hours was I out for?"

"Are you not normally gone for such a long length of time?" Julien asked.

"I don't think so. To be honest, nothing about that trip was normal."

"Speaking of the time, I have to bounce," Elliot said, but made no move to do so, his gaze subtly flicking between Julien and Cinn. Just what was his deal? And did Cinn even want to find out?

Darcy rose first. "I have a paper due tomorrow."

Julien cleared his throat. "Cinn looks tired. Perhaps we could crash—"

With a raised hand, Darcy silenced him. "Julien. I love you, but please go home to your apartment. It certainly costs you enough in rent to deserve to be used. Plus, you might be a freak that enjoys sleeping on sofas, but I doubt Cinn wants that old armchair."

Cinn could easily list ten far less comfortable places he'd slept in.

"I'll make some tea for you two, then you can be on your way." Darcy headed off, with Elliot trailing after her, pulling on his coat and giving Julien and Cinn one long last look. Cinn resisted the impulse to wave sarcastically at him.

Alone with Julien again.

Within seconds, a tangible tension descended between them, the rumble of Elliot's motorcycle reverberating as it came to life the only sound.

After a beat, Julien shuffled closer to the fire. The glow from the flames caught his light hair, creating a halo of golden strands. He worried at a loose blue thread on the rug before gazing upwards at Cinn.

"Thank you for today."

What to reply? *No biggie, mate? Sure, anytime?*

"We've been trying for months to reach her. Even resorted to some... unorthodox approaches. There's a couple of obscure methods that are purported to temporarily grant you access to the shadowrealm. One of them, Mortalisfade, an elixir of sorts, involves near medical death. In a controlled manner. Both Elliot and I had a go at it... and it didn't go well."

Cinn found himself shaking his head slightly. The pure desperation of these three to contact Béatrice was so intense that it was quickly rubbing off on him. "Julien," he said softly, reaching out to touch his knee. "She was so lucky to have you guys."

Julien smiled sadly, sliding Béatrice's locket off his neck and un-latching it to reveal a miniscule black-and-white photograph of a young woman, her arms thrown around two children. "This photograph miraculously survived the blast, even though the locket took a hit."

"That your mum? She looks nice."

"She was. She's also"—Julien swallowed—"not with us any longer. But she was incredible." Julien ran his finger over the photo. "Just me left now."

"And your dad."

The locket shut with a snap, and Julien's leg stiffened, prompting Cinn to remove his hand.

Oops. A rapid change of conversation was needed. "Why are you so convinced Béatrice was murdered, anyway? Even before her connection to the Arcane Purifiers was confirmed yesterday?"

Julien turned to face the fire, mouth downcast. "We still don't know that she was connected to them."

It seemed pretty likely, but Cinn clamped his mouth shut.

"Although, she was acting very unlike herself the last couple of months before she died. She withdrew from all of us, and her other friends as well. Often she'd tell us she was going somewhere, or had been somewhere, and we'd catch her out in a lie. We thought she was in some sort of illicit relationship or something." Julien's lips quirked upward, the movement changing his entire face.

Slipping quietly into the room, Darcy returned with a tea tray. She placed it down on the coffee table, gave Julien a quick, sad smile, then left without a word to bang around in the kitchen.

"Elliot had the wildest theories about which mysterious lover she'd taken up. Anyway, things took a rapid turn about ten days before her death. There were giant black bags under her eyes, she was deathly pale, and Darcy heard crying coming from her room. I tried to talk to her about what was wrong, and she... *s'est fermée comme une huître.* Closed like an oyster. Or 'bit my head off' if you like."

There was something about this Julien, so honest and warm and open, that made Cinn want to keep him talking infinitely.

The lilt of his suave, sophisticated voice, that Cinn enjoyed the sound of.

The way his eyes sparkled when he smiled.

The subtle pull of his magnetic force, drawing in everyone around him.

Those damned dimples.

Cinn shuffled his body, stretching his leg out so his calf grazed Julien's. The contact was completely accidental, of course.

"So she died in some sort of blast?" Although Cinn was reluctant to probe, the more he learned, the more he understood he needed the full picture.

"She went on this aid mission to the Philippines. Lots of Auri did. There's a team made up of different departments that often sends out crisis-response crews. Our sister organisations from America and Asia do the same. I was so proud of Béatrice when she signed up for it."

"Didn't you want to do it with her?"

Julien laughed, touching the locket, back around his neck now. "My skills weren't quite as necessary. She was always the better half of us," he said quietly. "The Philippines mission was her first, after a lengthy training process."

Images from watching the news in the break room at work emerged from the depths of Cinn's memory. "I think I saw it on TV. The hurricane?"

"Yes. We sent over a few units of medical support and a division to help them rebuild infrastructure and key buildings quicker."

Remembering their drinks, Cinn reached for the teapot and poured, relieved to see normal tea coming out rather than the weird stuff from the other day. He offered a cup to Julien, whose fingers lingered around his own for a fraction too long. Cinn shuffled his leg even closer, pressing it firmly against Julien's own. It probably wasn't the time—if ever—to be playing this game, but despite his better judgement, he couldn't resist the warm comfort touching him offered.

"And nobody ever notices when people are magically healed and buildings miraculously get repaired overnight?"

"You'd be surprised. People in these crises rarely have time to stop and think about these things. Plus, we're very adept at hiding our processes. Anyway, Béatrice's body was found alone at the top of a mountain by one of her friends. The details are all a bit murky, but Auri's autopsy examination reported enigmatic wounds consistent with motepower trauma. They concluded there was some sort of 'blast', because..." Julien stared intently into the fire, body very still, clearly reliving some of the worst days of his life. Cinn's hand twitched to reach out to him.

"Large patches of her skin were burned off. Mostly around her chest and arms. The conclusion was that she channelled too much motepower at once," he finished, then scoffed.

Cinn drained his tea in four gulps, then dared to ask, "So... why is that suspicious?" tensing while he did so.

"Very few deaths have ever been blamed on channelling too much motepower." Julien's eyes crinkled. "Heard the word *moteblown* yet? It's what we call it when we channel too much. It can be dangerous, occasionally causing one to faint or even require medical aid. It's rarely fatal though. And it certainly doesn't cause physical trauma such as that found on my sister."

Three knocks on the slightly ajar living-room door.

Cinn instinctively jerked his leg away, then glanced at Julien to see if he noticed, to find him wearing a knowing smirk.

He scowled back in return.

"It's my bath and yoga time!" Darcy called through the door. "Time to go!"

"Anyone would think it was her house or something," muttered Julien, rising to his feet.

Darcy waited by the door to see them out, a slip of paper in her hands. "Auri reopens tomorrow. Madame Sinclair sent this note to my bedroom fire to pass on to you. Shall we pick you up tomorrow at nine?"

Sent a note to a bedroom fire?! But Cinn had absorbed enough information for one day, and didn't have the strength to question it.

"If it's not too far out of your way," mumbled Cinn, glancing at Julien. He wasn't exactly sure how he'd get to Auri without him.

"Oh, and let's do lunch," Darcy continued brightly. "We'll show you the café we usually eat at. They do the best pastries. Even Julien approves of their *choux à la crème*."

She passed him the handwritten note, which informed him he had a meeting with Noir in the morning and another with Eleanor Sinclair herself in the afternoon.

Good thing he had no other plans.

As Cinn slid the note into the back pocket of his jeans, Darcy and Julien exchanged a hurried glance, worry laced on Darcy's face.

"Don't..." started Julien. "Don't mention today to Eleanor. Or anything about Béatrice."

"Why? I thought she was your close family friend or something?"

"It's complicated."

Of course it was.

Cinn rolled his eyes and bit his tongue. If they still wanted their secrets, they could have them.

Nine

JULIEN

Waving goodbye to the others, Julien's feet dragged him towards the Cerulean Auditorium, unable to resist its macabre pull.

He joined the trickle of people making their way there, all wearing sombre faces and pulling their coats tighter to their bodies in the cool morning chill.

The auditorium was, unsurprisingly, a ruin.

A haunting silhouette against the bright sky, the charred remnants of the building still stood in the centre of Auri, although in a sorry state. Amidst the blackened debris and rubble, mourners had placed bright flowers—petals of white, crimson, and gold interwove with the edge of the desolation, providing a stark contrast. The very subtle shimmer dusting the flowers, was a telltale sign they'd been grown in the Verdant Conservatory, and would likely remain beautifully fresh for many months.

There would certainly be many months of mourning ahead for Auri.

Huddles of people gathered around in small groups, soft cries coming from many of them. Snatches of sentences containing the words 'Arcane Purifiers' drifted over to him on the light breeze.

His father was right. They'd gone too far this time, with three people dead, many more injured, and a treasured building obliterated.

How could Elliot and Darcy possibly think that Béatrice had been involved with them? She'd once cried when she stepped on a snail, for fuck's sake. The possibility of her writing *Jour J* into her diary with the intention of supporting the Arcane Purifiers in literally murdering people was ludicrous.

Once he'd left the scene to head to his first task, he encountered a subdued atmosphere on every street. People appeared to be walking slower, physically burdened by the events two days prior.

It was a relief to reach Eleanor's office.

He knocked, pushing open the door without waiting for her invitation. After all, he didn't have an appointment. Poking his head around the door, he smiled at Eleanor, who raised one dark eyebrow in return. "I wasn't expecting you."

"It's just a quick one," he promised, closing the door behind him.

Eleanor's office was truly a reflection of the woman herself. Monotone, sparse furniture with a sprinkling of decoration, each chosen and placed with evident, deliberate design. The only thing he approved of was her taste in art—she had several captivating Rothko canvases proudly hung on her wall, their colour gradients and subtle complexities adding a refined allure that he itched to add to his own collection.

Perhaps if he complimented them enough, he'd be left them in her will.

As he sat down opposite her on a burgundy leather wingback chair, Eleanor's face remained expressionless, stoic. Not a single strand of hair was out of place, not even in her box fringe. A fraction of understanding of why others found her intimidating struck him.

"I just wanted to check in with you about my reference. I had a letter this morning from MEET saying they were still waiting for it."

His promotion to a permanent position as a lead project coordinator within Mote-Enhanced Engineering and Technologies was practically an assured deal. After all, he'd been a junior associate there for years, working on various projects alongside world pioneers, several of whom had already submitted outstanding references for him.

When he'd filled in the character reference information box, Julien had thought writing 'Madame Eleanor Sinclair' had been a stroke of genius. The icing on the cake of an exceptional application. He'd presumed she'd already written and sent it.

"It's two weeks late," he added.

"I'm aware," she said simply.

Julien dug his fingernails into his palm.

"I'm still finalising it."

He relaxed, infinitesimally.

"However, to be honest, Julien, I'm not convinced it's the right path for you."

Julien rapidly blinked at her. Not the right path? Was she joking?

"You were such a skilled channeller, back when you practised."

Julien pressed his lips together before saying, "You know I don't like talking about that. For very good reasons." What was Eleanor playing at?

"And you know that I think your reasons for not channelling are nonsensical. It baffles me that someone as intelligent and as reasonable as you still blames themselves for something that was—"

"Anyway," interjected Julien, dragging the conversation away from dangerous territory. "MEET is part of my ten-year plan to enter the field of quantum mote engineering." She knew this. His career path had been discussed many times with Eleanor around the dinner table, his father often being the one to bring it up.

For a moment, he almost considered bringing his father's expectations into the conversation—he wasn't sure what he would make of Eleanor writing anything but a glowing recommendation for the man who was practically a nephew to her. What stopped him was the determination to get where he needed to go all by himself, without any purposeful use of his family name.

References from friends of the family aside.

Peering at him over her glasses, Eleanor said, "Did you know that your mother tried to leave your father when you were five?"

Julien choked on his own saliva. "Excuse me?"

Eleanor stood up to wander over to her floor-to-ceiling window. The view from her tenth-floor office had always impressed Julien—the majority of Auri's awe-inspiring buildings were visible, each one its own work of art. Eleanor proceeded to stare out at the view as she continued, "One night, she met with me, the two of you in tow. Béatrice wouldn't stop screaming, but you were oddly quiet, with puffy eyes. She told me she'd had enough, and that the next day she planned to tell your father she was divorcing him and taking the two of you. She wanted my support. Financially. Practically." She expelled a breath so large, it misted the glass. "Emotionally."

"And what did you say?" Julien had no recollection of this event, but that didn't surprise him. There were many, many gaping holes in the tapestry of his childhood.

"I told her to think about her decision very carefully."

A long, tense silence filled the space between them.

Julien blinked back hot tears at the image of his mother returning home that night, her escape plans shattered. Had she ever tried again?

"Why are you telling me all this?" Julien spat. This was the last thing he needed right now. There were some things that he'd rather not know at this point, including that Eleanor, someone he trusted like family, had so badly let his mother down. "Have you had a dispute with *Père*?"

"Because, Julien, as much as you'd easily sit here and claim to despise your father—don't give me that look—you're already becoming a pawn in his game. His son climbing up the MEET ladder would be the queen's gambit in motion, checkmating every move before it's even made. There is already growing concern from many parties about his excessive influence over the consortium. Not to mention his ever-expanding collection of assets."

Julien blinked at her in disbelief. Her distaste for his father, never before detectable, was fleetingly splashed all over her face before she pulled her expression flat.

"Did you know he now owns ninety percent of all motetech patents, if you factor in all of the smaller companies that have aligned themselves with HorizonTech?"

Julien shrugged. "Sounds about right." His father was relentless in his acquisition of anything with the slightest bit of buzz around it.

A beat of silence as a bird flew close to the windowpane, stretching its wings to full span. Then, "And do you think that's morally right, one man having so much power?"

He bit back a laugh. "*Non*, obviously not. But unless you've got more than a few million in the bank, there's nothing you or I can do about it." He narrowed his eyes. Whatever reaction Eleanor wanted out of him, she was likely disappointed. "Unless you want me to poison his wine? I can't deny the thought has crossed my mind from time to time."

Turning away from the window, she walked back to perch on the edge of her desk, inches away from him. "I think about that conversation with your mother all too often. I would do anything to go back in time and change my actions. I'll carry that guilt to my grave now. It may be too late for me to change Isabelle's fate." Eleanor rested a hand on Julien's shoulder in a rare moment of physical contact. "But it's not too late for you. I'll write you that reference. Not that you really need it. They know you're a brilliant young mind. However, you need to make sure you're doing this for you, not him."

I am.

It was true—the world of motetech fascinated him, and most importantly, he was good at it. Excellent, in fact. The fact that it fell in line with the business interests of a father he hated was purely coincidental. Wasn't it?

Not trusting himself to speak further on the topic, he nodded. His mind reeled, the multiple shocking revelations swam around his head like sharks, threatening to drag him under.

Julien combatted it with a rapid change of conversation. "Why are you meeting with Cinn this afternoon?"

Eleanor frowned at him, circling round to sit in her chair. "Viktor Sturmhart has instructed me to oversee his progress. Check his support network is working for him." She gave him a pointed look. "Make sure he's on track to assist us with the umbraphage onslaught. Of course, I'll wait until Noir gives me the all clear that he's emotionally ready before I divulge that information to him."

Julien scratched the back of his neck. *Putain.* "He... he may already know a smidge about them. And about how Auri hopes he may be of assistance." He braced for fire.

Eleanor's smile froze icily on her face. "Does he now? And how did that come up in conversation?"

"The Arcane Purifiers." The lie slid easily off his tongue. "He was asking lots of questions, and it came up that AP blame the appearance of umbraphages on mote usage."

"And you decided to fill him in on the rest?"

"Well..." He stalled, brain stumbling. He really should have made coffee before leaving the house. "He asked how we were fighting them, and Auri's theory on shadowmotes came up..."

Eleanor shook her head. Sighed. "To be honest, I don't really care as long as that boy stays put and agrees to help us in due course. Are you being nice to him?"

Julien flashed her his fox-grin. "Since when am I *not* nice?"

"Did you see the images from the latest umbraphage attack?" she asked abruptly, reaching within her desk. "Last week. Outskirts of Seville. Ten people dead before we could dematerialise it. That fucker better not reform anytime soon."

Their biggest problem with the umbraphages was that they currently appeared unstoppable, permanently at least. That, and their numbers grew by the month.

"Want to see what we're up against? I'm sure you've heard about MEET's progress in developing a range of weapons for us to trial." Eleanor slid a cassette into the tiny television that sat in the corner of her room and hit play.

Shaky footage from a handheld camera filled the screen. The recorder's panicked breath coming in short bursts obscured any other sounds. The camera pointed at a pavement littered with junk. Then, the view jerked up to reveal a woman's lifeless body, coated in blood, floating in mid-air, her limbs arching backwards.

"They're invisible within video footage."

With a sudden jerk, the woman dropped to the ground, and the videographer stumbled backwards, screaming bloody murder. They evidently dropped the camera. The view of the street bounced around wildly until only a patch of concrete was visible. Then, a limp hand engulfed the frame, fingers twitching one last time before falling very still.

An eerie garbled sound came out of the TV that Julien struggled to assign meaning to. The umbraphage?

"The camera was... *recovered* from an eyewitness. The concealment team had quite the task this time. Over twenty people needed their memories tampered with. It's a good thing they now have the LMD to work with."

The Lumimeld Memory Disrupter project had taken Julien's team over eight months. The peculiar-looking headpiece harnessed the unique properties of various motes, blending them to create a powerful and targeted memory manipulation effect.

The effectiveness of it varied—particularly if not used immediately after the event that needed to be wiped—but it usually got the job done. In clinical trials, volunteers were often left with migraines lasting many weeks, but the consortium hadn't seemed particularly concerned about that side effect.

Eleanor's attention remained captured by the footage, which she was rewinding to play again.

"Did you see AP's statement printed in the morning paper?" Julien asked pointlessly. The idea of Eleanor not having access to it before it hit the press was unfathomable.

"Yes," she said simply.

"And? Do you believe their claim that it was a subgroup gone rogue? That the auditorium was never meant to be damaged?"

A tiny crack fractured Eleanor's emotionless mask. "Does it matter, when five lives were taken? Even if the majority of AP never intended the result, their name is now tarnished with blood." Her lips pursed as if tasting something sour. "Even if they originally had good intentions."

On the screen, the woman's body was again contorted into an obscene shape before being thrown to the ground. The scream sounded again.

"So, what's the consortium going to do about it?"

A bark of hollow laughter. "Rest assured, Julien, they will be dealt with. You focus on keeping your head down and your eyes and ears open."

"Indeed," said Julien, rising to his feet. "I won't take up anymore of your time. Thank you in advance for finishing the reference."

Bracing himself for her to say something else about his parents, Julien was surprised when she only nodded, and said her goodbyes before turning back to replay the video footage.

Julien wandered over to Aurelia Library, mood sombre. Like all mote-blessed, the umbraphage threat terrified him. Being powerless to help, he preferred to distance himself from any news of them. However, their presence was getting harder and harder to ignore. How much longer until their existence could no longer be covered up to the general population?

His spirits lowered even further when he discovered their favourite study room was occupied by a group of four people in mid conversation. Someone was sitting in Béatrice's armchair.

Ignoring their stunned looks, he entered the room anyway, spreading his papers over half of the central table and tapping his pen loudly against the wood.

After a minute, they wordlessly gathered their belongings and filed out of the room, their quick, pointed glances at him as they did so burning holes in his head.

Oh well. He hadn't *asked* them to leave. Although he couldn't deny it was likely because they knew who he was. Or rather, who his *father* was.

Lucien Montaigne.

CEO of HorizonTech Enterprises.

Wealthy and powerful beyond most people's wildest dreams, but never satisfied.

One of the most influential moteblessed to hold a seat within the consortium, and also the most feared.

Rumoured to have world governments in his pockets.

Julien sighed, the empty room feeling large and lonely without his friends filling it with him. He glanced at the navy-blue Morris chair that Béatrice would never again sit on.

Pull yourself together.

Julien pulled the paper that he'd planned to review yesterday towards himself—the proposal for mote-powered steam engines, aimed initially at the cargo ship production sector. His father was about to invest a large amount of money into the company and wanted his opinion.

A pawn in his game, Eleanor had said. She was wrong. Julien was completely in control of his own actions, his own destiny. It was his choice to read this proposal regardless, to further his own knowledge in the latest motetech developments.

After two hours of being completely absorbed in his task, the bells of St. Caelum's chimed noon. With haste, he snapped his notebook—now full of his scribbled thoughts—shut, and was ready to leave within moments.

Had he ever been quite so eager to meet his friends for lunch? Probably not. However, today Cinn would be there. He hadn't been able to get him out of his mind since their conversation in Darcy's garden, where Cinn had caught him off guard with the depth of his loyalty to his friends. And then, of course, there was the experience of inking his skin, which had become unexpectedly sensual....

Taking massive strides, Julien reached Curio Café Collective in record time, motivated mostly by finding out how Cinn's meeting with Noir went. Plus, there could be more opportunities to subtly tease him again, and make him blush or bite his lip.

As usual, the large eatery was overcrowded, every table jam-packed. Scanning the room, he spotted Darcy's mane of auburn curls and Cinn's grey beanie, despite the sweltering room temperature. God, did the guy ever take it off? He smiled as he took a step—

He froze.

There weren't two bodies sitting at their table, but three.

The third occupier certainly wasn't Elliot—he would be the most recognisable of them, with his wild hair, and besides, Elliot would arrive fashionably late.

He meandered towards them, trying to identify the stranger. He could only see the back of their head, but what he *could* see was Cinn's beaming smile, bright as sunlight, directed at the invader.

Julien slid into the empty seat next to Cinn, eyes snapping straight to the person Cinn was so captivated by.

Eric.

Fuck. His heart sank like a ship.

Eric's laughter died in his throat. Darcy looked between the two of them, body twitching like she might get up and leave. Julien couldn't blame her.

"Julien," Eric said, voice light but eyes full of daggers.

All Julien's usual energy for putting on performances disintegrated as he stared at Eric's expressionless face. "What are you doing here?" he snapped flatly.

Cinn's head swivelled towards him, but Julien didn't glance his way, avoiding the shock that would be written all over his face.

After a scoff, Eric replied, "I was just checking in with your new friend here. I met him at the Nexus Towers elevators the other day. He needed help using them, given that it was his first day here. Funny how you accidentally walked him to the wrong tower, eh?"

Julien wanted to close his eyes. Why did his day keep going from bad to worse? And had he really walked Cinn to the wrong tower? He could have sworn Noir's office was at the top of the Ivory Tower...

"Well, it was nice seeing you again, Eric. See you around," he said, before he could stop himself, causing Darcy to hiss.

"*Julien!*" she directed at him, while darting her eyes towards Cinn. Julien was embarrassing her. Embarrassing himself.

Eric's face darkened. "Fucking hell, Julien. After the way you ended things with me, I thought you were just deranged, but it seems like you're a genuine cunt."

Ouch. That one hurt. Just a little.

Cinn spluttered out some of the water he was drinking.

"Cinn, my offer still stands," said Eric, now intently focused back on Cinn again. He reached into his rucksack, pulled out some paper, and scribbled a number on it. A number Julien had called himself a handful of times. "Let's meet up at some point. I can introduce you to a friend who, a bit like you, was very late to discover she was moteblessed. Between us, we'll make sure you have everything you need."

"There's no need for concern, Eric. We're taking care of him just fine."

Under the table, Darcy's leg connected with Julien's kneecap. He winced.

Eric leaned over the table, pressing the paper into Cinn's hand before grabbing his forearm. "Honestly, Cinn, ring me anytime. It was lovely to meet you properly." Eric squeezed his arm as he stood up, and Julien was tempted to grab the butter knife that lay on the table.

"Thanks," mumbled Cinn, pocketing the paper. "I'll give you a call."

The hell you will.

As Eric ambled off, shaking his head, Julien fought back memories of Eric's naked body under his hands—oh, how his body had seemed sculpted by angels, a sea of smooth skin and firm muscles that Julien had thrown onto his bed before pinning his hands down...

And the thought of Eric doing that to Cinn—

"Julien Montaigne, I am downright embarrassed to be associated with you sometimes. Scrap that—*most* of the time, recently." Darcy had brought out her most disappointed expression. That was okay. Julien deserved it. "It's honestly no wonder you have a grand total of two close friends, if you go around talking to people like that." She banged the table with her cup.

"What... what was that?" Cinn asked weakly.

Darcy turned to Cinn, and took great joy in explaining, "Eric is one of Julien's many, many scorned lovers."

Julien winced, the butter knife seeming appealing again.

"Many, many is a bit of an—"

"Many, *many,* Julien!" she practically screamed, banging her cup on the table. "Many, *many!* We often can't walk down a hallway together without some girl or guy sending me a death look, thinking I've stolen you away from them."

Beside him, Cinn stared into his water cup.

"You were just disgusting to poor Eric. It's ironic that you were the one who was a complete twat to him, during your short *relationship* or whatever it was, and yet he was simply delightful towards you, and you were downright rude!"

Julien teetered on the edge of two choices: shutting down the conversation, which was his preference, as he never discussed his sex life with even his best friends, or defending himself. In the end, the latter won—he couldn't handle the idea of Cinn thinking he was some sort of narcissistic playboy who used and discarded others for fun.

He leaned back in his chair. Folded his arms. "Thanks for presuming it was entirely my fault that things ended badly, Darcy. It was actually slightly more nuanced than that, you'll be shocked to hear. If you want the full story, he started sleeping with his ex again, and only told me about it weeks later. Then I got... rather cross with him." Okay, that part was a slight understatement.

Darcy's mouth twisted slightly. "I didn't realise you were *together*, together with Eric, though."

"I wasn't." Julien never was, with anyone. "But I thought I'd made it exceedingly clear that while we were casually fucking"—Darcy cringed at the harsh language—"we were *exclusively* casually fucking." His voice rose near the end, and Darcy glared at him.

In order to further paint himself as the mature, mentally sane guy he would never really be, Julien said, "Anyway, you should call him, Cinn. It would be good for you to make more connections here," in his smoothest possible voice, fighting back roiling acid in his gut.

"What did I miss?" Elliot pulled out the empty chair with a scrape, throwing himself into it. "Have we ordered?"

Darcy's gaze pierced Julien's, a silent communication that the Eric conversation was over, lest they drag Elliot into it. Which certainly wasn't a good idea.

"I was just asking them what's good here," Cinn said, picking up a paper menu.

Elliot narrowed his eyes.

Julien pretended to also look at the menu, while side-eyeing Cinn. What on earth had he made of all that? Even without the Eric situation, Darcy's ridiculous exaggeration about how many people he'd slept with wouldn't be something he'd forget. *Why do you care so much about his opinion?* He clenched his jaw. *It's not like you want to date him or anything. Because you don't do that, do you?*

Although, when Cinn ordered the rösti upon his recommendation, and then proceeded to witter on about how much the head chef at his old workplace would have loved it, which somehow launched him into speaking about different types of English potato and their different uses for a full five minutes, Julien couldn't help but openly stare at him, his icy heart thawing ever so slightly.

When Cinn had finished every last scrap of his dish, Julien placed his own plate in front of him, offering him the last few bites, pretending he was done. He'd skipped breakfast earlier, so wasn't exactly full, but watching Cinn's face light up was worth it.

It had him calculating other ways to get that smile back. The smile that showed the slightest hint of teeth and crinkled the corner of his eyes. The smile that made something swell in Julien's chest at the sight of it, especially when Julien had been the cause of it.

Of course, the more Cinn liked him, the more assistance he'd be in contacting Béatrice.

Yes, solving his sister's murder was his only agenda here.

Well, and having a *little* fun. But one could certainly kill two birds with one stone, as the ridiculous English idiom went.

Which reminded him...

"The weekend after next is my father's birthday," Julien announced. "You know, that ridiculously over-the-top affair that is my annual torture. Darcy, you're actually invited to the party because my father thinks you're *la crème de la crème*."

Darcy smirked. "Well, I am, to be fair."

"Elliot, you're definitely *not* invited after last time, but you'll be gate-crashing."

With a laugh, Elliot ran his hand through his outrageously plush hair that Julien was frequently jealous of; it looked like a portable pillow. "Are you sure I won't be evicted from the premises the second he lays eyes on me?"

"And Cinn, you're my guest of honour," Julien said, trying to keep the twinkle out of his eye, and avoiding thinking too hard about the hint of displeasure that flashed across Elliot's face.

"Oh. I-I'm fine staying here," Cinn rushed to say. "Really, I'm sure he doesn't want me there. I don't even know him."

"He doesn't know half the people he invites to his birthday each year," said Darcy. "It's all a big facade to show off how important he is."

"You're coming," Julien said, nudging his leg into Cinn's. "It's decided."

Cinn bit his lip again. He bit it so frequently, Julien was already starting to predict the moments where his teeth would scrape across the plump flesh.

"Besides, you need to come. The primary purpose of our trip is to locate our next magnet item, for when you try again, Cinn. If you're there, you might be able to help decide which item will be best."

Julien had already decided what item they would leave with, but there was no need for Cinn to know that.

"And where exactly will your father's birthday take place?" asked Cinn, but the way he tensed expectantly told Julien he knew the answer.

"Paris," Julien said, with a flourish of his hands. "The most beautiful city in the world. According to delusional tourists. Don't say I never spoil you."

Ten

JULIEN

The discord sown by the Arcane Purifiers attack on the Institute didn't last long.

Life swiftly settled back into its usual pattern, with the added feature of heightened security around the Institute. This included extra guards on patrol around the campus, as well as the requirement to 'sign in' with a team of clipboard-wielding officers once you'd parked or arrived by bus.

As November trudged along, Julien's daylight hours shrank but his workload grew. His team at work had been assigned the task of designing and manufacturing a simple register device that would allow the user to press their palm onto a salt-rock disk as they passed through a checkpoint.

Eleanor sent Julien regular fire notes, thinly veiled reminders for him to keep tabs on Cinn—but this particular task required very little effort or hardship. Cinn drove to Auri with them every day, and more often than not spent time with them whenever someone was free to be with him. Noir had set him an extensive library list, so Darcy would often march them all there for a couple of hours—although Cinn tended to listen to music and doodle rather than actually read the books they'd located for him.

However, Julien's favourite times were when the four of them would end up back at Darcy's for dinner, where the conversation often turned to finalising their Paris plans.

"Why can't we at least *try* to get access to the Displacement Baths? Then we wouldn't have to travel at all," Elliot whined one evening.

"A weekend break in Paris isn't going to get us the documentation to access them," retorted Darcy. "You know that. Also, we couldn't take our stuff with us."

"We could ship the stuff and it could meet us there."

"Like *that's* a sensible and practical idea!"

Cinn tapped a foot against the floorboards. "Is this that... transdimensional travel thing? Because I'm not sure I trust the concept of that, anyway."

"Julien, weren't you flirting with one of the staff who manages the Baths the other day?" A scowl flashed across Elliot's face. "Surely they'll let us in."

Julien winced. "I... I think I burned that bridge when I didn't return their call."

With that method of travel out of the question, they debated the merits of driving—which Julien was primarily in favour of, as he'd enjoy driving Maz all the way there, and then they'd have her with them in Paris.

"The journey took over twelve hours when we drove there last year. Remember that hold up at the border? And then that massive traffic jam?" Darcy said.

"Plus, we can just use one of your father's gazillion fancy sports cars," added Elliot.

"It's literally ninety minutes to fly there."

And so Julien agreed to fly to Paris, which resulted in Cinn declaring he wasn't coming, as there wasn't 'a chance in hell' he was flying again. Apparently, he hadn't enjoyed his one experience of air travel, but then again he had just been kidnapped...

After Cinn refused all of her offers of various drugs to help with the flight, Darcy pointed out if he ever wanted to go home to England again, flying would be much cheaper than the numerous train tickets he'd need to buy, including the astronomically expensive Eurotunnel. It was at this point Cinn had stormed out of her living room to bang around in her kitchen.

After ten minutes, Darcy went to check on him, coming back to inform them that Cinn was stress-baking.

"You're actually letting Cinn use your kitchen?" asked Julien. "I'm impressed."

"He wants to make cookies. How could I say no? Don't worry. He'll come to Paris. He'd miss us too much not to."

Although it was true that Cinn had spent a lot of time with them since his arrival, weeks ago now, Julien suspected he'd be perfectly fine alone for a weekend. He'd probably end up hanging out with Eric, who he'd met up with at least twice. Not that Julien was keeping track, or anything.

Cinn burst back into the living room fifteen minutes later, covered in flour. "I don't have a passport," he announced proudly, with a grin.

"Eleanor is already sorting that," Julien said cheerfully, which sent Cinn storming back into the kitchen. "You'll get it way before next Thursday evening!"

Thursday evening came around quickly, and soon they were driving to the airport in Zurich to catch their eleven p.m. flight.

After locking Maz up, Julien stroked her bonnet. "Sorry I'm not allowed to bring you, girl."

Darcy hooked her arm around his and dragged him away.

At the very last moment at the check-in booth, Julien realised a slight oversight of his, and reached out to snatch Cinn's ticket off the counter before Cinn did. Three days ago, Cinn insisted he pay Julien for his flight tickets, so Julien made up some random figure that probably wouldn't even cover an economy seat, let alone the business-class seat he'd purchased for him. When he'd lied to Cinn about the price, he'd forgotten it would be printed on his boarding pass.

But hell would freeze over before they travelled economy.

"I'll keep hold of it for you," he told Cinn who, understandably, shot him a confused look.

As they battled their way through throngs of passengers, Cinn became more and more miserable, looking up at the numerous sign-posts for various gates with wide eyes.

Julien supposed he'd bypassed the many necessary airport steps when he'd flown on Viktor Sturmhart's private jet with Eleanor. "They're going to X-ray our bags now," he explained to Cinn as they entered the security section.

"I'm not a fucking idiot," Cinn snarled. "I know how airports work."

Darcy and Elliot snickered and nudged Julien with their elbows.

"I can't wait for the live demonstration of how to fasten a seatbelt in a minute," Elliot said.

"Well this serves me right for making a conscious effort to be nice," Julien mumbled.

Elliot had somehow brought with him three different carry-on bags, each containing a different illicit item that had to be confiscated. He waved goodbye to his pocket knife, a box of straight razors, and, curiously, an aerosol can of spray paint.

"Honestly, I can't take you lot anywhere," huffed Darcy.

Once they reached their gate, Darcy and Elliot beelined straight for the business-class funnel, bypassing the large crowds. Cinn slowed, gawking at all the hundred-odd economy passengers queueing miserably until Julien pressed the small of his back to hurry him along.

Cinn looked between the busy queue and Darcy and Elliot, who were already through the barrier, frowning. "I need my ticket now," he said. His clenched jaw spelled trouble.

"Don't be mad," Julien said, throwing the ticket at him, then sprinted towards the inspection desk before Cinn could explode at him. He turned to find Cinn's mouth slightly ajar as he studied the ticket.

"You absolute—" Cinn stumbled with his words, turning bright red, which made Julien laugh, which made Cinn even angrier.

"You'll thank me when strangers aren't coughing on you and babies aren't screaming in your ear," he shouted, slipping past the barrier to join Darcy and Elliot.

After literally dragging Cinn up the boarding stairs, they followed a friendly attendant to their seats, two pairs of seats opposite each other. Julien gestured for Cinn to take the window seat before throwing himself down next to him. Cinn pulled the blinds down on the two nearest windows.

"Those need to stay open for take-off and landing," Elliot said, taking the seat facing Cinn. "It's going to be pitch black, anyway."

Cinn reopened them miserably.

Darcy patted her hand luggage. "Are you sure you don't want anything, Cinn? To help you relax? Completely *medicinal,* I swear."

"No. I've told you before, I don't take *anything.*" He squirmed, before adding in a low voice, eyes downcast, "I used to self-medicate using whatever I could to try to stop my... episodes. "I've seen first hand what a slippery path that could be. I'll be fine. I'll just try to sleep throughout the entire flight."

A shred of guilt pierced Julien at his discomfort. He'd basically forced Cinn onto this plane. Although, Cinn *had* suggested he would love to visit Paris on the night they'd met... Hadn't he? Sort of?

"What?" said Cinn, staring at Elliot, who did have a peculiar, distant look on his face.

"Sorry. It's just... Béatrice always sat there when we used this airline. She was always opposite me, next to Julien."

"Should I swap with one of you?" Cinn asked.

Sarcasm or genuine question?

That line of enquiry quickly disintegrated, however, with Cinn's growing panic. Evidently, he hadn't exaggerated his fear of flying. As his eyes darted between the window and the growing number of passengers taking their seats, Cinn's leg tapped out morse code for SOS loudly against the floor. He pressed his fists to his head.

"Calm down." Julien reached for his arm, tugging it away from his head. To Julien's surprise, Cinn grabbed his hand and squeezed it tight, before quickly releasing it, horror on his face. "You can hold my hand anytime." Julien winked, offering it back to him.

"Why did you make me do this?" Cinn hissed. "This will be the end of all of us. Have you seen how flimsy those wings are? They're shaking in the wind!"

Julien waved a flight attendant over. "Five double whiskeys please. Preferably Irish." To his surprise, she went to fetch them with only the slightest shake of her head.

When the shots came, five glasses of amber liquid, Cinn didn't hesitate before knocking one back, then slamming the glass onto the metal table. Then another, another, another, and another. Julien had intended for the rest of them to have one each, but clearly Cinn had other plans.

"Does alcohol not count as self-medication, then?" Elliot flashed Cinn a snarky grin.

"Let me have my one vice."

"What's your smoking habit then, a pastime?"

Julien stifled a laugh.

Ignoring Elliot, Cinn glanced back to the table laden with empty shot glasses, eyes widening. He shot Julien a panicked look. "I can't actually pay for those."

Chuckling, Elliot leaned back in his chair. "The entertainment you're about to provide us with should cover it."

"When does it take off again?" Cinn rocked his whole body forward and back.

"Probably not for another thirty minutes or so. Preflight checks and such," said Darcy.

Cinn moaned, pressing his hand to his face. From his rucksack, he whipped out his Walkman, then violently shoved his headphones over his head. "Goodbye," he announced, squeezing his eyes shut and slamming his head back against the headrest.

The three of them burst into laughter.

The sound of Cinn's godawful music could just be heard over the ruckus of other boarding passengers; he'd turned it up to maximum volume.

When the plane finally started to manoeuvre across to the runway, an attendant looked poised to reach over to Cinn, and Julien's arm shot out to block her.

"Sir, he really should listen to the safety briefing."

"He's a frequent flyer," Julien said, shooting her his most charming smile, and she scampered off to bother someone else.

The take-off was uneventfully smooth, and their cabin became quiet as the captain dimmed the lights, passengers talking in hushed whispers. Cinn continued to squeeze his eyes shut and jiggle his leg, all the way through it, until his movements became slower and slower.

Darcy nodded her chin at Cinn. "I think he's asleep."

Indeed, his head now lay slumped against the side. The combination of the adrenaline crash with the alcohol must have knocked him out. He wouldn't be their delightfully drunk entertainment after all. Julien would far rather he slept through it, however, and his mouth couldn't help but twitch into a smile at his peaceful face—his expression carrying none of its usual tension—as he leaned over to close the window blinds.

Julien gestured towards Elliot's similarly slumped form. "So is he. He was up at four a.m. though, with an early training session to make up for missing tomorrow's."

"Do you ever miss it?" Darcy said quietly, referring to the period of time where Julien had studied the practice of physically channelling motes alongside Elliot. The period of time forever known as 'before' in his head.

"Not the intense physical regime of it all, no." But... there was *something* about the feeling of channelling that he'd never forget, never completely get away from. A feeling of invulnerability. Of power. Of security.

Eleanor's words from their last meeting resurfaced. Had she spoken to Darcy? "Why do you ask?"

She nudged her leg against his. "Only because it's my job to look out for you. Sometimes, when Elliot is talking about his day, you get this faraway look in your eye."

"Motetech is what I'm good at."

"Sure. We all know you're on track to become some sort of tech prodigy. However, Elliot always says how insanely good you were at channelling."

A tiny dash of turbulence rocked the aeroplane, and Julien's gaze flashed straight to Cinn, bracing for him to wake up in terror. Still fast asleep, he only shifted from leaning against the window to landing his head on Julien's shoulder, mumbling something incomprehensible.

Julien became very still.

Cinn's breath ghosted across his bare neck, sending a chill down his spine. Beneath the smell of smoky whiskey, Julien could faintly detect vanilla, from the specific cookie recipe he was now making routinely at Darcy's house, trying to nail the formula. He was certainly giving Darcy a run for her money.

If Julien moved his mouth an inch, he could kiss the top of Cinn's head. Well, his beanie anyway.

Not that he'd be doing that, of course. That would be wildly inappropriate.

However...

Julien slid Cinn's headphones off—the tape had finished—and carefully wrapped the wire around them like he'd seen Cinn do a thousand times. Then, he reclined their seats slightly.

"What are you doing?" Disapproval flashed across Darcy's face.

"Making him more comfortable so the turbulence doesn't wake him." Julien arranged Cinn's head gently against his chest. A crop of thick brown curls poked out of his beanie. Julien tucked them back under. They were just as soft as they looked.

He looked up to find Darcy seething. He could practically see smoke coming out of her ears. "Julien, you absolute *psychopath*. Stop touching him right now or I'll wake him up."

"You wouldn't do that to him," he said, but moved his hands away.

Instead, he snaked his arm around Cinn's body to pull him even closer towards him, enjoying the warmth of his head and the rise and fall of his chest as he breathed heavily.

Why did this feel so abstract, so unusual?

It hit him with a visceral punch—he'd never wanted this much body contact with anyone before, ever—well, not while clothed at least.

But every rise and fall of Cinn's sleeping body only compounded Julien's desire to never let go of him, to keep him trapped under his arm forever.

What was wrong with him? How had he been so easily bewitched by Cinn's big brown eyes and his heart made of gold?

Julien's fingers found their way over to play with the drawstrings of Cinn's dark hoodie. The garment hid a body that Julien knew all too well now, after he'd drawn on him with the aethraven ink. Toned muscles blessed with a surprising amount of gorgeous tattoos that Julien wouldn't mind investigating further. With his tongue.

Darcy's eyes widened further. "Jul— wait. I *thought* I saw that look in your eye the other day. No, Julien. Absolutely not. *This*"—she gestured wildly between him and Cinn's slumped form—"is not a good idea."

A pinprick of annoyance threaded through Julien. Who was Darcy to police his actions? Or Cinn's for that matter. Cinn wiggled under him, pressing in even closer, his left hand moving up to latch onto a handful Julien's shirt.

"Seems like he disagrees with you."

"Julien, this isn't funny!"

"Christ, woman, calm down," Julien snapped. Surprised by the heat in his tone, he flinched, then blinked at Darcy's stunned face. "Where did *that* come from?" he wondered quietly.

"I think I know," she replied.

At once, he was transported to a fractured memory of his childhood. His father had said the exact same words to his mother. Béatrice and he had been huddled together in the corner of an adjacent room, joined by an archway. Too scared to interfere, but too scared to go upstairs and leave their mother completely alone with him. A wine glass was smashed against the floor, some of the little pieces landing under the arch, littering the dark wood like stars.

The next day, a purple bruise encircled his mother's forearm.

"Can I take that back?" he whispered to Darcy, revulsion at the dark shadow of his father's language surging within him.

"Well, you've still got your one daily take-back left," she said, referring to the ongoing system from their university days, when the four of them would fight all the time. She smiled, and just like that, Julien knew all was forgiven, and she'd never mention it again. "Seriously, Julien, Cinn's not a shiny new toy for you to play with and break."

"And what if he's a broken toy I want to fix?" Julien replied, knowing full well what she'd say back.

"You're too fucked up yourself for that, and you know it. This one is already too delicate for you to fuck with, Julien. I'm not joking. *Stay away.* He deserves better than that."

"Ouch. You wound me." Julien clutched his heart. "I'd say he's a lot stronger than you think."

"Yes, he is. He's going to be absolutely fine as long as you don't mess with his mind. He acts like a tough nut, but I can sense he's crumbling inside. I, for one, really like him, and I'll be pissed at you if you scare him off from us. In fact, I'll disown you as a friend and take his side in the divorce."

"Mess with his mind? What do you take me for?"

Darcy pursed her lips. "Seriously, Julien, *please* don't go there. We're the only stability he has in his crazy new life."

"Okay, okay. I was just messing with you. He's not my type, anyway."

"Not your type? You mean he doesn't have a pulse?"

"Your humour just goes from strength to strength tonight, Darce."

Across the aisle, out of a window, Julien could see the glittering lights of Paris in the far distance. Almost there.

Darcy tracked his gaze. "There's something so special about coming back here, isn't there?"

Julien blinked. For her, Paris was only fond memories of them all attending La Sorbonne and living together in their inner-city apartment. Of late nights, bright lights, and one or two too many glasses of red wine. For him though, it was where he grew up. Where his mother died. And now, where Béatrice was buried, next to her.

"It certainly has some charms."

"Where shall we take Cinn?" she asked, all excitement—so much so that he caught a fraction of it himself.

Julien glanced down at Cinn's sleeping head, still resting on his chest. Likely he'd want to do all the usual tourist rubbish. *Joy.*

Becoming lost in thoughts of how he could avoid the particularly tragic ones, Julien zoned out until Darcy said carefully, "Maybe it would be best for Cinn to stay with us at the hotel. Elliot, my parents, and I are all on the same floor. We can try and get another room for him."

At the thought of dealing with the experience of his family home solo, of being left alone for hours and evenings and mornings when the others were at their hotel, liquid ice shot through his veins and his heart lurched into freefall. Having Cinn accompanying him throughout the weekend was the only reason he wasn't in a depressed spiral about the whole thing.

"No need."

"But Julien, your father—"

He groaned. "Will be perfectly polite towards him. He's going to be thrilled to meet our infamous new shadowslipper. Give me two more hours of not thinking about him, please."

The lights flickered on in the cabin as the crew prepared for landing, but Cinn remained blissfully asleep on his chest, his warm head and his steady breathing soothing Julien's now-anxious mind.

He even remained unbothered when Elliot woke up with a yawn, took one glance at them, then scowled before composing his expression into one of nonchalance.

"I didn't want to wake him by moving him." It was the truth. Mostly.

Elliot's leg shot out, in an arguably accidental stretch, to jab Cinn's own. He jolted awake, instantly pushing himself up from Julien's chest.

"Sorry," Cinn mumbled, a dash of mortification breaking through his sleep-drunk, hazy expression. He leaned back against the headrest.

Julien gritted his teeth, purposefully avoiding looking at Elliot.

He never could have anything nice, even for a moment, apparently.

Eleven

CINN

C inn stumbled through Paris Orly's passport control and customs, attempting to speak as little as possible. Which was easy, given that his whiskey-operated brain had nothing useful to say, anyway.

Head down, he followed the three pairs of feet as they swiftly traversed the airport and headed out into the chilly night.

Someone pushed a bottle of water into his hand, and he looked up to see Darcy's kind eyes twinkling. "I would blame Julien, but to be fair, he didn't actually tell you to drink all five double shots."

He downed the entire bottle, the icy cold doing nothing to clear his head.

"Get a good night's rest," Darcy continued, ushering a tired Elliot into the nearest taxi with its sign illuminated green.

Feeling like an abandoned child, Cinn's arm itched to stretch out to keep her with him. Why couldn't they all stay at Julien's together? He was more than slightly nervous to meet the formidable Lucien Montaigne. He spun to face Julien too quickly, resulting in powerful arms steadying him.

"How are you this much of a lightweight for your size?"

Cinn scrambled for a witty response but became paralysed by Julien's grip on his arm. Julien's captivating grey eyes locked on his. Julien's dimples as he smirked.

"I..." he started, then pushed Julien off him to stride towards the next free taxi without looking back.

Julien laughed as he followed him, tugging off Cinn's rucksack for him to hand to the driver. Then he slid into the back of the taxi, and Cinn bounced on the balls of his feet for several moments.

He should join him in the back, like a normal person.

But.

He needed to be as far away from Julien as possible while he was this plastered.

Cinn took the passenger seat in the front, sliding his beanie down over his eyes like that could make him disappear.

Once they'd sped off, Julien and the driver started a rapid exchange of French which, even in his inebriated state, he sensed was about him.

"Il a un problème votre ami?"

"Six, en réalité. Un voyage en avion traumatique et cinq double shots de whisky."

By the end of the journey, a headache had replaced most of Cinn's haziness. Looking out of the window, the soft glow of landmarks and winding foreign streets caused a tiny flicker of excitement to catch light within him. This was the third country he had ever set foot in—though he could barely count Switzerland, as he'd only been to Auri, Talwacht town centre, and the corner shop down the road from his house.

He managed to go the entire journey without saying a single word to Julien, and their silence continued as the taxi slowed down and came to a stop outside a black gate. Cinn climbed out—trying not to feel sickened by the enormous wad of notes Julien passed the driver—to find a single building on the road.

What the fuck?

To call the 'house' grand would be an understatement.

The elaborate carvings on its imposing facade bore a striking resemblance to the intricate stone detailing on London's Natural History Museum, where he and Tyler had spent many an hour wandering around, mainly in the dinosaur section.

And the windows! There were too many of them to count, their expensive panes gleaming in the bright moonlight.

In the middle of two colossal flaming torches, a black metal gate adorned with intricate designs blocked their path. If that wasn't ridiculous enough, through the grates, Cinn saw the icing on the cake: water fountains.

Internally, he howled with laughter. How was this his life?

"Please tell me you don't actually live here? It's not a house, it's a bloody *palace*!"

Cinn had known Julien was rich, but this was *rich*, rich. Filthy rich. Disgustingly rich.

Perhaps he should ask for the tiny scrap of aeroplane-ticket money back?

"It's not as central as I'd prefer, personally. That's the price my father pays for having an ostentatious mansion." Julien slid a packet of cigarettes from his pocket, lit one, took a deep drag, and passed it to Cinn.

"Cheers."

A long puff in, the cigarette's tip flashing red, then Cinn tipped his head back and blew the smoke at the stars.

"But if my palace doesn't suit you, there are many alleys you can test out. Just don't blame me when you wake up naked."

Cinn scoffed. "Are you telling me *all* French people are as sexually depraved as you?"

Julien accepted the offered cigarette, wrapping his lips around it with a deliberate sensuality that made Cinn want to rip it out of his mouth.

To put it back in his own mouth, of course.

Nothing else.

"I meant the homeless Parisians would steal your clothes, but yes, I'm sure they'd find you irresistible. Especially in that hat."

Their eyes locked, and Cinn's breath caught in his throat.

Julien passed him the end of the cigarette, which he finished in two long drags, all the while continuing their intense staring match.

Just when he was going to flick the butt on the ground, Julien snatched it carefully from his hand. "It's bad to litter," he said, tutting. Julien threw it into one of the fiery torches with impressive aim.

Was it bad that Cinn wanted to be punished?

That's enough.

Cinn shook his head violently to clear it. It was decided: he was never touching whiskey again.

Julien turned to the gate, but instead of locating an intercom system, he stepped on a shiny part of the ground Cinn had presumed was a drain cover.

Incorrect.

Two flashes of brightness lit the night sky as a fervent energy surged through the fire torches. A strange glow seeped up from the ground, curling around the iron bars.

Slowly, the gates opened with a slight screech, dragged by swirling flecks of light.

"Are those... motes? Did they recognise you and open the gate? Oh, also, are motes 'alive?' Like, can they see and hear us?"

Julien laughed. "I think there are a few chapters debating that, within that book from Noir that you're currently meant to be reading."

"I brought it with me," Cinn muttered. "No need to be the homework police."

"Definitely not. That sounds awfully dull."

Increasingly awestruck as they approached the house, Cinn couldn't shake off a sense of severe dissociation—not for the first time since he left London. He was about to sleep in this 'house', meet Julien's prestigious family. He was in *Paris*, of all places!

The ghost of a palm against his cheek. *"One day, you'll escape this fucking cycle, Cinn. You're too good for this rat race. You deserve the world."*

At the time, Cinn had shaken his head at Tyler, who was high as a kite on whatever he'd been able to buy that day. Now, approaching the mansion, he found himself echoing that action.

Tyler. He hadn't been able to reach him this morning. Tomorrow, he'd try again.

"Excited to be home?" Cinn asked Julien, as the double doors somehow sensed their presence and flung open for them.

After a moment's pause, Julien cast a sad smile toward him. "This place," he remarked softly. "Hasn't felt like home in quite some time."

Exhaustion weighed Cinn down with every step as he followed Julien down a maze of corridors, their shoes against the marble the only sound.

Up two flights of stairs, to the guest wing—honestly, who needed a guest *wing*?—and finally he was delivered to his room.

"How will I, uh... find you tomorrow?" said Cinn, not bothering to hide his panic.

"I'll come get you. Unless you'd rather come sleep in my bed?" A wide, gleaming white predatory smile.

Cinn rolled his eyes and closed the door on Julien's face.

"*That* is for making coffee? I have one of those in my new house."

"How do you not know what a *cafetière* is?"

"Heard of a little thing called Nescafé?"

"Ah, that granulated disappointment, the mud-like residue of regret? Yes, I've heard of it."

Julien passed Cinn a steaming cup of coffee, then obliged his request for milk, but drew the line at sugar.

Cinn's eyes widened as he took in the sheer expanse of the room. Stainless-steel appliances gleamed against expansive countertops, and an oversized island stood as a centrepiece. His fingers itched to use the industrial-sized gas stove, which sat below lines of gleaming pans hung from the wall.

"You realise this kitchen is basically the same size as my old restaurant, right?"

Julien shrugged. "Our chef never complains."

Your chef?!

At the look on Cinn's face, Julien continued, "You can judge her cooking tonight when we eat dinner with my father. You can give her your culinary feedback."

Cinn scowled.

"My father sends his apologies, by the way. Organising tomorrow's birthday event is keeping him and Carrie from the house until this evening."

"Why do you always say that? *My father*, in that weird voice?"

The purse of Julien's lips shut down that conversation. Cinn followed Julien through the house into the conservatory, where beaming sunlight bathed the room in a warm, golden glow. According to Julien, they had two hours to kill before they met the others in Paris, in which Julien had work to do. So before leaving his room that morning, Cinn reluctantly delved deep into the bottom of his rucksack to find the library book he was supposed to have already read.

In the centre of the conservatory, a substantial walnut table dominated the space, its polished surface reflecting dappled sunlight. Cinn slid out a high-backed chair, sinking into the plush navy upholstery. Maybe he could just chill here with his music instead of reading. He glanced over to the other side of the table and flinched.

Julien, already studying his paperwork very intently, had slipped on a pair of glasses, circles of thin golden wire that Cinn couldn't tear his own eyes away from.

Why, *oh why*, was this development causing his heart to tap dance against his ribcage?

Every flutter of Julien's long lashes had Cinn resisting the urge to reach out towards him. Touch his face. Slide his hand down to the patterned wool cardigan he was wearing over his buttoned shirt. Maybe take the cardigan off. Maybe take some other stuff off too.

No.

Cinn needed to stamp down these dangerous waves of attraction. Because even if Julien looked like he'd stepped out of a magazine with those dimples and that gorgeously touchable shiny hair, and even if he possessed a voice made of honey with that French accent that did all sorts of things to Cinn's insides—

"What? What's the matter?"

"Nothing. You look strange in those glasses."

You look hot as hell in those glasses.

"Read your book."

Cinn forced his head down to the colossal tome that awaited him—*Motecraft: Unveiling the Arcane Threads*—glaring at it like *it* was the problem. He opened it to page three.

He read a sentence. Had a few more sips of coffee. Read another sentence. Read the first one again. Was that a raven outside the window, or a crow? Julien would probably know.

"Cinn, you've been staring at the same page for ten minutes."

"Why are you watching me?" he snapped. "Do your own work."

"You're tapping your foot and look like you're going to throw that book through the glass. It's distracting."

"Is that a raven, or a crow?"

"What's wrong with the book?"

"I think it's a crow because I heard somewhere that crows are more common in urban areas, and this place seems more like a crow kind of neighbourhood. Plus, crows are smaller, right? This bird looks not as big as those ravens you see in movies. So, yeah, probably a crow."

"Cinn."

He looked at Julien. "What?!"

"What is wrong?"

At once, Cinn burst out of his chair, book in hand. "This book is fucking stupid! I can't even read the first fucking sentence!"

He threw the book onto the table, where it bounced. Calmly, Julien reached over and opened it.

"Motes exhibit a characteristic oscillation between spectral frequencies, akin to the ethereal dance of cosmic energies."

"Exactly! What does that even mean? I was expecting practical information, not this... this... poetic nonsense!"

Julien blinked at him.

"I'm *not* stupid. But all these books Noir sets for me are stupidly written in ways that don't even make sense... and the text is so bloody small that the letters keep jumbling about."

Cinn collapsed back onto the chair, pressing his forehead to the table. Julien was silent, so silent he eventually forced himself to sit back up. He found that Julien was scrutinising him carefully, fingertips pressed together in an arch.

Abruptly, Julien stood, and said, "Stay here." Then left the room for an eternity, in which Cinn sulked, lightly kicking the table legs.

When Julien returned, he carried a thin, rectangular object, like a giant bookmark, translucent yellow in colour with a thin blue line across it. He picked up the book to return it back to Cinn, leaning over behind him to open it on the table, the smell of the fancy coffee *just* detectable on his warm breath.

Julien placed his... thing.... on the first page, and instantaneously the text under the overlay magnified, and even seemed to magnetise to the blue line, preventing the words from jumping around. There were subtle tweaks to the font as well—larger spaces between words and the bottom of the letters looked a bit thicker.

Cinn removed the overlay, then placed it back onto the book again. Then he openly gaped at Julien.

"Okay, wow."

"Helpful?"

"What... is it?"

"Béatrice was diagnosed with dyslexia when she was twelve. I made it for her quite a few years back. It utilises a blend of lumenmotes and stabilimotes to trick your vision. You can have it now. Were you ever tested for dyslexia?"

"I don't think so?"

They'd mentioned it a few times to him in juvie, when he complained about finding the lessons hard, but nothing was ever done about it. Julien rested his hand on Cinn's shoulder. He fought the urge to rest his own on top of Julien's.

"Sounds like your school teachers were the stupid ones then, not you."

"Well, to be fair, I didn't go all that much."

"Do you want me to ask Eleanor to tell Noir that he needs to teach you this stuff himself, not give you 'stupid' books to read?"

Cinn eyed the book in question. "I'll try again. With your thingy. Thanks."

With a squeeze, Julien released his shoulder. Then, curiously, he tugged lightly on Cinn's beanie hat, an almost absent-minded, affectionate gesture.

"Oh shit, before I forget, can I use your phone to ring Tyler quickly?"

A few days after he'd provided Julien with Bradley's bank details, Julien gave him the receipt for the transaction. Cinn had called Tyler to confirm the money had gone into his friend's account, and Tyler babbled grateful sobs down the phone to him.

Cinn was elated until Tyler had asked when he was coming home.

And so his routine of ringing him every few days had started.

Asking him how he was, how his day had been.

Of course, Tyler knew what Cinn was really asking: how are you, and did you use today?

Julien's eyes narrowed almost imperceptibly and for a moment it seemed like he wasn't going to reply, but then he gestured to the corner, where a bright red desk phone lay waiting on a marble pedestal.

Cinn slid the number out of his wallet. "Will your dad mind the international call charges?" He was banking on Auri covering the astronomical charges that he was surely racking up on his own line. With a raised eyebrow, Julien gestured broadly to the space they occupied. "I think he'll just about be able to afford his newspaper still, yes."

Phone to his ear, Cinn paused. "Is it still the same number at the beginning, to make it connect to England? What button do I press next?"

Julien sighed, walked over, snatched the receiver and scrap of paper, and proceeded to jam the buttons. Passing the phone back, he returned to his seat. After a long silence, the phone rang.

And rang.

And rang.

And rang.

It disconnected.

"I'll quickly try once—"

"Well, we have to go now, anyway," said Julien, snapping his work shut and catapulting up.

"I thought we had anoth—"

"I've just remembered how long it takes to walk there. We don't want to be late."

Cinn placed the phone back into the holder. "Okay..." he said slowly. "I'll go get my coat."

Although Julien's palace seemed to float by itself in some distant rural location, the walk to civilisation was strikingly quick. With every step, Cinn's excitement at the prospect of sightseeing grew.

"Oh, can we go to the—"

Julien put his hand up. "*Non*. Don't say it."

Cinn scowled. "You don't know what I was about to ask."

With arms crossed, Julien sucked in a deep breath before declaring, "You were about to ask me to take you to that giant iron eyesore that blights Paris's skyline. The epitome of overrated tourist traps. Who in their right mind would want to spend precious time staring at a bunch of metal beams stacked together?"

"I actually thought we could go *up*—"

"And the crowds! There are so many other beautiful places in Paris, but no, everyone just has to go gaga over that rusty lattice. It's a symbol of hype over substance, and I refuse to contribute to the madness."

Cinn snapped his mouth shut as they continued onwards. The long walk into the city centre seemed to be suspiciously convoluted, but what did he know? He allowed Julien to drone on about annoying tourists, the 'decrepit' Parisian metro system and their overflowing rat and pigeon problems all the way to a bike rental store, where they met Elliot and Darcy.

To his surprise, Darcy threw her arms around him. Cinn weakly returned the gesture, patting her back.

"You survived!" she said.

Julien cackled. "Well, he hasn't actually met my father yet, so..."

Their first activity of the day was to hide in a side alley with their rented bikes, while Julien installed some sort of new invention he was trialling on the spokes of each of them. Attached to the hub, it looked like a twenty-four legged spider.

"They should give us a little boost," he said with a proud grin that Cinn couldn't help but smile back at.

"We're not entering the Tour de France today, Julien," said Elliot. "I'm sure we could have managed."

"Now we can *manage* even more effortlessly."

Dodging weaving traffic and navigating through the chaotic maze of honking horns and impatient drivers, they cycled in tandem across frighteningly busy city streets. The mopeds whizzing past, pedestrians darting unpredictably, and the cacophony of street sounds created a pulse of frenetic energy that was almost overwhelming, even for a seasoned Londoner like Cinn.

When they reached the Seine, hopping off to push their bikes alongside the river, Cinn breathed a sigh of relief.

"Well?" Julien demanded. "Did it work for you?"

Cinn pressed his hand to his heart. "Too well. I went so fast I thought I was going to start flying."

"Maybe that will be my next project."

Meandering along the riverside was a serene contrast to the city streets, although still busy to bursting.

"*L'île Saint Louis.*" Julien pointed across the river.

"A little island," translated Darcy. "We need to cross through it."

Two bridges, one coffee stop, and several horrendous main roads later, they were at their next destination: an extraordinarily busy glass pyramid, next to a water fountain where parents were letting their children splash around in the freezing water.

Cinn nudged into Julien. "Thought you weren't a fan of overrated tourist traps?"

"I make an exception for the Louvre." He winked. "It's Paris's greatest jewel."

Once they'd descended under the pyramid, Cinn gaping at the impressive architecture, Julien swiftly paid for all of their tickets in the spacious underground lobby before leading them down a corridor to the exhibits.

The echoing footsteps of other visitors and the hum of quiet conversations reverberated through the grand halls, and soon they were surrounded by centuries of artistic expression that Cinn couldn't even fathom understanding.

At once, Julien and Darcy entered full-on art-historian mode, heads pressed closely together as they discussed brushstroke techniques, cultural references, hidden symbolism, and the subtle nuances of the paintings that surrounded them.

Cinn trailed after them for a few rooms, attempting to listen to the duo passionately debating artists' influences until his sense of being out of his depth, a novice in a world of masterpieces, forced him to retreat to a red velvet bench in the corner of the Denon Wing.

"Don't worry, they usually run out of energy after about six hours here."

Elliot joined him on the bench, initiating their first time alone together. Cinn side-eyed him, instantly tense. In their few weeks in each other's company, Elliot had given off strong 'don't bother with me' vibes, and Cinn was happy to oblige him.

Elliot pulled at one of his many dark blond corkscrew curls. "When we had Béatrice, the two of us would drop them here, then fuck off down the road to a coffee shop. This was never our scene."

"Really? I kind of imagined Béatrice like Julien."

"What, a pretentious twat?"

Cinn snorted, the sound loud compared to the quiet hush of the other tourists, and quickly covered his mouth.

"Béatrice was far more into practical stuff. She was one of those people who was always learning a new skill. She even got me to teach her how to ride my motorbike. Julien doesn't even trust me enough to ride pillion."

"He probably wouldn't want to cheat on Maz."

Elliot gave a soft chuckle, then gazed over at Julien's back with a faraway look in his eye, a sliver of a smile on his lips. "Did you know he's working on this side project, a mote-powered special varnish that's invisible and undetectable to art conservators? It's to help preserve and even restore art to its original form." Elliot's voice dripped with so much pride and admiration, Cinn couldn't help but suck it up like a sponge.

Elliot, chattier than Cinn had ever seen him, seemed like he was in a sharing mood, and questions about the exact nature of his relationship with Julien danced on the tip of his tongue. His infatuation—or whatever it was—seemed one-sided, but had it always been? Was Elliot counted alongside Julien's 'many, *many*'?

Abruptly, Elliot stood. "Come on. I'll take you to see the *Mona Lisa*. Julien refuses to go to that bit."

Cinn rolled his eyes. "Of course he does."

Elliot darted off, forcing Cinn to chase after him. As he soon discovered, 'seeing' the *Mona Lisa* was a challenge. Not only was the woman herself bloody tiny, crowds of tourists clambered over each other to get to the artwork. Eventually reaching the front, Cinn faced the small painting encased in glass, not really understanding the fuss, but feeling the weight of the crowd's collective awe, nevertheless.

"Now let's go to the only exciting bit," Elliot announced, leading Cinn on a ten-minute march, all the way to a large open space within the Richelieu Wing, where glass ceilings bathed a bountiful collection of statues in natural light.

Now these *were* impressive. Their colossal size, the way the sculptors made the stone seem like it could be soft fabric or real muscles... Cinn's fingers twitched to reach up and touch the marble, only held back by the security rope.

When they got to *Hercules Fighting Achelous Transformed into a Snake*, Elliot initiated a silly game where they personified the statues, dramatising their thoughts out loud.

At *Psyche Revived by Cupid's Kiss*, Elliot declared, in a truly ridiculous voice. "Oh, woe is me! Cupid, darling, did you have to wake me up with such drama? A shake would have done the trick." Cinn bit his fist to suppress a roar of laughter.

Then at Venus de Milo, Cinn pretended to lean on the armless statue, saying, "Oh dear, oh dear, I used to hold something fancy but it got so heavy that my arms fell off. Now I look like a T-Rex who wants some hugs. Plus, I can't even flex anymore!"

Elliot's whole body shook, and the pair of them gave up any pretence of respecting their surroundings to howl with laughter.

"What on earth?"

They turned to find Julien, mouth slightly parted and eyes wide.

Cinn tensed. Even if Julien wasn't bothered by their childish behaviour, his unpredictable jealous streak might rear its head.

But then he *smiled*.

Julien raised his hand to his mouth, pretending to look shocked. "Having fun without me? Surely not."

Cinn's face broke into a smile of its own.

After the Louvre, their final mission was to cycle to a long row of *pâtisseries*, where Darcy and Elliot spent ten minutes arguing about which one to go into. Cinn eventually chose for them by walking into the nearest one. Named Stohrer, it held a small sign bragging about being Paris's oldest *pâtisserie*. However, what drew Cinn in was a thick crowd packed together at the back, watching a live demonstration of a pastry chef in action.

Crossing the quaint *pâtisserie*, he resisted the rows of meticulously crafted desserts with their glossy glazes and delicate toppings that promised indulgence in every bite to reach the plump, moustached man in the show kitchen. He was combining sugar and water to create gently sizzling caramel, demonstrating precise timing and skill as he dipped cream-filled choux puffs into the molten delight to create a shiny coating.

"He's making croquembouche," whispered Julien into his ear, startling him. The crowd had increased further, and perhaps this was what forced Julien to press up against Cinn's back. Then a light pressure on his left hip registered, and he glanced down to see Julien was securely holding it, his fingertips drawing tiny circles in the waistband of his jeans.

Cinn swallowed, fixing his gaze back onto the demonstration. "What's that dessert again?" he mumbled.

Over his shoulder, Julien leaned his face in even closer. "It's a tower of temptation," Julien breathed, his voice a seductive murmur, and Cinn shuddered so violently against him he surely felt it. Julien's other hand slid up his thigh to rest on his right hip. Then he pressed himself even closer to Cinn's back, closing any remaining space between them.

Cinn made no attempt to shuffle free; his strategy of simply ignoring Julien's flirtations had been working well for him so far. However, if the princeling kept holding him so firmly for much longer, he might end up with a larger problem, if the subtle ache in his groin was anything to go by. He forced himself to focus on the pyramid of glossy balls being assembled in front of him.

Julien continued, his lips brushing against Cinn's earlobe as he whispered, "Each bite, a sweet surrender."

The low, husky sound of his voice sent a jolt straight to Cinn's dick.

Nope. That was enough for one day.

Cinn wiggled out of his grip, weaving through the throngs of captivated watchers to dive out of the shop, straight into Elliot and Darcy.

"We got you two these chocolate éclairs." Elliot held them up. "What were you doing in there for so long?"

Cinn snatched one out of his hand, turning his flushed face away from everyone to eat it in three hungry bites.

After another hour or so of aimless wandering, they returned their bikes—sans mote-powered spider things—and said goodbye to Darcy and Elliot.

"See you tomorrow at the party." Elliot grinned at him and offered him a fist bump. "If I manage to break in, that is."

The victorious feeling Cinn experienced at earning some shard of Elliot's approval felt pivotal—he hadn't even known how much he wanted it. Turning to say goodbye to Darcy, he pleaded, "Can't you two come back to Julien's?"

The apprehension surrounding his evening back at Julien's mansion had only grown since the bakery.

She barked a laugh. "Not a chance in hell I'm signing up for extra Lucien Montaigne time. You'll survive him for one dinner though." She stepped back, adding, "Won't you?"

Cinn glanced at Julien, standing apart from them, watching passersby. *I'm not so sure.*

The setting sun painted Paris in deep shadows and gorgeous orange hues as they walked back. Trees were shedding their last few stubborn leaves, a few falling on them as they walked.

Julien brushed one off Cinn's shoulder. "So, now you've experienced true Parisian culture, I'm sure you have no regrets about not going to visit the metal beam monstrosity?"

"Nope. I still want to visit it, I'm afraid." Cinn smirked at Julien. "There's just something about overrated tourist traps that I can't get away from. Comes from being a Londoner, I guess."

With an exaggerated sigh, Julien ran his hand down his face. "I always forget Londoners have no taste."

Twelve

CINN

The imposing grandfather clock in the middle of the corridor loomed over Cinn. Five minutes to six. His fisted hand wavered over Julien's door. At least, he *hoped* it was Julien's door. Julien had shown him the way before dropping him off at his own room earlier, but his elaborately sprawling mansion was impossible to navigate.

The door swung open.

"Why are you standing there like a lemon, as Darcy would say?"

"How did you know I was there?" Cinn crossed his arms.

Julien leant forward, sniffing, to say, "You smell like a lemon, too."

Cinn scowled, tugging his beanie down lower on his head. "It's the only shampoo the corner shop sold."

Julien motioned for him to come in. Crossing the threshold, it became evident that 'Julien's room' was actually 'Julien's suite'—the living room he currently stood in housed four separate doors leading off it.

The centre of the room was airy and spacious, whereas the walls were jam-packed—rows and rows of bookcases, a half-filled wine rack beside a globe drink cabinet, a handful of small sculptures in display cases. The largest Persian rug that Cinn had ever seen covered the hardwood floor, its light blue and mustard yellow adding subtle dashes of colour to the dark room.

Eyeing the glistening chandelier in the centre of the ceiling, Cinn said, "This is... nice."

Julien smirked, eyes twinkling. "*Oui, nice* was exactly what I was going for."

"What do you want me to say? To be fair, I just spent the day at the Louvre. My standards are higher now."

With a laugh, Julien walked backwards, gesturing for Cinn to follow him through the nearest door. "If it's more art you're after, I put all of my favourite pieces in my bedroom. Come see them."

Resisting a joke about being lured into his bed, lest he encourage Julien's line-crossing, Cinn followed Julien to find the space just as opulent and luxurious as he'd imagined. The queen-sized four-poster bed hardly took up a fraction of the floor—in fact, Julien's numerous wardrobes dominated the room.

Remembering he was here to see the art, he followed Julien to the far wall, practically a gallery in its own right. He wasn't sure what sort of paintings he'd expected to see hung on Julien's walls—more classical pieces, perhaps—but these surreal and abstract canvases surprised him.

Cinn's eyes magnetised to a painting where eerie shadows danced across a desolate landscape, the skeletal remains of twisted structures looming in a haunting display of despair.

He moved down the wall. Each piece, clearly by the same artist, contained abstract settings, intimidating creatures, and distorted forms. A gathering of skeletons around a crackling fire, bones bleached white, eye sockets staring out at the viewer. A monstrous head with a gaping maw, out of which humanoid spiders were clawing their way. A large, gnarled tree with many skeletal hands emerging from its trunk and branches, reaching out in different directions, as if grasping at something unseen.

Cinn reached out to hover his fingers a few centimetres away from one canvas's brushstrokes. *Julien, why the fuck do you want these in your bedroom, you absolute freak?*

"They're a bit... doom and gloom," Cinn said, moving to the final painting, which featured predominantly red hues. The nightmarish, dystopian tableau reminded him so strongly of his visit to the shadowrealm, he clutched his golden bangle to make sure it was still there. "This one looks particularly similar to where I went when I tried to find Béatrice," Cinn said. "Who painted these?"

"Zdzisław Beksiński." Julien's hands ghosted across the canvas. "He once said, 'I wish to paint in such a manner as if I were photographing dreams'."

"Well, I love his use of expressionistic colour," Cinn said, sounding very smart indeed, but Julien snorted.

"Good job listening to me and Darcy today. For five minutes, anyway, before prattling around with Elliot."

"What's this one called?"

"He left most of his works untitled. So as not to impose a specific narrative on them."

"Sounds like something you would do."

Julien's infectious cackle made Cinn's heart beat ever so slightly faster. His laugh was quickly becoming like a drug to Cinn—he was unable to resist chasing it, knowing how it would light up Julien's eyes, cause his nose to scrunch up slightly, deepen his dimples.

Cinn inched closer to him. "Don't you want all this in your Talwacht apartment?" Over the last few weeks, Cinn had found himself increasingly curious about where Julien went after he dropped him off each day.

"Eventually. I don't really like the apartment, though." Julien's lips pursed, and he flinched as if he'd said too much.

"Why don't you take Béatrice's old room at Darcy's cottage?" Cinn regretted the stupid question even before he caught the look of horror that flashed across Julien's face. "Sorry, sorry, ignore me."

Julien walked out, with Cinn awkwardly following him to the sumptuous chaise longue in the middle of the sitting room. He really should be on his best behaviour now, but he couldn't resist touching a large ring-bound sketchpad lying on the coffee table.

"Can I?"

Julien appeared hesitant. "They're all old designs... but if you really want to."

Flicking through the pages, Cinn discovered dozens of incredibly detailed drawings of what he could only presume were motecraft inventions, each with numerous scribbled annotations in Julien's messy French scrawl.

A compass-like object, possibly to guide the user to sources of large quantities of motes. Goggles that appeared to give the wearer the ability to see through solid objects. A cross-section sketch of a pillow, containing five different layers, with doodles coming off a sleeping woman's head—an illustration of a sun, a book, and a dog. Some sort of happy-dream device? Cinn would kill for that.

"Julien, these are incredible."

"You don't even know what you're looking at. Half of these are impossible. They're just fantasy."

Cinn rolled his eyes. "God, you're so difficult. Just take the compliment."

"Oh, I did, don't worry." Julien drifted across the room to the full-length mirror. "We should head downstairs now." He combed a hand through his hair and straightened the collar on the smart white shirt he was wearing.

Cinn stood to copy him, hovering behind him. The other day, Darcy had accompanied him into the town to help him buy relatively nice clothes for this weekend. As he'd saved the fanciest shirt for the birthday party the following evening, he was in the cheaper black linen one. It itched his neck.

"Oh shit. Can I leave this here?" Cinn went to pull his hat off his head—it surely wasn't appropriate to wear it to dinner in this fancy palace. Even *he* knew some level of social etiquette.

Catching his arm, Julien pushed it down, then tugged on his beanie like he'd done the other day. "No, no. Keep it on. You're all good."

Cinn opened his mouth to protest, but then shut it. Without the hat, he felt stripped of his shield, as silly as that sounded.

As they traversed the maze of corridors into the main body of the mansion, a ball of nerves bounced in Cinn's stomach. Just how had he ended up here? "Anything I should know about them? Your dad and step-mother? Do I need to do anything special?"

Julien turned to him. "Just be your normal self." He flashed him a grin. There was a hint of *something* in the smile. Something that doubled Cinn's anxiety as they turned the final corner to reach the drawing room.

Around a roaring fireplace, a collection of armchairs sat arranged in a perfect semicircle, with figures occupying two of them. Upon their approach, they stood up to greet them. The woman swiftly kissed Julien's cheeks, while the man shook his hand. His father. He possessed Julien's wiry frame, but that was where the similarities ended.

It was hard to pinpoint what gave the man the air of authority he exuded. Perhaps it was his short-cropped grey hair and beard, in addition to a sprinkling of fine-line wrinkles. Perhaps it was his reputation. Or perhaps it was the way he moved—like he owned the world.

"Julien," he said, in a far thicker French accent than Julien's, then turned to Cinn. At first, Lucien Montaigne squinted at him with a frozen smile, like Cinn was an enigma, a lost stray that wasn't meant to be there. Then he composed himself, reaching over to firmly shake Cinn's hand, his gaze scrutinising every inch of him, hovering a few too many seconds on his eyebrow piercing and beanie in turn.

"Lucien Montaigne," he declared.

Behind his father, Julien wore an infuriating smile. Like he had set the stage and now was ready for the performance to unfold.

For fuck's sake, Julien. What have you done this time?

The woman—at least a decade Lucien's junior, but surely his wife, Carrie—seemed far less fazed, reaching out next for his hand. Dressed in a long purple evening gown, her bright red lipstick reminded Cinn of the shade his mother used to wear on the nights she went out and left him with their crazy cat lady neighbour.

"English, yes? Who do we have here, then?" Carrie's light, musical voice didn't fool him; her eyes were as calculating as a poker player holding a winning hand.

Cinn's head snapped straight to Julien, heart rate spiking. Had he not even told them his *name*? Did they even know he was staying here?

"I was promised that Julien was bringing home a date, but it's always delightful to meet new friends. Especially after that last *friend* he introduced us to."

Elliot? It had to be.

"Cinn Saunders," Cinn said, cringing at the waver in his voice. *It's just one dinner. You can get through one dinner.*

Carrie smiled, but a shadow darkened Lucien's face. Did he know about him? *What* did he know about him?

"Well," Lucien drawled, his fingers elegantly navigating his perfectly groomed beard. "*Quelle surprise.* I didn't expect to be meeting the infamous shadowslipper so soon. You'll forgive us, Cinnamon, for not being adequately prepared. My son seems to have a penchant for forgetfulness amidst the brilliance of his mind."

At the use of his real name, Cinn grimaced, biting his lip for a millisecond before remembering everyone was focused on him. *Don't give them an inch, Cinn.*

"Actually, his name is Cinn," stated Julien, moving to stand near him. "He doesn't go by Cinnamon at all."

Heat shot across Cinn's face. "Anything is fine," he mumbled.

"Cinn," Carrie repeated, slightly scrunching up her face. *It's a damn sight better than Cinnamon, woman.*

Julien pressed the small of his back, and Cinn had to fight not to jump away from him at the touch, fiery anger coursing through his veins.

"Let's sit," Julien said, pushing Cinn towards a chair.

Cinn stared into the fire as Lucien set about pouring drinks for them from a sidebar. Usually, the fireplaces at Auri brought him great comfort—he'd never lived or even visited anywhere with an actual fire in London—but this one seemed set to reach out to devour him.

The sound of liquid being poured into glasses filled the suffocating silence. Lucien set a silver tray with four wine glasses onto a small table.

"Oh, *Père*, Cinn isn't a fan of red wine. Do you have any beer?"

Julien's face was the picture of innocence as Cinn shot him his most furious glare. "Red wine is absolutely fine. Great in fact," he babbled, reaching for one. He searched his mind to recall Julien and Darcy's conversations about expensive wine—which occurred with alarming frequency. "Is this Château Margaux?" he added, butchering the pronunciation.

After a calculated blink, Lucien emitted a brief, disdainful laugh. "No, this is merely a sneak peek at a new collection from an emerging vineyard. However, I can extend an offer for *Château Margaux*, if that aligns more with your preferences?"

"No, no, this is great."

The look in Lucien's eye told Cinn he hadn't fooled him, so Cinn took a large gulp of his drink to prove he liked it. He almost choked. *You sip wine, Cinn,* he chastised himself, glaring at the dark red liquid. How could a liquid *dry* your mouth?

"So, Cinn, how have you found the Aurelia Institute so far?" Carrie asked.

His mouth dried further, descending into sandpaper territory. "It's been... okay."

Carrie continued examining him, clearly expecting more than a three word answer.

"It's very different from London. I mean, obviously London is a city and Auri is... whatever Auri is."

"And Eleanor tells us you knew nothing of motecraft or of your rare ability until she came to collect you?"

Eleanor. How had he forgotten Eleanor was best friends with these people?

"That's correct, ma'am." Cinn cringed at his own odd formality.

Lucien swirled the wine delicately within his glass, savouring the moment before taking a deliberate sip. His piercing blue eyes, devoid of warmth, appeared hesitant to detach from Cinn, casting an unsettling sensation upon his skin. "I trust my son and his associates have been providing you with the appropriate level of care," he remarked.

Grabbing onto the easier topic of conversation, Cinn said, "Yes, Darcy has been very welcoming." *Your son is a bloody nightmare, though.*

At the mention of her, Lucien's face lit up. "Ah, Darcy Beaumont!"

"Don't start waxing lyrical about her again, *Père*," said Julien, who had sunk so deeply into his armchair he was barely visible in the dim light. "Cinn may get the wrong impression of you."

Carrie made a tiny sound of discontentment, covering it quickly with a sip of her drink.

A woman, dressed in a double-breasted chef jacket, apron and neckerchief, appeared in the doorway, greeting them in French.

"Marie," said Carrie. "We have a special English guest with us this evening."

The chef offered Cinn a wide smile. "Pardon me. Good evening. If you would please follow me into the dining room."

With a sense that his hellish evening was only getting started, Cinn forced himself to his feet to follow behind the others.

"It's a pleasure to see a new face," Marie said as she showed them to their seats.

I bet it is.

"Hungry?" whispered Julien into his ear, his breath tickling the back of his neck.

Throwing Julien the sharpest of daggers, Cinn responded with, "Don't even dare. I'm so fucking furious at you it's unreal." Then he slid into the seat next to him, opposite Lucien and Carrie.

The mammoth dining room table was meticulously adorned with fine linen, crystal glasses, and several candelabras alight with flickering glows. Each place was set with a ridiculous amount of polished silverware.

While Lucien spoke to Marie, Julien turned to Cinn, glancing down to their place settings and opening his mouth.

"If you even *think* about trying to explain this cutlery to me, I will cut you," Cinn hissed, tapping the handle of the steak knife for good measure.

Julien smirked. "Why would I need to explain cutlery to a Michelin star chef such as yourself?"

Cinn was about to pick up the knife anyway when Lucien and Carrie's attention gravitated back towards them.

"Julien, one would assume you've received correspondence from MEET by now concerning your application," Lucien said, his tone one of condescension.

"*Non, Père.*" With a glance at Cinn, he added, "Mote-Enhanced Engineering & Technologies."

"I know what MEET stands for by now," Cinn mumbled. "You don't shut up about it."

Lucien chuckled. "My ambitious son has always possessed a talent for relentless chatter. Speaking of MEET, however..." Lucien's gaze narrowed in on Julien. "You still haven't offered me your thoughts on the steam-engine proposal."

"There wasn't too much to say. Besides, I heard through the grapevine your people had already motioned to acquire it before anyone else had the chance to pick up up their pen."

The older man stared at the younger as if he could burn him with his gaze. "Of course. Improving the efficiency of cargo ships will only benefit the entire planet, especially those populations in developing countries whose economies rely on exporting goods."

"*Oui*, but it doesn't *need* HorizonTech's stamp on it to do so."

The tension in the air was beyond palpable. Cinn stared down at the table, unable to maintain the back and forth.

"May I remind you that HorizonTech—"

"Gentlemen, save the business talk for the party tomorrow," interjected Carrie, with a nod to Cinn, who couldn't help but flush.

Lucien smiled a flash of sharp teeth. "Quite right dear. Now, Cinn, as you find yourself assimilated into the institute, do you harbour any grand visions for your future with us? Perhaps some objectives?"

Visions?! *Objectives*?! Was the man joking? Cinn's only plan was to keep his head down and hope they somehow forgot to ever ask him to go and banish those terrifying monster things to the shadowrealm, or whatever the fuck they actually wanted him there for.

Marie gifted Cinn a precious few moments to prepare his answer by presenting their amuse-bouche, the existence of which caused Cinn to wonder just how many courses he was going to have to sit through, and distracting him from producing his answer for Lucien.

"Um..." he started.

Julien interjected with, "Eleanor and Noir are formulating an agenda for Cinn to spend some time shadowing at various Auri departments."

They are?

"That's a splendid plan," commented Carrie. "A great way to immerse him in how things work."

Resisting shaking his head, Cinn used the soup spoon to scoop up his hors d'œuvre from its shallow bowl. This was the most awkward dinner of his life, but he couldn't deny the single, bite-sized truffle-infused oyster velouté with caviar was tasty.

Determined that Julien wouldn't be his mouthpiece, Cinn added, "I still have lots to learn about shadowslipping from Noir first, before I think about anything else." He glanced down at the golden bangle around his wrist, the life-changing device that suppressed unwanted slips. If only he'd been given it from the beginning. He'd have grown up unafraid, and four lives wouldn't have been taken.

Lost in his thoughts, Cinn didn't catch the name of the next dish, some sort of duck liver with a fig compote. If *he* were in the kitchen, he would have added a touch of balsamic reduction, but he certainly wasn't about to tell Marie that.

When the next dish wasn't the main, but a soup, Cinn wanted to scream. Marie's lobster bisque with saffron and chervil oil turned his stomach even before his first mouthful, the pungent seafood aroma overwhelming him. *Fish do not belong in soup,* he thought miserably, placing a miniscule amount on his spoon.

He tuned back in to hear the phrase, 'Arcane Purifiers', spat from Lucien's mouth.

Hoping he wouldn't be asked his opinion, Cinn glanced at Julien to catch the twinkle in his eye. The twinkle that meant he was about to cause trouble. "However *Père*, you can't deny that the evidence is there. Since the Calamities of Nineteen Sixty-Five, the rise in natural disasters has been fully consistent with our constant increase of mote channelling and mote application. And, now, with these new umbraphage creatures attacking people on city streets..."

With cold, flinty eyes bulging, Lucien elevated his chin. "Don't you dare extend sympathy towards their narrow-minded crusade within this household, *mon fils*. Their misguided, ill-informed quest poses a threat to the stability of the moteblessed community. They are nothing short of terrorists. I would have expected, especially after witnessing their work first-hand recently, that you wouldn't utter a word in defence of their cause." His words cut through the air with an authoritative sharpness.

Cinn suddenly found a fresh wave of appeal for his soup.

"What do you think, Cinn?" Julien asked, in a pleasant tone, as if they were debating tomorrow's weather.

Cinn chewed on his bread. Swallowed. "I couldn't possibly comment."

Once this dinner was over, he was going to murder Julien. Murder him, then slip into the shadowrealm and murder him all over again.

"*Père*, what did Béatrice think about the Arcane Purifier movement? Do you know?"

Eyes closed, Cinn murmured a silent prayer to any deity that might be listening.

Carrie's musical lilt filled Lucien's silence. "I hardly think our guest is interested in this topic of conversation."

But Julien wasn't letting it go. Shoulders drawn back, he seemed oddly tense, his unwavering gaze directed straight at his father. "Did she ever say anything on the matter to you?"

With a clatter, Lucien dropped his cutlery onto the table. "*Assez. Tu sais que Béatrice partageait mon point de vue sur ce sujet. Tout comme toi, je l'espère. Maintenant Julien, si tu pouvais arrêter d'embarrasser ta famille, je t'en serais gré.*"

Red splotches of colour dotted Julien's cheeks. His grip on his cutlery turned his hand white. A shred of sympathy shot through Cinn—just the teeniest fraction.

"*En parlant de ta très chère fille, pourquoi cela te déplaît-il autant de me voir enquêter sur sa mort?*" Julien replied.

He couldn't understand a word of it, but what he did know was that this was all too much. Far too much.

"Excuse me for a moment." Abruptly, Cinn stood, and before anyone enquired if he needed directions to the nearest bathroom, he dashed off towards the kitchen.

He found Marie instructing two assistants, elbow deep in potatoes. Her eyes widened as he approached.

Before he could be ordered out, he said, "*Please* let me do something for you. Just for five minutes. I'm a trained chef. Well, semi-trained chef."

Likely at the desperation in his eyes, she nodded towards a pile of leafy asparagus. "Wash and trim those. If you don't fuck that up, you can blanch them for me." She studied him, eyes roaming up and down. "What's a *semi-trained chef* doing dining with the Montaignes this evening, anyway? You don't look like their normal victims."

"I was coerced into this horrific event by their son, purely for his entertainment, it seems."

She laughed, a genuine hearty laugh that was music to his ears.

For a moment, he focused only on the noises of their combined efforts in the kitchen and pretended he was back at Rosewood Parlour with Sarah whispering gossip in his ear when she was supposed to be washing dishes, and Benny barking orders. Any second now, the head chef would shout out one of his stupid rhyming commands. *Less chatter, more batter! Less stressing, more dressing! Less clutter, more butter!*

"Not bad." Marie admired his line of uniform asparagus. "If I ever crack under the pressure of working for my exasperating employers, you can have my job."

A shadow at the doorway told him his time was up. Cinn washed his hands before pushing past Julien, deliberately not looking at him. He'd deal with him later. He just had to make it through three more courses.

When he returned to his seat, Lucien inquired, "Is everything alright?" His tone didn't invite any deviation from 'yes'.

As Julien slid back in next to him, Cinn nodded. "Marie just wanted some extra help in the kitchen, that was all." They'd know it was an excuse, of course, but couldn't challenge it. "And I'm training to be a chef." *Not exactly true, not anymore.* "I mean, I was. In London."

Carrie's face brightened with delight. At least the woman was good at feigning interest. "Oh, how... lovely!"

"Yes. It was." Cinn aggressively dunked his baguette slice in the now-cold soup, imagining he was punching Julien's face.

"Cinn is giving Darcy a run for her money with his cookie making skills."

"I'm just messing around in her kitchen. I'm not really a baker."

Neither Carrie nor Lucien seemed equipped to continue a conversation about cookies, so a tense silence fell between the four of them.

Then he felt it.

The lightest brush against his ankle.

Cinn shuffled slightly across, giving Julien more room.

Then, another nudge came, followed by small circles on his lower calf, before Julien hooked his foot around Cinn's, pressing their legs together.

What in the world? How did Julien have the audacity to attempt to play footsie with him under the table right now?

With all the force he could muster, Cinn shot out his leg to kick Julien, who lurched forward, dropping his knife with a loud clatter. Mission success.

Plastering his best butter-wouldn't-melt expression on, Cinn asked, "Are you okay?"

And that's when Cinn realised his error. Because he'd forgotten something vital—Julien loved games. Lived for them, seemingly.

The smile Julien flashed him was as bright as the sun, and he was Icarus, about to burn.

Thankful that Lucien and Carrie had struck up their own quiet conversation, Cinn leaned in close to Julien to hiss, "If you touch me *one more time*, I'll announce I'm feeling ill, go grab my stuff, and walk to Darcy and Elliot's hotel if I have to."

Hell, he'd sleep on the street if it came to it.

"Pardon. It was an accident." However, Julien didn't look anywhere near as guilty as he should, his eyes still shimmering with a hint of amusement. Oh, what Cinn would do to smack that expression off his face.

He narrowed his eyes, attempting a contemplative look. "Maybe Elliot will let me sleep in his room."

A flash of *something* crossed Julien's face before he composed himself, and Cinn counted that as a win. For good measure, Cinn shuffled his chair away from him. The loud scrape was worth it.

The rest of the meal was uneventful. Cinn was too stressed to enjoy the impressive main, which Marie announced as châteaubriand steak with béarnaise sauce, truffle mash, and asparagus bundles. At least each bite helped him count down the seconds until he could escape. Lucien continued to ask him questions about his experience of Auri, then launched into random speeches about the consortium he held a chair of, but Cinn didn't even attempt to follow, nodding in random places in agreement.

As for the dessert, a Grand Marnier soufflé delicately flavoured with orange liqueur, he was far too full by then and only managed three bites before admitting defeat.

"Shall we retire into the drawing room with our coffee?" Lucien asked, once what Cinn had assumed were the final dishes were cleared.

Coffee?!

Too quickly, Cinn stood up, causing his chair to screech again. "Actually, thank you so much for the lovely meal, but I'm rather tired after sightseeing today, and I want to be refreshed for your party tomorrow."

"Of course." Carrie gave him a tight smile. "We look forward to seeing you there. It will be a great chance for you to meet important people within our community."

Another evening of absolute torture. Maybe he should see if he could change his ticket and head back to Switzerland tomorrow morning. Alternatively, he was now incredibly close to England...

"I am also feeling tired," announced Julien.

I bet you are, after that ludicrous show.

After dragged-out farewells, Cinn was finally free to leave the room, Julien hot on his tail. He darted down the halls, retracing their earlier steps.

Of course, their earlier steps led him straight to Julien's rooms.

Cinn stopped outside of it. Shaking with rage, unable to even meet Julien's eyes, he said in an unsteady voice, "What the actual *fuck* was that?" The skin under his golden band tingled with warmth.

"Dinner with my darling father and his wife."

"No, that was an absolute shit-show that you dragged me to for your own entertainment."

"Oh, come on, it wasn't that bad, was it?"

Something inside Cinn broke.

He'd had enough of this entitled princeling who thought he could fuck with him.

Closing the space between them, Cinn forced Julien to take two steps backwards until his body pressed into the door.

"Are you joking? It was awful," he snarled at Julien, blood turning to lava as it pulsed angrily through his body. "You're such a prick. Did you stop to consider for one moment how shit it would be for me to sit through you deliberately winding him up? You didn't even tell them I was staying here for some fucked-up reason."

Cinn unleashed an angry, strangled scream, slamming his fist against the wood beside Julien's head, lest he smash his stupid pretty face in.

Julien wasn't smiling anymore. Rather, his face had gone very blank, and any shred of colour drained from it.

"And this is all after I forced myself on a bloody aeroplane to be here to help you."

A flinch.

"Which I didn't mind doing, because I'd do anything for my friends. But if this is how you treat yours—"

"It's not." Julien's voice was so quiet, he barely heard it.

A pause.

"Well?" Cinn spat. "Aren't you going to say anything else?"

Without warning, Julien pushed the door handle down, throwing his weight backwards to open it, sending them both stumbling through the doorway.

Thirteen

CINN

C inn fell into Julien, who caught him with strong, steady arms. He spun him around so that his body blocked Cinn's exit, then clicked the door shut for good measure.

Right then. If he wanted it like that.

Cinn lunged for him, gripping Julien's shirt with two hands, before pushing him against the nearest wall, hard. If it took more than words to make his message clear to Julien, so be it. "I've had more than enough of this fucked-up game you've decided to play with me, Julien."

He expected Julien to push him back, or taunt him at least. What he got instead was a bewildering blend of expressions flashing across Julien's face. Panic, alarm... fear?

Cinn loosened his grip slightly and shuffled backwards.

"I'm trying to apologise." Julien's tone was a calm breeze compared to the tempest Cinn was riding. "If you'll give me the chance." He placed a hand on Cinn's chest, lightly pressing against it. "Will you let me? Please?"

The pleading, slightly haunted look on his face had Cinn's hands releasing him. Julien slipped away from the wall, opened his drink cabinet, and pulled out a half-full bottle of golden whiskey. Throwing the stopper to one side, he took several deep gulps before offering it to Cinn.

He should have probably refused, but being sober seemed rather unappealing presently.

Julien moved to the sofa in the middle of the room. Leaving a great deal of space between them, Cinn perched on the other side of it. After burning his throat with several deep swallows of the whiskey, he said, "Start talking then."

"My friends are incredibly precious to me. So the fact that I've hurt you has upset me. I feel awful, genuinely."

"I'm so sorry," Cinn said, laying the sarcasm on thick. However, searching Julien's eyes for any sign of manipulation, Cinn found none. It wasn't possible he was seeing Julien in his most candid form right now, right?

"You've coped so well with everything that's been thrown at you so far. I guess I didn't think that you'd find that dinner so stressful. I didn't think at all." Cinn opened his mouth. "I know, I know, I was stupid. I was a prick." Julien reached across for the whiskey, twirling the bottle before taking a swig. "I've been dreading this weekend for weeks. The only thing that kept me from spiralling was the knowledge that you were staying here with me. It made me almost... look forward to it." Then he muttered quietly, as if to himself, "But then I fucked it up."

Some of Cinn's anger began to dissipate, chipped away at not by Julien's words, but by the way he looked right now: sombre, morose, but most importantly, remorseful.

"I wouldn't have minded being a buffer if you'd better prepared me. And hadn't used me as a surprise. Why were you dreading it so much, anyway?"

"My father is truly insufferable. You've only seen the tip of the iceberg. He cares very little about me. About anyone but himself really, and his business. And the power he holds with the consortium. He didn't care when my mother died, and barely seemed to care about Béatrice's death. Now all he cares about is what I can do for him."

He drank two more large gulps of whiskey before Cinn could grab it off him. "Do you know the first thing he suggested to the consortium once the Lumimeld hit production? That it could be sold to governments to wipe the memories of prisoners of war, after they'd been interrogated."

"Fuck," was all Cinn could say.

"I don't know why I was surprised. He was so... *cruel* during our childhood." Julien's voice dropped to a whisper, and he broke eye contact to look at the floor. "Especially towards our mother." He rubbed at the shoulder Cinn slammed into his wall moments earlier.

A wave of nausea shuddered through Cinn. Remembering the confusing way Julien had reacted to being thrown around, he fisted the hands that he'd allowed his anger to control. "Oh God—" Cinn started, before his throat closed. "Julien, I shouldn't have..." His eyes flicked to the wall.

"What?" As if clearing his mind from a trance, Julien shook his head. "Oh, I didn't mean to imply—genuinely, that wasn't meant to be a guilt trip. It's me that should feel bad. I shouldn't have brought you here, Cinn. I'm sorry for being so selfish. I'm a worthless piece of shit sometimes. You've every right to hate me. I'll book you on a flight for tomorrow morning, if that's what you want."

A pensive silence filled the space between them. Cinn's lingering fury from earlier was now at war with the deep melancholy in Julien's expression. This new Julien alarmed him. He'd have taken any other version right then, if it meant freeing Julien from the prison of this one.

Cinn took one last sizeable gulp of the smooth honey whiskey before setting it on the coffee table. Julien hadn't moved a single inch in minutes. Shuffling closer to him on the settee, Cinn reached up with gentle fingers to tip Julien's chin towards him, resting his hand on his thigh. Grey, unblinking eyes stared at him.

Cinn's anger dissipated like a sunbeam piercing through fog. "It's okay," he said, against his better judgement. He'd likely live to regret letting the princeling off so easily, but he couldn't cope with those sad,

sad eyes. "Fucking hell, I don't hate you. I... I can forgive you. But stop all the bullshit. If you want me as a friend, treat me like one."

"I don't expect your forgiveness."

"Well, you've got it, so don't waste it."

Julien sighed, running a hand over his face. "I won't. Promise."

Cinn dropped his hold on Julien's chin, but kept his hand on his leg, unable to pull it away from where it was tethering them together. "Why don't you just cut your father out of your life?"

"He's too fucking influential within Auri's consortium. All the chairs are meant to hold equal weight, but his motetech business liaison role has made him untouchable. He's wormed his way into everyone's pies, so to speak. It could mess up my future if I go too far against him. Anyway. Let's not spend any more energy talking about him."

Julien wrinkled his nose in disgust before reaching over to grab the whiskey from the table. He wrapped his mouth around it to drink from it, pulling off it with a soft *pop,* all the while giving Cinn an almost challenging stare. Then he did it again, dipping his lips down a little lower on the bottleneck.

"What are you doing?" Cinn groaned. *This fucking guy.*

"What?" Julien asked, with a bat of innocent eyelashes.

Cinn reached for the offending object. "Give me that."

Like he was fluid liquid himself, Julien ducked away from him, sliding off the sofa and taking two large steps backwards. "What, this?" Julien took another gulp.

"You're going to be completely sloshed if you keep that up."

A familiar glint in Julien's eye. "What are you going to do about it?"

He should have whiplash from the abrupt change in dynamic, but instead he was only relieved. Maybe it was the whiskey. Or maybe he enjoyed Julien's attention more than he wanted to admit.

He dove for the bottle, narrowly missing it as Julien darted away from him, tossing the liquid to the back of his throat. His next lunge was successful—his arms wound around Julien's waist, and he snatched the whiskey from him. Pushing Julien against the wall, the writhing man twisted in his arms in time for him to see Cinn finish the bottle off, pouring the alcohol into his mouth so quickly, much of it spilled down his neck.

Laughter erupted out of Cinn, cathartic and cleansing.

It died in his throat when he felt the hot press of Julien's tongue against his neck. Licking a drop of liquid from his collarbone to his jaw. The bottle fell to the floor with a *clink*.

A small involuntary moan came out of Cinn's mouth before he could stop it. "Julien," he started, tangling his hand in his blond waves and making no effort to gently push him away. Both of Julien's arms wrapped around Cinn to clutch the back of his shirt.

"I don't think this is a good idea," Cinn said, his voice weak to his own ears.

Julien's mouth moved next to his ear. "Why not?" With the gentlest of caresses, he brushed a thumb across Cinn's cheek.

So, so many reasons why.

Strangely, none of them were coming out of his mouth.

He should remove Julien's hand from his cheek. He should tell Julien not to touch him. He should take five steps back.

But he didn't.

"Why... why are you like this?" What exactly he meant by this, he couldn't articulate, so he flung his hands in the air instead.

"This?" Julien whispered, one hand still cupping Cinn's cheek, the other sliding up the nape of his neck to entwine his fingers in his hair, knocking his beanie to the floor in the process. "What am I right now, Cinn?"

You're about to make me lose my damned mind.

Cinn shut his eyes, half stumbling towards Julien. His hands hit the smooth plaster of the wall on each side of Julien's head, his body pressed up against his.

Darcy's words—Darcy's *warning*—about Julien's many, *many* lovers echoed through Cinn's head.

Even so, the world faded around him, the dimmed lights seeming to darken as he was further pulled into Julien's orbit. All that remained was the feel of Julien's warm, lithe body, the electrifying tingles dancing across his scalp from Julien's skilled fingers, the racing of his pulse. As Julien traced the features of his face, brushing over each eyebrow like it was a work of art to be worshipped, Cinn accepted his path had been set for him. His fate had been sealed.

Julien gently pulled his head close to his mouth, to whisper, "Do you trust me?" his fingers brushing over Cinn's cheekbones in a reverent dance. "Let me show you how good I can make you feel."

In response, Cinn closed his eyes and leaned into Julien's touch, traitorous legs trembling.

"Give me complete control, and I promise you"—he nipped at Cinn's earlobe, making him cry out softly—"you won't regret it."

Over his dead body would he give Julien complete control. But now Julien's hot tongue was in his ear, thrusting itself into it. "Fuck you," Cinn gasped.

"I'm trying to."

Cinn attempted to shove Julien again, a half-hearted endeavour that only ended up with him fisting Julien's shirt with shaking hands.

They were so close he could feel every hot breath of Julien's ghosting across his face.

"Shhh." Julien used both hands to tip Cinn's chin up, then kissed his cheek. The strong honeyed scent of whiskey on Julien's hot breath, warmth and spice, only served to heighten his arousal.

Julien tightened his grip on Cinn's head. "Trust me. Follow my instructions and I promise you, I'll make you come harder than you ever have in your entire life." A shaky breath escaped Cinn's lips. "Then I'll do it all again."

Subtle pressure applied to his shoulders had him dropping to the floor so quickly, his knees hit the wood with a thud. It may have been Julien's hands that pushed him down, but it was definitely *his* hands fumbling with Julien's belt, his hands palming Julien's hard length through his trousers, his hands reaching around Julien's thighs, dragging him closer.

Cinn tugged down the layers of fabric, and Julien's erection burst out of his briefs, slim yet lengthy, an echo of his tall, lean body, nestled within a groomed crop of dark hair.

"Hands behind your back," Julien commanded, again in that honeyed whisper, and Cinn found himself doing exactly that, any last scrap of resolve to stay in control abandoned in favour of the heedless pleasure his body so desperately wanted to take.

When Cinn's mouth dived straight for his cock, Julien laughed, lightly grasping Cinn's hair to control his head, tugging him back so he couldn't quite reach it.

Fucking maniac.

"Do you want me to suck your dick or not?" Cinn snapped, staring a challenge into Julien's grey eyes.

Lifting it with his hand, Julien traced the outline of his closed lips with his swollen member. "Open up for me."

Cinn obliged, parting his mouth to allow his tongue to dart out, to lick only the very tip before retreating again, pressing his lips closed.

If Julien wanted to play games, then he would get what he deserved.

Although, he couldn't deny that the soft moan he elicited from Julien went straight to his head, to his own balls, his own cock further swelling, scraping almost painfully against his jeans.

Julien's fingers flew to Cinn's mouth—trying to force it open?—but Cinn ducked his head away, diving for one of his balls.

He inhaled it into his wet, waiting mouth.

Sucked it.

Nipped it ever so gently.

Julien brought up his other hand so that both now clutched Cinn's head, nails digging into his scalp as he gasped.

The tiny hint of this Julien—a version of him not entirely in control, even though he'd claimed to be—drove Cinn to see how far he could take it, to see how undone he could make him.

Drenching his tongue in as much saliva as possible, next Cinn mouthed up the entire underside of his cock, dragging his tongue as slowly as he could make himself, pausing on every inch of soft, velvety skin, licking and swirling. When he eventually reached his girthy head, leaking thick, salty precum, Julien's grip on his hair became painfully tight, a slight tremble vibrating through his hand.

If Cinn was to become one of Julien's 'many, *many*' sexual conquests, then at least he would make sure he was one to remember.

"What should I do now?" Cinn asked innocently, gazing up at Julien's flushed face, batting his eyelashes. Before Julien had a chance to answer, he pressed his tongue into Julien's slit, one deep, long lick, taking the hot liquid into his mouth.

In answer, Julien pushed himself deep into Cinn's mouth in a single long thrust, his tongue gliding along the silky underside of his cock until it hit the back of his throat, then kept going.

A thump and Julien's head hit the wall, chin tilted upwards, face a picture of bliss. He pulled out a little before then pushing back in, impossibly further. Almost gagging—it had been a while, a long, *long* while—Cinn sucked in air through his nose, swallowing around Julien as he threaded his fingers through his hair, rhythmically, as if petting him.

"Look at you," Julien breathed, stroking his cheek again. Then Cinn's lips joined to the base of his cock. "Don't deny how much you've wanted this, too." Two ragged uneven breaths. "My cock in your mouth."

Fucking hell.

Cinn could only increase his fervour in agreement, sucking and swallowing with renewed frenzy.

"From the moment you pulled my hair that night we met." Three ecstatic gasps, taken in quick succession. "You were mine."

Tiny prickles of tears emerged from the corners of Cinn's eyes as Julien continued his punishing assault of his mouth.

As if he could sense it was becoming too much, Julien pulled out, leaving just the tip inside, a moment's reprieve. Cinn inhaled greedy gulps of air, his heart racing impossibly fast as he collapsed against Julien's legs, hands still clasped behind his back, beginning to ache.

Julien wiped away the single tear that had tricked down his cheek.

Then, after flashing Julien a gratified smirk, he was ready to continue.

Squeezing his eyes, he swirled his tongue once around Julien's head before opening his jaw as wide as possible, inviting Julien to thrust inside him again.

And that he did.

Julien struck up a punishing rhythm, slamming himself again and again against Cinn's face.

"I want to see your eyes, beautiful."

Cinn found himself powerless to disobey, fluttering them open to find Julien gazing down at him with... lust? Desire? And maybe, just *maybe*, a hint of adoration?

"That's much better."

Julien went slower then, gently tilting Cinn's head back so he could burrow deep into his gaze, the eye contact so intense it sent a ripple of anticipation through him.

And when Julien said, "Look at you," the outrageous sound Cinn made around his cock was one he'd never heard himself make before. Needy. Desperate. Hopeless.

Julien moved the tip of his length to Cinn's tongue. Jerked his hand in frantic movements.

"Swallow," Julien whispered, a heartbeat before he came, and Cinn did, attempting to match every spasm of Julien's cock with a greedy gulp. Ignoring Julien's earlier command, he unclasped his hands to grab both of Julien's thighs, to balance himself as a frenzy took over, his sole determination to suck Julien dry, to lick up every last drop that dared escape him.

Julien's soft humming noise continued to soundtrack their escapade, until his dick finally fell soft, his grip on Cinn relinquished in favour of stroking the nape of his neck, in a manner almost absent-minded. Again, Cinn found himself collapsing against Julien's leg. Now that he'd freed his hands, one shot straight to his own aching length, desperately rubbing it through his thick jeans.

Sliding down the wall, Julien captured Cinn's wrist, before pushing him backwards onto the Persian rug. He sank his head backwards, staring up at the intricate crystal patterns that refracted the warm glow across the room.

His body was no longer his own.

He was completely at the mercy of Julien.

A terrifying notion.

Yet, a sense of euphoria enveloped him, as if he were drifting weightlessly on a cloud.

Almost like being high.

Agonisingly slowly, Julien unbuttoned Cinn's shirt, then positioned his limbs as if he were a doll to tear it off him with a flourish. Cinn reached out to do the same to Julien's but quickly found his wrists clasped tight together, forced above his head, as Julien pushed him down flat on the floor.

"Keep those there." Kneeling with Cinn's legs between his, Julien trailed his hands down the underside of Cinn's arms, squeezing the firm muscles of his biceps, then cupped his cheek briefly before pressing his fingers deep into his left pec, where his ouroboros was inked into his skin. The first tattoo he'd ever gotten.

Julien's lips danced over the design before he scraped his teeth against it, following the shape of the tiny red snake eating its tail.

When Cinn groaned, attempting to buck his hips upward to little success, Julien held him firm. "You're going to need a lot more patience than that, darling. I'm nowhere near done yet."

Indeed, he wasn't. Julien's lips traced a feather-light path back up to his right arm, spreading electrifying tingles across his skin, to mouth his Pixies tattoo before lavishing it with attention from his tongue.

Next came the lyrics that curved alongside the bone of his ribs, from Fleetwood Mac's "Go Your Own Way". His mother's favourite song, played so often in his childhood it had never left him. His tattoo artist had thought the words a dig at her, a mantra of his independence, but that had never been his intention.

Julien continued his exploration of Cinn's tattoos until the only one he hadn't discovered was the inkwork on his shoulder blade, the near-identical match to the tattoo all of his Feltham Young Offenders crew had given each other—a tiny spider web, as intricate as their poke and stick kit allowed.

And, *fuck*, now he was thinking of Tyler again. Of his bare shoulder pressed against his chest night after night in their cell together. For almost a year, they'd slept together like that, cocooned in their bed of warmth. Of love.

He swallowed, forcing himself back to the present moment.

Thankfully, that wasn't particularly challenging, as Julien now had his left nipple between his teeth, tugging on it with the perfect amount of pressure. As he writhed on the floor, a low groan tore itself out of Cinn's mouth.

Fuck, how much longer was Julien going to make him wait?

"If—" he started, interrupted by Julien tweaking his other nipple at the same time. "Fucking hell! If you don't touch me soon, I'm going to—"

Lifting his head up, Julien devoured him with his eyes. "Going to what?"

"I'm going to..." A pause, punctuated by his panting gasps. "Scream your fucking house down!"

He smiled wickedly. "Be my guest."

And with that, he pressed a hard kiss to Cinn's forehead, sucked his eyebrow bar between his teeth, then nipped along his chin, placing his lips everywhere aside from Cinn's own, even though Cinn had his mouth slightly parted, his waiting tongue desperate to meet his. However, when Cinn leaned forward to capture Julien's mouth, he ducked his head, moving down to his neck, licking across skin until he found a spot above his collarbone, sucking hard.

It was okay though, because finally, *finally*, Julien's hand was touching his twitching cock, tracing the outline of it through his jeans with gentle fingertips.

"*Please*," he choked out. "Is that what you're waiting to hear?" Because he'd quite happily beg at this point, his desperation for release nearing blackout levels.

But Julien only kept sucking his neck oh-so-softly now while his fingers matched that same pressure.

More tears sprung out of his eyes. He was so far gone; he didn't even care.

The sensitivity from his rock-hard erection had cranked up to maximum levels, every tender touch making him lose another fragment of his mind until he wasn't sure if he was fully conscious, time blending and bending as gentle, torturing waves of euphoria enveloped his body.

Distantly, he became aware that the golden bangle around his wrist had warmed, blocking his body from slipping. Sex hadn't ever been a trigger before, but there was a first time for everything, particularly when Julien's tongue was involved, apparently.

"Julien, *please.*" He tried again. "I... need you to..."

"Shhh." A finger was placed on his lips, and he opened his mouth to lick it, desperate for some act he could control. "You're going to come just like this," he said simply, so matter of fact, then returned to sucking the spot on Cinn's neck.

Cinn screamed out a noise of outrage, wiggling down the rug, trying to get under him to buck up against him. "I can't," he spat.

"*Oui*, you definitely, definitely can."

Slamming his head against the rug in frustration, Cinn released his arms from their position above his head, but before he could touch himself, Julien had pinned both of his wrists back to the floor, using both of his hands.

His face filled Cinn's entire vision, his smile wicked. "If I have to restrain you, then I won't be able to touch you."

"I'm going to *fucking kill you.*"

His aching, torturous pain continued, with Julien mouthing tiny kitten licks in that same spot above his collarbone and applying his excruciating pressure to his throbbing bulge.

"Come for me, Cinn," Julien whispered into his ear, and then, squeezed his cock hard, just once, but that was enough for Cinn to erupt into his jeans, his blissful ejaculation taking an eternity and a half, Julien *finally* using his palm to rub him with firm strokes.

As Cinn whimpered, cursed, then whimpered again, Julien released him, using his hands to brush the tears from the two paths they streamed down his temple.

His mouth came to his ear again to breathe the word, "See," into it. "Maybe you'll trust me more next time."

Next time.

The sound of his zip being undone. The sensation of his jeans being ripped off. *Now* Julien wanted them off?!

Once Cinn had lifted his hips, brain too scrambled to even question what was going on, Julien slid his briefs off, rendering him entirely naked, sprawled spreadeagle on the rug. Entirely naked, with Julien entirely clothed.

Julien kissed all the way down Cinn's stomach, which clenched in anticipation, until he reached his twitching cock. When he licked it—wet and hot tongue sliding over the entire length of it—Cinn cried out, barely resisting shouting Julien's name.

Where the fuck had he found this absolute demon?

With devout attention, Julien licked every inch of his dick, his balls, his thighs, hands moving back to knead the fleshy muscles of his butt while he did so. Hours could have passed, days even, and just as Cinn thought he was going to pass out with the onslaught of fresh waves of ecstasy, he felt the muscles of his cock begin to reharden, his member twitching back to life.

"Oh," said Julien. "Well, that's a nice surprise."

Cinn groaned as Julien popped the tip into his mouth and sucked lightly.

It took an embarrassingly short amount of time before Cinn was writhing on the floor again, another round of cum bursting out of him straight into Julien's mouth.

As Julien's last tiny, soft moans of pleasure and Cinn's raspy breathing created an unholy symphony of sounds, Cinn brought his hands down to Julien's hair, running his fingers through the long strands, his fingertips stretching out, grateful for being used again.

Cinn laid there, utterly exhausted and spent, as Julien's body slid upwards to lie next to him on the rug. Cinn turned his head, mouth reaching for Julien's, but he ducked out of the way, nudging Cinn's chin up with his cheek, returning once again to that spot above his collarbone for one last suck.

Cinn laughed weakly. "What are you, a vampire?"

After a light nip with his teeth, Julien relinquished him, shuffling slightly away. "When you want me to be. So," he said, eyes gleaming in the dim light. "Did I live up to my promise?"

"If your promise was to absolutely torture me and make me regret my every choice that led me here tonight, then yes."

Julien made a pleased hum before stretching both arms. He yawned, opening his mouth wide. "We better get some sleep to be refreshed for the stupid party tomorrow. Can I offer you another drink before you head off?"

Cinn's mouth dropped open as his heart stuttered. Tongue frozen, all he could do was shake his head.

Just what had he expected, though? To crawl into Julien's queen-sized bed with him—tantalisingly visible from their position on the rug—and cuddle with him all night? *Maybe just a little bit.*

Lyrics from "Wicked Game" flew through his head.

It hit him all at once.

For years, he'd repressed this side of himself that craved physical intimacy. That wanted to be held, and loved, and cherished.

There had been Tyler, beautiful Tyler, who had made him feel safe during the darkest of times. The relationship with him had changed the course of Cinn's life.

Then, there had just been him, and he'd quickly closed the door on anyone that showed the slightest interest in it being opened.

And now, *this* door had just slammed itself open wide. With a bang.

It didn't necessarily lead to where he wanted it to go, however.

In a brisk manner, he jumped up, tugged on his beanie and resigned himself to shoving on his damp jeans, stuffing his underwear in his pocket.

"I'll see you tomorrow," Julien said, still lying on the floor.

Not trusting his voice to reply, Cinn took a step towards the door.

"Oh, and Cinn?"

Cinn turned, positioning his face into a blank mask, because he had a feeling he knew what was next.

"You probably know this, but I can only do casual."

There it was. A tiny pinprick, straight through his heart.

Many, many, *Julien!*

Well, he couldn't say he hadn't been warned.

"Sure," Cinn said, spinning on his heel. Face burning, heart pounding, he had to force himself to close the door with a quiet click before rushing down the corridors to reach his own room.

Any fire alarms be damned, he swung open his window and lit a cigarette, breathing the frigid night air and the blissful release of tension inhaling the smoke offered him.

He had dropped to his knees, followed Julien's every command... and loved every second of it, yes, but... oh God, *what had he done?*

It was okay. He would resolve this. Tomorrow, he would make it crystal clear to Julien that tonight was a one-time thing.

A moment of weakness, never to be repeated.

Fourteen

JULIEN

Something was wrong with Cinn.

He hadn't come to Julien's room that morning, so he eventually headed to the kitchen to make coffee for them, then brought it into the conservatory where they'd worked yesterday morning. Then he waited. And waited.

Earlier, in a sleep-addled haze, Julien had woken up reaching for him, heart skipping a beat when his hands found an empty mattress, rather than a warm Cinn to wrap himself around.

Why had he sent him back to his own room again?

So he didn't start expecting something you can't offer him.

Now, in the cold light of day, Julien could see how that had probably appeared slightly—okay, *incredibly*—rude.

He softly banged his head against the table. *Why did he keep fucking this up?*

What they'd done together last night had been amazing. Julien couldn't stop replaying every moment in his mind. The elation he'd felt at exploring Cinn's body. The tattoos adorning the exquisite expanse of olive skin he'd relished running his tongue over. The feeling of Cinn squirming underneath him, desperate for his touch, and his only. The taste of him.

What if Cinn regretted what they'd done?

Just when he'd reached boiling point and decided to go knock on his door, Cinn slunk into the room clutching his book, headphones around his neck. He barely met Julien's eye when he mumbled hello, sliding into the same seat as yesterday before quickly opening his book before Julien could strike up a conversation.

The tension was palpable, and the distance between them stretched with every passing second.

Every so often, Cinn tugged up the neckline of his hoodie, which—mostly—covered the lovebite that Julien had marked him with last night.

"You can't see it, and besides, it's just me in the room."

Cinn flushed beetroot-red, glueing his eyes to his book.

"How's the reading going today? Seems like it's easier?"

"Please stop talking."

So he *was* angry with him.

"Why are you upset with me? Because of dinner still?"

Cinn sighed and closed his eyes, pressing his fingers to his temple. "No."

"I've realised it was probably very rude of me to assume you'd want to go back to your room." *I'd have far rather woken up with you in my arms.*

Cinn turned the page of his book, placing his overlay on the next sentence.

A sickening jolt passed through Julien's heart. Whatever he'd done, Cinn seemed extremely pissed. What if he *never* forgave him?

Mind-blowing sex aside, Cinn's tentative inclusion into his tiny circle of friends was more important to him. Too important to fuck up. Even though he'd only been in his life for a handful of weeks, he'd feel his absence like a missing puzzle piece. And so would the other two.

Why, oh why, had he not listened to Darcy?

"Cinn?" he practically whined, unable to keep the panic out of his voice.

Cinn's eyes snapped upwards, angry storms swirling in them.

"You didn't tell me if you were clear, yesterday."

Julien blinked. "You didn't tell *me*, either."

"Well, I don't go around sleeping with every Tom, Dick and Harry! Plus whatever their female equivalents are."

"What? Who are they?" He was fairly confident he'd never slept with a man called Dick. He'd remember that.

"It's an expression! It means you fuck around a lot."

Julien winced. "Really, Darcy was exaggerating that the other day."

"Just answer the question."

"I'm clear."

"You sure?"

"One hundred percent. I'm actually offended that you think I'd endanger you like that. Who do you think I am?" *Someone that sleeps with every 'Tom, Dick, and Harry,' clearly.*

Cinn placed his headphones over his head, turning the volume on his Walkman up to what must have been maximum. His eyes returned to his book, jaw clenched. A frown etched a deep canyon into his forehead that Julien itched to smooth with his thumb.

Look at what you do to the people you care about.

Unable to bear the oppressive atmosphere, Julien scooped up his papers and slipped out of the conservatory. His feet led him past his rooms, and up another flight of stairs, to Béatrice's.

Her childhood bedroom was, of course, exactly how she'd left it: lilac frills and a forest of memories. She watched him from the corner of his mind as he collapsed onto the silky sheets of her bed, reaching for her one-eyed stuffed bear. Bernard Bear.

The toy stared at him judgmentally, burrowing deep inside his soul.

Why haven't you found her yet? Bernard grumbled at him, in the gruff bear's voice his mother used when she'd wiggled him in the air.

The ghost of Béatrice's laugh echoed through her room.

Another person he kept letting down.

A drop of the grief he kept so tightly bottled up leaked out. Panic crept in. If he allowed his sadness to spill out of its airtight container, it would flood him, sink him under, drown him like it had done for that first month after she died.

Béatrice had been his rock, his anchor through the shitstorm of their childhood, and then she'd been his very best friend. The only one that truly understood him.

The grief he'd felt after Béatrice's death was nothing like the grief he'd felt for his mother. His mother's passing had been a tempest, a relentless storm lasting years that battered his soul, leaving behind a landscape scarred and barren, where every memory was tinged with sorrow.

Béatrice's departure was different. It was like a quiet mist that randomly descended upon him, subtle yet suffocating, wrapping around his heart with delicate tendrils of loss. While his mother's absence, in the years after her death, pounded into him like thunderclaps, reverberating through the chambers of his being, Béatrice's absence was more akin to a silent scream. He often found himself trapped in a vacuum, an emotionless state that left him suspended in a haunting stillness.

Julien moved to sit at her white wooden dresser, staring at the sea of makeup she'd stopped wearing once she hit her twenties. Whereas he'd updated his Parisian living quarters over the years, she hated coming home even more than him, and as a result, hadn't bothered to redecorate. Julien's gaze dropped to a shoebox, its contents spilling out of it. He crossed the room to open it.

It was a treasure trove of trinkets.

Old photos of the two of them, sometimes with their mother as well, and a rare few of the four of them. Black and white smiles and silly faces. That boat ride down the Seine. Underneath, a collection of letters, postcards from their travels—New York, Malaysia, Australia—a scrap of material from her baby blanket, a child-sized silver Irish Claddagh ring.

Any number of these possessions would likely make an effective magnet item, yet Julien had something even better in mind.

But that was later.

Julien picked up the telephone in the corner of Béatrice's room and dialled the number for Darcy's hotel from the business card she'd given him. The receptionist put him through, and moments later, her voice burst through the receiver.

"It's me."

"Julien? Is everything alright?"

"*Oui*. Well, not entirely. Can you come around here today before the party? I'm worried about Cinn and I think he'd like to see you. He's not... very happy with me."

A pause.

"What the fuck did you do?"

"I don't want to tell you."

"Julien!"

"Can you come? I miss you."

"I'm spending the day with my parents, Julien," she said, but her tone was softer now. "I'll see you at the party venue, okay? Leave Cinn alone for a bit. Don't push him."

"Fine. See you at the party. Oh, and don't wear heels."

"What? Why?" And then, "*Julien*?"

He hung up the phone.

Julien appraised himself in the mirror.

Hair brushed until gleaming. *Check.*

Dark suit, wrinkle-free, just one top button undone. *Check.*

One slightly less grumpy companion, lurking in the shadows of the room? *Check*.

Once Julien had made it back to the conservatory earlier, Cinn suggested they go out for a walk. As if by some unspoken rule, neither of them mentioned any more about last night. Cinn slowly unfurled throughout the day, and by nightfall he was practically back to normal. As long as they continued to ignore any elephants that stampeded through the room.

Cinn had, rather sensibly, left his beanie hat off this evening. His head seemed naked without it, brown curls bouncing free, and Julien resisted crossing the room to run his fingers through them again.

"Here." Julien threw him a suit jacket of his, navy blue with white embellishments. It matched the tie that Cinn looked so strange in. Even more strange was the brogues he wore instead of his usual battered trainers. "Ready to go? Our car should be here soon."

When Julien picked up two bags, one oddly large and rectangular, and one a tatty rucksack that certainly didn't belong at a high-society party, he glanced at Cinn expecting a comment, but none came.

Their destination was on the outskirts of the side of Paris. The traffic was awful, making them blessedly late—the less time at this ostentatious affair, the better—but their taxi eventually pulled up at the venue. Cinn's eyes became so saucer-wide, Julien could easily see the building reflected in them: a majestic mansion adorned with ornate wrought-iron balconies and cascading ivy, and soft, golden light spilling from arched windows.

Impeccably dressed attendants launched into their efficient checking-in process, ticking their names off lists and taking their coats. Julien dragged Cinn straight through the grand lobby, which housed so many fresh flowers it made his nose itch.

Staff ushered them through to the heart of the party, a spacious ballroom with towering ceilings featuring intricate mouldings, already crowded with people. Beautiful, beautiful people, a vision of refined fashion, the very definition of haute couture. Men donned impeccably tailored tuxedos, complete with bow ties and cufflinks that glinted in the light. The women created a sea of bright colours with their flowing evening gowns, sequins and lace galore.

"See, I told you we wouldn't be overdressed."

When Cinn didn't reply, Julien spun around to find him frozen still, clear panic on his face.

"Look, Darcy and Elliot are over there," Julien said, even though he hadn't located them yet.

Scanning the massive space was a challenge, but at last he spotted them—Elliot looking sulky and Darcy in a floor-length emerald-green-silk gown that accentuated her coppery hair, mostly wrestled into an elegant bun.

Like divers swimming for treasure, they crossed the busy ballroom, the ambient murmur of polite chatter underscored by the clink of crystal glasses.

"I told you not to wear heels," was the first thing out of Julien's mouth.

"And I've told your ego complex again and again, that you don't control the actions of everyone around you."

They exchanged cheek kisses.

Elliot lifted champagne glasses for them all from a server's tray. Cinn downed his entire drink, bubbles be damned, then swiped two more from another tray. Darcy gave Julien a look that said, *look after him or die.*

Cinn gravitated towards a small stage area, with Julien reluctantly trailing after him. He'd always hated theatrical entertainers channelling motes as cheap party tricks. This one was juggling fireballs that turned into watery ball-shaped whirlpools on every third rotation. *Child's play.* Yet Cinn was enthralled.

Tugging at Cinn's elbow, Julien guided the two of them over to his father to pay their respects, to 'extend their best wishes' like every other guest. Better to get it out of the way early.

His father, sitting on a throne-like chair surrounded by his usual loyal subjects, stood up to greet them both with handshakes. "Jonathan Steele is around here somewhere," he said to Julien, nodding meaningfully.

Parfait. Julien was sure the director of MEET would love to be personally harassed about his application this evening. Likely, his father had already dropped some 'subtle' comments, anyway.

Upon noticing Cinn, Carrie immediately took it upon herself to sweep him away to introduce him to their 'most important' guests, many of whom Julien had already caught surveying Cinn with curiosity.

"I'll stick right by you," Julien whispered into Cinn's ear, fully expecting some sort of sarcastic comment back. What he got instead was a quick grateful smile, plastered over a terrified expression. Julien brushed his hand over the small of Cinn's back in reassurance. Had he forgotten it was Julien's fault he was there in the first place?

The first guests happened to be Darcy's parents, the Beaumonts.

"Alexander and Fiona are both completing pioneering work in the medical field," said Carrie, by way of introduction. "And this is Cinnamon, or Cinn, Saunders."

Fiona's eyes—the exact same green as her daughter's—lit up as she gushed about how much Darcy had spoken about Cinn that day. Cinn relaxed an infinitesimal amount—his shoulders slightly unfurled, and he wasn't clutching his champagne as if it were a life support any longer.

Just as Alexander finished describing to Cinn how he and Fiona were developing a mote-powered pacemaker, funded by HorizonTech, Julien's father's company, Carrie brought over more guests to speak to them, each consortium chair-holders at Auri. These next three were not as tactful, however, and as soon as conversation turned to Cinn's shadowslipping—their beady eyes raking over him like he was some sort of spectacle—Julien tugged him away, pretending his father needed them elsewhere.

After about an hour of this, a hush descended upon the room.

Viktor Sturmhart had arrived, fashionably late.

All eyes turned to the German man, whose commanding presence overshadowed even his formidable size. Although he'd passed sixty, he'd very few wrinkles to show for it, and only a peppering of grey in his dark hair. *Motecraft cosmetics.*

A quiet, low whistle. "Who the fuck is that?" asked Cinn.

"Viktor Sturmhart. He basically governs Auri's consortium, even though it's supposed to be leaderless. The man thinks he's God's gift to the universe and that he deserves to be in charge. He and my father are in each other's pockets, of course."

"What's his actual role meant to be?"

"He's supposed to manage and support the moteblessed we've placed in governing political parties across Europe, and be Auri's representative on the world stage. As you'd imagine, he relishes the second part of his role."

As if sensing his name, Sturmhart eyed them from across the room and strode purposefully towards them. Julien shuffled closer to Cinn until their arms touched.

"Julien! And of course, Cinnamon Saunders," Sturmhart boomed, even though he was standing close enough for his nauseating cologne to assault their nostrils. "When Lucien told me you were attending, it made my day. I trust Eleanor has been taking care of you?"

Julien held back a scoff.

"Yes," was all Cinn said.

"I look forward to hearing great things about you." Sturmhart clapped Cinn on the shoulder before striding off to the right—straight to Julien's father, who was now with Jonathan Steele.

Julien observed them for a moment. Something about the trio's dynamic was off, and Julien couldn't tear his eyes away. The three men leaned in close to exchange words before his father nodded his head upwards. Was he suggesting they meet privately upstairs? To discuss what?

"Those three look pally." Cinn swirled his champagne.

"*Oui*. The third one is the director of MEET. They need to discuss confidential motetech business away from prying ears. Jonathan probably wants a cash injection from HorizonTech for some sort of project. And Viktor Sturmhart just wants to have his finger in every pie."

Cinn snorted. "Sorry. That sounded weird. What sort of stuff does your father fund again?"

"There's an arm of the business that deals with standard tech, but his main focus is on owning and controlling development of each and every motetech product that gets approved. He's made millions from it. Most of it is sold on to normal companies who have no idea about our world, and motecraft."

Cinn gave him an incredulous stare. "Like what?"

"More subtle stuff, like mote-infused metal to lay railway tracks, guaranteed to need less maintenance. Same with building materials. There's a fair bit of agricultural tech. Tear-resistant fabric. Medical equipment. More efficient solar panels and batteries with longer lifespans. You get the picture."

The three men headed for an exit, and an appealing notion of attempting to eavesdrop struck Julien, but he squashed it. He doubted Cinn wanted to be hiding in closets with him any time soon, sadly.

Once his father had rounded the corner, Julien started to turn away, then paused. Someone else was following them out of ballroom, slinking against the wall, fox-like. A woman. He'd recognise that gleaming white power suit anywhere. *Eleanor Sinclair.*

She glanced ever so casually over her shoulder before she slipped through the archway.

Now this *was* interesting.

Just as Julien was opening his mouth to make the case for a covert mission after all, Cinn loosened his tie, before fanning his face with it. "Can we go outside for a moment? It's so hot in here."

With effort, Juilen tamped down his burning curiosity. Who cared why Eleanor was skulking after the three most influential moteblessed people in Europe? Definitely not him. After all, he had attractive men to re-seduce.

Catching Elliot's eye across the room, Julien gestured to a door, and soon enough the four of them escaped the stuffy ballroom to sit in the courtyard garden, surrounded by lumenmotes dancing in cages. A light show flickered across one vine-covered brick wall—balls of various coloured lights creating rainbow patterns. A party guest reached out to touch it, and the motes responded to the contact, rippling outwards away from her hand.

Cinn raked a hand through his hair. "When does this thing finish again?"

Elliot chuckled. "Having fun then?"

Rearranging the collar of his shirt, Cinn shuffled on the bench. "Those people are all..."

"A bit much?" said Darcy.

At the same time Julien retorted, "A bunch of assholes?"

After sliding a cigarette out for himself, Julien tossed the packet of Gitanes on the table, and soon four wisps of smoke rose into the crisp night, Elliot whipping the wind around them ever so slightly to clear the air.

"Remember that year"—started Darcy, before taking a puff—"that Lucien held his party in that field in Epernay, with all those white horses?

And we all had to compete in that horseback archery contest? They all looked so unhappy, the poor things."

Julien shook his head. "It was nowhere near as bad as the year he hired that band—the one that had motetech instruments that could be heard wherever you were within a mile's radius. I woke up with a migraine the next day."

"Next year, rather than drag all of us here to suffer with you, perhaps you could just bail. Send him a birthday card in the post." Elliot smirked, and Julien imagined his father's face if he did indeed do that. Tempting.

This annual occasion *was* useful though: it was reliably a hive of whispered snippets of gossip about investments, consortium seat changes, mote-use policy proposals, and more. If he didn't have to watch his father lord over the whole thing, he'd probably enjoy it.

"I kept overhearing stuff about the umbraphage attack from a few weeks ago," said Cinn. "It sounds pretty awful, what with so many people dying." He took in a long drag, eyes on the crescent moon hanging in the sky, seeming lost in thought. "I guess they'll want to try to use me to help pretty soon."

Use me. A sudden spike of terror shot through Julien at an image of Cinn being shipped off to deal with one of the enigmatic, deadly creatures. The way he'd awoken from his shadowslipping trip didn't fill Julien with confidence that Cinn was the missing key to defeating them. Plus, he wasn't sure how much he trusted Eleanor to keep him safe.

"There's no way we'll let them make you do anything you don't want to, Cinn," Darcy promised, her face sombre.

Julien silently agreed—if anyone started a fight, they'd get a *war* before they wielded Cinn like a weapon.

Finishing their cigarettes, they headed back in, Darcy and Elliot peeling off from them to find food.

"I'm going to the bathroom," Cinn announced, and Julien swallowed his suggestion to accompany him.

Before he could even blink, Carrie filled Cinn's empty space, eyes narrow, face pinched. "Julien. I can't help noticing that man over there bears a striking resemblance to the friend of yours that Lucien said he wished to never see again. One Elliot Pérez."

Julien overtly scanned the room before his gaze landed on Elliot, then he whipped out his best surprised act. "Oh! So he does! What a strange coincidence."

"And how do you suppose his name got on the guest list?"

"Well, I suppose someone must have written it down on it."

Taking a step forward, Carrie lowered her volume, hissing, "This is your father's birthday, Julien. The event he looks forward to more than anything else." *And my yearly torture.* "It would be extremely embarrassing for this family if any... *scenes* were to happen."

A bat of his eyelashes. "Wouldn't it just?"

A warning flash swept across Carrie's face. Then, her expression morphed. Jerking back as if electrified, her lips parted as she stared at Julien's neck. Before Julien could react, her hand lurched forward, and for a horrible second he thought she was about to strangle him. Instead, she tugged on Béatrice's locket chain until she freed the silver oval from under his shirt.

Holding it in her palm, she lifted it higher into the light. "How... how did you get this?"

The odd note of rage in her voice only irritated him further. "That's none of your business. It's not like Béatrice would have left it to you!"

Composed Carrie returned like an actor slipping on a mask, and she stepped away from him. "I simply wasn't aware that it had been returned to you."

Julien stared at her, mind whirring. Cinn chose that moment to return to him, sending Carrie scuttling off with a fabricated smile.

"What was that all about? Why was she touching your locket?"

"I'm... not sure. She asked me how I obtained it."

"Did Béatrice leave it to you?"

"Well, no." Julien grimaced. "Who do you know our age who has a will? It was with her body when they found it. The gendarmerie's investigation department held her corpse for weeks while her death was investigated, and I asked and asked for it to be returned to me, but they refused. I wasn't even allowed to see her body..." Julien became momentarily lost in hazy memories as the colours of the bright room swam around him.

The feel of Cinn taking hold of his elbow brought him back to reality. "So how *did* you get the locket?" he asked, but something in his face told Julien he already knew the answer.

"Creative methods." Julien winked. "A breaking and entering... of sorts." It had actually involved a bottle of scotch, half seducing a security guard, five rounds of strip poker, and a specially made motetech device to unlock a fortified door, but specifics weren't needed here.

Cinn rolled his eyes. "I can imagine. So Carrie wanted Béatrice's locket?"

"*Non!* They hated each other. But that was certainly strange."

Reaching out to brush his fingers over the locket, Cinn said, "I've just realised we're going home tomorrow and we haven't even looked for the magnet item for Béatrice. You know, the whole reason I was dragged along this weekend."

You were dragged along for many, many reasons, darling.

"Oh, we're getting that this evening. Very shortly, in fact."

Cinn's forehead wrinkled. "What? How? We're not even at your house."

"I'm aware."

Tugging Cinn by his sleeve, Julien led him over to Darcy, who was watching Elliot scoff down macaron after macaron with obvious disdain.

"Follow me to the lobby," Julien announced. "We're bailing on this pathetic excuse for a party."

"We are?" asked Darcy.

"We need to go and collect Béatrice's magnet item."

The three of them shared confused glances with each other.

Julien couldn't help but love every second of it.

They trailed after him to the now-quiet lobby, the two security guards facing the night sky. In the corner of the room, a plush red velvet sofa awaited them. Julien fell to his knees, dragging out two bags from underneath it.

One was his usual rucksack, although stuffed with unusual items. And the other...

"What...?"

And then, out of the enormous zipped bag Julien had brought along in the taxi's boot—and then paid the driver a hundred francs to ensure it was placed under the sofa closest to the door—he lifted an enormous shovel. With a theatrical flourish, he wiggled it in the air. "We're going to need this."

Darcy gasped. Even Elliot looked shocked.

"Huh? Where are we going?" asked Cinn, who, unlike the other two, hadn't caught on.

"Père Lachaise Cemetery." He flung the shovel over his shoulder.

"No!" breathed Darcy. "No Julien, not that! Anything but that! That's... the literal definition of sacrilege!"

Watching Cinn's face change as he put the puzzle pieces together was the highlight of Julien's night. So far.

"You mean... we're going to go and... dig up Béatrice? From her *grave*? And... take one of her bones home with us as a magnet item?"

Despite the look of horror on Cinn's face, Julien beamed at him. *"C'est ça!"*

"Elliot, back me up here. Tell Julien he's deranged." When Elliot didn't say anything, Darcy shouted, "Elliot!" She snapped her fingers.

"Darce, Béatrice would probably find it quite funny. Besides, we can put it back afterwards. Julien is on to something here. What could possibly be a stronger magnet item than her freaking bones?!"

A scream of exasperation. A pursing of her lips. The tiniest stamp of her foot.

Darcy wasn't happy, but she'd come.

Julien turned to Cinn, expecting resistance from him also, but clearly they'd corrupted him, as he just threw his hands up in an 'I give up' sort of way.

Fifteen

JULIEN

The four of them wordlessly stared up at the high perimeter fencing of Père Lachaise Cemetery, each spike glinting menacingly in the moonlight.

Even having removed their ties, they weren't quite dressed for this breaking-and-entering adventure.

Cinn bit that beautiful bottom lip of his. "Julien, I can't get arrested for this. Not with my record."

Julien was pretty sure Eleanor had instructed his record to be wiped clean, but he grabbed Cinn's hand, thumb trailing over his knuckle, and dropped his voice to a low murmur. "I give you my word that I won't let that happen."

With one sharp, decisive nod, Cinn squeezed Julien's hand before releasing it.

In case he wasn't completely convinced, Julien swung his rucksack around, unlatching the top to show Cinn the interior. "If the police do suddenly arrive, I have multiple weapons in my arsenal."

Cinn's jaw fell slack.

"Not to kill them!" God, what did Cinn take him for? Lighting a cigarette, Julien inhaled a lungful of smoke before passing it to Cinn's eager fingers. Did Cinn also feel the tingle of sensation where their skin had briefly touched? Was Julien alone in the slight increase to his heart rate?

Most importantly: was Julien forgiven yet?

If only he could reach inside Cinn's mind to unravel its mysteries.

Reaching the tall metal gate, secured by a chunky iron chain held by a sizeable padlock, Julien smiled—he was prepared for this. He reached inside his rucksack, seeking his compact, silver capsule that would align the padlock's tumblers and spring the lock free.

However, as his fingers closed around the object, Elliot, in an annoyingly languid way, lifted his hand, and channelled windmotes into a powerful, tight tunnel of pressure, flinging them at a specific link in the chain.

Blasted apart, the chain and the padlock dropped to the ground.

Darcy tutted, but before she could complain, Elliot said, "What? I checked for CCTV. We're clear."

"Woah!" Cinn exclaimed, still staring at the broken chain, and Julien shook his head softly. Cinn had seen the Arcane Purifers blow a building to smithereens with motepower, but now Elliot's simple pressure blast was impressing him?

Seemingly in tune with Julien, Elliot laughed. "My friend, that was nothing."

"That was *not* nothing!"

"Please, Julien and I could do that trick by the time we were ten. Although he always had far more precision control than me. When we were kids, his greatest joy was thrashing me at our camp's tournament every summer, then tormenting me about it for the rest of the year."

Elliot jostled Julien with his shoulder, but Julien didn't respond, only sighed in dismay at Cinn as he absorbed Elliot's words, looking between him and Julien with pinched brows. *Goddamn Elliot and his big mouth.*

Cinn blinked at Julien. Tugged on his beanie. Then stared at him some more.

Julien braced himself for the inevitable question that poured from Cinn's lips. "How come I've never seen *you* channel any motes?"

A gust of wind blew behind them, sending a tin can hurling noisily down the street. Elliot and Darcy waited for him to answer, likely wondering what script he'd give Cinn. He considered outright ignoring the question, but Cinn's big golden eyes were so intent on him, he found himself unable to.

"I can't channel anymore," Julien said at last.

Elliot snorted, shaking his head. "He means he *won't*."

Stop talking, Elliot, please *stop talking.*

Ignoring his silent plea, Elliot turned to Cinn. "He was, well *is*, well, could be, the very best channeller our generation has seen. That's what our coaches used to say."

How did Elliot not understand that the warm pride Julien could hear in his voice made it five times worse?

Curiosity coloured Cinn's face as his head snapped towards him. "So why don't you?"

Julien's stomach tumbled. He scrambled for a simple answer that would placate Cinn. A moment later, Darcy saved him—Darcy, who'd been scrutinising him carefully for the last minute.

"Can we just get on with this whole grave-digging thing before I change my mind about rummaging around in the dirt for our best friend's bones, please?"

Darcy pressed on the wrought-iron gate, leaning all of her weight against it to push it ajar.

The sliver of moon offered little light to guide their journey as they weaved through rows of silent tombstones, a sepulchral maze. Rustling leaves and the occasional hoot of a nightbird were the only sounds as they passed weathered mausoleums and engraved benches.

Nearing the spot where Béatrice was buried alongside their mother's own grave, a sudden realisation struck Julien. He hadn't yet seen her headstone, recently installed. Before he had time to prepare, the thing filled his vision, a solemn sentinel standing tall and resolute above many of the others. He paused in his steps, frozen by the name Béatrice Montaigne, inscribed in large, looping cursive, on a slab of gleaming white marble.

Flowers still remained from her funeral—next to his father's white roses lay a bundle of black and purple lilies, still as fresh as the day Julien had placed them there months ago, shimmering with everglaze.

Her epitaph read: *Our Brightest Treasure, Your Star will Forever Shine.*

Imaginary Béatrice snorted and shook her head in amusement.

For weeks, Julien and his father had warred over burying her in the family plot, or cremating her and splitting the ashes between them. Julien wasn't even sentimental, but the notion of his father controlling Béatrice's death had tipped him over the edge. Well, he may never get her ashes, but he was about to be in possession of something even more macabre.

Père, this is one battle I'm now glad you won.

Darcy ran her fingers over the letters etched deep into the marble. For a while, nobody spoke, until Darcy tipped her head backwards at the starless, cloudy expanse of the sky. "Though my soul may set in darkness, it will rise in perfect light," she said.

"I have loved the stars too truly to be fearful of the night," Julien finished, moving forward to squeeze Darcy's arm.

"Shall we graffiti it on top of your father's unsentimental crap?"

"Tempting."

Cinn had positioned himself slightly apart from them, hovering back, eyes downcast. Sometimes Julien forgot Cinn had never met Béatrice. And yet he was here, standing in the middle of a cemetery, about to commit grave robbery for her. For *him*.

Even after Julien had been an absolute prick.

Julien briefly ran a hand over his mother's headstone, far less grandiose than Béatrice's. *"Repose en paix."* Be at peace.

Then, one quick unzip of the bag, and the shovel was ready to go.

"Don't tell me you actually want to spend five hours digging?" asked Elliot.

Julien balanced the shovel on his shoulder. Smiled. "Not particularly, but it seemed pretty important to bring it. For aesthetics, if nothing else."

Elliot raised both hands out in front of him. It was good fortune that it was a blustery evening—the windmotes would offer him more power behind them to channel. Cinn's eyes widened once again as the wind whipped up around them, creating a strong current of air that escalated into a small tempest.

When Elliot manipulated the wind with supreme precision to slice into the grass, creating a neat rectangle of turf, every molecule of Julien's essence ached to join him, imagining the feel of the windmotes underneath his fingertips. How they'd bend for him so easily. The elation, the *high* that came with channelling.

And as Elliot manipulated the windmotes underneath the rectangle he'd so masterfully created, to lift it four feet in the air above him, it took all Julien's energy to block out that tiny voice whispering in his ear: *he's better than you, now.*

Some loose dirt still remained above the casket, and Elliot removed that in clumps, creating small earthy tornados that deposited the soil in a pile next to the gravestone.

Then it was done, and Béatrice's silver casket shone in the feeble amount of moonlight the clouds let pass. And underneath it? By now, she'd have very little flesh left, if any. Her teeth may well have fallen out. All this he knew from his month-long obsession with researching corpses when his mother died.

"Right, Julien, what now?" Elliot asked.

Time suspended as three pairs of eyes sought his for instruction. This was his plan, but now that he was actually here, about to tear a bone from his sister's skeleton, it didn't seem like a very good idea at all.

"Umm..." he started.

Darcy said, "If you've changed your mind—"

"I haven't. This is our best chance to get the strongest magnet item possible."

"I guess I can do it," said Elliot, but he looked less than enthusiastic, eyeing the casket warily. "I could even try to use the windmotes again."

"Or me," said Darcy, glancing at Elliot, face pinched with worry. "I think I'd handle it best of all."

Julien looked between the pair of them. Now was the moment where he stepped forward, to insist there was no way he was letting either of them be the one to mutilate his sister's corpse.

Then Cinn stepped forward, arms crossed in steadfast resolve. "I'll do it. I've seen enough dead bodies to last a lifetime already. One more can't hurt." He shrugged. "At least this one will be stationary and won't try to attack me."

Julien waited for Darcy or Elliot to protest.

They didn't.

Cinn moved towards the grave.

"So, what do we want? A finger? A toe? A kneecap or two?" Cinn's attempt at humour was offset by the slight shake to his voice.

In a quiet voice, hesitant and unsure, Julien replied, "A rib."

Something that her heart touched.

Cinn nodded, tossing his jacket to Elliot and rolling up the sleeves of his shirt before dropping to the ground next to their dirt pile.

Julien couldn't watch.

He'd set this whole thing up, dragged them here, made them all do the dirty work, and now he couldn't even *watch*.

Facing away from the scene of their crime, Julien set about counting the abundance of headstones in his peripheral vision, focusing on the task like his life depended on it.

But even so, he heard it all.

The creak of the casket opening.

The tearing of clothes. *That awful blue dress Père insisted she be buried in.*

Cinn's strained grunts of effort.

And finally, the heart-wrenching snap of bone.

Julien didn't turn around until the rhythmic thud of Elliot redepositing earth on top of Béatrice's coffin rippled through the night.

When he did, he found Darcy cradling a canvas bag close to her chest, hugging it delicately, eyes shining with tears.

If the bone turned out to be useless as a magnet item, Julien would suffer some serious guilt from the PTSD he'd surely inflicted upon everyone tonight.

Cinn moved away from the grave, approaching Julien with slow strides.

When he was close, Julien reached for Cinn's arm. "What... what did she look like?"

Cinn gazed straight at him with those amber pools, and for a moment Julien basked in their golden warmth. "Beautiful," he said, solemn and soulful. "She looked beautiful."

Without overthinking it, Julien reached over to wipe a dusting of mud from Cinn's chin. He didn't restrain his hand from lingering on his face. "Thank you," he whispered.

Sixteen

JULIEN

"What now? Back to your father's party?" Cinn asked Julien.

He blinked, unsure for once; he'd reached the end of his roadmap for their night.

"Let's go out," suggested Darcy. "Show Cinn Parisian nightlife." At this, she grabbed his hand and spun herself around into his arms. He looked far less than comfortable.

"Well, there's no way we're going anywhere playing trashy pop music." Elliot gave one long shake of his head. "No offence to that crap that leaks out of your headphones, Cinn."

"It's mostly R'n'B, actually," Cinn mumbled.

"What about Café Crescendo, that jazz fusion bar we found last winter?" Julien interjected and was promptly ignored.

"And I'm not going to any of Darcy's places," Elliot continued. "Shit gets crazy in her drum and bass basements."

"God, that was one time!" Darcy moaned, rolling her eyes. "And nobody *forced* you to take that random pill from the stranger you met in the bathroom."

Cinn shuffled on his feet. "I second no drum and bass. Tyler's dragged me to a few gigs, and I hated every second of them. There's no—"

"There's no soul," Julien chimed in. "We want none of that synthetic beat nonsense. Café Crescendo has the perfect vibe—smooth jazz, low lights—"

"No!" shouted Darcy and Elliot simultaneously, so loud Julien flinched.

"Sounds like you're picking then, Elliot, doesn't it?" Julien wouldn't sulk. It was beneath him.

After flagging down a taxi, and taking a quick detour so that Darcy could store Béatrice's rib in her hotel room, and change out of her muddy heels—why did she never listen to Julien?—they were dropped in the heart of Paris's Le Marais district, which Darcy argued would please everybody.

Tall, centuries-old buildings lined the narrow road, with people smoking out of balconies and wooden shutters, leaning their bodies over to watch the merriment below.

One look at the neon lights, rainbow flags, and scantily clad revellers spilling out into the cobblestone streets, clinking drinks and shouting loudly, and Cinn took a full step backwards, as if he was about to take flight.

"This isn't really my scene." Panic wrote itself all over Cinn's face.

Julien raised his eyebrow. "Isn't it?"

Darcy linked her elbow through Cinn's and dragged him across the street to the nearest bar, which was pumping heavy music and teemed with people.

Cinn froze at the threshold. "But aren't we overdressed?"

"Darling, in the city that lives and breathes fashion, one can never be overdressed," Julien replied with a smirk, pushing Cinn the final few steps.

Inside, the dance bar throbbed with the pulsating beats of electronica, disco lights enveloping dancers in a kaleidoscope of colours. Fog from a machine merged with smoke from cigarettes to form a hazy mist, transforming swirling figures into intangible shapes.

Straight to the bar, of course.

"Five double whiskeys for you then, Cinn?" Elliot shouted over the cacophony.

Shaking his head, Cinn looked less than impressed, but Julien smiled to himself—Elliot had certainly taken his time warming to Cinn, but the two of them seemed to be becoming fast friends.

Julien easily jostled his way to the front of the queue, to order two Hennessys for Elliot and Darcy, a Kronenbourg for Cinn, and a glass of red for himself—wrinkling his nose at the selection of wine on offer.

Sans Elliot, who'd slipped away from them, they headed into the narrow alleyway garden, where Darcy immediately jumped at the chance to join in with an impromptu poetry slam that was being held. Her floor-length green gown did indeed stick out next to the casual attire of the others. She rocked it though, naturally, throwing her head back and gesturing wildly as she spun out rhythmic prose far easier than Julien could ever dream of, even though she was speaking a second language. If Béatrice were here, she'd be clapping along, encouraging Darcy to climb on top of the bistro table to perform on a makeshift stage.

"What are they shouting about?" Cinn furrowed his eyebrows, head cocked to one side, attempting to glean meaning from the rapidly spoken French.

"Oh, just the fervent echoes of discontent. Societal injustices, the sting of inequality, that sort of thing."

"Just that, then, huh?"

Julien chuckled and pushed him back inside to the warmth, leaving Darcy to her new friends.

Within moments, Cinn's jaw hung slack. Julien followed his gaze to find Elliot dancing with a stranger, bodies pressed tightly together as they danced to a rhythm all of their own. Elliot had his tongue deep down the tall, pretty-looking man's throat, clasping his long blond hair, which was not dissimilar to Julien's own...

"That was... fast," Cinn quipped, averting his eyes from Elliot but not quite meeting Julien's. And then, said so quickly it was as if the words were burning his tongue, Cinn asked, "What's the deal with you and him, anyway? I mean, have you ever...?"

One week ago, Julien and Elliot sprawling together on Darcy's rug, several empty bottles of red wine on the coffee table.

Cinn and Darcy asleep on the sofa, mirrored snoring twins.

Elliot, staring into the fire, blurting out, "Are you going to fuck him?"

Julien considering replying, "Who?" but settling for silence to give Elliot the answer he didn't want.

Elliot leaving the room, and Julien turning to watch Cinn's sleeping form, studying the rise and fall, rise and fall of his chest.

"*Non*," said Julien, emphasising the word with certainty. With two fingers, he gently tilted Cinn's face to meet his. "He's my best friend. But we've never. And will never."

Cinn's golden eyes drilled into his. "And how does Elliot feel about that?"

"Well, he certainly isn't sitting around crying about it." Julien gestured to Elliot, who was now grinding against the stranger with remarkable enthusiasm.

From the day they'd met over a decade ago at summer camp—the day Julien had thrashed him at every activity, and Elliot had grinned in delight in response—Julien had loved Elliot. Just not in the exact way Elliot wanted to be loved. However, their relationship had long since moved past the barriers that the situation had created. Mostly.

With a subtle shift of his body, Julien crowded Cinn against the shallow alcove they'd found themselves in. He plucked the beer out of Cinn's hand and placed it on a shelf.

"What are you doing?" Cinn asked, but the slight hitch of his breath made it clear he knew exactly what was happening.

He didn't resist when Julien pushed him so far back he hit the wall, Cinn's hands snaking around to rest on Julien's hips. Needing no other encouragement, Julien pressed himself into his space, so close their chests collided, and he could feel the *thump, thump, thump* of Cinn's rapidly increasing heartbeat, that seemed to correspond with his own then sync with the upbeat tempo of the music.

Julien cupped Cinn's face with one hand, and Cinn leaned into the touch at once, closing his eyes and placing his own hand on top. Sliding his hand free, Julien brushed Cinn's jaw with his knuckles before dusting his thumb over his collarbone, then dipped lower to find the bruise his mouth had marked Cinn with last night. Eyelashes fluttering against Julien's cheek, Cinn slid slightly down the wall when Julien pressed on the mark while taking the tip of Cinn's ear between his teeth.

Pulling him upright, Julien stepped back, gripping Cinn's wrist to drag him past the bar, across the dance floor, out the front door, up the busy street, and down a quiet side alley, a whirlwind journey that knocked the breath out of them.

Face dazed, Cinn half stumbled as Julien perched on a low wall and tugged him onto his lap. Julien smiled against the soft skin that was back against his, where it belonged. He hooked his fingers through the belt loops of Cinn's trousers, then pulled on the material of his shirt until he'd freed it from his trousers, to slide his fingers up the expanse of warm skin he'd craved since yesterday.

But Cinn had fallen very still, freezing Julien's exploration. Cinn leant his forehead against his. In the quietest of voices, a whisper in the cool wind that whistled down the cobbled alley, he said, "I can't." And then, still with his forehead touching Julien's: "I'm sorry."

In lieu of a reply, Julien froze stone still himself, hoping to calcify the feeling of Cinn's weight on him, the warmth of his minty breath, the subtle shift of his forehead rocking gently left, then right across Julien's own.

If Julien didn't move, perhaps they'd remain suspended in time, and he wouldn't have to hear Cinn's next words.

"I can't. I want to. God help me, I want to so much, but I can't."

"Why?" Julien whispered.

"I can't do *casual*, Julien. It's not me. I haven't actually been with anyone else since Tyler, and that was years ago now."

Swallowing his choked sound of surprise, Julien considered his next words, twisting them around his tongue.

What if—

You don't—

But we could be—

If I—

Maybe this time—

He'd taken too long. Cinn was unwrapping himself from him, sliding away, away from *him*, and then he was pressing his lips to Julien's forehead, the spot where they'd just been touching, and walking away without looking back.

When he turned the corner, Julien expelled an almighty gasp, as if he'd been punched in the stomach. The visceral ache in his chest saw him sliding off the wall, onto the ground, to lean his head back against the cool brick.

What had just happened? Why did it feel like Cinn had just stabbed him in the heart? Julien had only been seeking physical intimacy from him anyway, and he could get that anywhere. This was no great loss. They would simply go back to being friends.

Then, Cinn's golden-hazel eyes filled his mind, blinking once, and Julien reached out his hand into empty air to tug on a beanie hat that wasn't there.

He shook his head at himself. Waves of dissociation collided with unrecognisable desires of *wanting. Longing.*

Julien didn't have many people in his life he was close to. Scrap that, he had only two. A potential three if Cinn didn't get sick of him. But two very special, treasured jewels he'd do anything for. He felt no urge to ever surround himself with a wider group of people who'd never truly know him.

Within his inner circle, he had trust. Security. It was so easy for a lover to drop out of your life—this he knew first-hand. He'd done it to others, when he'd gotten too close to them. Here one day, then gone the next, as fleeting as a passing breeze. Don't get attached, don't get hurt.

Yes, having a partner was a risk. A risk he'd never taken.

And wasn't the ache in his chest right now the perfect reminder why? If he felt this awful now, what would he feel like if he had his already-fragile heart broken?

Béatrice's dismayed face appeared in his mind, shaking her head sadly. *So your plan is to be alone forever?* she said. *Sounds great.*

In response to the figment of his imagination, Julien tore at his hair, expelling an almighty groan. *Calme-toi. Je suis ridicule.*

Forcing himself to his feet, he dusted himself off before using two hands to pull his cheeks upwards, forcing his lips into a smile. Because Julien didn't skulk in alleys after being rejected.

He could go back onto the main street and find a different bar, pick up a different body to fill the void inside him.

However, Cinn was staying at his house, and he couldn't simply abandon him. The thought was unthinkable.

Plus, you don't want anybody else. You only want him.

But he couldn't have him, because Julien had fucked it up. Messed up any chance of being with him, because he was clearly hell-bent on self-sabotaging any chance of happiness.

You'd have only hurt him in the long run. It's better this way.

Rare tears, hot and angry, threatened to burst out, so Julien squeezed his eyes shut.

He'd give himself one more minute, then he'd drag himself out of the alley, plaster on his best smile, and go and pretend the last hour hadn't happened.

Julien could do that.

He was the master of pretence.

Seventeen

Cinn

"Today I want to explore the origins of your shadowslipping, Cinn."

Noir leaned back into his chair, already puffing away on his silver pipe. Cinn still didn't know what the old codger smoked, but it certainly wasn't tobacco.

"Sure," Cinn replied, like he had any say on the agenda, anyway.

"Specifically, I want us to go back to your childhood."

"What is this, a therapy session?"

Noir exhaled a massive plume of smoke. "If you need it to be."

Crossing his arms, Cinn pushed back slightly on the desk, wheeling his chair away from Noir. "I don't."

With an upward quirk of his moustache, Noir said, "Very well, then. You've previously shared with me your first ever experience of shadowslipping, where you had morning tea with that pleasant gentleman."

Cinn nodded.

"I wondered if you were aware by now, perhaps enlightened by some of the literature I've prescribed, of the speculated origin of the shadowslipping ability, the *cause* so to speak."

God, Noir and his damned books. Didn't he know there was music to be listened to, cookie recipes to master, troubled ex-boyfriends to call, beautiful yet complicated men to daydream about?

"I didn't get to that part yet."

A crinkled smile. "Well, allow me to spoil it for you. I want you to think back to the time shortly before your first trip."

Cinn stared at him. "Okay…"

"Did anything happen to you, Cinn, in the weeks or months prior?"

Many things. Many, many things. Most of them bad.

"You're going to have to be more specific."

"Well, our limited research into the handful of shadowslippers ever recorded suggests that a near-death experience often triggers the ability. Specifically, where the person is medically, or at least very close to, dead for a short period of time."

Noir allowed him time to process his words, rearranging items on his cluttered desk.

"Do you recall such an event, Cinn?"

He did.

He recalled the feeling of sinking ever deeper into the icy water, the frantic, uncoordinated kick of his legs to no avail, the lungfuls of river he inhaled, to choke on. He recalled the burning sensation in his legs, then chest, the sting of his eyes. He recalled the odd sense of relief that washed over him when the world had faded to black.

"Cinn?"

There was no way in hell he was in the mood to spill his guts about one of the worst days of his life to Noir, as friendly as the mentor had been so far. Cinn didn't have enough energy to face the judgement and pity that would be clear as day on Noir's face. So he remained silent.

Noir sighed, running a hand through his beard. Hopefully, he'd got the message that Cinn wasn't in a sharing mood. "If that is too much for today, perhaps we could return to our project of recording your experiences?"

By 'our' project, Noir meant *his* project, but fine. At Cinn's nod, Noir brought out his large leather-bound notebook and his silly fountain pen with the ridiculous feather on it. Apparently, biro was too pedestrian for Noir.

He flipped to the next clean page. "So, we've covered your first episode with the newspaper and the gentleman, then we recorded the encounter with the fireman outside the burned-down department store near your house. Yesterday, you mentioned that your third trip was... less than pleasant?"

Noir looked up. It was Cinn's turn to talk.

"Yes." He tugged on his beanie. "Although most of them were pretty awful, from that point onwards."

"Take me back to that day. Paint me a picture." Noir waved his fountain pen in the air with a flourish and Cinn glared at him.

"It was a couple of months after the first episode on my thirteenth birthday. My mum and I were running late, so we were running for the bus."

"Where were you going?"

"Is that bit important?" Noir didn't respond, so Cinn continued, "Anyway, we were sprinting, so my heart was already racing." He paused to allow Noir to note that down. Adrenaline increase seemed to be part of the trigger, for him at least—Noir rarely discussed any of the shadowslippers that had come before him. "If you must know, we were on our way to one of Mum's medical appointments, and I remember we were late the last time, then she wasn't allowed in, so this time she was determined to be on time and she made us run super fast."

Even from discussing this early part of the memory, Cinn's heart beat faster in anticipation of reliving what was yet to come. He twisted the golden band around his wrist.

"So, we make it to the corner shop, and Mum looks at her watch, and says that we need to speed up. She's dragging me by this point, I can barely breathe... and—" *And she got cross with me for slowing her down.*

"Anyway, at the next crossing, we have to dart out onto the road without pressing the button."

"The button?"

Cinn frowned. "Yeah, to change the traffic lights to red."

"Right, right," said Noir. "Carry on."

"Anyway. Mum... forgot... to look." He cringed, but Noir didn't look up from his notebook. "And then this white car comes speeding round the corner. Genuinely, Mum said he was going way over the limit, and—"

The scrape of metal against paper stopped. Perhaps Noir had realised where this story was going. "Cinn, I didn't realise quite how traumatic this particular incident could be to retell. Shall we take a break? Skip this one for now?"

Cinn gritted his teeth. There was no point stopping now. "No, it's fine. So, the white car sees us, but it's going too fast, *way* over the speed limit, and..."

The blaring of a horn, the screeching of tyres.

"It crashed into a lamppost. So hard the lamppost bent. After that, there was lots of screaming. Someone ran into the corner shop to call nine nine nine. I sat down on the pavement, unable to stop looking at the car. I remember my mum shouting at me that we needed to go, but I couldn't move."

"Is that when the slip began?"

"Yeah. This one was interesting because it was the first one where I understood I was in a memory, but we didn't go there straight away. So, I felt myself fade away, and I guess it felt like I was *slipping* or whatever into the pavement. But it didn't click at first that I'd slipped, because I was still on the main road. Although, everybody had disappeared, and the world went sort of... grey and blue. I kept looking at the white car until the back door opened."

"And someone got out?"

"A young girl." He studied Noir's reaction, but the man schooled his expression. "There was... blood all over her head, and her arms were all bent. I didn't learn this until later, but she hadn't put her seatbelt on."

"And you're certain this was her spirit form you were seeing at this moment? I only ask because of her appearance. We've discussed how usually, the spirits don't present with the injury that killed them."

"It depends," said Cinn, wiping his hand over his face. "You should have more answers than me, anyway." Noir didn't take the bait, and waited for Cinn to continue. "So she stumbles up to me, and I stand up to catch her. She's a couple of years younger, maybe like, ten? She's wailing, almost screaming. I can touch her, and for some stupid reason, I try to straighten out her arms, like she's a doll I need to fix."

"Did you manage to?"

Cinn scowled. "Of course not, it just made her screaming worse. She started howling so loud, I grabbed both of her shoulders to calm her down. And then... I guess you could say I slipped *through* her. I felt myself falling towards her... almost like she was a magnet, sucking me in. The road faded away, and when I woke up, I was in a garden."

"Ah," declared Noir. "So, this is the *memory* part?"

"I think so? The girl—her name was Emma, I found out after—her injuries were all gone. She was smiling. Emma grabbed my hand and pulled me to her swing set. She wanted me to push her. So I did. I remember her black pigtails flapping in the wind, again and again as she flew up into the air."

"Did you ever see her parents? At the roadside, or in the garden?"

"No. They both survived the crash." Well, their bodies did, at least. With their only daughter dead, however...

"And how did the slip end?"

"I remember watching Emma swing forward and back, forward and back. And like a pendulum, I started to feel sleepy. My eyes started closing for longer and longer, and eventually, they stayed closed."

Noir's furious scribbles dashed across the page. "And how did you return?"

"To my mum shaking me."

"*Shaking* you?"

"Yeah, because I was asleep! Well, I was to her, anyway."

"I would have thought she'd have got a paramedic to look at you, as you were unconscious."

"I don't know, maybe she did!" After a breath, Cinn consciously returned his volume to normal to continue, "I woke up, and we went home."

"Did the police want to talk to her about the crash?"

"What? That's got nothing to do with this... record," Cinn said, gesturing to Noir's book.

With a snap, Noir closed his notebook. "Quite right. I suppose, what I really wanted to say, was that you shouldn't carry any guilt with you about that girl's death, Cinn."

"I don't!" A sour taste arose in the back of his mouth.

Two bushy eyebrows flew up in time with two palms. "Alright, quite right. I think we should leave it there for today, then. You've got plenty of reading to be getting on with, anyway."

Cinn half stood, but then sat down again. He'd almost forgotten something. Something very important, ahead of their next attempt to contact Béatrice tonight.

"Before I go, I wanted to ask you what you knew about how shadowslippers bring spirits back to this realm with them. Like I accidentally did when those four people died." He bit his lip. He still wasn't *completely* convinced his secret plan to find a way to bring Béatrice back to talk to the other three directly was the best idea. Although, it did hold a certain appeal—the look of elation on Julien's face for one, plus then Cinn needn't panic about asking her all the right questions.

"You shouldn't need to worry about that, not with your warding device." Noir nodded at Cinn's wrist.

"I know, I know, but say I *wanted* to bring someone back, for a short amount of time—" He cut himself off at Noir's rapid blinking, his pipe frozen on the way to his mouth. "I mean, completely theoretically. Before, you said you'd do some research into how exactly I was able to bring spirits back, the very few times I've done it."

"I am still in the process of that research."

Great. He'd alarmed Noir for no reason.

"It seems that very, very few shadowslippers have ever experienced that particular quirk. In fact, there's only one record of such a person."

For a moment, his heart inflated with the hope of meeting someone else like him. Then he remembered he was the only shadowslipper currently alive.

"Shall we reconvene tomorrow, hmm?" The old man appeared deadly serious as he reached forward to grasp his arm. "I hope you're taking care of yourself, Cinn."

After promising that he was, Cinn freed himself and let himself out, rummaging around in his rucksack for his A Tribe Called Quest cassette. His hand paused, however, at a shadow slinking out from behind a corner. Cinn fought to suppress a smile. This was the third day in a row—making it *every* day since their return from Paris—that Julien had been waiting for him when he'd finished with Noir. And just like those other times, Julien had in his hand a black coffee from Curio Café Collective, ready to pass to him.

"Thanks," Cinn said, beginning the long walk down the many sets of spiralling stairs. He still avoided the so-called 'elevators'. Surely they weren't suitable for coffee carrying, anyway.

Cinn wasn't sure what sort of message Julien was trying to communicate with the coffee, exactly.

'Yo, I'm your friendly coffee-bringing buddy who can one hundred percent be just friends with you?'

'I didn't want to kiss you when we fucked, but now I'll bring you coffee every day to fuck with your feelings?'

Except he couldn't quite get an image out of his head. A snapshot of the expression Julien had worn on his face moments before Cinn left him alone in that alleyway in Paris. Surprised, yes, but underneath it, the unmistakable hint of despair, and even regret.

So, Cinn wasn't sure what to think of either of their 'feelings' anymore.

Once they reached the street, they walked a few steps in tension-laden quiet, until Cinn cracked and stopped abruptly in the middle of the pavement. He opened his mouth, but Julien beat him to it, to say, oddly, "Before I forget, I got this for you."

Julien dipped his hand into the front pocket of his over-the-shoulder messenger bag to reveal a fistful of olive green material.

He tossed it to Cinn.

It took him a few blinks to recognise it as a hat.

"It's only because I was sick of seeing that ratty grey one on the top of your head," Julien said, mouth perfectly straight, eyes guarded.

Cinn let out a short, unsure laugh as he stuffed his old hat into his bag, and tugged the green beanie onto his head. It was far warmer, fit him perfectly, and was as soft as kitten fur.

"It's bamboo fabric blended with organic cotton," Julien said in a rush. "But if you hate it, I won't care. I just saw it in passing when I was out doing something else."

Cinn stared at Julien, his heart doing an odd sort of tap dance. Where on earth did beanie-hat-gifting fit into the ever-shifting dynamics of their relationship?

"Thanks," he said at last. Then opened his mouth to see what would come out next, only to shut it again, since Darcy was charging towards them, scarf flapping in the wind, lips pressed in a grim line.

Eighteen

Cinn

Darcy's face, blotched with pink, broke into relief at the sight of them. Out of breath, she leaned on her knees, and Julien reached out his hand to steady her. "Great timing. Madame Sinclair just sent a message to Noir's fireplace, but sent me running here in case you missed it." She checked her watch. "Elliot's about to be sent out with the gendarmerie. He's already at the Baths."

"What? What's going on?" asked Julien.

"There's been another umbraphage attack. In progress. Right now. But this time... this time, there's *two*." Darcy stared at Julien, her emphasis on the number heightened by the tight clench of her jaw. "At once."

"And Eleanor wanted us to know Elliot was being sent out... why exactly? He's been sent to expel them before."

"Well..." Darcy started, glancing at Cinn.

In an instant, Julien's arm flew out in front of Cinn to create a barrier. "She's got to be joking."

"She only wants him to *observe* from the background. To see what he makes of them. See what reactions he has."

"*Oui*, Eleanor can have a *reaction*, alright—"

Cinn pushed Julien's arm down. "It's fine, Julien." And then said to Darcy, "I'll come."

The tight press of Julien's lips suggested he wasn't happy, but it really had very little to do with him, so Cinn angled himself away from him to address Darcy. "It's why I'm here, isn't it? If there are people in danger,

I guess I should try to help," he said, surprising himself in the process. Truthfully though, he was getting rather tired of long interviews in Noir's office, and attempting to read books half as heavy as him. He'd always learnt best practically, so what was the harm in a little fieldwork?

"I'll walk Cinn to the Baths. We might still be able to catch up with Elliot," said Darcy.

A short, sharp laugh burst out of Julien. "I'm coming too. I'm going with him."

"Good luck persuading the operators that you're on the list."

Julien only smiled wickedly. "They can try to stop me if they dare."

Darcy folded her arms. "Well, if you're going, I'm coming as well."

"Fine."

"Fine!"

Cinn coughed. "Well, shall we...?"

"Even if we somehow get clearance, the bath operators won't be pleased with us tagging along pointlessly during emergency protocol," Darcy said as they started their brisk journey.

"I don't care," Julien replied.

Cinn slowed his walk. "So, just to clarify, when we say *baths*..."

"Oh, yes! Sorry Cinn. We're going to travel via the Displacement Baths." Darcy's eyes danced with *delight*, of all things. The snippets Cinn had heard about these strange devices did not make him jump for joy at the prospect of using them. "Elliot uses them all the time for work travel."

They cut through the centre of Auri, past the ruin of the Cerulean Auditorium, past St. Caelum's, with its towering spires, past the library's cobbled courtyard, until they were a few steps away from a modern-looking building, all shiny metal and gleaming glass, the faint scent of chlorine wafting out from its edges.

Abruptly, Cinn halted his following of Darcy's rapid pace and slowed to a crawl.

Julien grabbed his shoulder. "You okay? Have you changed your mind?" He seemed rather hopeful.

"Do I have to... *swim* in the baths?"

"No. They're not that big at all. You couldn't even if you wanted to."

"Will I have to go underwater?"

"It's not water exactly... you'll see. But, yes, you'll need to be completely submerged."

Cinn worried at his lip. Would he actually be able to cope with this without having a public meltdown? Although, he supposed he'd gone all the way under the water a few times in his fancy bathtub at his house, and *that* had been fine.

Julien's grey eyes turned oddly tender—for him—and he used his thumb to nudge Cinn's bottom lip out from his teeth. His warm hand remained on Cinn's cheek when he said, "Let me tell Eleanor maybe you'll go next time. This is all too sudden."

At a more appropriate time, he'd have to instigate a no-touching rule, as his silly little brain couldn't cope with any level of contact and traitorously craved more and more of every morsel Julien gave him.

"I want to do it," Cinn said with as much conviction as he could muster. And a large part of him *did* want to—he was becoming increasingly curious about these so-called 'umbraphages' that were terrifying the moteblessed community with their existence.

"Are you coming in?" Darcy called from the revolving-glass entrance, with clear impatience.

Apparently, yes, he was.

The Displacement Baths were a... process.

First, they'd been in a crowded lobby, cramped, with dozens of people jostling each other to be further ahead in the queue for the check-in desk. The no-nonsense receptionist took Cinn's name first, then pointed to a metal turnstile gate. He'd hovered to the side, waiting for Julien to finish his long 'explanation' of why he and Darcy weren't on today's access list, but then was called through the barrier by a woman in a white lab coat and a clipboard.

Julien, noticing that he'd passed through without them, shouted after him, but all Cinn could do was give him a helpless shrug. Hopefully, he'd find Elliot on the other side of the Baths, wherever that even was.

Marched to a changing room, the woman ordered Cinn to strip completely naked, slip into the provided robe, and put every single possession in a locker. After eyeing the cabinet unhappily, he wrapped up his headphones and buried them deep in his bag before carefully folding his new green beanie, pushing it down securely so that it wouldn't catch in the bag's zip.

The woman closely scrutinised Cinn's earring and eyebrow piercing, holding several metal bars to them in a series of tests. Whatever she was doing, they appeared to pass the checks.

Next came the inspection of his golden bangle, which he warned her was not coming off, in the hope she wouldn't question it too closely. The way the woman kept glancing at her clipboard clued him in to the fact she was prepared for this, however, and she made no further comment.

The emergency code on the top of his form warranted Cinn be sent straight to the front of the queue for transportation, and this displeased the attendant, who could see from her notes that it was Cinn's first visit. The name 'Madame Sinclair' was muttered unpleasantly under her breath.

When she informed him that the usual process involved watching a one hour instructional video, but that he wouldn't be doing that today, it did *not* make him feel better.

"I'm going to quickly break down the procedure for you. When called, you will enter the chamber number stated. Place your feet on the markers on the tiles. The chamber will fill with Aerofluid. The rising liquid will pause at your neck. The operator will confirm you are happy to proceed. Next, the Aerofluid will rise above your head, fully submerging you. Keep *very* still. Oh, and don't forget to take a deep breath before-hand—deep as possible, until your lungs are filled to bursting."

He gave her a *look*.

"You'd be surprised at how many people forget. There's a red panic button within arm's reach. Pressing it will empty the chamber within five seconds. If it's not pressed, shortly after the chamber's capacity is reached, you'll be displaced."

And what exactly does that entail? he wanted to scream at her, but she was already gesturing for him to follow. Keeping his thin white robe—would there be clothes on the other side? Surely there would be?—firmly wrapped around him, he followed the stern lady down a corridor, joined by other robed people coming out of changing cubicles. Combined together, he was struck by the uncomfortable sensation that the lot of them were sheep being herded.

He swallowed.

The funnel poured out into a spacious, high-ceilinged room with ugly brown tiles, cool to the touch of his bare feet. Its centre housed eight benches that created a square that faced the four walls, each featuring rows of doors inscribed with white numbers.

Now he was in this final chamber, the chlorine smell increased to almost nauseating levels. He'd visited swimming pools several times fol-lowing the years since he'd almost drowned, and always left ashamed he hadn't made it past the shallow end.

But you're not swimming today, you're simply.... standing.

The wait on the bench was agonisingly slow. Various names were called out over the loudspeaker, each instructing the traveller to enter a numbered chamber. Cinn studied the faces of the people near him. Some seemed tense, but nobody else was having the near panic attack he was.

"Cinnamon Saunders, chamber four."

He didn't even have enough energy to cringe at his real name.

As he forced his unsteady legs to take the handful of steps to the numbered door, a voice called out his name, and he turned to find Darcy waving at him from the entrance, she and Julien in their own stark white robes. Shoulders untensing somewhat, Cinn smiled to himself; Julien had talked their way into the Baths after all. Of course he had.

However, Julien still looked pissed off, and a fissure of annoyance crackled through Cinn. Why had he insisted on coming if he was just going to sulk the entire time?

He had no more time to ponder the mysterious workings of Julien's mind, because now he was in the tiny chamber, no bigger than a cupboard under the stairs in width, and the heavy iron was closing automatically.

The four sides of the chamber were lined with metal so shiny, Cinn could see his reflection. He scowled at the robed, wide-eyed fellow with tangled hat-hair. Positioning his feet exactly on the two red crosses on the tiles, he straightened his posture, and waited, a pool of anxiety eating at his stomach.

A tinny voice filled the small space. Cinn couldn't see a speaker in sight. *Motecraft?*

"Starting displacement sequence. Stand by."

From thousands of miniscule, pinprick-sized holes near the bottom of the chamber, a liquid started pouring in, wetting the bottom of his feet. The lukewarm fluid was... strange. It was clear like water, but with a slight haziness to it. Once it had reached his knees, Cinn marvelled at the light airiness of the fluid splashing against his skin. There wasn't a single hint of chlorine now—instead, the liquid held a vaguely earthy, floral scent.

Everywhere the fluid touched, his skin tingled with a not unpleasant sensation; it was almost like being tickled with a feather. The liquid rose higher and higher, until it had reached the hem of his robe. To his utter surprise, the material completely disintegrated upon contact with the Aerofluid, dissolving into it without a trace. He watched, fascinated, as the water level rose quicker and quicker now, and took his robe with it.

It was when the fluid reached his chest that the panic started.

Memories of battling for his life against that cold, murky river resurfaced, and he recalled those horrible, horrible moments where his body forced him to swallow the dirty water instead of breathing air.

Fighting against the nervous shake in his leg, Cinn took manual control of his breathing to slow his rapid heartbeat. *It's not even water. You probably can't even drown,* he lied to himself. *It will all be over within seconds,* he continued, even though he hadn't the faintest clue.

He bit into his lip so hard, a metallic tang filled his mouth.

The Aerofluid reached his collarbone. A tiny involuntary moan crept out of him, and the red panic button, easily within reach, tempted him.

However, he'd look simply ridiculous to Julien and Darcy if he backed out now and didn't join them on the other side.

Plus, he'd have to leave the chamber completely naked.

Yes, that sealed the deal.

The rising fluid paused at his neck, exactly like the woman said it would.

"Please audibly confirm you wish to proceed."

Terror gripped him with a vice-like fist. "Wait! Nobody has actually told me where I'm going yet!"

The bored, monotonous voice declared, "Chambers one to five are rigged up to our portable receiver baths."

"Huh? What?"

"Sir, are you ready?"

No! "Yes?"

Squeezing his eyes shut and praying he didn't open them to find himself in the Atlantic Ocean, Cinn inhaled the largest lungful of air he could, imagining his lungs were a balloon that could always inflate that *tiny* bit more.

The cool tingle of the strange substance danced across his chin, cheeks, forehead, until Cinn's hair was lightly tugged upwards by the rising liquid. He knew when the chamber had reached capacity—his feet were lifted off the ground.

He was floating.

And then, he was *flying,* engulfed in a shimmering dance of bright colours that penetrated his closed eyelids. Weightless, untethered to time and space, the fabric of reality folding and wrapping around his form.

For a fleeting moment, he questioned whether he even existed at all, fearing he may have even shadowslipped, as the familiar sensation of disassociation washed over him.

Then, he wasn't floating, or flying, but falling, *dropping*, although not necessarily *downwards*, hurtling towards *something*.

The multicoloured lights converged, collapsing into a brilliant point of focus, and Cinn hurtled through a tunnel of sorts, until the lights faded and he was left with the black of his closed eyes.

The Aerofluid relinquished its firm hold on him, gently releasing Cinn into the new space. Once his body felt the chill of air rather than liquid, he tentatively peeled his eyes open.

Cinn inhaled the biggest breath of air he'd ever taken.

Then, an awful sense of vertigo consumed him when he realised he wasn't actually standing anymore, rather, lying down horizontally.

Slightly rusty corrugated metal was the first thing Cinn saw, then, as his vision cleared, a series of overhead shelves, each holding boxes and containers, came into focus. The scent of industrial materials and a hint of engine oil permeated the air.

He sat up so quickly, his head swam.

He was in a van. An enormous van.

Secured crates were dotted in between what could only be described as bathtubs, each connected to the van by thick metal tubing. Uniformed people ran up and down the centre aisle, barking orders. What did he do now?

A towel hit his face.

"Get dressed," Darcy's voice instructed him.

Using the towel to hide as much of himself as possible, he asked, "Into what?"

She dumped a pile of navy fabric on the crate next to him. "Congratulations. You've been promoted into the gendarmerie for the day. I hope you're shoe size nine."

"How did you beat me here?" Cinn said to her fully clothed self, frowning. Even her hair, although damp, looked immaculate, tied back in a neat ponytail. "And why am I now in an actual bathtub?"

"The journey timings are very unpredictable. And the portable displacement systems have to be flat for space-saving purposes."

"And where's Julien?" Cinn would rather he didn't end up stark naked in front of him, all things considered. However, Darcy had seen someone more important than him, and left to chase them down the van's interior.

After drying and changing—facing the van's wall—Cinn pushed past the throngs of people to access the van's rear door, open to the world, with a ramp allowing access to a paved surface.

The van's interior sprawled out into a small, circular, makeshift base: more supply crates, workbenches, chunky medical kits, a massive radio antenna. A couple of grainy screens connected to humming power generators displaying wavy lines of data. A collection of metal caches, some of them propped open to reveal strange looking devices that could only be weapons.

Nobody glanced at Cinn, standing in the middle of the organised chaos, not even once. He was a ghost, floating over the whole scene, watching down from above.

What on earth did he do now?

"Hey," said a voice, and a hand pressed into the small of his back.

Cinn couldn't deny the cascade of relief that coursed through him when he turned to find Julien's face filling his vision, offering him a tight, dimpled smile.

"Hey." His breathy reply probably gave his elation away. If it didn't, the way Cinn grabbed the sleeve of Julien's navy blue shirt definitely did.

"Enjoy the journey?" Julien said, then smirked. "Or was it as traumatic as Auri's elevators?"

"Better than the elevators. Aside from the whole having-to-be-naked bit."

"*Oui*, I'm sad I missed that," Julien said, eyes twinkling. "If only I was a few minutes faster, eh?"

Cinn gave him an exaggerated eye roll and dropped his grip on Julien's arm. Julien laughed, looking pleased.

Darcy saved Cinn from further torment by materialising, Eleanor Sinclair in tow. Cinn blinked, not expecting her presence here even though she'd demanded his. It was striking seeing her in a standardised uniform, rather than the power-suit combos she tended to favour. Even more strange was the absence of her black thick-rimmed glasses, which she must have had to leave behind at Auri.

Eleanor looked straight past Cinn to Julien. "I'm still not entirely clear what you and Darcy are doing here," she said pleasantly enough, but the edge to her undertone made Cinn's stomach tense.

Darcy's gaze fell to the ground like a reprimanded child's, but Julien remained unaffected. "How can I support MEET in developing motetech to handle these umbraphages if I've never seen one?"

"Ah, so the director of MEET approved the paperwork? Funny how Jonathan Steele managed to do that, within ten minutes, while being out of the country."

Darcy now looked like she wanted to die, to sink into the ground and never return.

Cinn stepped forward. Cleared his throat. "It's my fault, ma'am. Darcy came to take me to the Baths, and I panicked about going alone. I begged them to come with me. Sorry if they should have checked with you first."

Julien didn't blink an eye at his lie, but Darcy looked up, looking even more horrified.

Eleanor made a clucking sound. "Well, we're all here now. But this isn't a school trip. You'll follow the instructions from the unit commander to the letter. These things are dangerous. The two umbraphages have already killed six people, one of them ours."

"Elliot—" started Darcy.

"Is fine. Now follow me."

The three of them fell into step behind Eleanor, who left the vicinity of the van to march them down the road. For the first time, Cinn took in their surroundings—a residential area, three-storey terraced houses on either side of them. When they reached the end of the road, a line of orange blockades prevented access to the left.

"We've evacuated every house in the surrounding blocks, citing a critical gas leak," Eleanor said. "We were forced to use the LMDs on a couple of residents who saw too much."

"Lumimeld Memory Disrupter," Julien said quietly. "My team and I designed them." The evident pride in his voice made Cinn smile to himself.

Two turns in the road later, the first traces of noise became audible. Shouting mainly, but some other indistinguishable sounds as well. Cinn's pace slowed as Eleanor's quickened. He really wasn't sure what to expect from these elusive creatures that Auri believed he held the magic key to turning the tide against. What he *did* know however, was that they were likely to be very disappointed when he turned out to be useless.

What would happen if that happened? Would they send him back to London? With his golden band on, he wouldn't be a danger any longer.

Although, when he imagined himself slotting back into his old life—well, he'd probably need to find a new restaurant to work at—a pang of loss twinged through him. Which in turn triggered a wave of guilt, because Tyler needed him there.

It had alarmed Cinn to get a phone call from Tyler yesterday. Just past nine a.m., but Tyler joked he hadn't been to bed yet. Cinn hadn't found the manic note in his laugh funny at all. When he'd accused Tyler of being high, Tyler had muttered something under his breath before hanging up on him. Cinn knew Tyler better than the back of his hand. Tyler felt abandoned, and confused about what exactly Cinn was doing in Switzerland, and hurt by the lack of information he could offer him.

"Hey, this is exactly where that umbraphage attacked the other week, isn't it? Outskirts of Seville?" said Julien. "I recognise it from the video you showed me."

"Yes," replied Eleanor. "We dissipated it, but it's returned to the exact same place, which is unique enough as it is. But this time, it's brought company."

The noises increased in volume until it was clear they'd almost arrived. Turning the last corner, Cinn braced himself.

Nothing could have prepared him for what he saw.

His breath caught, and he reached for both Julien and Darcy's arms simultaneously as he observed the spectacle unfolding before him. Two of the creatures, suspended in mid-air above a sea of navy-blue uniforms—Auri's gendarmerie. The umbraphages, black silhouettes that emitted a dark, otherworldly glow, writhed and contorted like shadows come to life. Their formless bodies ebbed and flowed, a dance of darkness that seemed to mock the efforts of the brave team confining them below.

The gendarmerie formed a circle in the wide road, and enclosed the creatures in a barrier made of, or at least powered by, some sort of motes. Millions of tiny flecks of vibrating movements, all working together to create a half sphere of protection.

"They'll compress the light net smaller and smaller until the umbraphages disintegrate," Eleanor informed them. "It's only a temporary measure, however. They'll be back. We've started recording the tiniest individual difference between them, you see. Each of them emits a unique energy signature. That one on the right is the same one that was here before. The other is new."

As the combatants clashed, tendrils of inky blackness lashed out, and occasionally momentarily broke free of the glowing light barrier, unleashing a round of panicked shouts as more effort was required to channel motes to fill the gap in the barrier it created, and to push the tendril back inside.

Julien gestured towards something, prompting Cinn's confusion until he clocked Elliot's wild hair at the far side of the action. Elliot had his feet planted firmly on the ground, left leg bent in front of the other, but he was clearly feeling the strain of whatever he was doing to support the light barrier, as his outstretched arms trembled.

"We're not going any closer." Julien positioned himself slightly in front of Cinn. Hilarious, as the chances of him charging into battle like a knight in shining armour were as improbable as a snowman dancing in hell.

A long inky tendril suddenly whipped out of the fractured barrier, the scent of sulphur increasing as it did so, and an umbraphage succeeded in wrapping itself around the upper arm of some poor fighter. The man made a harrowing sound: a scream that reverberated through the air, before punching straight into Cinn's soul. A spray of blood decorated the concrete before the team could push the umbraphage back into the light cage.

Falling to the ground, the man wailed in agony. Two gendarmes lifted a shoulder each to carry him away, towards where the four of them stood. Dashing towards them from the left were two paramedics, and Cinn jumped backwards to allow them quicker access to their patient.

Eleanor stepped forward to examine the wound over the shoulder of the doctors. "See that?" she said, as one paramedic cut a sizeable chunk out of the officer's uniform to allow access to his entire limb.

The laceration that the umbraphage made ran deep into the man's arm. Scarlet-red blood ran freely from it, dripping onto the ground. And then, Cinn saw what Eleanor was talking about—tiny flecks of black ink swimming in the blood, as if alive. Looking even closer—as close as he dared—it appeared that the veins around the injury had blackened too.

"It makes the wounds a nightmare to close," said Eleanor. "Occasionally, some of our gendarmes have needed full blood transfusions because so much of the stuff got into their bloodstream, it poisoned them."

The man fell to his knees, clutching both hands to his head, to the dismay of the medics who'd been trying to clean out his wound. Without warning, the man's wailing suddenly increased in volume and he shook his head violently, as if trying to clear it of something. Cinn shuffled back.

"And this," continued Eleanor, as if giving a lecture. "Is another side effect of our lovely new friends. If you get too close, or if one strikes you, it can sometimes trigger the person to experience delusions. We've even had some reports of them projecting nightmarish visions into the minds of their victims. In rare cases, the affected individual has become trapped in a state of psychosis. Even if you're a fair distance from the umbraphage, they can intensify feelings of fear, sorrow or anger in their proximity."

Were they a 'fair distance' from them right now? Perhaps the light barrier was protecting them. Even so, the umbraphages emanated a chilling aura, tainting the air with an oppressive weight.

Cinn cautiously retreated from the disturbed man sprawled on the concrete. Paramedics hovered over him, administering an injection while Darcy whispered something to Julien.

Taking small, uneven steps, Cinn stumbled backwards until he hit a garden fence.

These umbraphages. They were... too much.

Eleanor... Julien, Darcy, Elliot... the rest of Auri, hell, potentially the rest of the *world*, were relying on him to sort this out? No chance.

The reality of the challenge slapped him in the face like a bucket of icy water. He crumbled against the fence, crumbled under the weight of everyone's expectations.

Julien and Darcy approached.

"This is why—"

Darcy interrupted Julien with a sharp, "Don't."

"So, are they similar to what you saw that day in my cottage, Cinn? When you shadowslipped?" Darcy asked.

Cinn glanced over to the action again, where the ongoing struggle with the umbraphages was still unfolding like a desperate ballet, light battling darkness on a blood-soaked stage.

"Similar. Not exactly the same, no. But they... feel the same," he said, his voice trailing off to a near whisper. "I'm so sorry, but I really don't think..." He stared over at the two deadly creatures of darkness throwing themselves at the barrier.

Darcy dropped to the ground beside him, with Julien following closely behind. "*Please* don't worry about that right now," she said.

Julien nodded, his lips tightly pressed together. "Let's go home. I'll talk to Eleanor. You'll never have to see them again, if you don't want to."

"Don't promise him that, Julien!" snapped Darcy.

Cinn looked away from the pair of them, up into the sky. The sun was still visible, but its light appeared dampened, diminished.

Another scream, another person down, this time a woman.

As Eleanor walked towards them, frowning, Cinn climbed to his feet.

"I think we'd all better return to the va—"

Before Eleanor could finish her sentence, an almighty inhuman screech tore through the air, and everyone's heads snapped towards the light circle, where one umbraphage had fashioned its form to create two long limbs, working them together to create a rip, a tear in the barrier. Within a heartbeat, it had completely freed over half of its shadowy existence, causing a wave of outcry from the gendarmes below.

"We need to run," Julien said, yanking Cinn's arm so hard that a jolt of adrenaline shot through him, his heart pounding in sync with the urgency in Julien's voice.

It was too late.

The umbraphage was completely clear of the barrier, not a single wispy trace of it left behind. Several gendarmes came together to create a flat surface of light, one last futile effort of defence, but it easily surged upwards, rising high until it was above the chimney line.

Distantly, his mind registered Darcy and Julien's shouts, but Cinn tuned them out. Because the umbraphage was... *looking* at him. He couldn't explain how he knew this; the creature had no face, no eyes with which to seek him. But it *knew* him.

And it was coming for him.

Like a bird of prey diving for its next meal, the umbraphage flung itself towards the ground.

An agonising heat seared through Cinn's left wrist, and he tore his eyes away from the umbraphage to his warding band. It had become lava-hot, radiating scalding heat, and all at once it was as if molten sunlight coursed beneath his skin. As the inferno deepened, already causing blistering red marks, he unleashed a primal scream. He tried to rip off the band with his other hand—*stupid, stupid!*—which only doubled his pain when the flesh of his fingers and palm joined his wrist in burning, practically melting his flesh away.

"Give me your wrist!" shouted someone—*Julien?*—but Cinn had enough sense to spare them his agony, and swung his arm in the opposite direction.

Then, a new sensation began. One of terror. One of dread, creeping slowly through him.

Limbs failing him, he tumbled to the ground, looked up to find most of his vision consumed by black, the umbraphage's form spreading out in front of him like an angel of death.

And then, all pain, all the noise, every single sensation faded away, as he slipped away from the world.

Nineteen

CINN

This shouldn't be happening.

The band was supposed to protect him.

Instead it *burned* him, and allowed him to shadowslip at the worst possible time, leaving everyone else to die.

He'd have presumed he was dead himself right now, if it wasn't for the fact he recognised where he was: back in the ruined red city of death. Crumbling skyscrapers rose above him, the alien red vines devouring them with their insidious grasp. An odd rumbling reverberated around him, causing a slight shake to the cracked ground. He looked up to the sky. Yup, the moon was still fractured into shards. At least it was reliable here.

The only silver lining was that his bangle was icy cold, its blistering burn ceased, his skin unmarred.

"Where are you, little motes?" he said aloud, eyes searching the sky for his shadowmote friends that had helped him last time. They were nowhere in sight.

Well, he'd better go find them then, before it was too late.

Forcing his legs into action, he picked a random direction and started walking. It was unsettling how detailed this version of the shadowrealm was. Just like a real city, it had trees, although dead and splintered, and cars, some parked neatly against the pavement, others sprawling at odd angles in the road.

Something about the shape of the cars seemed strange to him, but he struggled to put his finger on it. The vehicles appeared sleek and streamlined; the contours were too smooth, the angles too... something.

A tiny tickling sensation, not unpleasant, brushed against the back of his neck. A miniscule shadowmote flew in front of his face, so close that for a moment Cinn thought it was going to act like a butterfly and land on his nose. Its impossible black glow flickered as it hovered in place.

"Hello there," Cinn whispered.

In reply, it bounced up and down before zipping off to the left, then pausing. Cinn stepped towards it, then it zoomed off again.

Did it want him... to *follow* it?

Well, he had no other plans.

Always remaining several metres ahead of Cinn, the shadowmote led him down a littered alley, ground covered in sharp shards of glass.

Two more turns, and they reached the beginning of a bridge, its skeletal remains stretching across a dried river, the bed of which was a deep drop below him. The corroded metal and fractured concrete only hinted at this structure's past life.

As he stared at this desolate, decaying monument, his mind whirled.

It was then the lurching sense of familiarity hit him.

He almost couldn't believe he hadn't recognised the city before now, because it was his very own: it was *London*. This wasn't any old bridge: this was the remnants of *Tower Bridge*.

Looking across the riverbed, his eyes scanned for the recognisable silhouettes of other landmarks. Where was the Tower of London, standing proudly on the north bank?

A heavy sense of sorrow settled over him when he finally identified what remained of it. The historic castle, like everything else in this London, now lay in ruins, its medieval walls crumbled after succumbing to the oppressive red vines that choked it. They wrapped around the shattered stones, their vibrant hue in stark contrast to the desolation that surrounded them.

He'd never been able to afford the entrance fee for The Tower of London since that one time he'd visited on a school trip. His experience of the day had been marred by shadowslipping in the middle of the inner ward. He'd collapsed on the grass, perhaps under the weight of too many spirits compressed into one place. Comparatively, it was a relatively 'good' trip—the dead that he'd met had been surprisingly friendly, considering most of them had been executed there.

The shadowmote danced across his vision.

"Did you want to show me this, little friend?" he asked, reaching his hand out. The mote came to sit on the palm of his hand. "Why?"

Before the mote could offer any sort of response, an inexplicable force tugged at his very essence. It was as if his insides were being wrenched outside of him. This wasn't like the usual sensation of shadowslipping, which was often akin to drifting from one place to another.

No, this time he was being *yanked, forced.*

His surroundings blurred and flickered like a fading dream. The world seemed to lose its grip, fragments of the ruined city dissolving like mist.

He closed his eyes, gave into the phenomenon, and let himself be pulled away.

Twenty

JULIEN

Moments Julien would never forget:

The sight of Béatrice's dead body, burnt and broken, after he'd insisted he be the one to formally identify it.

The first day of university, when a single ray of sunshine had shone through his impenetrable darkness.

The day he'd killed his mother.

And now, the collection of these present ones:

The umbraphage making its relentless charge towards the four of them, the rising sense of terror increasing as it closed in.

Cinn's scream of sheer agony as his gold band burned blisters into his skin.

Julien attempting to wrench the fucking thing off his body by any means possible but being pushed away.

The nightmarish shadow creature lunging itself at Cinn, a hair's breadth from touching him.

Julien urging himself to reach for the motes so easily within his grasp, within his control, but doing nothing. Nothing to save him.

Nothing, nothing, nothing.

Elliot miraculously appearing next to them, pushing Cinn and Julien out of the way to throw himself in front of the umbraphage, hands manipulating a sphere of lumenmotes.

And then, the sight of the monster lashing out at his best friend's chest, splitting his torso open in a gruesome gash that Julien himself felt every inch of, a visceral echo of anguish.

The next few moments were a black hole in his tapestry of memory. At some point, he must have realised Cinn had shadowslipped, because next he was half carrying, half dragging his limp body as far away from the scene as he could, before collapsing with him in a long narrow path between two houses.

Then he'd simply sat there, back against a wall, breathing hard.

It could only have been moments before Darcy, breathless and wild-eyed, came rushing up the path. "Elliot is okay. Genuinely. His wound isn't that deep. The paramedics are treating him now. And they've managed to get the umbraphage back into the light cage. Though now they've knocked out our radio signal somehow. Eleanor is supporting the commander, and I'm running back to the van to tell them what's going on. Stay here with Cinn."

Julien blinked at Darcy's ramblings until they started to sink in. Sickening panic at being left alone to protect Cinn's lifeless body gripped him, and he almost begged Darcy to stay, but then he nodded.

"You could try this," Darcy said, uncertainty lacing her tone as she rummaged through a first-aid kit she must have borrowed. "I know it's not really the time to be experimenting, but..."

She tossed him a vial of thick, milky blue liquid.

He eyed it suspiciously. "What is it?"

"Zenolique. It's a calming drug most often used in our psychiatric wards. It should reduce his adrenaline levels."

He was fairly certain Cinn would have hesitations if he were awake to have an input, but he wasn't, so Julien nodded. "I'll see how we go."

Carefully, Julien rearranged them so that Cinn was slumped against his chest, in between his parted legs. He pressed Cinn's head to his ribs, keeping it there with a hand that rubbed soft circles into his scalp.

With his other hand, he gingerly peeled back Cinn's left sleeve to look at his wrist. The gold band, still slightly warm to the touch, had left a canvas of destruction on Cinn's soft skin. A circlet of grotesque, raised welts, with the surrounding skin charred and blistered. Julien brushed his fingers near the burn that was furthest up his arm. His skin was too hot—even the air around his wrist was warm with residual heat. His stomach twisted in sympathy at the pain he'd felt—he'd surely *feel*—once he woke up. There would be damage to Cinn's hand too, where he'd tried to remove the band, but Julien couldn't face looking at that right now.

"Mon ange," he murmured into Cinn's hair, gently lowering his ruined arm. Cinn shifted in his arms, but didn't wake. Julien pressed his palm against Cinn's forehead. He felt cold. Too cold.

How much longer was Darcy going to be?

What if she didn't make it in time?

At any moment, one of the umbraphages could escape again, find them here in this alley.

And Julien would be powerless to protect them.

"I'm sorry," he said to Cinn, torturing himself by replaying that moment earlier where he didn't reach for the motes at his fingertips, didn't protect him, only stood there and awaited fate.

Wasn't that what he was doing right now, really?

He twisted the vial of Zenolique around in his hand. Darcy was correct, now wasn't the time to be experimenting, but neither was it the time to be unconscious and defenceless, slumped against a wall.

He tipped Cinn's head back and placed the vial at the back of his throat, emptying every last drop of the milky blue substance into him.

Wait. Darcy hadn't told him how much to administer. What if it was only meant to be a drop? Making a strangled sound, Julien clutched both sides of Cinn's head and pressed it to his lips. *What have you done?* His fingers flew to Cinn's pulse point on his neck, but the fumbling shake of his hand made the effort futile.

Should he stick his fingers down Cinn's throat?

Although, what if that caused him to choke on it?

Cursing himself every vile name under the sun, he pulled Cinn tightly against him, leaning his head against his shoulder now, and resorted to praying.

Then, he felt it: the smallest stir of Cinn's body, the slightest tickle of a fluttering eyelash against his cheek. Julien gasped, pulling back Cinn's head to see his eyes were *open*. Beautiful hazel-gold orbs of pure sunshine. Eyes that were looking at him sleepily, dazed and disorientated. Relief coloured his face as he gazed up at Julien.

His expression was also communicating something else. Something else entirely. The slightest flicker of longing. A soft, lingering gaze that dropped to Julien's lips before looking back up into his eyes with dilated pupils.

Cinn's bottom lip slid between his teeth as he gave him a barely perceptible teasing smile that played at the corners of his mouth. Then Cinn's hand reached up to fist Julien's shirt, as if steadying himself, tethering himself to him.

Julien swallowed.

Wordlessly, they stared at each other, existing in the space between heartbeats, each frozen still.

Anticipation hung in the air like static electricity.

As one, they moved their heads towards each other, drawn together by an invisible force, magnets irresistibly pulled toward each other.

When their lips touched, the rest of the world faded away.

Their first kiss was trembling, tentative. Cinn wrapped his arms around Julien's chest, anchoring himself in his lap, as Julien brushed his lips over his, feather-light, basking in their glorious softness, as soft as they'd always looked. Cinn exhaled an unsteady breath, and for a heart-wrenching moment, Julien feared he was about to push him away, to get up and walk away again, but then Cinn pressed his lips firmly against Julien's own. Then he did it again. And again.

Julien needed no more encouragement. He fused his mouth to Cinn's, allowing no space between them. He cupped Cinn's neck, then glided gentle fingers through his hair while his other hand ran up and down his spine.

Julien's teeth sought out the plump swell of Cinn's bottom lip, pulling his lips open so his tongue could slip inside. The delightful taste of mint sweets danced across his tongue. Mint sweets and sunlight breaking through clouds. Moving his tongue slowly in a gentle caress, he felt the delicious sensation of Cinn's own moving against it.

Cinn ran his hand up Julien's arm, gooseflesh erupting in its wake. Then Julien was weightless, floating with an expansive feeling in his chest, as if Cinn was filling him with air. Filling him with life.

Out of Cinn's mouth came a tiny sigh of contentment, and Julien wanted to swallow it, devour it, devour Cinn.

So he did.

He lost himself completely to the kiss, feeling the world spin around them and enjoying the dizzy whirlwind they'd created. Julien pulled Cinn's body even closer to him, gripping his hip as hard as he dared. He wanted to melt into him, to climb into him. He settled for exploring every inch of Cinn's mouth, carving into it with his tongue, his hand now fisting Cinn's hair as he pushed their lips together.

Julien broke away to kiss Cinn's forehead, drag his lips over his jaw, kiss the pulse point on his neck, blissfully beating. Then he pulled Cinn back into his chest, to feel his warm, alive body against his. *"Mon dieu merci! J'ai cru... J'ai cru que je t'avais perdu, Cinn,"* he breathed into Cinn's hair, feeling his own heartbeat finally slow down in time with his deep, shuddering breaths.

Cinn's fingers brushed against his cheek. Wiping them. "Why are you crying?"

Julien hadn't realised that he had been. "I thought I'd killed you."

"What? You *saved* me."

"*Elliot* saved you. I just dragged you here." After he himself was as much help as a potato. "Elliot…" he managed, before his guilt forced his throat shut. "We need to go find him. The umbraphage sliced his chest open."

Cinn slowly unpeeled himself from the cocoon he'd made in Julien's arms. As he stood up, he sucked in a breath of air, wincing and holding up his damaged wrist. "The burns hurt where the band is touching them."

"Take it off," said Julien, reaching for Cinn's injured palm to assess it. At least *that* injury wasn't as bad as he'd thought—raw, red skin, yes, but no welts. He brought it to his lips. "We can move it to your other wrist."

Cinn held the band for a moment, closing his eyes in concentration as he widened the metal, then slid it off himself with great care not to touch his skin.

He held it up in the light. "I guess the umbraphage… overpowered it somehow? But I better keep it on," he said with reluctance, slipping it onto his other wrist.

"He's awake!" came a shout from the path's entrance, and Darcy's beaming smile appeared like the rising sun. "Did you use the Zenolique?"

Julien nodded, hoping Cinn didn't ask what questionable substance he'd forced down his throat.

"Elliot's been taken back to the van. The rest of them have finally dispersed the two umbraphages. For now, obviously." She frowned. "Madame Sinclair said that it was the trickiest battle against them so far. There was one more casualty. One of Elliot's friends, I think. They became moteblown, collapsed unconscious, and then one went for him."

"They channelled too much?" Cinn asked.

"Channelled motes for too long, or in too large a quantity. It rarely kills you, but you can become seriously weakened. Moteblessed that focus on physical channelling spend hours training and priming their body, but it still occasionally happens." Julien recalled those gruelling days all too well. He and Elliot would often spend hours and hours together, at the camp they both attended every summer as teenagers, pushing their bodies to the limit as they challenged each other to channel more at once and for longer.

Returning to the van, they found things in a state of disarray, with many wounded members of the gendarmerie slumped on crates. Even the uninjured officers looked awful, displaying the telltale signs of over-channelling—pale, trembling, disorientated. They were lucky only one of them had become moteblown.

Finding Elliot wasn't hard. He came charging towards them, a disgruntled paramedic shouting after him. He was shirtless, his torso wrapped in white bandages. Inwardly, Julien let out a sigh of relief, gazing up at the heavens in thanks. What he'd have done if Elliot had died because of him, he couldn't begin to fathom.

"It's just one more battle scar," Elliot was saying to Darcy's fussing.

Julien shuffled forwards, to quietly say, "Thank you."

"I was hardly *not* going to rush to your rescue, was I? Especially as Cinn decided to have a nap on the ground."

Cinn scowled at him, but there was a playful edge to it.

What Elliot *should* be doing was calling Julien out on his shortcomings. He should shout at him, tell him he should have reached for the lumenmotes himself, even though he was extremely out of practice, to at least have *attempted* to protect the three of them.

Of course, Elliot wouldn't do that to him. Julien offered him a grateful smile, which he returned, albeit with eyes crinkled with worry.

Eleanor appeared, barking orders at them to go and find a bathtub, shooting Julien a withering glare. Yes, it was true, they'd definitely been more hindrance than help today, but Julien was still glad he'd forced his way into the Baths. Because if he hadn't, who else would have been there to drag Cinn out of danger?

And then cuddle him until he woke up, to be kissed half to death?

Julien's eyes slid sideways to Cinn. For an electric moment, their gazes burrowed into each other, until dots of dark pink bloomed on Cinn's cheeks and he looked away.

"I can't. I want to. God help me, I want to so much, but I can't," he'd whispered to Julien in Paris.

Later, Cinn would likely inform him the kiss was a temporary lapse of judgement.

A one-time thing, never to be repeated.

For now, Julien would cherish the lingering feeling of his lips on his.

Twenty-One

CINN

"No, it wasn't like that." Cinn fought to keep the impatience out of his voice. He'd been trying to explain his latest trip to the shadowrealm for at least half an hour, and the exhaustion of the day was getting the better of him.

As soon as they'd returned to Auri, they'd driven straight back to Darcy's cottage together, all piling onto the rug on her living room floor, jostling to be closest to her fireplace. Darcy had lost the battle, so went to make tea. Upon her return, the recount had began.

"What I'm still trying to figure out," said Julien, wrinkling his nose. "Is what version of the so-called 'shadowrealm' you went to if there were no spirits there to shape its form? I know Béatrice was there last time, but it can't have been an imprint of her memory, or a *projection of her reality*, or however Noir phrases it to you." Julien took a noisy slurp of his tea, and Darcy shot him a dirty look.

"I've no idea," Cinn replied, facing the fire. He'd pointedly avoided any level of eye contact with Julien since their return. Already he was plotting how to delay the inevitable conversation they'd now have to have, following their... *entanglement* earlier. He could only hope by the time it occurred, he would have found a more eloquent way of phrasing 'that was the hottest kiss of my life, but please don't kiss me again because my stupid brain can't handle it'.

"Could it be..." Darcy started.

"Spit it out." Elliot leaned forward to take another cookie. They were Darcy's pistachio nut creations, sadly not the vanilla ones with dark chocolate chips Cinn was determined to perfect.

Darcy dragged out the pause before declaring, "What if... it's the *umbraphage's* projected reality?"

A charged silence as everyone considered her words.

"That... makes a lot of sense," said Cinn.

It also raised a lot of questions, which Julien soon voiced. "But why did he go there that first time when there wasn't an umbraphage about? And why do they live in that nightmarish version of London?"

Elliot rose to his feet, rolling his shoulders that surely ached after his earlier efforts. "I'm going to head off. We still on for Béatrice attempt number two tomorrow afternoon? I have the day off."

Julien's eyes shot to Cinn. "I'm not so sure that's a good idea anymore."

"What?" Elliot snapped. "You mean we ripped a rib off her dead body for nothing?"

Julien winced. "But the umbraphages—"

"Can't hurt me in the shadowrealm," Cinn said, with conviction he didn't truly feel. "Besides, I want to go back. The shadowmote had more to show me, I'm sure of it, before you made me return."

"*Oui*, I'm so sorry about that," said Julien sulkily. "Next time I'll just leave you to your precious version of London, where the fucking moon is fractured and red ivy has eaten everything. And stop touching that." Julien leaned over to knock Cinn's hand away from his now-bandaged wrist. The burns underneath the fabric itched like hell, despite the strange concoctions Darcy had smeared on it.

Elliot shot the pair of them a quick half smile. "See you tomorrow," he said, before abruptly turning to leave. Darcy started stacking cups, and a few moments later, the muffled roar of Elliot's motorcycle reverberated through the walls.

"It's almost midnight," said Julien to Darcy, a slight pleading tone seeping into his voice, before yawning dramatically.

"Oh, for God's sake, fine, you two can stay. But use the *spare* toothbrush, *not* mine. And help me get the blankets out of the cupboard."

Julien jumped up, beaming so wide Cinn almost laughed, to follow her out of the room. Shortly after, a hissed argument was faintly audible from the corridor. "I mean it, Julien!" Darcy's voice warned, followed by a door closing.

Hovering just outside the bathroom, Cinn waited for Julien to be done brushing his teeth, accidentally locking eyes with him multiple times in the mirror. And *fuck*, did each time do something to him. Julien's subtle smirk as he handed over the toothbrush told Cinn he knew exactly what he was doing.

Cinn rinsed it for a full ten seconds before putting it in his mouth.

When he re-entered the living room, Julien was dumping an armful of blankets onto the rug. "You're on the sofa, I'm on the floor."

Cinn was about to protest, but it *was* Julien's choice not to drive them back to their own beds. If he wanted to wake up tomorrow with a bad back and a cricked neck, so be it. He did leave Julien the softest-looking blanket in exchange, though, choosing a patchwork quilt that looked rather handmade. A closer inspection revealed the initials BM stitched into the corner.

As Cinn settled into the admittedly comfortable sofa—no wonder Julien loved sleeping on it—a nicotine craving hit him, but entering the garden alone with Julien, out of the safety of Darcy's earshot, seemed like risky territory.

He lay on his back, facing the ceiling with its rustic wooden beams, and traced with his eyes a route of tiny imperfections in the wood.

"Can I ask you something?" Julien said, and Cinn wanted to sink into the sofa's shell.

"Yes," he finally replied, every muscle held tense. He really didn't have the energy to talk about *the kiss* tonight.

Julien paused, then said, "Earlier, when you stopped outside of the Displacement Baths. You were freaking out about being fully submerged in water."

Cinn's tired mind reeled from the unexpected direction of the conversation. "Is that a question?"

Julien laughed. "Fine. *Why* were you freaking out?"

"I have a very reasonable fear of drowning."

"Yes, I inferred that part. I was just wondering why."

Because I can't fucking swim.

Cinn sighed and twisted around on his side to face Julien. "This is weird, because Noir tried to make me retell this exact story earlier today."

"I didn't realise the two of you were close enough to make swimming plans together."

An involuntary smile tugged at the corner of Cinn's lips. "Noir and I have the best time together. It mostly involves braiding each other's hair."

"Sounds like I'm missing out. So you didn't tell Noir the story because...?"

Because I can't stand people's reactions to it, when I tell it truthfully, the way it actually happened.

"It's not a very nice experience to relive."

"Fair enough. Don't worry then," said Julien. He'd also rolled over, and now the two of them were doing the exact thing Cinn had wanted to avoid: staring into each other's eyes.

Well, at least telling the story would keep Julien's eyes from undressing him. Potentially.

Cinn sighed. "It was about two weeks before my thirteenth birthday—you know, that day I had my first slip. In fact, Noir told me today that this near death experience actually triggered my shadowslipping ability in the first place." That was a whole *other* thing he hadn't had time to process. "It was February, and freezing cold, but we'd been stuck inside all weekend and I really wanted my mum to take me to the park."

This is where he had the choice of how much to sugarcoat, how much to change. He'd told a dozen different versions of this tale, each much more palatable than the truth.

However, something about Julien's enraptured focus on him made him fight the impulse to lie.

"If I tell you the exactly accurate version of events, I don't want any over the top reactions, okay?"

Julien frowned slightly. "Okay."

Cinn exhaled. "So, it was Sunday afternoon, and I wanted to go to the park. Yes, I know I was twelve, but I still really loved feeding the ducks that lived on the river."

"Adults can enjoy feeding ducks, too, you know," Julien interjected, smirking.

"Well, on this occasion, my mum was not at all on board. She'd already made plans with the TV and the bottle of wine she'd drunk half of already that day. Though eventually, she agreed." Cinn studied Julien's face for a reaction, but none came. "I guess I shouldn't have pressed so hard," he said, almost to himself.

"You were her child. It was her job to take you!" Julien burst out, and Cinn gave him a warning look. "Sorry."

"Well, we went to the park. But the wine came with us. My mum sat on the bench at the top of the riverbank, and I took down our dried up bread to feed them."

His usual lies danced on the tip of his tongue.

Then, an old man had a heart attack, and my mum had to run over and give him CPR.

Then, a lost dog darted past her, and she had to chase it down to make sure it was okay.

Then, she turned around to sketch a picture of this really beautiful tree behind us.

"Then, she drank the rest of the wine, and fell asleep."

"Cinn..." Julien started, but Cinn ignored him and pushed on.

"I looked back and saw her eyes were shut, and she was slumped across the bench. I should have woken her up." Julien made a noise of protest. "But I was so angry at her for making me feed the ducks by myself, I just let her sleep. It was often best like that. I finished throwing all the bread to the ducks, then I sat down by the river to watch them. The ground was so damp. I remember thinking my mum was going to be angry about the mud on my trousers. So I thought I'd quickly splash some water on them, to get the worst off, at least."

"Sounds very sensible," said Julien, and he didn't even sound sarcastic.

"Yes, well, my twelve-year-old brain thought so. I leaned forward to cup some water into my hand, but... somehow stumbled. It was quite windy, so that didn't help. Anyway, I tumbled straight into the freezing cold river. I panicked and splashed around, of course, but not loud enough for my mum to wake up. The current wasn't that strong, but the river was so deep I couldn't stand."

"And you didn't know how to swim before this?" Julien said, clearly trying to keep his voice neutral.

"Do you know how expensive lessons are?" Cinn did. He'd saved up all his tiny scraps of pocket money to try to pay for them. Unsuccessfully, because his piggy bank was routinely raided. "We needed all our money to buy things like clothes and food." *And wine. And vodka.*

"Fair enough," Julien said, but the judgement was plainly written all over his face.

"Anyway, I ended up sinking under, even though I was kicking like mad, and in my panic I started to swallow water, then choke on it."

Would he ever forget that horrible sensation? The *burning* in his lungs, the *terror* gripping his heart.

"Then I must have passed out. Next thing I knew, I was on my back on the riverbank, and this random man was giving me mouth-to-mouth. I think I threw up on him."

"And your mother?"

"She was awake by that point. She was standing behind the man, crying."

"I bet she was," Julien said bitterly, then pursed his lips.

"Remember, you promised."

"That wasn't an overreaction. That was an *under*reaction, if any-thing."

Cinn sighed. "She wasn't a saint, but she wasn't altogether a bad mother." He could see Julien was about to disagree, so he jumped back in. "I never found out if I had actually *died* that day, but what Noir said earlier makes me think that I might have. Or was very close to dying, at least."

Julien let out a breath. "Cinn, I'm so sorry. I didn't realise what that story entailed."

"Oh, I'm sorry, I'll drown on a holiday to the Bahamas next time, while swimming with dolphins."

"That's *not* what I meant!" An angry flush appeared on Julien's cheeks. "I just meant, I feel terrible for you having to go through all that. It sounds awful."

Cinn stared at Julien. "You realise this story is just the tip of the iceberg, right? The geezer who saved me reported my mum to child services. They already had tabs on her from my school, so that was the last straw. I was placed into foster care five months later. My childhood, hell, most of my adult life even, was pretty fucking traumatic. You know I ended up in jail, right?"

The lack of surprise in Julien's eyes didn't shock him. He'd predicted Eleanor had given Julien the full rundown on the English hooligan he was charged to babysit. "*Oui*," Julien said. "I can only imagine how difficult that was."

Yeah, *imagine*. The privileged princeling would never be able to empathise with Cinn's lifelong battle against poverty. A very good reason to stay the fuck away from his dangerous dimples and his even more dangerous dick.

"But I want to hear more about it," Julien quietly continued. "Your life, I mean. So I can properly understand." His grey eyes had gone soft and sincere, rendering Cinn powerless against them.

"Sorry. I didn't mean to bite your head off."

Julien laughed. "I always find that phrase so ridiculous."

Cinn joined in, finding a cathartic release of tension within the laughter.

"Thank you for trusting me with all of that," Julien carefully said, in the quietest of voices. "That means a lot to me."

Julien's eyes bore into his until the electric charge between them returned, so Cinn rolled over to face the ceiling again, hearing Julien do the same, but with a tiny chuckle.

"Just so you know, I'm trying really hard not to climb up there with you right now," Julien whispered.

Cinn closed his eyes. *Now I'm trying really hard not to beg you to do just that.*

And now Julien had said that, his mind was overrun with images.

Julien's naked body, accentuated by the firelight, crawling on top of him.

That predatory dimpled smile he'd use, the one that would make Cinn melt.

The heavy, glorious weight of him as he pressed Cinn into the sofa.

The way his lips would surely go straight to the love bite on Cinn's neck. The one that was almost healed, to Cinn's slight regret.

And then his mouth would go lower and lower—

"Cinn?"

"What?"

"You just made a weird sound."

Oops.

For a while, neither of them spoke. Then, the question blurted out of him before he could stop it.

"What if... what if they try to send me back to London? Once Eleanor realises I'm not the asset against the umbraphages everyone hoped I'd be."

The creak of a floorboard as Julien twisted onto his side, with Cinn mirroring his action.

Julien's grey eyes were deadly serious when he said, "Then I'll have to fight them for you. I could knock Eleanor out, any day."

Cinn had doubts about that, actually. That woman was *terrifying*.

"You're not going anywhere," Julien whispered, and held out his hand.

Cinn offered Julien his bandaged wrist, and Julien gently interlaced their fingers.

"Promise?"

"Promise."

The soft crackle of the fire, and the steady beat of Julien's breath, lulled Cinn's eyes into closing. He relaxed every other muscle, but he squeezed Julien's hand firmly against his, as if he were a life raft, and Cinn was drowning all over again.

Twenty-Two

CINN

When Cinn awoke, hand dangling off the sofa, he was alone in the living room. The fire had dwindled to embers overnight, leaving the room enveloped in a chilly stillness.

Tugging on his hat, then throwing the blanket around his shoulders, he wandered into the kitchen to find the others making tea. Julien smiled at him over Darcy's shoulder. Nothing extraordinary, only a brief flash of teeth, yet a subtle warmth spread through Cinn's chest, and he found himself busying himself with dishes before he did anything ridiculous.

Of course, Julien followed him to the sink, sipping his tea. He reached out to touch the blanket, running his thumb over Béatrice's initials. "Still up for later?"

Cinn nodded. *Béatrice, you better be ready to talk this time, now we've bloody dug up your grave.*

The next part of the morning was taken up by Darcy, unimpressed when Julien used up all the cottage's hot water during his shower, arguing with him over the need to let him install some sort of fancy-sounding motetech heating system in her boiler.

"If you'd just sleep at home like a normal person, then it wouldn't be an issue," she snapped, which concluded the discussions.

Julien, who unsurprisingly had a stash of spare clothes at Darcy's, agreed to drive Cinn home to shower and change after he'd refused to borrow anything.

The drive quickly led into the next argument of the day: Julien persistently suggesting Cinn take pain medication for his burns, which pissed him off to no end. The salved wounds weren't pleasant, but he'd dealt with injuries five times worse before, especially during his stint in juvie.

"Why do you care so much?" That eventually shut him up.

Julien waited in the car for him, then drove them straight back to Darcy's. He didn't say much on the return journey, but he *did* let Cinn choose the radio station, so that was something.

Upon their return, they set about preparing for their second attempt to reach Béatrice, with Cinn helping Darcy drag materials up from the cottage's basement. As soon as they opened the ancient trapdoor in her pantry, Cinn's senses were assaulted by a heady blend of exotic, aromatic herbs. The rungs of the oak ladder they descended, creaky and uneven, bore weathered marks of time. A string of giant lightbulbs ran across one wall, and when Darcy touched one, each came alive with the bright glow of dancing lumenmotes.

Everywhere he looked, bundles of dried herbs hung from wooden beams—lavender, sage, and many other mysteries. Jars lined wooden shelves, some oddly empty aside from a strange shimmer within. He picked one up, squinting and holding it to the light. Tiny specks of dark green and maroon were dancing together like fireflies in hidden currents.

"Can you see those?" asked Darcy. "They're floramotes combined with terramotes."

"I didn't realise people kept motes in jars." Cinn spun the jar around in his hand, watching the motes spin with it. They were pretty. Maybe he could decorate his house with some.

"How else would we keep them? That's not any old jar, by the way. Don't drop it, they're expensive."

Like a child in a toy shop, he put it down and picked up something else from the shelf underneath. A large flask with a thin neck, it bore a label proclaiming it Mortalisfade. Its liquid, a deep indigo reminiscent of the midnight sky, appeared to swirl and writhe within the confines of the container.

"Woah! What's this?"

Darcy snatched it off him so fast her arms were a blur. "That needs to stay on the shelf. Not only is it deadly dangerous, but it took me three weeks to brew." With care, she set it back, then stared at it, as if entranced. "This is the elixir we were experimenting with before you came. The one that causes a temporary state very similar to death. If used correctly, in conjunction with some other elements, it's *said* to allow us ordinary moteblessed access to the shadowrealm."

"But it never worked?"

"No. Elliot and Julien took turns almost killing themselves with zero results. I hated every second of it, but they threatened to do it without me if I didn't supervise." She muttered something that sounded like 'fucking children' under her breath. "I had to revive them from flatline several times." She eyed Cinn. "We are *not* going down that route again."

Cinn stared at the dark swirl of liquid. Would there ever be a scenario where he'd risk his life in order to communicate with someone one last time? "Béatrice was Julien's sister, but Elliot..." He left his thoughts unfinished.

"She was his sister too, in lots of ways," Darcy said quietly. "Don't tell Julien I said this, but they might have been just as close. He understood her in ways that Julien never could. Especially when Julien was being the overprotective big brother. You've seen how in denial he is about her involvement with the Arcane Purifiers, right?"

Snorting, Cinn said, "Yes. I'm scared he might not believe me if I ever manage to deliver a message from her."

Seizing a crate from the damp floor, Darcy darted through the basement, swiftly loading it with an assortment of items. "Well, let's hope she's got some answers for us. It's bad enough he already carries guilt over the death of his mother, without all of this Béatrice stuff for him to also beat himself up over."

"What? How did his mother die?"

Darcy's hands paused. "That's his story to tell."

The dining room table was cleared.

The candles, lit.

Elliot, late.

"Take the book to copy from and the aethraven ink to get that bit done, at least." Darcy handed Julien the pot of dark fluid. A phantom itch spread across his skin, a reminder of the last time they'd done this, and he'd awoken in agony. At least the ink had done its job however, and prevented him from bringing back the umbraphage with him.

"There's no point getting on the table yet. Elliot could be hours longer. Come lie down in Béatrice's room. Maybe it'll be good luck to do it there."

The sofa would probably also do the trick.

But he couldn't refuse his chance to peek inside Béatrice's eternally closed door.

When he followed Julien through it, the air hung oppressively heavy with memories. Pure eclectic chaos, shelves overflowed with novels, walls were plastered in arty photography and snippets of illustrated poetry, lots of it French. It was as if the room had inhaled a deep breath when Béatrice had left, and had held it in this whole time, awaiting her return. He didn't want to touch anything here—felt uncomfortable even standing in it, in fact—let alone lie down on her rumpled bed.

A quote on the wall caught his eye: beautiful typography surrounded by hand-painted golden stars. *Though my soul may set in darkness, it will rise in perfect light. I have loved the stars too truly to be fearful of the night.* The words were familiar, but not from his English classes. "This is what you and Darcy said in the graveyard, when you were staring at her headstone."

"*Oui.* She loved poetry. She wrote several herself. Performed them even. That poem was her favourite, I think. I had to battle my father to be allowed to read it aloud at her funeral."

Cinn attempted to move towards Julien, but tripped over a stray mug, its long-evaporated contents leaving a dark ring behind within it.

Julien laughed, setting the ink and book he carried on Béatrice's bedside table, pushing a stack of trinkets to one side to make room. "She's a lot messier than me. Was. She'd often bribe me to tidy her room for her when we were children."

An image of two golden-haired children playing together passed through his mind. He'd never had a sibling—both a blessing and a curse—and was acutely aware he'd never been able to fully understand Julien's loss.

As if in a trance, Julien wandered over to a half-finished knitting project that lay sprawled on the desk, needles still embedded in black yarn. Never to be completed. "This was meant to be a scarf for me, I think." Julien sighed and ran his hand over his face. "I actually forgot how much I hate coming in here. Sorry."

"Shall we—"

"*Non.* It's fine. It's just a room."

Just a forest full of memories, each a pine needle to the heart.

Julien opened a small drawer in her desk. "This is where we found her diary. The one that said *Jour J.*" He stared at the offensive item with a sour look on his face. "Anyway," he said, slamming the drawer shut, then turning to look Cinn straight in the eye. "Take off your clothes and lie on the bed."

Bloody hell. He couldn't be in this dead girl's room and hear those words. Not with Julien looking at him like that. Tamping down his body's inappropriate reaction, he tugged off his hoodie and shirt, pulling his beanie back onto his head when it slipped off.

As soon as his bare skin felt the cool draft of air that drifted through the room, his body viscerally *felt* Julien's eyes magnetise to it, shuddering in response. Remaining on the far side of the room, he eyed Julien warily, who wiggled the ink bottle in response.

"Come on. I don't bite," he said, all predatory dimpled smile.

Fuck yes, you do.

When he reached the bed, he kept his feet planted on the floor, and lay on his back, tensing every muscle as he awaited the feel of cool ink on his skin.

"Relax," said Julien softly. As if it would be that easy, especially with Julien using *that* voice. The one with the exact cadence as that night in Paris.

Without warning, fingers started gently kneading into the firm muscles of his abdomen.

Cinn groaned. "This *isn't* going to help me relax."

Ignoring him, Julien widened the circumference of his endeavours, extending his slow circles towards his ribs, then dipped lower and lower, scraping tantalisingly close to the waistband of his jeans.

"If you carry on doing that..."

"Then what?"

When Cinn didn't answer, Julien pressed a kiss to the top edge of his V-line. Cinn's hands, that had remained still by his side, finally gave in, and reached to wrap themselves in the tangles of Julien's hair.

A silent battle still warred inside him. Julien's touch, Julien's lips, Julien's *attention,* was a spellbinding caress of his body, his soul. Cinn was Eve who'd had a taste of the apple, and now couldn't resist another bite. And everyone knew how that story turned out.

"Julien…" The rational part of Cinn's brain screamed to stop him, to push his head away, halt the path of feather-light kisses that were circling his hip bone. That fragment of resistance soon short-circuited however, silenced by Julien scraping his teeth along his sensitive skin, the waves of euphoric shivers erasing each and every thought from his mind.

"You just promised me you didn't bite," Cinn half gasped.

Julien looked up, grey eyes dual tempests. "*Oui*. But those sorts of promises are made to be broken."

Holy fuck.

With panther-like grace and power, Julien climbed upward, until his head hovered above his, consuming his vision. Cinn's head spun in dizzying waves as his heart beat impossibly fast.

Julien placed a teasing kiss upon his jaw, before he had time to stop him.

That wasn't right; he didn't *want* to stop Julien.

But he *needed* to stop Julien.

"We should—"

He was silenced by his mouth, soft yet firm, insistent yet tender.

He pushed him back, just an inch. Looked him in the eye to say, "Julien. Listen. We can't just keep kissing like this."

A tiny kiss on the corner of his mouth.

"Why not?"

"I told you in Paris."

"We did plenty more than kiss in Paris." As if to emphasise his point, Julien rubbed Cinn's overtly hard cock through his jeans, and Cinn threw his hand to his mouth to suppress his groan. *Please let Darcy be back in her basement somehow.* How had Julien tricked him so easily into this unsupervised space?

"Don't do that," he said, but the desire seeping through his words was laughable.

"You don't sound particularly convincing right now."

Using his elbows to wiggle backwards, Cinn dragged himself up so he was semi-upright. "Okay, yes, let's talk Paris. Where we did plenty more *without* kissing, and then you told me you didn't do relationships."

Silent for an eternity, Julien seemed to be on the edge of some sort of precipice, holding the weight of his potential words on his tongue, before finally whispering, "Well, some promises are made to be broken."

Time suspended. Each of Cinn's heartbeats battled with the gravity of the statement. In this moment, it was only the two of them in the universe, two damaged souls being increasingly entwined in a fragile dance of possibilities.

He wanted nothing more than to swallow Julien's words, let them burrow inside him and allow his growing attraction to him to bloom into something concrete, something real.

There was one question looming large that Cinn couldn't move past, however: *What if you just want me because you can't have me?*

Julien didn't do relationships. Cinn wasn't special. Apparently Julien had no qualms about dropping his lovers like discarded toys.

So how long would Cinn hold his attention for once he'd given in?

Their worlds were too different, silk and sand. Julien's, a world of motecraft, ambition, art, science, control. Cinn's... He was simply trying to carve out a piece of this crazy life for himself. Build a fortress of his own design.

Julien was silent, awaiting his response with a shocking amount of patience, for him. Expectation burned in his eyes. Expectation, desire and... was that the tiniest whisper of fear?

Questions danced on Cinn's tongue. *Why me? Why now? And why don't you do relationships, anyway?*

A series of sounds from the corridor: the cottage's front door being opened with a click, the bang of it being shut, Elliot's voice shouting hello.

Saved by the bell.

There was the smallest window of time for Cinn to shuffle away from Julien, and for Julien to grab the ink and paintbrush, to hold it convincingly in mid air when Darcy threw open the bedroom door.

"How have you not finished yet?"

A guilty flush was surely written all over Cinn's face, even if Julien's composed mask remained in place, so he threw his head back onto the mattress.

"I've almost finished," Julien said.

"Looks like it."

Darcy left again, leaving the bedroom door wide open.

Wordlessly, Julien propped open the book against a pillow, and began his task, eyes flicking between the rune-like pictures and his canvas, Cinn's skin.

Closing his eyes, Cinn focused only on the cool sensation of the ink against his muscles. He slowed down his breathing, forcing his heart to do the same.

He soon heard the soft muted pop of the stopper being placed back into the bottle, and the book being snapped shut. He sat up to find Julien looking at him, but not like before. Warmth had replaced desire, and a crinkle in his eyes had replaced his wolfish smile.

"Thank you again for doing this," Julien said, placing his hand on top of Cinn's. "I can't explain how grateful I am."

Julien's sincere words caused another shred of doubt to slide into him: what if Julien was leading him on only so that he kept helping him? The notion twisted his insides into knots, and words tumbled out of him before he could clamp his mouth shut. "This isn't why you keep..." He couldn't quite say it, so finished up with, "Right?"

Julien's face froze, eyes wide, as he pieced together the intended question. He removed his hand from Cinn's so fast, it was as if he'd burned him. "*Merde!* How could you think that?" His hurt was so evident that

Cinn instantly wanted to claw the words back, turn the pain inwards on himself. "Who do you think I am?"

Before Cinn could gather himself to apologise or explain, Julien stormed out of the room.

"You fucking idiot," Cinn mumbled to Béatrice's ceiling.

Once Cinn climbed onto the dining room table, all that was left to do was bind Béatrice's rib bone to him. Ready with her mortar full of powered luminaquartz, Darcy held in her other hand the canvas bag she'd placed the bone into, back in Paris.

She looked between the two objects in her hand until Julien gently released her from both of them. "It's my turn."

Cinn had forgotten about the apparent need to use saliva to turn the powder into a paste, so his stomach gave a lurch when Julien spat into the mortar before using the pestle to mix it together. Julien was going to have to rub his spit into the part of Cinn's stomach outlined with the inked circle. But then he supposed he'd had far more involvement with his other bodily fluids, so this should pale in comparison.

If their bedroom conversation hadn't ended so poorly, Cinn might have found Julien's fingers back on him sensual, but Julien completed the task with precision and haste.

When the rib bone came out of the bag, he couldn't help but stare at it in the light of day. It appeared delicate yet robust, its ivory-white, subtle curvature gleaming gently. He'd held it in his hands, that night he'd snapped it from Béatrice's corpse. The sickening sound of its reluctant yield would be one he carried to his own grave.

The moment he'd jumped down into the casket and surveyed Béatrice's skeleton in its entirety was something he'd never forget. Layers of silky blue material forming a puffy dress, encasing off-white bones that mapped out the body of a girl so loved they'd dug her grave up.

It had certainly been an experience he was glad he'd spared Julien from.

As Julien scooped the rest of the paste onto his fingers to spread on the rib, the slightest shake to his hand gave him away. Elliot attempted to take over, reaching his hands out towards him, but Julien batted him away, finishing the job quickly and pressing the rib to Cinn's stomach.

"Sorry. Is that okay?" Julien asked Cinn without looking at him.

Cinn removed his gold band. "It's fine. I'm ready."

Darcy came forward and wiggled a bottle of creamy lotion at him. "I've got this ready for if the ink starts to react with your skin again. And here." She presented the stimulant, the vile-tasting crystal powder for him to rub into his gums. He licked his finger before pressing it into the tin.

"See you on the other side," he said to the three tense faces. Julien opened his mouth, on the verge of saying something, but Cinn quickly swiped the crystals around his mouth and sank back onto the table.

He'd accidentally consumed far more of the powder than last time, and he felt it. A gasp tore out of him as his adrenaline levels shot up alarmingly quickly, every nerve tingling with a sudden surge of electric intensity, his heart pounding in his chest like a thunderous drumbeat.

The others might have been expressing concern, but he couldn't hear them, the familiar low buzzing the only sound. The world greyed. Cinn closed his eyes and let himself fall. Let himself slip.

Twenty-Three

CINN

When he awoke, not to his ruined red hellscape city, but instead into a field of daisies, the tiniest shard of disappointment threaded through the realisation. Even though the shadowrealm London was not the slice of home he'd ideally want to visit, he couldn't deny his excitement at recognising it last time, and starting to unravel its mysteries.

So, where exactly was he, then?

He climbed to his feet. The field was vast, an expanse of white flowers that stretched for a mile. The bright sun warmed his bare back, while a light breeze pleasantly brushed across the ground, sending the daisies waving back and forth.

All that was missing was an ice cream, and he'd be set for a nice afternoon.

Shame that he was here to interrogate a dead woman.

He spun, about to choose a direction at random, when a childlike laugh came bursting out from a treeline on his right.

"Béatrice?" he called, and was rewarded with another gleeful laugh.

Moving quickly, he darted towards the sound, entering the crowded thicket of trees. A sense of urgency enveloped him. Sunlight played hide-and-seek through the leaves overhead as he wove between towering trunks, a rhythmic crunch of twigs beneath his hurried footsteps.

Every time he thought he was about to close in on the laugh, it sounded again, equidistant from him.

Then, he saw it: a flash of white fabric that disappeared behind a large pine tree. He shouted her name again to no avail—she was gone by the time he reached it.

Gritting his teeth, he pressed forward. If he woke up and had to tell the others he'd spent the entire trip lost in a forest, he'd not be pleased.

A soft, golden glow began to filter through a diminishing canopy. Sunlight hit on an earthy path, as if revealing it to him. Emerging from the woodland shadows, he found himself on the threshold of another green expanse, this time a vast greenery alive with a sea of poppies, scarlet petals greeting him with their dancing wave.

More laughter, but this time more than one voice. He squinted across the field to spot three figures in the distance. Taking tentative steps towards them, he soon saw a family: two blonde children, around ten years or so, sat on a red checkered picnic blanket, on either side of a beautiful blonde woman, vaguely recognisable from Béatrice's locket. Their mother.

Was this a memory, or an imagined projection from Béatrice? He hoped it was the former. The trio's enjoyment of the day was irrefutable—Julien was merrily munching on an apple, legs kicked out, looking up at the clouds as they drifted languidly across the blue sky.

If only it had all stayed this way for you.

As expected, neither Julien nor his mother looked Cinn's way as he approached them. They wouldn't be able to see him—he'd learnt that the hard way during his first handful of trips. He turned to Béatrice, who was plucking poppies from the field and placing them in a pile on her white dress.

Her head snapped up to him, her grey eyes so similar to Julien's, he was momentarily stunned.

"What took you so long?" she said.

Before he could reply, she'd jumped to her feet and sprinted off. Not sparing a second, Cinn charged after her, fully prepared to tackle the small girl to the ground, if that's what it took.

She was fast, but he was faster.

Grabbing on to the back of her dress, he yanked her backwards. Her small body stumbled backwards, touching his. He reached to gently wrap his arms around her, her sun-kissed skin warm.

A single intake of breath and an ethereal energy pulsed through her into him. She continued to fall backwards, impossibly further *into* him, the boundaries between their forms blurring.

Then he wasn't in a field. He was Béatrice, eleven years old, hiding under a table, behind a tablecloth. He was terrified. Terrified of the glimpse of feet he saw pounding across the floor. *Père,* her voice said in his head. *Don't let him find me.*

"*Où est-elle?*" her father said. Where is she?

And then another set of feet came into view, and another voice—familiar, albeit younger. Julien. Their father repeated the question, but Julien seemed unwilling to give the answer he desired.

As Béatrice, his heart hammered with fear and guilt. He needed to come out from under the table. He needed to help Julien, before it was too late.

Then Julien's feet were being lifted off the ground to be shaken like a rag doll, and all Béatrice could do was to press her fist into her mouth and silently scream. *Julien*!

Another pair of shoes thundered into the small sliver of floor, attached to thin legs. A woman's voice unleashing a distressed series of French curses.

Then the legs went flying off to the right.

Reality flickered.

The sun was back.

He was back in Paris, on the bank of the Seine, if the glimpse of the Notre-Dame towers were anything to go by.

He—Béatrice—was older now, thirteen, and was sitting with their back pressed against someone. He turned to find Julien again, his shock of blond waves longer, his boyish face offering a glimpse into its future form. Julien smiled his dual-dimpled grin at Béatrice, before returning to his task: sketching the river. As his hand flew across his drawing pad, the slightest hint of his tongue poked out.

He shuffled back around to return to pressing his back against him, savouring the peaceful afternoon. Gazing up at the beaming sun, he desired to stay here forever, in this tiny slice of happiness.

Maybe it was because he already knew he wouldn't cope with whatever came next.

The dread started in the pit of his stomach, growing until it consumed every piece of him. He opened his mouth to protest, to say something to stop Béatrice from taking them away from this place. Because where they were off to next was the worst day of her life. He could feel it.

"Please," he whispered, shutting his eyes.

The gentle sounds of the river and Julien's pencils faded away, replaced by a growing hum.

When Cinn pried his eyes open, there was a crimson lattice adorning his palms. The sound of someone sobbing—Julien, of course it was Julien—tore his eyes up to find him, barely older than in the last memory. This Julien screamed, a horrific sound of pure devastation, as he sat by the unmoving body of their mother, who was face down on a tiled floor.

All around them lay debris, the air thick with dust and acrid smoke, assaulting his eyes and making them water. Forcing himself to look through the haze offered glimpses of stained-glass shards across splintered pews, their vibrant colours muted by layers of grime. It was only when Cinn looked up to see the splintering beams of the vaulted ceiling shaking above them that their location became clear: they were inside a large church, its once-grand architecture now crumbling around them.

Béatrice was injured. One leg in particular throbbed, and he held it limp behind him as he forced her body to move towards Julien, whose face was pure devastation as he shook his mother and screamed nonsensical things in French.

"It's okay," Cinn tried to say as he attempted to place his arms around him.

Julien shoved him off, sending Béatrice tumbling backwards onto a shard of fractured stone.

"Julien," Cinn croaked, as tears freely poured down his cheeks. Béatrice's cheeks. "I'm so sorry."

He climbed to his feet on shaking legs, stepping towards Julien again, this time kneeling behind him to wrap his arms around his stomach. Julien's whole-body sobs reverberated through his embrace, each shuddering breath piercing a knife a little deeper into Cinn's own heart.

"Tout ça c'est ma faute!" Julien screamed. It's all my fault.

"No!" Cinn said. "Don't say that."

Julien continued to sob in his arms.

Pressing his face against Julien's back, Cinn squeezed his eyes shut, inwardly demanding to Béatrice that it was time to leave.

She agreed. Julien's warm body faded from his grasp, and Cinn felt its loss like a tooth.

Cinn had lost Julien, but he'd lost Béatrice, too. He felt her drift out of him, leaving him empty. Sightless, he drifted through an eternity of time and space. Everything was fluid, formless, a boundless expanse of intangible whispers he couldn't quite grip on to.

Then, wetness.

Wetness under his face, his hands, his body. He reached out to grab a handful of sand. He'd washed ashore, somewhere. A dark beach, lit only by starlight.

He stood up, instantly dry, and strode towards Béatrice, sitting alone on a rock. Just them this time, then. Behind her rose a towering cliff, its sharp edges jagged.

She was crying, knees drawn up, head in her lap.

"Hey," Cinn said, touching her shoulder. There was no response, and a jolt of anxiety shot through him—what if she couldn't see him now? He studied her. An adult now, far taller, and with even longer golden hair. "Béatrice. Listen. We might not have much time. Julien has sent me."

At the mention of Julien's name, her breath hitched, but she didn't pull her head up, only continued with her soft sniffles. Sighing, Cinn threw himself down on the sand next to her, facing the ocean. Its smooth waves gently lapped the beach, its expansive depths reflecting the blanket of stars above.

Stars.

He twisted, reaching up to cup her head with two hands. "Though my soul may set in darkness, it will rise in perfect light. I have loved the stars too truly to be fearful of the night," he recited.

A gasp. Béatrice's muscles tensed. And then, she lifted her head up to face him.

"Who are you?" she whispered.

"A friend of Julien's. And Darcy's, and Elliot's."

A single tear trickled down her cheek. "I miss them so much. It's cold here. And lonely."

"They miss you too," he croaked. "Have you just been... here the whole time?"

A faraway look entered her eyes as she stared at the sea. "I've been... lots of places."

He felt the tiniest tug within him, the smallest signal that his time here was drawing to a close. "I need to ask you some questions, Béatrice. Julien believes that your death wasn't an accident." Béatrice did know she was dead, yes? Cinn tensed, but no reaction came. "He wants to find out if you know anything that might help him. Help us."

Béatrice said nothing for a long time, and Cinn itched with impatience. But then, from under her patchwork jumper, she brought out her locket. "It was this," she said, gripping it tight in her fist.

"Your locket? How?"

"Something was wrong with it that day." She opened her hand to show him the metal oval, turning the side adorned with the moon and stars over to the back, the metal charred black and warped. Just like he'd always seen it. "I was up in the mountain. Trying to find survivors." Cinn frowned, recalling the hazy details of the aid mission she was on. "I found one of those... dark creatures up there. It... it—" She cut herself off with a choke.

"An umbraphage?" he said. This was new information, as far as he could remember.

"I started channelling and that's when it happened. The locket... did something to me." Her face crumpled. "I'm sorry. I'm finding it hard to remember."

"Take your time," he said, even though they had only moments left, he was sure of it.

"It was like it was taking all my power and amplifying it. But it was too much. Then, I was floating. Then, I was... burning," she whispered, horrified, looking down at her arms as if she could see phantom flames still licking her skin.

"What was wrong with your locket? Do you know?"

She shook her head.

"Had you noticed anything odd about it before?"

Another shake. "I rarely took it off. I don't know what happened to it."

A giant tug within him, lurching his consciousness back to reality. *No. Not yet.*

There was one more question he couldn't leave without asking, even if the answer would kill Julien. "Béatrice, what was your involvement with the Arcane Purifiers?"

She blinked at him.

"Could they have done this—murdered you?"

"What? Why would they do that?"

"Julien found a note in your diary. It marked the day they attacked Auri. You have to tell me. Were you working *for* them, or against them?"

A silence. A breath held in anticipation.

"Is Julien going to be very angry with me?" she asked, her grey eyes as wide as the moon. "When he finds out?"

Cinn grabbed hold of both her hands. "No. Julien loves you very much."

She suddenly stood, dragging him up with her. "Don't leave me here. Take me back with you."

Stunned, it took him a moment to reply. "Béatrice, I can't."

"You can. I can feel it."

"They've warded my body with this ink stuff. It won't let me bring anything back with me."

"Please, just *try*," she said, more tears streaming down her face. "I don't want to be here by myself."

"Okay," he said, to appease her, and she threw herself into his arms, clutching him tightly to her, burying her face into his neck.

He tipped his head back at the night sky. The stars shimmered, brightening. Then he noticed a shadowmote, dancing above Béatrice's head.

"Where have you been?" he whispered to it, holding out a hand. Another appeared, then another, and soon there was a tornado of darkness encircling the pair of them.

They were the eye of the storm.

Cocooned in a tempest of shadows.

The shadowmotes' pace increased, and so did Cinn's grip on this reality. He pressed Béatrice tightly to him, as the shadowmotes circled ever closer to them, until they were brushing up against them, a rush of wind and black.

Then, they were spinning, spinning alongside the shadowmotes.

Spinning, spinning, spinning.

Twenty-Four

JULIEN

T he grandfather clock in the corner of the dining room chimed eight p.m.

Darcy wandered back into the room from the kitchen. "Still dead to the world?"

"Yup. He's putting *me* to sleep now." Elliot yawned, slumping backwards on his chair.

Julien's eyes flicked straight back to Cinn. "I think he's twitching more. Look."

"You said that five times already." They fell back into silence until Elliot said in a soft, low voice, "I'm not blind, you know." He nodded to Cinn.

Oh God. Julien knew this was coming sooner or later, but the sudden lurch into this conversation threw him.

"Hmm?"

Darcy quickly slipped back out of the room.

"I can see the way you look at him. That he looks at you."

A moment of deafening silence.

"I'm sorry," Julien eventually whispered, more to the floor than Elliot, unable to bear any hurt in his best friend's eyes.

"You've got nothing to be sorry for. He's a cool dude. I like him. So much, in fact, I want him to stick around." Elliot's tone spelled out a clear message underneath his words. "But if there is something going on, I would rather you didn't hide it from me."

Julien nodded, and Elliot quietly stood up and walked out, leaving him alone with Cinn.

Exhaling a heavy, shaky breath, Julien moved closer to him. Asleep, he looked years younger, the stresses of life washed away from his face, leaving a boyish innocence in its wake. A freckle on his right eyelid that Julien hadn't noticed before drew his attention. He brushed his finger over it, lightly tugging it upwards towards the tiny metal bar that shot through his eyebrow.

Julien tucked some of Cinn's chestnut waves back up under his new beanie, running his thumb over the ribbed cuff. He smiled. Cinn had worn it every possible moment since he'd given it to him.

Mission success.

Of course, Julien definitely *hadn't* spent almost two hours browsing high-end clothing boutiques before finding this perfect hat on a corner market stall.

He'd definitely *not* spent an age considering how the beautiful shade of olive green would complement the earthiness of his hazel eyes.

And his heart definitely *did not* beat impossibly fast when he'd awaited Cinn's reaction to it.

"Julien, why are you touching him?" Darcy snapped from behind him, making him jump. "Just leave him alone."

Elliot's laugh almost distracted him from noticing Cinn twitch again, a brief spasm that raised his torso from the wooden table. Julien pressed two fingers against Cinn's neck, feeling the strong pulse of his increasing heart rate.

Another twitch, the tiniest of moans escaping Cinn's lips.

In the space of a blink, the symbols Julien drew earlier faded away, the ink seemingly absorbed to leave behind a blank canvas of light-brown skin.

"*Non!* What's happening? Darcy, put the band back on him, now!"

Darcy lunged for the golden bangle but froze when a strange sound emanated from Cinn's mouth. A cross between a cough and a grunt, Cinn's unconscious form abruptly heaved, as if he was choking.

"What the hell?" muttered Elliot.

"Turn him over," Julien called out, and rushed to do just that.

"The recovery position!" shouted Darcy, but Julien and Elliot only blinked in response. "Oh, for goodness sake," she snapped, pushing Julien out of the way to bend Cinn's arms and legs, creating a contoured L-shape.

His strange seizing continued, his eyelids fluttering slightly ajar. "I think he's coming back," said Julien, relief pouring into his voice.

One more almighty cough, and then miniscule flecks of darkness came bursting out of his mouth all at once, a thousand or more floating balls, impossibly emitting the darkest form of light.

Stunned, Julien could only watch as they appeared to organise, swirling and glueing together to fashion some sort of shape.

"Shadowmotes?" Darcy flinched away from them. "But—"

They all gasped as the shape became distinctively animalistic. Four legs, three tails. Two ears. A writhing shadow-creature of darkness, although only a small one. A touch bigger than the average cat, and still expanding, the shadowmotes multiplying to create a denser form.

It stopped.

It arched its back in an unmistakably feline way. Cocked its head—a subtle elongation to its jaw, shallow dips where eyeballs should be—at them.

"Uh... guys? What the fuck is that?"

Only now realising they'd left Cinn unattended on the table, Julien spun to find him sitting up, pale, eyes wide and stunned. Then he slid to the floor, crossing the room, hand extended.

"Don't touch it!" hissed Julien, reaching out to stop him.

"It's... it's Béatrice!" Cinn said.

Julien laughed, manic and high-pitched.

"No, really, it is!"

Julien studied the eyeless monster, which was crouched low to the floor now, ears flattened as its head flicked between them. It hissed, an eerie, guttural sound that no normal animal would be able to produce. Then, with one final snort, it spun and darted into the kitchen, using its four legs in sinuous, shadowy strides.

Cinn threw himself towards it, but his legs gave way, sending his knees to hit the wooden floor with a heavy thud.

Julien rushed to his side, jumping out of the way of the other two, who charged after it.

"It's gone out through the window!" Darcy shrieked. "Get it!"

Then there was the click of the back door handle and the pounding of Darcy and Elliot's footsteps fading as they chased the creature.

Still on the floor, Julien heaved on Cinn's arm to pull him up. There was still a slight tremble in his legs.

"Sorry. I always forget it takes a while for my body to behave again," he muttered.

Julien pushed him towards a chair, and when he was seated, he could wait no longer. "So what happened? Did you find her?"

"Yes," Cinn said, and the relief that coursed through Julien was enough to almost knock him to the ground. "I did."

"*Merci,*" Julien breathed, pressing his palms together.

"I had to chase her for a while. She was a little girl, in a white dress. I watched you guys have a picnic in a field. Then we went on a... trip through some of her other memories for a while." Julien tensed. "You were in them. Every single one." Cinn stared directly into his eyes. Swallowed as if choked with emotion. "She loved you so much, Julien. I could feel it."

A prickle of goosebumps tingled across the back of Julien's neck. "Which... memories did you see?"

Julien waited as Cinn considered what to relay to him, his hesitation obvious.

There were so many miserable memories he and Béatrice had experienced together and then, of course, there was the icing on the cake.

Please, please, not that one.

Cinn rose from the chair, then gently clutched Julien's arm. "I didn't realise—" he started in a whisper, but Julien raised his hand.

"*Please*," he said, begging him with his eyes. "I can't right now."

Nodding, Cinn kept hold of him. "Okay," he whispered, then pressed a quick kiss to Julien's forehead, before offering him a shy smile and ducking his head.

The intimate gesture froze Julien momentarily, knocked him off kilter. Before he had a chance to recover, there were footsteps in the hall—Elliot and Darcy had returned.

"She's miles gone by now, little minx," said Darcy, panting and shaking her head. "Not a chance in hell we're catching her. Maybe we should buy some cat food, leave it out?"

Elliot snorted, folding his arms. "I'm *not* convinced it's Béatrice."

"It *is*," said Cinn. "I know it's her. They *felt* the same. Had the same energy."

At Elliot's raised eyebrow, Julien said, "If Cinn says it's her, then we'll have to believe him." He glared at him to close the matter.

"Obviously, you'd want to believe it," Elliot protested.

"I'm not sure I'd want to believe that Béatrice has returned to us as some sort of eyeless cat demon thing," Julien said, voice raised. He wasn't in the mood to argue.

Darcy stepped into the middle of them. "Let's not worry about it right now. I'm sure whatever it is isn't dangerous," she said, looking far less than sure. "We can ask... someone about it. I'll do some reading."

Ushering them all into her living room, Darcy poured them out some tea she'd brewed while Cinn was gone. This trip had taken him almost six hours. Julien had remained at the table, watching the rise and fall of his sleeping body, tensing at his every twitch, whereas Darcy had eventually gotten restless and wandered around her cottage.

Cinn collapsed in the emerald armchair, exhaustion evident, plain as day. A shiver tore through his body.

Julien touched the back of his hand. "You're freezing. Come sit by the fire."

An eye roll. "I'm fine."

Julien grabbed the blue blanket that was spread across Darcy's sofa to drape it around Cinn's shoulders. Cinn pulled it around him, mumbling his thanks without looking at him, tiny rosy splotches dotting his cheeks.

Julien sat on the rug by his feet, and as he looked up at him, he was struck by the memory of this same arrangement on the day they'd met him. A lifetime ago now. If he could go back in time to that moment, what would he say to himself?

This one is different.

Don't fuck it up.

"So, you talked to her then?" asked Elliot. "Tell us what happened."

Cinn sighed, wiping his hand over his face. Then he opened his mouth and began his tale.

A field of daisies, a field of poppies. A picnic Julien couldn't remember, as idyllic as it sounded. That was okay. He would love to pretend that it had happened.

A tapestry of memories, briefly outlined, with several glances at Julien throughout, asking, *is this okay to share?*

Cinn kindly summarised the final memory as 'the day their mother died'. Yes, it was the day their mother died. However, it was also the day a piece of him died, too. A day that altered his future in countless ways. It was the end of his childhood.

When Cinn described talking to Béatrice on a star-filled beach, Julien edged closer towards him, every muscle tense from anticipating what might finally be revealed. Listening to his recount, the Béatrice he'd described meeting didn't sound quite right. She sounded too... childlike. And clearly, she was somewhat confused.

Some information had been gleaned, however. Julien held up Béatrice's locket as Cinn relayed what she'd said about it.

"So, her locket was tampered with?" Julien wondered aloud, brushing his finger over the damaged side. "It's what caused her to..." *channel so many motes that she burst into flames.* "If that's true, then it fits with the difficulty I had getting the locket to be released to me. Someone high up was blocking the request."

Darcy slid off the sofa to inspect it. "But who could have done that if she never took it off?"

Cinn leaned forward. "How did she get to wherever she was? What country was it again?"

"The Philippines."

"She might have taken it off to use the Baths?"

"Oh!" gasped Darcy. "They didn't travel directly to the Philippines. They don't have any receiver baths there." Darcy's eyes came alive in the way they only did when she was on the verge of solving a puzzle. "I'm pretty sure the entire aid taskforce was displaced to the Ho Chi Minh Baths, in Vietnam. Then they would have flown across the ocean, I think. So you're right, Cinn!"

Julien wanted to kiss her. And kiss Cinn. Though that wasn't anything unusual.

"Their stuff would have followed by cargo plane a day later," said Julien. "Plenty of time for someone to tamper with it."

"But *what* did they do to it?" Elliot drummed his foot against the floor. "That's the question."

Yes, in addition to who, and why. And all of the other millions of questions that still remained.

Julien's gaze returned to Cinn. "Was there anything else about the locket?"

He shook his head.

Julien steeled himself. "And did you ask about... the Arcane Purifiers?"

Cinn's face shifted subtly as he controlled his expression, but gave himself away by biting his lip. Clenching his fists together, Julien pressed until he could feel the sting of his fingernails.

"I did. She didn't want to tell me anything about them. I mentioned the attack on Auri, and then she asked if you were angry with her."

A sudden lump in his throat had Julien turning to face the fire, unwilling to allow the others to see the emotions that were brimming underneath his surface, threatening to spill.

A hand fell upon his shoulder. "Hey. Come with me for a cigarette?"

Julien rose to follow Cinn out of the room, the pair remaining silent all the way to the garden bench.

There was only one cigarette left in the packet that Cinn offered him. Julien lit it, inhaled, then passed it to Cinn.

Cinn leaned back against the bench, blowing rings of smoke into the sky. "I'll never get over being able to see the stars here," he said dreamily. "I didn't know what I was missing in London."

"They're beautiful," Julien murmured in response, forcing his gaze up to appreciate them, and their gentle twinkle calmed him at once.

"I told Béatrice that you weren't angry at her at all. I told her how much you loved her."

Julien swallowed. "Thank you." The thought of her alone in death believing that was too much to bear.

"Do you think we can help her... move on, eventually?"

Cinn snorted. "What, into 'the light'? I did try that for a bit, a few years after I started slipping. None of the ghosts I've ever spoken to have ever seen any light. I don't think it's actually a thing. Anyway, apparently she wants to be an ugly cat for a bit, anyway."

"She didn't really like cats," Julien mused. "She liked dogs more."

"Well, an eyeless dog would be even more terrifying, so I'm glad she went cat."

Julien considered him, smiling. Cinn grinned back, and for a stretching moment, they remained like that, two paralysed statues, each awaiting the other's next move.

Then Cinn shuffled across the bench towards Julien to hook his ankle around his. "I'm sorry about earlier. When I accused you of only wanting to fuck me so that I'd keep trying to reach Béatrice."

Julien flinched at the memory, the crass language. "Maybe it's not entirely your fault. I clearly don't always give off the right impression."

"No—"

Silencing Cinn by grabbing his hand, Julien continued, "I want to clarify that it's one hundred percent *not* the case. I have many, many reasons for wanting to fuck you, and none of them are related to my sister." Julien interlaced their fingers. *Besides, I want to do so much more than fuck you, beautiful boy.*

Cinn flicked the remnants of the dead cigarette into the ashtray. "What sort of reasons?"

His eyes were molten pools of gold that Julien wanted to swim in. Closing the space between them, Julien tugged on Cinn's hat.

"Your beanie look is kind of cute, even though that grey one was so ratty and definitely needed a wash." *Preferably burn it, and keep my one on your head forever.*

A cackle of laughter, eyes sparkling with delight. "Wow, your bar is really low if all it takes is a ratty beanie hat."

Julien dropped his hand to cup Cinn's cheek, stroking his bottom lip with his thumb. "Your smile is fucking gorgeous."

Cinn wasn't laughing now. He was staring at Julien like he was the first one to ever say that to him. And Julien hoped desperately that it was true.

Clutching Cinn's baggy hoodie, he continued, "You dress like a ragamuffin but I sort of love it. And you've got a heart of gold. So much purer than mine could ever be."

Julien brushed his knuckles across Cinn's jaw, relishing the way his eyelashes fluttered closed in response.

"You call me out on my shit. You see me." *And I think, if I managed to let you in, you'd make me feel safe.*

Cinn licked his lips, opening his mouth to respond.

The shrill screech of Darcy's house phone sounded from the open kitchen window. Three crisps rings, then the faintest *'hello?'*.

"I... don't know what to say to this," Cinn eventually whispered into the space between them. He buried his head in his hands.

Say that you'll give me a chance. That you'll let me try.

The back door flew open, and Darcy leaned out of the frame to shout, "Cinn, it's for you."

Jerking backwards as if electrocuted, Cinn spluttered, "What? Me?"

An uneasy feeling came over Julien, an inexplicable sense of dread.

"Your friend Tyler must have written down this number at some point, because now this guy Bradley is on the line."

The feeling intensified.

"What does he want?" asked Cinn, jumping to his feet.

Julien was one step behind Cinn all the way to the living room.

He watched as Cinn picked up the red receiver from its rotary telephone base.

Then he paced up and down, the one sided snippets of conversation he overheard sending his brain spiralling.

"What did he do?"

"Fuck, they took *all* of it?"

"Is he hurt? Is he in danger?"

Darcy grabbed Julien's wrist as he passed her on his frantic path around her living room. "Julien, sit down," she hissed. "What's wrong with you?"

He stared at her, not understanding how she could be so calm.

Then Cinn's phone call appeared to wrap up, with him promising, "I'll be there as quickly as possible."

What? Would he? Where? London?

And if he went there, would he come back?

When Cinn hung up the phone, face pale and ashen, Julien announced in a rush, "I'm coming."

Cinn blinked, then shook his head slowly as Elliot and Darcy glanced at each other. He ignored them. They'd come. He needed them.

"Tyler's fucked up. I don't know all the details, but he somehow ended up owing Heino Richter money again. He was dealing for him again and then somehow lost a lot of product." He sat back on the armchair and slammed his fist into the soft armrest. "*Goddamn* it!"

Darcy flew to his side even quicker than Julien. "Don't worry," she said. "We can send some more money."

"No, I need to go there. ASAP. Apparently, he's in a state, and asking for me. He's hurt. Richter is out for blood this time. But it's okay. I don't expect you guys to come with me." He looked between them and the slightest glimmer of hope in his eyes said otherwise.

"We'll all come," said Julien, putting force behind his words. There was no way Cinn was going to London alone to drag his ex out of danger. He'd like to finally meet Tyler face to face, anyway. The man taking centre stage in so many of his stories. The man that made Cinn constantly worry about him. The man he'd do anything for.

"Elliot?"

Elliot slowly nodded. "I'd miss a training session, then some work shifts," he said. "But if it's that important..."

"As much as I hate to miss out, I really think someone needs to stay here and keep looking for that... *cat*. Or at least be listening out for any news of... cat attacks." Darcy grimaced, twitching back her living-room curtain as if the creature would be right outside, waiting to be let in. "I'm tempted to say we need to turn ourselves in, but we might have a lot of explaining to do." She turned to Cinn. "Beside, I wouldn't be terribly useful in London. Definitely take Elliot, though. I'd worry if you didn't."

Darcy's words were a sudden jagged knife slice across his skin. They were true—Elliot could keep them safe in ways Julien could never—but it stung, nevertheless.

"Thank you," said Cinn, looking between them all, a small smile playing on his lips that Julien itched to trace over with his fingers. "I would love for you to come."

Twenty-Five

JULIEN

The London Underground wasn't as bad as Julien feared. It certainly wasn't as dirty as the Paris Metro and also had significantly fewer people rudely barging into you.

Their flight landed an hour late, catapulting them straight into the five p.m. rush hour. Julien had tried to reason with Cinn, citing the benefits of taking a black cab, but he'd rolled his eyes and headed straight for the underground sign. When Elliot smirked and followed Cinn, Julien knew the battle had been lost.

As they descended onto the platform, the distant rumble of an approaching train echoed through the tunnels, accompanied by the distinct smell of grease and an announcement shouting at them to mind the gap over and over. Flickering fluorescent lights overhead bathed the diverse mix of commuters in a surreal glow.

When they finally pushed their way into an overcrowded carriage, Julien tentatively clutched the slightly damp handrail. "How long are we on this thing for?" he said, making no effort to stop his nose wrinkling in distaste.

"All the way to the end of the Northern Line, High Barnet."

The train came to an abrupt halt, sending Julien's body jerking forwards.

"Think you can survive that long, princeling?" Cinn's eyes sparkled.

"What? *Princeling?*"

Cinn only laughed.

Scowling, Julien jumped out of the way of a throng of people now pushing their way off the carriage.

Cinn, gliding in between the moving crowd like water through fingertips, said, "There are seats now, so stop your tantrum."

Elliot howled with laughter, and Julien wondered at what point he was going to have to intervene with the union they'd clearly formed, one that took great joy in teaming up against him.

The carriage was still packed, forcing Elliot to sit a few seats down from the two Cinn and Julien took, side by side. He instantly struck up a conversation with a stranger who was carrying a motorcycle helmet.

"How does he do that?" asked Cinn, with a slow shake of his head.

"*Why* does he do that?" replied Julien.

Cinn snorted, then rubbed his hand over his face and slumped back into his seat.

"Are you okay?"

"Just anxious to get there and see what the situation is."

"What do you think we're going to find?"

"Sounds like he's deep in it this time. Both the drugs and his debt to Heino Richter."

"Have you ever met him?"

Julien conjured images of Cinn with the heinous crime lord he'd heard a bit about, but he couldn't quite make it work.

"Once. When I was helping Tyler clear his last debt, and I agreed to his plan of letting his men rob Rosewood's safe."

Cinn's eyes shot straight to his shoes, and he rubbed the back of his neck.

"I'm sure it seemed like a good idea at the time," Julien said, in lieu of his actual thoughts on the matter, which was quite the opposite. To Cinn's credit, his loyalty to those who he cared about certainly knew no bounds.

"It helped that although I loved the team at the restaurant, the owner was a wanker. I kind of figured he could claim the money back on insurance. Serves him right for paying us minimum wage on twelve-hour shifts with stupidly short breaks."

Julien brushed his hand over Cinn's. "I'm not judging your decisions, honestly."

"Thanks." Cinn's smile didn't meet his eyes. "I judge myself enough for both of us, though. I ended up killing four people, after all."

"The murderous ghost did," Julien corrected.

Cinn didn't argue, only slumped back further into the seat, arms folded.

Diverting the topic, Julien said, "Has Tyler ever sought professional help? For his addiction?"

Eyeing Julien warily, Cinn answered. "He's been in a few free programs. It's hard to get into them, and they're quick to kick you out for any reason under the sun."

The line further emptied, leaving the seats opposite them free. Julien's gaze flicked to Elliot, but he was waxing lyrical about motorbike tyres.

"*Oui*, I'm sure, but he can't continue to rely on you to drag him out of his shit every time he fucks up."

He'd said the wrong thing by far. The look on Cinn's face chilled him. "I don't mind him relying on me. I never have. I'll always be there if he needs me." He narrowed his eyes. "I told you that you didn't have to come with me for this, you know."

But if him relying on you ends up with you being coerced into committing crimes, surely it's time for you to rethink your approach.

"I only meant that Tyler needs to learn to stand on his own two feet."

"Yeah, of course, and I'm trying to get him there."

By dropping everything to save the day for him, every single time?

He knew that he should bite his tongue, but Julien couldn't resist replying, "But what if he needs to be allowed to fall before he can learn to pick himself up?"

A red flush burst across Cinn's face, and that was how Julien knew he had gone too far.

"*Fall*? You think he hasn't fallen enough already? Christ, Julien, you have no idea what it's like to watch someone you care about spiral downwards again and again, hitting every damn rock on the way. So no, I won't watch him crash and burn just because of some twisted sense of tough love. This isn't about letting him fall. It's about lifting him up when he's too damn broken to stand on his own. You've clearly been lucky enough that you've never been in the position of loving someone drowning in their own demons, so you're in no position to judge."

Stunned into silence, Julien could only stare at the blackness rushing past them outside of the window. A few lines of defence threatened to escape his mouth, but he swallowed them.

There was one question ricocheting around his mind that refused to be silenced, however. He studied Cinn's reflection in the darkened glass across from them, asking the question, "Do you still love him?" Every fibre of his being held a breath in anticipation, every muscle in his face tensed, a perfect blank mask that would show no reaction to Cinn's answer.

Fiddling with the drawstring of his hoodie, Cinn exhaled a breath, then said, "Tyler's my blood. Have I even told you that we met in juvie? Anyway, he saved me in there. I wouldn't have made it through without him. We grew up together, that year we spent in Feltham, then the years that followed. I'll always feel connected to him in some way. But to answer your question, no. It's not like that between us any longer. Hasn't been in years." Cinn hesitated before continuing, "For me, at least."

Julien allowed some of the tension to dissipate from his body. "Does he still love you?"

Cinn took a moment. "In a complicated way, maybe? His attachment to me is all wrapped up in how much we depended on each other in the past. He's never been able to move on with his life like I have. He had an even shittier start to life than me, though," Cinn said forcefully, as if demanding Julien believe him. "It fucked him up more than you could ever imagine."

Julien offered one sharp nod, pursing his lips together.

"And he wants to get clean. He really does."

"I'm sure," Julien said.

Continuing to study their dual reflection in the window, the realisation hit him—he was now only a handful of minutes away from finally meeting this fabled Tyler. And he could only guess at what sort of opinion Tyler would have of him. He didn't give a damn, but what would Tyler say to Cinn about him? And what if he somehow convinced Cinn that he needed to return to London ASAP?

"You get that it's completely over between us, right? In that way?" Cinn said quietly, almost inaudible amongst the noise of the carriage. "You don't need to be..."

Their eyes locked upon one another in the reflection. *Jealous.* The unspoken word hung in the air, its toxic tendrils poisoning the atmosphere.

Julien didn't do *jealous*. After all, you couldn't possibly get jealous if you never had relationships.

"I'm not," Julien replied, dripping confidence into every syllable, turning to flash Cinn his wolfish smile.

Of course he wasn't. He didn't need to be. Cinn wanted him. He saw it in every quick glance towards him when Cinn thought he wasn't looking, the way his eyes sparked with desire whenever they touched, the way he fell into step with Julien whenever they walked, his arms brushing his on every other stride. He saw it whenever he pulled on his olive-green beanie, the tiniest of smiles gracing his lips as he positioned it on his head.

Cinn wanted him, and as soon as they flew home, Julien was going to show him exactly how much he wanted him in return.

Three knocks on the door, followed by silence.

"Sure we've got the right address?" asked Elliot, eyebrows crinkled as he scanned the dilapidated exterior of the small block of flats. An array of small windows, all dark, sat above window sills featuring peeling layers of glossy paint.

The curtain of the window nearest to them twitched. Moments later, heavy footsteps sounded behind the door. Julien hovered behind Cinn with Elliot, shuffling his weight from one foot to the next.

The door opened a crack.

Then flew wide.

"Buns! You came!" A young man stood in the doorway. He ran his hand over his buzz-cut blond hair. "I knew you would."

Elliot snorted. "Buns? Please don't tell me... like, cinnamon buns?"

The man grinned, friendly and warm. "Gave 'im that name his first day with us. He never did make them for us though, eh, Buns?"

Cinn groaned and let out a tired sigh. "Please forget you heard that immediately."

After clutching Cinn to him with a whack on the back, the stranger reached out his hand to shake Julien's. "Bradley. Cheers for coming all the way here."

Bradley. *Bradley Harrison.* The name Cinn had given him, to transfer the money Tyler needed.

After following Bradley down a tiny corridor to the interior entrance to his flat, they were shepherded into a small kitchen. The room was a chaotic blend of mismatched dishes piled precariously in the sink, crumbs scattered across a chipped linoleum floor, and faded wallpaper peeling at the corners. A burnt toast smell hung in the air, even though it was almost eight p.m.

Julien pushed himself against a cupboard, hard pressed for standing space. The flat wasn't warm; all three of them kept their coats on.

Bradley flicked his kettle on, then turned to them. "So, you're that Julien, eh? Tyler often talks to Cinn in here." Bradley nodded towards a phone on the wall. "Your name crops up a lot," he continued, giving Julien a mischievous look that he interpreted as, *not that Tyler enjoys it.*

Bradley turned to Cinn, flashing him a grin. "Tyler's been tight-lipped as ever about what the devil you're up to in Switzerland. All hush-hush, is it?" His gaze shifted between Julien and Elliot, a touch of scrutiny in his eyes.

"Something like that," Cinn said uneasily.

"Well, beats heading back to the slammer, I reckon," Bradley remarked with a sigh. "I was proper gutted when I heard you got pinched. As for Tyler, mate, let me tell you, he was crushed. Took off like the wind, and I didn't lay eyes on him for days."

"Where is he now?" Cinn rifled through Bradley's cupboard, producing four chipped mugs.

Bradley's eyes darkened. "I'm sorry to tell you that Richter's got him. That bastard. I warned Tyler a thousand times to steer clear of dealing for him again. But did he listen? Hell, no. Stupid fucker. I would throttle him, if Richter wasn't doing it for me, anyway." Bradley banged his fist against the counter. Perhaps Julien would have an ally in Bradley.

"What do you mean, Richter's *got* him?" Elliot said. "As in, he's locked him up somewhere?"

"Somewhere, yeah. He grabbed him off the street yesterday. I told him not to leave the house as well. No clue where he is. I keep my nose well clear of that world now." A hint of bitterness tinged Bradley's tone. "I only got the information about Richter grabbing him through a friend of a friend."

Cinn passed out the mugs of tea he'd made, then closed his eyes in a dreamlike state to take a sip. Julien almost laughed. Apparently, any tea bag they found for him in Switzerland wasn't the same.

Cinn set his mug down, then leaned against the table, crinkling his forehead. "I think I know someone who can relay a message to Richter. A kid that works for him. I was with Tyler when he spoke to him a few times. We can head out in a minute, see if he's at his usual spot."

"Worth a try, then," said Elliot, who glanced at the door, clearly already wanting to be free of the claustrophobic kitchen.

"You lot can crash here tonight," Bradley offered, and Cinn promptly expressed his gratitude, leaving Julien little room to politely decline. Elliot shot him a panicked look, but Julien shrugged in defeat. There was no way he was leaving Cinn here unprotected. "There's a single in Tyler's room, then there's a sofa and a floor."

Bradley opened the kitchen window and lit a cigarette, blowing the smoke out into the cool night air.

"Alright. We'll be back later, then," said Cinn. "Thanks, mate." Draining the last of his drink, Cinn yawned before heading to the door, tugging his beanie further down on his head.

Once they were back in the freezing, early December chill, Julien and Elliot trailed behind Cinn as he marched them through numerous residential streets and a small play park to reach the top of a high street.

"Oh!" said Elliot. "There's a fish and chip shop over there."

The smell of grease wafted out from a shop that had a sign more battered than the fish they sold.

"We're not here to play tourist, Elliot," said Julien, but Cinn's eyes lit up.

"I love that one! Maybe we can bring that kid some chips to butter him up."

"Butter him up? What is he, toast?"

Cinn rolled his eyes and headed straight into Cod on the Corner. El-liot shot Julien a smug, victorious smile. Yes, intervention was definitely going to be needed.

The takeaway restaurant was at least warm from the fryers. Julien studied the menu. Several of the price labels had fallen down.

"Why would you want your peas mushy?" Julien hissed into Cinn's ear. "And what on earth are 'scraps'?" When he reached the battered sausage, he groaned. "*Mon ami*, please don't tell me these are all typical English delicacies?"

Beside him, Cinn shook with laughter. "I'm ordering for you."

"I'm honestly not hungry," Julien pleaded, but Cinn ignored him, reeling off a list of menu items.

When he was finished, they huddled in the corner to wait, watching the steam blur the view out of the window. A loud, stern lady soon shouted at them that their order was ready. Cinn passed Julien a small greasy box, a tub of dark sauce, and a wooden fork. He eyed the cutlery with disdain, its cheap splintered edges seeming likely to leave him with a mouthful of wood.

Julien raised an eyebrow at the gloopy curry sauce, handing it back to Cinn with a bemused expression. "I'm *not* putting curry with fries," he declared firmly.

Elliot snatched it out of Cinn's hands. "You guys ever tried deep-fried pickles? I've only ever found them back in the states."

"I fear my taste buds are not prepared for such transatlantic eccentric-ities. Let's go find our friend then," Julien said. The server was glaring at them for taking up valuable space.

He opened his box to find a surprising top layer of cheese. Certainly a bizarre choice. Underneath, the fries were far too chunky and salty for his taste, and drenched in vinegar, of all things, but Julien still wolfed them down—they hadn't eaten any dinner. Cinn led the way all the way through the high street to a supermarket car park. He paused near a trolley stand.

"I think that's him over there," Cinn said quietly, jerking his head subtly towards two figures lurking by a bush. "Let me do the talking."

"What are you afraid I'll say?"

"Pretty much anything," Cinn replied, and Elliot snorted.

As they approached the pair of youths, Cinn slowed his steps. The duo, a girl and boy, instantly stopped their conversation to study the three of them.

"Hey, mate. George, right?" said Cinn, stepping under a streetlamp to reveal himself clearly. "I doubt you'll remember me. I'm Tyler's friend."

The girl maintained a suspicious gaze, but George flashed a smile. "Course I remember you. You're that geezer who lent me a tenner. Need it back?"

Cinn shook his head and raised the paper bag. "I've come with an offering of chips in exchange for a favour. Tyler's in trouble with Richter again. You still working for him?"

George eagerly accepted the bag, opening the box and handing it to the girl. She used her bare hands to scoop a large mouthful up. Julien stared at the pair of them, who couldn't be much older than sixteen. They were dressed well enough, but their faces were slightly gaunt.

"Yeah. I heard about Tyler. Can't believe he fucked up again. The story is that he was lugging around enough white to fill a damn swimming pool, but some slick crew rolled up and snatched it right from under his nose." Even though there was nobody around, George dropped his voice to continue, "Richter's proper pissed at him, mate. He owes him big time now. I'm worried for him, man. You know what happened to Hawk, don't you?"

"What?"

"Let's just say Hawk's wings got clipped real short. The skies won't be the same for him now."

Cinn flinched. Did he know this Hawk fellow? Julien moved closer to him, and George's eyes flicked to him and Elliot.

"Who are your mates, anyway?" George asked, wariness colouring his voice.

"They're here to help Tyler. Think you can get a message to Richter for us? We need to tell him we'll get him the money."

George snorted, shoving a chip into his mouth. "You sure about that? I reckon it's a hell of a lot more than last time."

The girl, grease all over her lips, added, "I dunno if you wanna stick your nose in. He's really cutting loose right now. It's not just Hawk that's felt it. Word is on the street that he's taken care of this woman named Sally. She was his girl, until she tried to leave him."

"Taken care of?" Julien said, and the girl flinched. Cinn shot him a warning look.

"She was my mate's mate. Nobody has heard from her in weeks."

"What did the police say?" asked Julien, and George and the girl burst into laughter.

George grinned. "Where did you find this one, mate?"

"It's a valid question," said Elliot.

The girl eyed him with interest. "You American?"

Cinn glared at Julien and Elliot as if to say, *I told you not to open your mouths.*

"The police are *looking into it,*" the girl mumbled through her final mouthful of chips.

"We need a time and place from Richter. We'll meet him and Tyler with cash. That's the deal."

George leaned back, a sly grin on his face. "Time and place, eh? Sounds like this is a rush job. I could head there right now, but I'd lose money if I left this spot."

Dear George didn't seem to be teeming with customers, but Julien bit back that retort to say, "We can cover your loss for the evening, I'm sure."

When Cinn didn't protest, Julien found his wallet. Luckily, they'd had the sense to exchange some money at the airport. As he handed over a handful of twenty-pound notes, George's sleeve shuffled far enough up his arm to reveal a line of purple bruises.

George's eyes widened in surprise at the amount, which he quickly tried to cover. "That *should* do it."

"That will *definitely* do it," said Cinn. "We'll come back here at noon tomorrow for his response." He paused. "Roughly how much money are we talking?"

"About thirty I'd say?"

Cinn failed to hide his reaction—he grimaced, then bit his lip.

"Shall I tell Richter that might be a problem?"

Julien brushed up against Cinn's arm. "No. And don't tell him anything about us that you don't need to."

George nodded, and then he and the girl headed off into the shadows.

Elliot filled their space. "Are they actually going to come back here at noon tomorrow, or will they go on a bender with that hundred pounds?"

"They'll be back. He's a good mate of Tyler's. He'll want to get him free."

"Did you see those bruises on his arms?" Julien mused. "They looked nasty."

Cinn shot him a dejected look. "At least he's not dead or half-dead like Sally and Hawk."

"This guy can't be just walking around killing people! What is George even doing, working for a man like that?"

"Know any ethical kingpins?" Cinn said, then snorted. "In his world, things aren't that simple."

As the wind picked up, Elliot wrapped his coat further around him. "So, are we actually going to give that monster a load of cash, or are we going to give him his just deserts? You know which option I'd prefer, Julien."

A worried frown crossed Cinn's face. "You guys don't need to have any more involvement. I can—" He hesitated. "*Borrow* the cash from you and meet him by myself. It's easier if we don't cause trouble."

"Not a chance," said Elliot before Julien could. "We'll all go, and I'm more than happy to have a nice long *conversation* with our friend Richter."

"What about Auri?" asked Cinn. "Would they be cool with that?"

Elliot shrugged. "How would they find out? Don't you want to see that fucker punished for what he's doing?" He looked to Julien for backup.

"We are *not* killing him, Elliot," Julien said, pressing his mouth into a firm line. "Cinn's right. We can't take that risk. Let's go back to that flat and come up with a plan. I'm sure we can find a way to sort this."

The relieved smile Cinn gave him sent a comforting wave through Julien; the warmth radiating from him permeating through Julien's ice-cold skin. As they fell into step, Cinn's hand brushed against Julien's several times before Julien grabbed it, squeezing it tightly, then ran his thumb over it reassuringly.

"This will all be over soon," he murmured into his ear.

Cinn didn't reply, but leaned into Julien's side to nudge his head against his, the simple gesture so intimate it made Julien's breath catch in his throat, his heart stumble, his mind whirl with possibilities.

Twenty-Six

CINN

Noon came, and noon went.

The three of them resorted to perching on the pavement on the edge of the supermarket car park, watching shoppers push trolleys for entertainment.

Well, the other two were. Cinn was bobbing along to the Fugees on his Walkman.

Until his battery ran out mid-song.

He dragged his headphones down to hang around his neck.

"He's even later than I usually am." Elliot tapped his watch. "It's almost two."

How much longer should Cinn give it before he admitted George wasn't coming back? He sighed, dropping his head between his legs. This whole day was turning into a nightmare.

Earlier, Julien had used the phone in Bradley's kitchen to contact his bank in France, causing Cinn no end of guilt. Demanding such a large sum of money be released to a foreign bank wasn't a simple action, if the clipped tone of Julien's French was anything to go by.

"Here." Julien's voice made him lift his head up. He offered Cinn a cigarette, which he accepted with grateful fingers.

Elliot rolled his shoulders, clicking his back. He'd drawn the short straw and ended up on the floor last night. "Shall we give it another hour, then call it?"

Cinn forced himself to nod in agreement. He couldn't make them sit outside on the pavement all day for someone that may never come. Then he saw him—dressed in dark clothes, hood up, crossing the car park to reach them. Cinn leapt up. "Shit, that's him!"

George was alone today. In the stark light of day, the unhealthy pinch of his face was more evident. Deep bags ran under his eyes. He offered Cinn a weak smile. "Sorry I'm late, mate. I had a long one last night. Here's everything you need."

Passing him a scrap of paper, George spun on his heels, and was walking away from them before Cinn had time to reply.

The paper held a scribbled address on it, a North London postcode that Cinn didn't recognise. Then, a time: nine p.m. Then, a figure: £50,000.

Julien let out a low whistle. "Reckon that kid told him how desperate you were?"

More likely, the hundred pounds Julien had so freely handed over had made George think that there was plenty more where that came from.

"Is that going to be a problem?" Cinn's whole body tensed. "God, I'm so sorry," he added, closing his eyes. This entire experience of practically begging Julien for money was mortifying.

Elliot punched his arm. "Dude, chill out. Julien doesn't give a shit about spending Montaigne wealth. His shithead father is at least good for one thing."

A cool gaze settled over Julien's face. "You know I don't rely on him for money," he snapped. "I haven't since I left for university. However, you're right in that it's not a problem. We will have to go and talk to the bank."

Three Tube stops later found them outside a large building, whose ornate stone facade exuded wealth. According to Julien, this bank was partnered with his one in France. "Stay here," he muttered, face set in determination, and went to join the long queue alone.

"What's the chance we'll hear angry French cursing in approximately ten minutes?" said Elliot.

It took double that before Julien re-emerged, footsteps heavy, face a scowl. A large padded envelope was now in his hands. "They would only give me ten thousand. Apparently that was very generous of them, and they made a special exception for me, as I'm such a loyal client of their partner bank. Anything more and it'll be a couple of days' wait."

"Looks like we'll be going with Plan B then." Elliot smiled like the cat that got the cream.

Cinn didn't share his enthusiasm. He'd only had one encounter with Heino Richter before, and the memory of his venomous, snake-like smile still turned his stomach. "We better go get ready."

Hovering at the edge of an industrial estate, Cinn re-examined the piece of paper. "It's that warehouse there," he said, nodding to a large single-storey building ahead of them, its corrugated metal exterior glinting in the moonlight.

Julien grabbed his arm before Cinn could take another step. "Remember the codewords?"

Cinn nodded. He didn't realise he was biting his lip until Julien tugged it free with gentle, lingering fingers.

"It's not too late to back out. We could tell Richter we need more time to get the money together."

What if Richter thought they would fail to come up with it? Cinn hadn't had a spare fifty grand the last time they'd met. Or worse, what if Richter realised they were organising a plot against him? Better to launch in now and take him by surprise than to drag this whole thing out...

"It'll be fine," said Elliot, who sounded almost bored.

"You do crazy shit like this for a living, Elliot," Julien snapped. "Give us a second."

"I'm usually part of a team sent to arrest moteblessed criminals. This is going to be a walk in the park compared to that. You two stay here, and I'll be back with Tyler in five."

"*Non!* We'll be burying bodies until three a.m. if you go in there by yourself, I know it."

Cinn picked up the duffle bag from the ground and left them to cross the quiet expanse of the estate, hoping they'd follow. Seconds later, Julien wrenched the bag out of his hand.

The three of them crept around the side of the building to find a doorbell. Elliot pressed it once, hard. An eerie hush descended as they waited.

A side door clicked open, a bear-sized man emerging. It was the man who'd escorted Cinn to Richter last time, in a different location. The man nodded, then beckoned another man outside.

"Arms up," the new one barked, and all three of them obliged them in their pat down.

"What's in the rucksack?"

Julien handed it to him to rifle through, and Cinn prayed that none of the items in it warranted suspicion. He'd packed a load of junk in it, in addition to the one item that mattered.

"That other bag the cash?"

With gloved hands, Julien quickly unzipped a tiny portion of the duffle bag to flash the men some notes. It seemed to appease them, and one held the door ajar for them to enter.

The spacious warehouse appeared to be a storage unit, when it wasn't serving as a drug lord's lair. Following Richter's men through a maze of shelves and crates, they eventually reached the other side. A blue door, light seeping out from under its crack, awaited them. The burly man took position outside of it, hand resting lazily on his belt. What weapons was he concealing?

"Buns?"

Cinn spun so fast he got whiplash. There, in the corner, slumped against a wooden box, was Tyler. Cinn was on the floor next to him before he took his next breath.

With unfocused eyes, Tyler reached out for his hand. "They came outta nowhere. Cobra's crew. They jumped me. No idea how they clocked I had all the white on me. Some fucker must have tipped them off."

That many sentences at once seemed to exhaust Tyler's energy; his head dropped against the crate. A piece of rope around his wrists that was attached to the crate was his only restraint—clearly he wasn't much of a flight risk in this state. A sheen of perspiration covered his forehead, and there was a slight tremor to his leg. Withdrawal. Now wasn't the time for lectures though. They could come later.

"Course I came. Julien and Elliot did too."

Tyler's hazy eyes flicked over to them. His mouth twitched downwards ever so slightly, and Cinn's stress levels further increased—hopefully Tyler wasn't about to embarrass him by saying anything even vaguely insulting about the two people about to literally save his life.

"They're lending me the money." Cinn raised his eyebrows at Tyler to impart a clear message.

Tyler nodded to them. "Class. We'll get it back to them."

"Richter will see you now," one man announced behind him. "Through the door."

A hand squeezed onto Cinn's shoulder. "I'll sit here with him," said Julien. "Take Elliot in with you."

Cinn hesitated—was that arrangement the best idea?—but having no other solutions, he climbed to his feet to head to the blue door, with Elliot stuck to him like glue.

Heino Richter was just as intimidating on this occasion as when they'd met before. Even though he was sitting on an office chair, his stature felt imposing, his steely gaze and salt-and-pepper beard betraying years of calculated ruthlessness that Cinn knew too much about. Dressed in a tailored suit that only amplified his authority, he exuded a quiet power that demanded respect.

The larger of Heino's men had followed them in, and now clicked the door closed. The cramped office was lit only by a single dim dangling bulb illuminating everything in a subdued glow. Stacks of boxes labelled with ambiguous codes surrounded a weathered mahogany desk cluttered with ledgers. Was this a regular meeting spot for Richter?

Cinn exchanged a quick glance with Elliot, who, despite his bravado earlier, seemed slightly rattled as they awaited Richter's greeting.

Richter didn't smile, didn't nod, only leaned back in his leather chair, fingers plucking a cigar from a metal box on the desk, whilst maintaining complete eye contact with Cinn.

Cinn swallowed, but met his gaze unwaveringly. *Don't give them an inch, Cinn.* It was Tyler's mantra that had got him through that year in prison and some of the hard times after. And now he was here to save his best friend, hopefully for the last time.

With a flick of his gold-plated lighter, Richter brought the flame to life, casting an amber glow on his face as he took a contemplative puff, fragrant smoke curling around him.

"So," he began, and Cinn wanted to cry in relief. "Here we are again, young Cinnamon Saunders. Our last transaction didn't exactly unfold as anticipated, did it? A stumble in the dance of business, my friend."

Cinn remained silent. Elliot, almost imperceptibly, moved closer to him.

"I didn't get my funds, and two of my finest associates met an untimely end," Richter stated cooly, his gaze piercing through the smoke-filled room.

Cinn snorted. "Ronnie and Spiky? Your *best* men? Anyway, I got the money to you, just a few days later."

"Yes, yes. Your diligence was certainly appreciated. But what I truly want to know." Richter leaned forwards, eyes drilling into Cinn's. "Is what exactly transpired that night at Rosewood Parlour? Four corpses, you tagged with murder, and then, poof!" Richter blew a plume of smoke at him. "You're released, scot-free."

"There was a miscommunication." Cinn set his jaw in a hard line.

"And has this miscommunication anything to do with your fancy new friends, Cinnamon?"

Cinn stepped forward. "I'm not interested in idle chit-chat. I've got the money in a bag. This is the deal: we hand it over, and Tyler never works for you again. None of your dealers will sell to him, even. He goes free, has a proper chance at getting clean this time."

Richter chuckled, a hollow, unpleasant sound. "You're aware he's the one pleading at my door every time, aren't you? It's not my fault he has the unfortunate habit of screwing up his line of credit repeatedly. I promise nothing. This is business, Cinnamon, supply and demand. There are always those that will win, and those that will lose. Loyalty is rewarded, and stupidity is punished."

A surge of fury consumed Cinn. "Like that kid, George, who you've got dealing for you? How did he get those bruises on his arms? Stupidity? And that girl Sally? What about her?"

Richter's laugh was unbearably loud. "Do you fancy yourself the saviour of every fuck-up in North London now, Cinnamon? And I thought you saved all of your hero complex for your faggot boyfriend."

If Cinn had harboured any small doubts about their plan, they vanished like mist.

He hadn't done much good for the world in his short life so far, but he could stop Richter from ruining any more lives.

A soft, strangled sound from Elliot, then, "You're a real piece of shit."

"Let's just get this over with," said Cinn, before Elliot decided to derail the scheme by exploding Richter's brain. He nodded at the door. "The money's outside. Let's make the exchange."

Twenty-Seven

JULIEN

J ulien studied the scrawny man tied to the crate.

The one he'd just witnessed Cinn fawn over, despite being the one to endanger them all. Tyler had assumed Cinn would come to his rescue, and he had. The guy hadn't even seemed that grateful, when Cinn was *risking his life* for him. When he and Elliot had dropped everything—including his dead sister's possible reincarnation into a demon cat—to help him, a stranger to them.

Julien clenched his jaw.

They hadn't said much to each other in the minutes since Cinn and Elliot had gone through the door. That was okay. Julien had very little to say to him.

Tyler's tangled dark blond hair hung over a pale face that was resting on one knee. He lifted his head up to say, "You're the one that wired over that money."

Is that... supposed to be a thank you?

Play the game, Julien, play the game.

Julien smiled. *"Oui."*

"The friend he's trying to help. With the dead sister."

"That's me." *The friend with the dead sister, apparently.*

Tyler coughed, an audible rasp to his breath. "So, when is Buns allowed to come home then?"

Julien's skin prickled. *Home is there, now. Home is us.*

"Surely you guys can't keep him in Switzerland forever?"

"He's told you what he's doing there. Auri is helping him learn more about himself." Julien didn't bother to hide his look of distaste. And then, because he'd let this infuriating man rattle him, he added, "Maybe you shouldn't assume he wants to come back."

Tyler lurched forward as far as the rope would let him. Julien glanced at the remaining guard, who seemed unbothered by their little spat.

"Of course he wants to come back. His life is here."

"Is it? I'm not sure his restaurant would rehire him after he robbed it for you."

If looks could kill, Julien would be dead meat.

Thankfully, at that moment, the door swung open, and Cinn emerged with Elliot and, presumably, the infamous Heino Richter. He instantly reminded Julien of his father: unyielding, untouchable. Someone who always got what they wanted.

Cinn's eyes shot straight to Julien's, a tiny but unmistakable smile on his lips when their gazes met. "It's cold in here," he said, the slightest hint of emphasis on the word *cold*.

"*Oui,*" Julien replied, crouching down to unzip the duffle bag with his gloved hands. Then, he positioned a certain couple of bank notes *just so*, so they would be the first ones to be touched. He kicked the bag into the middle of the concrete floor.

As predicted, Richter nodded towards it, and his two henchmen scurried over to it. Kneeling on the floor, one lifted the stacks of notes out of the bag, and then passed it to the other.

Perfect. Better than they'd hoped for, in fact, with *two* of them touching the money.

Moments later, one lifted his head, forehead crinkled. "Sir, there's no way this is fifty G. It's mostly—"

Newspapers. However, the man didn't get to finish his sentence, as his body fell slack. He crumpled back into himself, then tipped over onto the floor, eyes blinking in surprise. Soon, all he'd be able to do was blink, if he was lucky.

A round of shocked gasps from Richter and Tyler.

"Wh—" the other one managed, before finding himself in a similar fate. He dropped the stack of money he was holding. The stack with the slight dusting of white powder to the notes.

Thanks, girl. Darcy's ultra-concentrated Frostbite compound had come through, just as promised.

"Reynolds! Mitchell!" Heino Richter shouted, and for a moment Julien presumed they were the names of the fallen men, until he heard two pairs of footsteps pounding towards them through the warehouse.

Fuck.

"Elliot!" Julien shouted, already moving to Cinn, pushing him against the wall to stand firmly in front of him.

The overhead strips of fluorescent lights flickered as Elliot threw his arms wide. Sparks rained down upon them as he drew upon the lights, channelling every lumenmote he could towards him.

But the lights were weak—narrow, dim strips that barely lit the warehouse, and time was not on their side.

Two more men burst into the space, looking straight to Richter for direction.

"Kill them all," was the only thing he uttered.

With his entire weight, Julien pressed a cursing and very much resisting Cinn further back into the wall. Richter's backup security, knives glinting in their hands, looked between their fallen comrades and the three unarmed assailants with evident confusion before moving towards Elliot and Julien.

Julien's eyes darted to Elliot, face crumpled in pure concentration.

A part of Julien ached to reach for the motes himself, so close, so within reach. His body longed to feel them coursing through him. It would be so easy. They were right there, waiting for him. Julien's arms twitched, reaching up...

With an almighty crash, Elliot brought one of the light fixtures down from the ceiling, knocking one man down to the ground. Then, a flick of two wrists sent the lumenmotes he'd cultivated bursting in two directions—at the remaining gang member, and Richter himself.

An unseen current gripped their muscles, and tremors rippled through their frames, from the tips of their limbs to their cores. Collapsing to the ground, their bodies twitched with involuntary, jittery movements.

Tyler let out a low whistle, the first action of his that Julien approved of.

Cinn pushed Julien off him with a grunt. "I literally couldn't breathe, you freak." Though as Julien turned to face him, there was a tender softness to his expression that told a different tale.

With his trainer, Cinn nudged the shoulder of one of the men who'd been electrocuted. "What did the lumenmotes do?"

"Elliot converted them to electromagnetic waves to shock them." Something that Julien had done himself many times, in the controlled practice sessions of his youth. "They better not be dead, Elliot."

A smirk in response. "As if I don't have perfect control. Fuck, Richter had a gun on him," Elliot said, nodding to the handgun that lay on the floor.

"We'll dispose of that." Julien shoved it into the duffle bag, then retrieved his rucksack from near Tyler. Theoretically, he could have untied the guy at the same time, but he was busy. Busy sorting out his mess.

"Good thing Darcy didn't come," said Elliot. "She'd have *freaked* at all that."

Julien was pretty ruffled himself, adrenaline still freely jabbing at his beating heart. He rummaged in his bag to find what he was looking for.

To a casual observer, it was an oddly shaped metal headpiece.

To motetech experts, it was a powerful memory disrupter.

Elliot grabbed the nearest unconscious man under the shoulders to pull up upright.

"What the bloody hell are you up to?"

Ignoring Tyler, Julien continued to install the LMD onto the man's head. "Still up for what we agreed?" he asked Cinn, who nodded once, face set.

The Lumimeld Memory Disrupter was never *designed* to tamper with long-term memories. It had only been formally approved for memories obtained within the last twenty-four hours.

That didn't mean it couldn't be wielded for a range of purposes, in the right hands.

Connecting the headband to the palm-sized battery-powered controller, Julien began to charge the LMD.

Cinn, after untying Tyler, came to crouch down beside Julien. "So, they'll all wake up with no idea who they are, even?" he asked quietly.

"*Oui*. That's the plan. Let's hope they still have enough brain cells for bodily functions."

Cinn's face clouded as he stared at Julien's first victim, whose head was vibrating as the LMD worked its magic. "I don't give a shit about Richter, but these other men... We don't know their stories."

Oh, precious Cinn and his goddamn eternally caring nature. What was he going to do with him?

Julien turned down the dial.

It took fifty minutes to do all five of them. Julien took pleasure only in the one he'd saved for last: Heino Richter. Once he was done with them, Elliot and Cinn carried the bodies outside and dragged them to various parts of the industrial estate, in the hope they'd wake up separately.

Finally, it was done. He didn't even bother suggesting to Cinn they at least wipe the last twenty-four hours from Tyler's mind—he already knew what his response would be. Cinn had trusted Tyler to keep his own moteblessed ability a secret since he'd confided in him—Julien would have to hope Tyler would extend them the same courtesy.

Tyler, who'd been rather quiet throughout the whole thing, remained sheepish on the Tube journey back to the flat—hood up, eyes downcast unless Cinn spoke to him.

Now they'd accomplished what they'd come here to do, how much longer would they have to stay in London?

Silently filing into Bradley's kitchen, exhaustion was evident on everyone's faces. For a sickening moment, Julien imagined Cinn suggesting he and Tyler share Tyler's single bed, but then they found the note from Bradley, a scribbled message about working the night shift, and offering his room.

In a bizarre show of domesticity—considering they'd just taken down one of London's notorious drug lords—they took turns brushing their teeth in Bradley's tiny yet spotlessly clean bathroom.

Julien opened the door to let Cinn in, then flinched in surprise as he shut it behind him, bolting the door.

"Everyth—"

He didn't get to finish his question: Cinn's tongue in his mouth was a slight barrier to further speech.

Stumbling backwards, Julien's back hit the glass pane of the shower as Cinn pressed into him, his hands sliding around his back to grip his ass, hard.

When Cinn let out a tiny moan, Julien wedged his thigh in between Cinn's legs, and he quickly rolled his hips into him. Cinn then dragged his mouth from Julien's lips, to nuzzle his light stubble with his soft cheek.

"Thank you," Cinn whispered. "You don't know how grateful I am to you and Elliot."

"You're doing a great job of showing me," Julien quipped. Turns out saving someone's ex-boyfriend could be a well-rewarded venture. Good to know. "I hope that Elliot will be getting a slightly more condensed version of this thank-you message."

Laughing, Cinn leaned back in for another hungry kiss that had Julien's knees softening. Julien savoured the last lingering touch of Cinn's soft, velvety lips as he pulled away, savoured every inch of his shaky breathlessness.

Julien wrapped his arms around Cinn's back. "Where are you going? I was just about to turn on the shower. To cover up all the noise you're going to make."

One light squeeze of Cinn's hard length through his jeans had him falling further against him, Julien's name whispered on his lips.

Julien slid one hand up Cinn's arm to interlace their fingers before trailing a line of kisses up his jaw. "I can be quick this time. I promise."

Cinn's temptation to give in was almost tangible, but he groaned, letting his forehead fall against Julien's. "Don't make this harder than it already is," he said, grabbing Julien's wrist and placing it on his chest to wedge it between them. "Tomorrow," Cinn breathed into his ear. "Straight from the airport. Your house. It's closer. And it better be anything but quick."

Julien brought his hand up to run his thumb over the cuff of Cinn's green beanie hat.

"I'll make it worth the wait," Cinn continued, capturing Julien's hand to place his thumb into his mouth.

Three bangs on the bathroom door, followed by Elliot's gruff voice. Cinn didn't even flinch, didn't take his eyes off Julien's as his tongue licked slow circles into his thumb.

It was the single most erotic thing Julien had ever done with his clothes on. His dick gave a needy twitch, and for a brief moment he considered begging, a first for him.

With wide-eyed innocence, Cinn released Julien's thumb with a small pop of his mouth, a string of saliva following it.

"For fuck's sake!" Elliot snarled, followed by another bang. "You better not be doing what I think you're doing."

Julien pushed past Cinn and unbolted the door to reveal a grouchy-looking Elliot. "Since when is communal teeth brushing a crime?"

"When you're brushing each other's teeth with your mouths. Get the fuck out."

Cinn, flushed gorgeously pink, ducked his head as he exited the bathroom.

They hovered together in the corridor, outside Bradley's room, where Cinn was sleeping.

"Tomorrow," mouthed Julien.

The corner of Cinn's lips tilted up into a slow, soft smile. He stared unblinking at Julien as if he'd said something profound.

"Tomorrow," Cinn promised.

Tomorrow, and tomorrow, and tomorrow, Julien could only dream.

Twenty-Eight

Julien

The bitter scent of decidedly instant coffee, so kindly handed to him by Elliot, was Julien's rude awakening the next morning. If that wasn't bad enough, Elliot then delivered the delightful news that Cinn and Tyler had left the house to go on a walk together.

This resulted in Julien stress-cleaning Bradley's kitchen for him. At least someone would benefit from his strained mood. He stole a handful of tea bags for Cinn as payment for his efforts.

After an age, the front door clicked. Laughter filled the corridor.

"I just borrowed Bradley's phone to book our flight. It leaves in four hours," Julien informed Cinn when he and Tyler entered the kitchen, rosy-cheeked and windswept.

"Already? You just got back!" Tyler spun to face Cinn, clutching the sleeve of his hoodie.

Cinn's face crumpled. "We'll sort out that plan for you to come visit Auri, remember?"

Well, that's something to look forward to.

Julien said, "We'd stay longer, but we have a rather urgent cat problem to attend to, I'm afraid." *Amongst other things.*

Then, they only had an hour to kill before their taxi—Julien refused to even consider the underground again, pleading possible delays.

Cinn and Tyler were alone in the living room together when the black cab rolled up slightly down the road. As Julien entered, he caught the tail end of something like 'that posh French tosser' being muttered.

"Taxi's here."

Cinn and Tyler rose to their feet, with Tyler looking extremely displeased.

After shaking Tyler's hand as quickly as possible, Julien said, "Say thank you to Bradley for us?" Their generous host hadn't returned. Which was probably for the best, as Julien had got a little carried away reorganising his kitchen.

"See you soon, Buns," Tyler whispered emphatically, as he scooped Cinn towards him for a massive bear hug. Julien left them to hover in the corridor. The corridor which was decidedly unsoundproofed.

"This is it, Buns. From today, I'm clean. I'm cutting it all out. All of it. I swear to you."

Julien coughed loudly, which brought them both out.

Finally, bags shouldered, Julien followed Cinn and Elliot out of the flat. The other two were partway down the road when Julien froze at the entrance to the apartment block. He'd forgotten something—that slip of paper he'd scribbled down the flight booking reference on, then left next to the phonebook.

"*Putain!*" Julien cursed under his breath, and spun around to run back for it. By a stroke of luck, the front door to Bradley's flat was slightly ajar.

Please let Tyler have gone into his room.

No such luck. He was sitting at the kitchen counter on a bar stool, a packet of rolling tobacco in front of him. And a lighter. And a tiny plastic bag of *something*, something that quickly disappeared into his pocket as he looked up to glare at Julien.

Julien shook his head, turning quickly to hide his displeasure at Tyler breaking his promise to Cinn literally one minute after he'd left. "Just needed this paper," he said, holding it up.

"I wasn't actually going to take it," said Tyler. "Before you run to him and tell him lies."

Of course you weren't.

A calm rage consumed him, repressing any second thoughts, any *logical* thoughts, about what he was about to do.

"You know what? Here." Julien tossed the black duffle onto the kitchen floor. The one with around nine thousand pounds in it—the money from the bank sans the Frostbite-laden wads they'd disposed of. "Take this. If you care about Cinn at all, then you'll use it to check yourself into rehab and sort your life out so he doesn't have to fucking worry about you every day of his life."

Tyler stared at him. "He's heading back here to me in London as soon as he can, you know. Told me this morning."

You fucking liar!

Julien smiled his politest smile. "Oh, really?"

"I said as much yesterday, didn't I?"

It was the glint in Tyler's eyes and his stupidly smug, so-sure face that made Julien's temper flare to uncontrollable levels—bright, angry tendrils that began in his chest, and quickly wormed their way upwards to control his tongue.

One hollow laugh escaped Julien's lips. "Honestly, Tyler, I'd start moving on if I were you. I'm not sure what you think you heard, but he's not going anywhere. He belongs at Auri now, with us." And then, perhaps because his utter adoration of Cinn had fried the rational part of his brain, and perhaps because the look of pure determination on Tyler's face threatened his very core, he added, "He's mine now."

Julien pivoted so quickly his head spun as he fled the kitchen before anything else could happen, like a fistfight.

Although, if it came to it, he could take on Tyler with his eyes closed...

"What the hell was that?" someone hissed into his ear, and Julien froze.

Elliot.

Elliot, pressed up against the far wall of the building's lobby, a chasm-deep frown etched into his forehead.

"What are you doing?" Julien whispered.

Elliot stepped towards him. "I came in right behind you to refill my water bottle, then gave you two your space for your little showdown or whatever. But fuck, man. What was all that? You actually gave that addict a bucket load of free cash? Shouldn't you have checked with Cinn first?"

Ice slowly trickled through Julien's veins.

"Plus, what the hell was that at the end? Did you *want* to piss the guy off? That's Cinn's best friend. Are you insane?"

Yes. Julien was becoming very sure that he was, in fact, certifiably insane.

Wordlessly, he followed Elliot outside, where, down the road, Cinn had the taxi door open to stare up at them. "What's the hold-up?" he hollered.

Julien paused, glanced back at the apartment block.

Sighing, Elliot gave Julien a helpless shrug, then clapped him on the shoulder. "Let's go, you idiot. It's too late now. You'll have to tell him, though. About the money, at the very least. You know that, right?"

No, he didn't know that, because he hadn't quite got that far in his thought process.

Heart beating hummingbird-fast, Julien walked over to the taxi and slipped into the passenger seat. Closing his eyes, he pressed his palm against his forehead.

This is why you don't do relationships, a tiny voice said snidely into his ear. *You can't help fucking them up before they even begin.*

Twenty-Nine

CINN

Julien, Julien, Julien.

Cinn's brain had been well and truly broken by the princeling, because he couldn't get him out of his goddamn mind.

From the moment the taxi dropped them off at the airport, Cinn became engulfed by his all-consuming desire for him. As if Julien's gravitational pull had been magnified, and Cinn had to be constantly near him, preferably touching in some small way.

When Julien returned from the airport shop with a packet of batteries for Cinn's Walkman and those mints that he loved, he had to restrain himself from climbing on top of him.

He was significantly less restrained on the flight, however—the instant Elliot predictably fell asleep twenty minutes into it, Cinn burrowed his head into Julien's chest, tracing patterns on his knee with his finger.

The view out the window offered only the black expanse of the ocean. How long would it be until he flew back over it again? He'd made Tyler no promises earlier that morning, despite Tyler's heart-wrenching comments about how much he missed him. *Needed* him there in London, in fact. At least Tyler was eager to visit Cinn in Switzerland, if he could sort his passport out. Tyler was far less enthusiastic about spending more time with Elliot and Julien, and had some rather choice words about the latter man. Cinn's outright and unwavering defence of Julien—who'd been instrumental in saving Tyler's ass, he'd reminded him several times—only seemed to exasperate Tyler's dislike of him.

Cinn sighed, and Julien's arm wrapped tighter around his chest.

"Your fear of flying seems to have lessened, somewhat at least," Julien murmured into his ear.

"It's helping that I have other things to focus on." Cinn dragged his fingers up Julien's thigh.

"Well, if it's distraction you're after...." Julien tugged Cinn's beanie slightly off his head to expose his ear, ghosting over it with his teeth.

A low groan threatened to escape him. "You'll get us in trouble."

"Well, there's always the mile-high club."

Cinn snorted. "I can't imagine you tolerating an aeroplane bathroom even for a piss, let alone getting buck naked in there."

"Touché." Julien's body shook with laughter, and Cinn smiled.

The rest of the short flight to Zurich vanished like a breath of wind, carrying them to their destination.

Deboarding. Passport Control. Transfer bus.

Before he knew it, the three of them were marching up and down the parking lot, trying to remember where they'd left Maz.

Cinn had never been so glad to see her shiny black bonnet.

Elliot slid into the back before Cinn could offer the passenger seat. "The deal is that I can pass on any radio station you choose," he announced gruffly, once they were all seated. Cinn found a station playing British hits from the seventies, which seemed to appease the masses.

Once they were on the long road home, the glances between him and Julien began, subtle yet charged. They started small—a quick flick of the head, an almost imperceptible turn of the eyes. As the road stretched out before them, the stolen glances grew bolder, lingering a moment too long, weaving a heated thread of connection that tightened with every passing mile.

Instinctively, Cinn knew without question that Julien was counting down the seconds until Elliot left the car with the same frantic desperation he was.

By the time they'd reached his house, Elliot had also sensed the increasingly rising tension. "Have a nice evening," he muttered with an edge of amusement to his tone, before sliding out of Maz. "I'll ring Darcy and check on her, as I have a feeling you'll be too busy." Then he paused, hand on the door, to curiously state, "Julien, don't forget about what I said earlier."

Cinn glanced at Julien for any clue, but Julien only nodded as the door slammed shut, then he zoomed Maz away so fast that Elliot became a speck in the rear-view mirror before he'd reached his front door.

Julien's hand, warm against his skin, came up to squeeze the back of Cinn's neck, then remained there for the duration of the silent drive.

There were no discussions of where they were going next; neither of them had forgotten their promises in the bathroom yesterday.

It was only when they drove through an unfamiliar part of town, one composed of shiny, fancy high-rise buildings, that it hit Cinn—he was finally going to get to see Julien's apartment. Finally going to get a lot else too, but there was always room for icing on the cake.

Maz slid into an underground parking lot.

Her engine switched off.

Cinn and Julien both stared straight ahead, out of the pristinely clean windscreen.

Julien cleared his throat. "Listen, I need to tell you some—"

Before Julien could ruin it with his words, Cinn unclipped his seat belt and climbed on top of his lap, squeezing himself into the space between the steering wheel and Julien's body. After a small noise of surprise, Julien gazed at him with wide eyes, then reached down to pull the lever under the seat, sending the chair flying backwards.

"Cinn—"

Cinn silenced Julien with his mouth, then pulled back to whisper, "Let's talk tomorrow." Whatever Julien had to say could wait. He had already decided that even if Julien returned to his 'strictly no strings' mindset, Cinn would allow himself this one night of indulgence with him.

The very tip of Cinn's tongue teased open Julien's mouth. Then, letting go of all and every inhibition, he melted against Julien's lean body. Hands quickly roamed all over each other—running over hips, thighs, hair, urgent in their need to touch, touch, touch.

Needy, breathy little sounds that he didn't bother to hold back escaped Cinn as he rolled his hips into Julien's lap, relishing the firmness he found there.

Beep!

The hard plastic of the steering wheel dug into his butt.

Oops. He'd almost forgotten they were in a car.

Julien gently pulled Cinn's head back, muttering several curses in French. His swollen lips pulled up in a beautiful smile, both dimples flashing. "Come on."

Holding his hand every second of the way, Julien led him out of the car park, through a luxurious lobby, and jammed the button for the elevator with aggressive force. Then Julien dragged him through the barely opened doors.

"Please don't tell me you have the penthouse suite," Cinn groaned.

"Because you can't bear the thought of waiting that long for me to rip your clothes off, or you can't bear the thought of me being a rich asshole?"

"Definitely both."

Julien hit the button of the highest number with a guilty smirk.

As the doors slid closed, Julien manhandled Cinn against a mirrored wall, eyes predatory. He pressed his tongue to Cinn's neck, then nuzzled a path all along his jaw. "I'll make the time go quickly."

Surging need had Cinn shivering in anticipation, full body tremors that Julien could surely feel, given how hard he was pressing Cinn into the mirror.

If there was a CCTV camera in here, someone was getting quite the show. But damned if Cinn was taking his eyes off Julien to check.

Demanding hands dug into the flesh of Cinn's ass through his jeans, pulling him impossibly closer to Julien. Then, relinquishing the grip of one hand, Julien lifted Cinn's chin up to meet his gaze, and squeezed it lightly while he said, his voice low, husky, "I'm going to fuck you so hard you'll scream my name until your throat is raw."

Cinn choked.

Ping! The elevator doors slid open.

They had only seconds to spring apart, panting heavily on opposite corners of the lift as a cleaner joined them, wheeling a mop bucket into the middle of them while their eyes darted from one of them to the other.

Cinn wiped the excess saliva from his lips with the back of his hand.

The cleaner turned to face the elevator door, her chin tilted upwards, shaking her head to herself.

Heart pounding, Cinn focused on the button lights as the elevator travelled three floors upwards.

The doors opened. The poor intruder walked out.

Then, within a heartbeat, he was back in Julien's arms.

"I want you to fuck me," Cinn whispered, his heart reaching overdrive. "But you'll be my first."

Julien blinked in confusion, head cocked to one side.

Cinn's face flushed with heat. "With Tyler I always topped. And then, obviously, there were a few others," he said, not wanting to seem so dramatically under Julien in terms of the number of his sexual experiences. "But we didn't get that far," he mumbled.

"Okay," said Julien, eyes softening. He gently cupped Cinn's cheek to run his thumb over it. "Are you sure? We can do whatever you want."

One decisive nod later, the elevator doors finally slid open to reveal the top floor: a corridor, two apartment doors on each end. Julien squeezed his hand as he led him down to the left, unlocking the door with haste and ushering Cinn inside.

Passing quickly through the lobby, they entered a spacious, sparsely decorated living room, modern and sleek, although slightly more grey than Cinn would have predicted. "Nice place," he said, to be polite.

"It's really not."

A grand piano was easily the most impressive thing in the room, its red velvet stool offering a stark contrast to the high-gloss black finish of the instrument. Cinn's eyes roamed over to the open-plan kitchen, but Julien's arms wrapping around him from behind soon distracted him.

"You can evaluate my cookware tomorrow." Julien laughed directly into his ear, as his hand moved to cup Cinn's dick, giving his semi-hard length a light squeeze. "I'm hungry for something else right now."

Cinn leaned back into Julien as he rocked his hips up against Cinn, showing him exactly how starved he was.

Was it just Cinn, or was the whole room spinning? He swallowed. "Wait, can we put on some music first?"

He'd spied an extremely fancy-looking silver turntable on the other side of the living room. After an impatient hum, Julien released him, and Cinn went over to flick through the box of vinyls next to it.

"I've got nothing you'd know," Julien said, with a faint chuckle.

"Then put on your favourite album."

Julien kneeled beside him, then held up two vinyls, *A Love Supreme* by John Coltrane and *Kind of Blue* by Miles Davis.

Cinn wrinkled his nose. "Surely you have something other than jazz?"

Sighing as if Cinn pained him, Julien rifled through the box to the very back. "Béatrice got me this. I've never played it."

Cinn snickered at the familiar rainbow prism cover of the *Dark Side of the Moon*. "Thankfully for me, Béatrice had good taste in music."

Dark clouds covered Julien's eyes, so Cinn grabbed his face to kiss his forehead. "Put it on," he whispered.

With careful fingers, Julien placed the disk onto the turntable and delicately lowered the needle. The heartbeat sound of Pink Floyd's "Speak to Me" soon filled the room. Cinn climbed onto Julien's lap, straddling it. He placed one hand on Julien's chest. A soft smile broke out on Julien's face as he returned the gesture.

"You're really quite exceptional, you know." Julien tugged off Cinn's beanie to run his fingers through his hair. His tongue glided over Cinn's lower lip before he placed it between his teeth. Then Julien pulled back to meet his eyes. Gave him a considering look. "Did you like it last time, in Paris? Like me being in control?"

Far too much.

Since Paris, his late-night fantasies had often wandered in a Julien-shaped direction.

Fantasies of Julien's voice directing him, *commanding* him.

Fantasies of being tortured for hours as Julien made him wait and wait and wait to climax.

Fantasies of being tied up.

"You're all good," Cinn whispered. "I'll tell you otherwise." After a satisfied smirk, Julien's mouth reached for his lips. Cinn ducked his head away. "But are we going to do it on the floor again, or do I get treated to a bed this time?"

"I think you just about deserve a mattress," Julien replied with a breathy laugh. Then he looked Cinn dead in the eye to add, "Only so I can push your face into it, though."

An electric jolt shot straight to Cinn's cock and he groaned. Julien pulled them both to their feet, turned the music up to maximum volume, and led him through a door to the bedroom.

Taking backwards steps while still wrapped around Julien, his legs hit the frame of the gigantic bed. He fell back onto it, with Julien gripping the front of his hoodie, tugging it upwards. With haste, Cinn lifted up his arms, and Julien removed it and his T-shirt simultaneously. Warm hands eagerly explored the bumps and dips of his chest, while his fingers dragged through the light smattering of hair.

Hands ever so slightly trembling, Cinn fumbled with the buttons of Julien's white shirt, then pushed the garment off him to reveal his body for the first time, his heart rate spiking. Cinn's eyes traced the lines of Julien's pale, lean frame, a subtle strength beneath the surface of his lightly toned physique. In the soft, dimmed light, the contours of his body painted an enticing portrait that Cinn already ached to touch.

An appreciative sigh escaped him, and Cinn made quick work of Julien's belt. Julien shrugged out of the rest of his clothes, his impressive erection springing up from a nest of dark hair. Unable to resist, Cinn fell to the floor at Julien's knees, placed the tip of his length in his mouth, and gave him one hard suck.

With a possessive grip, Julien fisted Cinn's hair, forcing himself slightly further into his throat. He'd only had the guy's dick in his mouth twice in his life, but he was quickly becoming addicted to Julien's warm heat, the sensation of his weight against his tongue.

Julien's free hand began to trace the map of Cinn's face, gentle fingers in stark contrast to the increasing urgency of his thrusts. Cinn pulled back to tongue his cockhead, painting his lips with Julien's precum while his spit pooled down his chin. Then, he took him as deep as he could, swallowing around him, eyes watering.

As Julien extracted himself from Cinn's warm, wet mouth, Cinn whimpered at the sudden absence of him. A short laugh was quickly followed by Julien's growl in Cinn's ear. "You were too good at that, mon amour. Now, take your jeans off. Quickly."

At the flash of heat in his eyes, Cinn shed his shoes, socks, and trousers at lightning speed, before throwing himself backwards onto the middle of the soft bed. Cinn's own dick, now beyond fully erect and begging for attention, twitched in anticipation, and he took it in hand, desperate to relieve himself.

Before he could complete his second stroke, Julien's hand had clamped around his wrist, pulling it away with a tight squeeze. "That's mine," he growled.

Holy shit. Was it possible to come from words alone? Cinn would happily volunteer to find out.

Julien climbed on top of his legs, pinning Cinn to the bed. Then, with an obscene sound that rattled around Cinn's head, he spat on his dick. A firm hand closed around his aching cock, and he was soon thrusting in time with Julien's delicious wet strokes as cool fingers traced up his left side, to slip delicately in between his ribs. The pad of Julien's thumb rubbed gently over Cinn's slit on every upstroke, mixing the beads of precum with his saliva.

Cinn's eyes rolled to the back of his head just as Julien paused.

He made a very vocal noise of protest, but Julien continued his ascent until his face hovered right above his so that Cinn met his dark and wide eyes. "Do you still want me to fuck you?" he said, his hand reaching down past Cinn's dick to rub the length of Cinn's crease.

"Yes, yes," Cinn breathed impatiently. "Fuck, Julien, *yes.*"

Julien grinned, his sliver of white teeth glinting in the moonlight pouring in through the floor-to-ceiling window. "I'm going to make it so good for you," he promised, and Cinn melted back onto the mattress, panting with need.

Cinn already felt so, *so* good. How could he possibly feel even better?

"Should I use a condom?"

"Not unless you've fucked someone since you told me you were clear."

Julien reached up to cup his face. "Cinn. I haven't wanted anyone else since the moment I laid eyes on you." He pressed a single kiss onto Cinn's lips. "And I don't see that changing."

Cinn swallowed, wanting so desperately for those words to be true. "Same."

Julien kept one hand resting on Cinn's chest, stroking small circles onto it as he climbed over to his bedside table, to rummage around in a drawer for a painful amount of time. Finally, a bottle clicked open, and Julien removed his hand to squirt a large amount of lube onto his fingers.

Climbing back on top of him, Julien cupped his cheek with his other hand. "Spread your legs," Julien whispered. "Relax for me."

With conscious deep breaths, Cinn untensed every muscle, imagining he was sinking ever deeper into the soft bedding. Wet fingers traced a path down his thighs, and he jerked his hips upwards. A full-body shudder coursed through him as Julien pressed one finger to his crease, without breaching him. Then, one slicked finger slipped inside him, and Cinn released a guttural groan as he rolled his hips further into Julien.

With gentle, tender strokes, Julien worked him open, and he became more undone with every thrust. "You don't need to hold back," Cinn half gasped.

A tiny chuckle. "Trust me, I have no intention of doing that, *mon amour*."

Julien's mouth trailed a line of feather-soft kisses up, then down the column of Cinn's throat, before returning to *that spot* near his collarbone, the spot he'd claimed with his mouth in Paris. When Julien lightly nipped it with his teeth, Cinn wrapped his fingers around the tendrils of Julien's hair before pushing his face further into it. He wanted him to suck it. He wanted to be marked.

Cinn's heart rate surged impossibly faster, every inch of his skin tingling with an intense warmth. "More," Cinn gasped, and he didn't know if he meant more fingers, more pressure, more sucking of his tender skin. He just knew that he needed more, more, *more*.

Almost instantly, another finger pressed inside him, stretching him open with a small sting before they found their rhythm. Julien's fingers curled ever so slightly as they sought their prize. The first pass against his prostate had him crying out as warm, electric waves of pleasure racked his body. The second and third had his eyes leaking tears. The fourth had him clenching around Julien's fingers, streams of nonsense pouring out of his mouth.

The sound of his own blood rushing through his ears merged with the one of the wet squelch of Julien's fingers working absolute magic. Cinn's balls tightened to the point of pain. "Please," he begged, before letting out a pitiful whine. "I want you to be inside me when I come."

Semi-delirious with want and need, when Julien removed his fingers, Cinn began jerking his legs erratically, thrashing about on the mattress. Julien pressed two firm hands onto his hips, pinning him down with enough force and control that Cinn stilled, although with a low, desperate moan.

"Are you going to behave? Or do I have to make you?" Julien said, his tone so sultry it did nothing to help Cinn follow his instructions.

"I'll behave if you're quick about it."

"Oh, I'm anything but quick," Julien replied. "Didn't you learn that last time?" He released his iron grip on Cinn to lunge for the lube bottle again, squirting an obscene amount onto himself, slathering up every inch of his length. For the first time, a tiny seed of apprehension unfurled in Cinn as he took stock of what was about to enter him. One look at Julien however had that feeling evaporating into thin air—moonlight hit his face, accentuating his cheekbones above a soft smile that only held adoration. Cinn trusted Julien with this, one hundred and ten percent. Trusted him with his body, and increasingly, his heart.

So when Julien said, "I need you to promise you'll tell me to stop if it's too much," Cinn groaned. If only he hadn't overshared about his inexperience, Julien would be inside him right now, and he wouldn't be left with this empty, aching need while he waited.

"Julien, I swear to God if you don't give it to me right—"

Julien's lips silenced him with a searing kiss, his tongue delving deep into his mouth. "Promise me," he hissed.

"I promise," Cinn choked out.

"Start on your hands and knees," Julien instructed, with a slap to Cinn's thigh, and he positioned himself so quickly the world spun.

Cinn closed his eyes.

The only noise that could be heard above the faint music playing in the living room was Cinn's erratic breath. Then reality became nothing but his own panting breath as Julien pressed the tip of his slick cock against his crease, the euphoria of Julien stroking his dick as he inched ever deeper inside Cinn with tiny thrusts, Julien pausing to ask if it still felt good and Cinn encouraging him onwards, Julien pulling his hair ever so slightly too roughly, Julien's voice telling him he was doing so, *so* good, and then the pressure of Julien's thighs pressing against him as he bottomed out, filling Cinn completely.

Cinn gripped the duvet, steadying himself as he became consumed with the sensation, the feeling of fullness he'd never felt before. Julien used both hands to grab his hips, fingers digging deep into his flesh, gloriously pleasurable pain coursing through Cinn as Julien began to move, thrusting faster and faster, going impossibly deeper. As his body opened for Julien, he trembled, almost collapsing on top of the mattress.

"Non, mon amour," Julien murmured as he repositioned him. "Stay right like this."

Cinn was only able to whimper in response. Each movement knocked the breath out of him as he arched his back, pushing himself further onto Julien's cock.

"I can't"—Julien panted, his fingers dipping ever tighter into Cinn's hip—"describe"—a deep thrust tore a scream out from Cinn's mouth—"how fucking amazing you feel."

Cinn became lost in Julien's long smooth glides, movements that rubbed over every inch inside him, shooting bursts of ecstasy through his every cell.

When Julien ceased moving, and pulled him up into his arms, he didn't complain, only became a pliant bundle of limbs that sagged back against him, sighing happily.

"Turn around. I want to look into your beautiful eyes when I come," Julien breathed, releasing his tight grip on him.

Dazed, Cinn lay on his back, staring up at the dark ceiling as if in a fever dream until his vision was consumed by Julien's face. As Julien eased back inside him, he moaned, dragging his fingernails down Julien's back as he did so. With his arms bracketing Cinn's head, Julien captured his mouth, sliding their tongues together at the same pace as he pushed himself inside of him. Distantly, he was aware of Pink Floyd's ethereal vocals and haunting synthesisers reaching a crescendo.

To muffle his screams and incoherent babbles of pure pleasure, Cinn threw his hand over his mouth, to find his wrist being wrenched back onto the bed.

"*Non*. I want to hear what I'm doing to you."

Even though his eyes were squeezed tightly shut, tears freely streamed down his cheeks onto the mattress. The feeling of Julien's skin touching almost every inch of his was too much and not enough at the same time. "Julien," Cinn whispered like a prayer, tightening his legs around Julien's waist.

"Say it again."

Cinn opened his eyes. With a trembling hand, he brushed Julien's blond waves from his sweat-slick forehead, to reveal grey eyes that pierced his with a ferociously possessive gaze.

"Julien, Julien, Julien," he chanted, his dick throbbing with every syllable.

"Louder!"

"Julien, Julien!" he screamed, as Julien pushed inside him one last time to fill him with hot cum, and as if that was his own permission, Cinn released his own hot, silky ropes into the middle of them.

Collapsing on top of him, panting breathlessly, Julien smothered Cinn with his body, his fingers tangling in his hair as he whispered beautiful sounding things in French into his ear while he continued pushing him into the mattress, slowing the roll of his hips until he stilled.

Eventually, Cinn's limbs stopped twitching, and his pulse steadied. He burrowed his face into the crook of Julien's neck. "Holy fucking shit," he mumbled, and Julien laughed. Cinn hooked a leg over Julien's, entwining them even further. "Just so you know, if you try to kick me out right now, I will probably burn your apartment block down."

"That's funny, because I was about to say that if you even *think* about leaving, I'm not opposed to tying you to the bed."

Cinn trailed his fingertips down Julien's face, brushing his thumb over the dip of one dimple. "Why would I possibly leave when everything I want is right here?" he whispered.

Thirty

JULIEN

When Julien's eyelashes fluttered open, he was pressed up against warm skin.

Confusion gripped him, until the slow, steady rhythm of Cinn's breath reminded him of his presence. His presence here in Julien's *bed*. Shuffling back slightly on the pillow they'd somehow shared, Julien marvelled at Cinn's sleeping face. It had been years since he'd woken up with someone.

Over the years, Julien had engaged in numerous sexual escapades with many people, but last night with Cinn was by far the most intimate encounter he'd ever had.

Images replayed in Julien's mind.

The way Cinn had looked at him so trustingly, so adoringly.

The way he'd shouted his name, like it was the only word that belonged on his lips.

Then, the way he'd playfully sprayed Julien with the shower when they rinsed off, then jostled him for sink space while brushing their teeth together.

Afterwards, Julien had slipped under the covers and held his arms open, and Cinn had climbed in beside him, entangling their limbs in a warm embrace. The feel of Cinn's heavy head on his chest as they'd drifted off to sleep, Cinn's fingers firmly interlocked with his, had seared itself on Julien's soul.

There would be nobody else for Julien now. He was as sure as the stars in a clear night sky.

This is what it should feel like.

Lying still in the bed, Julien didn't move an inch, lest he disturb Cinn. He focused all his energy on capturing this moment in his mind, an imagined sketch of the two of them, sharp lines and soft contours fusing together to create a work of art.

At some point, he must have fallen back to sleep, because Cinn was gone when he next opened his eyes. He couldn't prevent the sickening lurch of his heart falling like a stone through water as he reached out to find the space where Cinn had been cold, the faintest scent of lemon lingering on his pillow.

And this is why you were afraid of it.

For a moment that felt like an eternity, he held in a breath, until a bang in the kitchen restarted his system, flooding him with blissful relief. He slipped on his dressing gown and headed straight to the kitchen to find Cinn, dressed only in his T-shirt and underwear, brown curls a tangled mess, grinning at him.

"I was going to cook you breakfast, but then I discovered you have no food. Like, none. Why do you have so many empty cupboards? Also, you don't have any instant coffee, so you'll have to use your fancy thing to make me one." Cinn gestured to the cafetière, eyes wide in expressive mock fury.

As Cinn continued to rant about various items in his kitchen, Julien's heart swelled full to bursting, to the point his throat tightened, and he had to swallow down tsunamis of rising emotion that threatened to spill out of him.

Ridiculous things wanted to climb out of his mouth.

You are the most beautiful thing, inside and out.

Stay here with me. Never go home. I won't hate it here if you're with me.

I think I'm falling in love with you.

Non, I know *I am.*

Cinn raised a blue mug, examining the golden patterns that ran through it. "This is pretty."

"It's motetech." Julien took it from Cinn and twirled it in his palm. "I made several of them. The embermotes in the gold veins keep your drink warm. Plus, they look really cool."

Cinn's warm laugh filled the kitchen. He picked up Julien's reading glasses from the counter and stepped towards him. "You are *such* a nerd." Cinn placed the glasses on his face, then beamed at him. "But a hot nerd, at least, in these."

A kiss on the tip of Julien's nose, then his cheek, then his lips, Cinn's tongue sliding in to meet his. Julien's back hit the countertop, and they soon became an entangled mess of limbs pressing against each other.

Reluctantly, Julien pulled away, running his hands through Cinn's hair to smooth out some of the kinks. "If we start that now, we'll never leave the house today."

A smirk danced on Cinn's face. "Fine by me."

"We really need to go check on Darcy. We just up and left her to look for that... cat." *Cat slash demon-monster slash Béatrice-reincarnated.* "You're more than welcome to come back here tonight though," Julien added in a rush, the thud of his nervous heart beating against his ribcage. *And tomorrow, and tomorrow, and tomorrow.*

"Okay," Cinn said slowly, and the light dancing in his eyes had Julien's soul singing.

Julien pressed a kiss to Cinn's forehead. "I'll take a quick shower."

The telephone was ringing.

He heard it from the bathroom as soon as he'd switched off the water.

The telephone was ringing, and Julien's heart was about to be impaled.

Of course, it *could* have been his father. Elliot. Darcy. Any number of other people.

However, Julien knew, without a shadow of a doubt, that it was him. Tyler.

And now, it was too late. He'd fucked it up.

He'd had ample time to tell Cinn by now, to present his side of the tale before Tyler did, but he'd pushed London to the furthest depths of his mind, to the point he'd tricked himself into believing it didn't happen.

Cinn's voice was audible now, getting increasingly louder, but not to the point Julien could make out the words. *Good.*

Julien faced himself in the mirror. Wet strands of hair pasted themselves to his cheek. *You're going to fix this*, he told himself. *It's going to be okay.*

Because if he didn't fix it—

Julien's throat tightened to the point he could barely breathe.

He dried himself, then changed into fresh clothes. There was only silence coming from the living room now. Had Cinn left? Surely he wouldn't...

Like a coward, Julien hovered in the corridor, playing his own game of Schrödinger's cat. Because until he went in there, everything was fine. Maybe it *was* Elliot that called, or—

"I can see your shadow," Cinn's voice snapped, his tone ice-cold.

Julien closed his eyes. Pressed two fingers to his temple.

"Get the fuck in here."

With confidence he didn't truly feel, Julien took the final few steps into the room. Cinn, seated on the sofa, had his eyes glued on the telephone on the side table rather than Julien. His expression was a picture of thunder—black storm clouds circled his head.

"That was Bradley. He rang Darcy's number, then she gave him yours."

"Okay…" started Julien. Maybe it was okay. Maybe Bradley was ringing as they'd left some socks behind? Maybe Julien had accidentally gone too far in his kitchen reorganisation, and Bradley couldn't find his tin opener?

"Tyler didn't come home last night. Bradley also filled me in on what happened yesterday with you and Tyler, when you went back into the flat."

"Cinn… I was going to explain. I tried to tell you yesterday," Julien began, his traitorous voice trembling.

Lightning flashing in his eyes, Cinn jumped to his feet, body noticeably shaking. He tore a hand through his hair. "Why, Julien, why? Why the fuck would you do all that? Why would you do that to him? To me?"

Because he goaded me into it.

Because he was saying the most ridiculous lies.

Because you've made me lose my mind.

Because I want nothing else more than you, and I was worried he was standing in the way.

Because I'm a selfish prick.

"I know," Julien croaked out. "I know I should have asked you before I gave him the money. It was a random last minute decision that I now regret."

"Why the fuck didn't you tell me as soon as you got in the taxi? Oh wait, I know, because you also told him some random bullshit about me never seeing him again and being *yours* now."

Julien's face flushed. "What?! I never said that! Well, not *exactly*." He definitely *had* said the last part. The semantics didn't matter now though—tears shone in Cinn's eyes and Julien hated himself. *Loathed* himself with every fibre of his being. "You're completely right. I fucked up. I have no excuses for my behaviour."

He stepped towards Cinn, fissures running through his stuttering heart when he flinched away from him.

"I'm not *yours*, Julien."

Julien's heart exploded into tiny pieces. He dropped to his knees, his throat closing so tightly he barely got out, "What if I want you to be? So badly it hurts? So badly I did a stupid, stupid thing?"

"Jesus fucking Christ! Did you ever think about... I don't know, just asking me out on a date like a normal fucking person rather than threatening and bribing my ex?" An awful sound of pure frustration poured out of Cinn's mouth as he tore his hand through his hair. "Do you realise that if Tyler's gone on a massive bender with that money, he could already be dead. *Dead*, Julien!"

Cinn stormed towards the door.

"Where are you going?"

"Home, to ring Bradley back. To see if Tyler's turned up yet. He took the entire stash of money out with him, so God knows where he's ended up."

Without a single glance back, Cinn marched out of the room, slamming the door behind him, then slamming the front door even harder a few moments later.

Silence.

Julien released a choked sob as his head hit the carpet. He pressed his knuckle into his mouth.

In the months that followed his mother's death, then the months that followed Béatrice's, he'd become very adept at forcing himself to disassociate, to float away on a hazy cloud of nothingness when his emotions got too turbulent.

There was no such luck today. Sharp daggers of pain assaulted every molecule of his being, twisting themselves into him again and again as his mind showed him only one image: the expression of pure hurt and devastation on Cinn's face.

Streams of tears poured out of him. Rivers. Oceans.

Then, from his position curled up in a ball on the floor, he spied a lump of soft, olive green material. He released a low, pathetic moan as he reached for Cinn's beanie, pressing it to his face to inhale the citrusy scent of Cinn's shampoo before clutching it to his chest.

What could have been hours passed.

Julien remained motionless, staring up at his ceiling.

The phone rang once, then again shortly after.

It wasn't until the banging on the door began that Julien pulled himself to his feet, rubbing his tear-stained cheeks.

Cinn? He stupidly allowed himself to hope, while fully knowing there was no way he was behind that door. Julien didn't deserve it.

"Julien!" Darcy's shrill voice boomed down the corridor through the letterbox.

"I'm coming!" he croaked, then dragged himself through his flat to open the door.

Face set into a grim line, she tornadoed into the apartment, dragging him by his arm to push him onto the sofa.

They didn't speak, not until she had made two mugs of tea, and pressed one into his hand.

"Elliot told me," she said, by way of explanation. "Well, Cinn rang Elliot and then Elliot rang me."

"Cinn rang Elliot?" Julien's voice was a hoarse whisper. "What did he say?"

Darcy gave him *a look*. "He asked if Elliot knew what you'd done in London. Then he shouted at him for not stopping you. Then he begged

Elliot to come check on you." Darcy glowered at him. "Because Cinn's a fucking angel and you're a complete twat."

"I know, Darce, I know," Julien moaned, pressing a cushion to his face. "So how come you're here and not Elliot?"

Darcy ripped the pillow from his grip. "Because it's been hard enough for Elliot watching you two grow closer and closer without him torturing himself by comforting you right now!"

A strangled scream emanated from deep within him, and he pressed his head to his knees. "I'm a fucking awful person. An awful friend. Just leave me. Go."

A sigh, then Darcy placed her hand on Julien's back and rubbed it. Even more tears leaked out of Julien's eyes. How did he even have this much water left in his body?

"You're not an awful person, Julien. You're just a complete mess. But you're *our* complete mess. And we'll sort this. Together." Darcy wrapped her arm around him and squeezed.

"I can't lose him, Darce," Julien said. *He was never yours to lose,* screamed his inner voice. "You're not going to believe this but, I genuinely care about him so much. Far more than anyone else I've ever been with. He's the only one I've ever wanted to *be* with."

Darcy petted his hair, smoothing it like he was an upset child. "I know, Julien. I know."

"Cinn said that Tyler might die because of me," Julien confessed in a whisper.

Darcy paused her strokes.

"What?" After a moment's further silence: "Darcy, what is it?"

"So, I wasn't sure if I was going to tell you—"

"Just spit it out!"

"Okay. But stay calm." She pressed her hands into his shoulders like she could contain him. "I rang Cinn before I came here, and he'd just heard from Bradley that Tyler *did* end up in the hospital—"

"Non!" Julien jumped to his feet, pressing his fist against his mouth. "Oh, God!"

"Calm down and let me finish! What happened was, he ended up gambling half of the money, losing it, and then got into a fight with two other drunk men. They knocked Tyler around a bit, that's all."

"That's *all?*" Sinking to the floor, Julien ran a hand over his tear-stained face. "Are you joking? That's awful. And there's no way Cinn will forgive me now."

"It sounded like Tyler will be absolutely fine. Just a few cracked ribs. You can't entirely blame yourself for this. It was his choice after all."

He stared at her. "I gave ten thousand pounds to a drug addict."

"Well, on the bright side, Bradley has confiscated the rest of the cash now!"

A low moan dragged itself out of Julien as he lightly bashed his head against the sofa.

"Julien, come here." Darcy grabbed his arm, tugging him towards her. Julien fell into her, letting himself be enveloped by her tiny frame embracing him.

"He could have died."

"Yes, well, we live and we learn."

"I don't deserve you," he whispered.

"Julien, my love, you deserve the world. You've just never believed it, and that is why you occasionally act like a total psychopath."

Julien reached for his tea, the warm liquid calming him with each sip. "What's my plan then? A boombox over my head outside his window? A thousand red roses? A flock of white doves that spell out 'I'm an idiot for almost killing your ex-boyfriend'?"

"No, no, and even more no," Darcy replied, punctuating each word with a slap to Julien's thigh. "You calm the fuck down and give him space."

"What?" Julien cried. "How's that meant to help? He'll just ruminate on how awful I am."

"Probably. Maybe you could start with a letter."

Julien groaned. "I'm not good with words in that way."

"That's why you're in this mess!"

"Fine!" he snapped. "Have it your way."

Darcy smiled that sickening winning smile of hers. "I always do."

Thirty-One

JULIEN

Julien stared over at Cinn, standing with Eric and his friends, amongst a busy crowd on the other side of the street. If Julien ducked under the tape that had cordoned off the road, where the festival procession would soon pass, he could reach him in ten seconds.

So near, so close, but for all Julien's futile attempts to catch his eye, he may as well have been on the other side of the planet.

Two weeks. How could anyone possibly stay angry, without even the slightest hint of reprieve, for two whole weeks?

Julien delivered what he believed was a very heartfelt letter through the door ten days ago now, and still, nothing. At least he knew Cinn was okay—he met with Darcy for coffee almost daily, to Julien's relief. And jealousy. At least she'd been able to find out that Tyler had left the hospital and was on his way to a full recovery.

Now, it was a waiting game, made more difficult when Julien found himself near him. The other day, Julien saw Cinn ahead of him, walking with Eric through Auri, and he'd had to walk in the opposite direction, lest he punch something.

"Stop staring at him," hissed Darcy into his ear, and Elliot snorted in amusement. "He's not going to look your way. He's as stubborn as you."

How much longer would this torture go on for? Aside from Julien's pathetic pining, which the other two were both vocally sick of, it had been a quiet two weeks, with zero cat sightings and slow progress researching who could advise them regarding Béatrice's tampered-with locket.

Julien had protested against attending the winter lantern parade this evening, but had eventually been dragged out of his apartment to witness the festivities, which marked the start of the holiday break for some Auri departments.

Later, there would be the spectacular display of mote-infused fireworks, where Darcy would likely monologue, for the tenth or so time, on how much effort they were to produce, and how wasteful it was of resources.

The procession began, saving Julien from the temptation of gawking at Cinn.

First there were the renowned lanterns, lots held by moteblessed children who were changing the soft, vibrant colours the animal-shaped paper creations emitted. Several lanterns, including an impressive penguin, floated gracefully through the air, travelling several metres above the child's hand, controlled by skilful windmote manipulation.

Next came the elemental performers, some of the gendarmerie mixed in with professional entertainers. Dancers in vibrant colours wove fire into intricate forms as if thread, and water responded to their movements like liquid silk, swirling and dancing in harmony to the background music provided by a live band on a nearby stage. Elliot muttered something under his breath. Julien smirked to himself. Every year, Elliot not so subtly hoped to be invited to participate in the annual display of talent.

"Salvatore Gallo has fifty francs on AP making some sort of scene tonight. Crying around about gratuitous mote use, etcetera," Elliot said, followed by a scoff.

A tut from Darcy. "I'm not convinced the chief of the gendarmerie should be lowering himself to such speculation."

Their attention turned back to the parade, where they were treated to artisans crafting intricate giant snowflakes out of thin air, freezing moisture to create crystalline sculptures that sparkled with a celestial glow. Each delicate snowflake seemed alive as the artists held them in place, suspended like frozen dreams waiting to be released into the night.

Animated ice sculptures followed, in addition to teleporting illusionists.

The wind picked up, and light snow—genuine, natural snow—flurried down from a lone cloud, falling on Julien's head. He shivered.

Despite his best efforts, Julien's eyes once again magnetised straight to Cinn, who now had a salted pretzel from a food stand in his hand. Cinn glanced up at the sky, and then ran a hand over his brown curls, flicking off the dusting of snow that'd settled there. Julien's heart leapt. He'd kept Cinn's green beanie in his bag, carrying it around for the right moment to give it back to him. What did it mean that Cinn hadn't gone back to wearing his grey beanie? Absolutely nothing, probably. However, if there was ever going to be an opportune time to attempt to give this one back, it was now.

Julien took a half step towards the barrier, then hesitated. If Cinn rejected the hat, or even simply pierced him with those icy-cold eyes like he'd done the day of their fight, that would be the final nail in the coffin for his poor broken heart.

But the more he studied Cinn—the light pink splotches on his cheeks, the subtle duck to his head, the slight distance he'd put between himself and the group he was with—the more his pull became irresistible.

"I'm going to go talk to him," announced Julien. "This is ridiculous. He doesn't even look like he's enjoying hanging with those guys."

Elliot chuckled. "He looks fine to me. But I'll admit to missing the dude. So, go make up already."

Turning to Darcy, Julien found her unsure. Her head flicked between Julien and across the street. "Why don't all three of us go over, and then it will make it a bit more casual?"

At the next lull in the performance procession, Julien ducked under the tape barrier and darted across the road, followed closely by Darcy and Elliot. Eric's pointed glare at Julien as they approached did not inspire the casual aesthetic they were aiming for. He ignored Eric and focused entirely on reaching Cinn, who bit into his lip as soon as he noticed their appearance.

Julien rehearsed his opening lines: *Hey, how have you been? Did you read my letter? Your head looks cold, and I just happen to have had your hat in my bag for the last two weeks.*

However, when Julien stumbled to a stop a handful of steps away from him, every word in his vocabulary vanished as he was confronted with the intricate blend of emotions manifesting in Cinn's expressive gaze.

Julien opened his mouth to say something, which was seeming highly likely to be a nonsensical babble of *I'm an idiot* mixed with *I miss you so much,* when the first scream sounded.

The sharp noise cut through the festive atmosphere, a discordant note against the enchanting melody the band was playing. The lanterns that were being held within the crowd flickered, as if nervous.

A ripple of apprehension shot through the parade watchers, and Julien's stomach lurched. The previously joyful parade sounds curdled into a symphony of hurried footsteps and anguished whispers.

Something was wrong.

Lunging for Cinn, Julien gripped his arm tightly, which prompted a fierce scowl. "I think—"

The air itself seemed to constrict, as if a vacuum had formed, stealing away any shred of warmth to create an icy chill. Every lantern dimmed to a feeble flicker. Shadows elongated, contorting into grotesque shapes that danced eerily across the snow-covered ground.

An uncanny hush fell over the crowd. And then, emerging from the heart of the parade, an umbraphage materialised like a phantom from the shadows, its form twisting and pulsating with malevolent energy. Inky tendrils unfolded, reaching hungrily toward a gasping crowd that immediately fell backwards in a collective rush.

Elliot swore, pushing Darcy behind him as Julien did the same to Cinn.

"Your wristband, Cinn," Darcy shouted. "Don't let it burn you again."

"It's already off."

Abruptly, a swarm of people stampeded in from their left, their faces etched with terror as they weaved through the panicking crowd. Julien caught a cry over the raucous noise. "There's two more near St. Caelum's!"

"You guys go," said Elliot to the three of them. "Quickly."

Julien clasped his shoulder and gave him a look that he hoped communicated volumes before Elliot launched himself into the fray of gendarmes that had already joined the fight.

Julien turned to usher Darcy and Cinn forward.

Or at least, he tried to.

"Wait." Cinn held his ground, staring at the umbraphage, eyebrows drawn together in intense concentration. He pressed a finger to his temple. "I can... *feel* it. Feel *them*."

Julien grabbed a fistful of Cinn's coat, tugging him in the opposite direction. "What?" he snapped. "That doesn't matter right now. We need to go."

Darcy quite vocally agreed with him, her panicked voice reaching a shrill peak.

"Hold on," spat Cinn, his tense body resisting Julien's efforts to drag him away. "I feel like I could... I could..."

Julien didn't hold back his noise of exasperation.

Darcy's eyes shot saucer-wide. She pointed behind Julien. "Another!"

Everything happened in slow motion.

The additional umbraphage, surging towards them.

Elliot's distinct shout from afar.

The rush of wind, undoubtedly motecraft in origin, knocking them out of the way of the monster's path. Slamming them into the ground.

Cinn being torn from Julien's grip.

The thud of his body landing some distance away from him, the sound reverberating through Julien in continuous echoing waves.

Julien's blood freezing as the umbraphage headed straight for Cinn, lifting his limp body from the ground as if a doll.

A smaller being, similarly shadowy yet distinctively *cat-shaped*, suddenly emerged, circling the umbraphage and hissing wildly.

Darcy's terror-laden scream could easily be heard over the commotion as the shadowy nightmare brought Cinn higher and higher, before lifting him to the part of the umbraphage's body that could pass as its head.

No!

A sudden impact blindsided Julien, an unseen blow to the back of his head, followed by a searing burst of pain erupting across his skull. Darkness rushed in, his senses overwhelmed as the world dissolved into a void.

Every inch of his being fought to stay awake, stay awake for Cinn, stay awake to save him, even if it was the last thing he did—he'd claw his way over there if it killed him—but the battle was futile, and Julien drowned in the blackness that enveloped him in deafening silence.

Thirty-Two

CINN

If Cinn was currently in the shadowrealm, it was no version he'd ever been to before.

This was... nothingness.

A soundless vacuum consisting only of unfathomable obsidian darkness that held him in a tight grip of paralysis. Any endeavour at movement was fruitless. Cinn attempted to force his mind to recall his music, any snatch of lyrics that would help to tie his floating consciousness back to reality, but none came. Even the sound of his own heartbeat was absent, leaving endless absolute silence.

Was he simply imagining the sensation of blinking? Was he presently staring at the back of his eyelids? Hard to say when his entire world was a blank canvas of blackness.

Time was an abstract concept here.

Hours, days, years could pass, could already *have* passed, and Cinn would be clueless, locked in this timeless cage of eternal limbo.

Cinn felt nothing. Nothing aside from longing. Not pain, not fear, not even curiosity, but *longing*.

He longed to hear the sound of his own breath, to feel the compression and expansion of his ribs as his lungs took in precious air.

He longed for his red city with its fractured moon, far preferable to this suffocating abyss of nothingness.

Longing, tinged with bitter regret.

He longed for the life he almost had, could have had.

He longed for the many people he didn't get to say goodbye to. Tyler. All of his other London friends. Darcy and Elliot. *Julien.*

If this was it, if he was dead, he'd spent his last two weeks alive torturing himself and Julien for nothing.

Julien? Cinn struggled to place the name. Distantly, he became aware that he was slipping away from himself. This should have panicked him, but the further he fell, the less he felt the sense of loss.

Fragmented memories danced at the edge of his consciousness, elusive and disjointed, teasing him with fleeting images that he couldn't even say for sure were his own.

A burnt-orange setting sun melting into London's horizon.

The stars dancing in a cloudless night sky, above a garden bench. *A garden bench...* a garden bench he could no longer remember the importance of.

The softness of olive-green cotton underneath his fingertips.

Two dimples, their quick flash throwing a blanket of bittersweetness over him.

Three of... something. Something good. Something whole. Three pillars, holding him up. Or was it four?

A fleeting feeling of warmth, of safety, of home.

And then, nothing.

Thirty-Three

JULIEN

Rubbing a hand across tired eyes, Julien repositioned himself on the armchair, battling another round of pins and needles from sitting on his legs for too long. Between his sore muscles and the head injury that needed stitches, he could easily be a hundred years old.

Next to him, Cinn's body lay on the hospital bed as still as it had been the day he'd been brought in, almost a week ago now. Heart-monitor wires criss-crossed his body, and a nasogastric tube slivered serpent-like out of his nose.

Sighing, Julien reached for Cinn's hand and squeezed, his gaze drifting, as it often did, to the inflamed burn-like mark adorning Cinn's neck like a choker, the aftermath of the umbraphage's direct touch.

Elliot and two other gendarmes had come to their aid as quickly as possible, once they'd seen Cinn suspended in the air, but not before the umbraphage had wrapped a black tendril around his neck. Although the gendarmes managed to manipulate lumenmotes quickly enough to save Cinn's life, he'd fallen to the ground, unconscious.

Julien knew all of this from secondhand information, of course. He'd missed it all, knocked out by something undetermined in the chaos and rendered useless while his best friends were in danger.

The umbraphages were eventually banished thanks to the amount of extra support pouring in from various other moteblessed hubs throughout the world, travelling to Auri as quickly as the Displacement Baths would let them.

That's not to say there wasn't a fair number of casualties, however. Forty at least from Auri, so Julien had heard, plus more from their backup support.

Then there was the long list of seriously injured, so lengthy that if they were attacked again today, there wouldn't be nearly enough gendarmerie.

Rain battered the window of Cinn's small private room within Auri's hospital. It had practically become a greenhouse with the amount of flowers Darcy kept bringing. He'd had several visitors, including Eric yesterday, who'd dropped a box of chocolates around for 'when Cinn woke up'. Elliot immediately started munching away at them in the corner of the room while Julien issued a short apology to Eric for his rudeness towards him in the café, followed by one for how he'd handled it when they'd ended things earlier that year. Eric had shrugged, admitting he shouldered some of the blame for their miscommunication on the terms of their casual arrangement.

"I can see it's completely different with him though," Eric said, voice soft, glancing at Cinn's lifeless form.

"Too bad I fucked it up," Julien whispered. "I broke his trust." *Ripped it to shreds and then stamped all over it. Permanent damage.*

Eric had given him a sad smile. "I think you two will find a way through it. It was clear how upset he was, how much he missed you guys, even though he refused to talk about you."

They'd had no visitors today—though Darcy was due any minute—but Julien had preferred it. He'd made friends with a nurse, a kindly older lady who now routinely brought him apple juice, and that was serving as enough social interaction for him.

Even though it was only seven p.m., Julien's eyes drifted shut, and he resigned himself to another night sleeping in the armchair.

His eyes snapped open at a knock at the door, followed by a head poking around it.

Albert Noir. He slid into the room to hover a good few metres from Cinn, nodding once at Julien. He'd not seen Noir since the third day, when he'd briefly popped in, then left again. As always, he was dressed in his dark robe-like coat that, along with his grey beard, always left Julien with the impression of a stereotypical wizard. He was yet to magically cure Cinn.

"I thought that it was Eleanor coming today," Julien said, jumping up and stretching his aching limbs. "She promised me she'd stop by."

"She's otherwise detained. Another umbraphage outbreak. Florida, following on the heels of a hurricane. Lots of our gendarmerie have already been sent."

A flash of worry for Elliot shot through Julien, before the knowledge that he'd been signed off due to his injuries soothed it smooth.

"How many this time?"

"Three."

"So Auri still holds the record, then?" There'd been five in total that night, in the end.

"For now." Noir moved closer to Cinn's bedside to snatch up his charts, then began flicking through them. "What's with the music?" he asked, one grey bushy eyebrow raised at the headphones over Cinn's ears, plugged into his Walkman on the bedside table. The faintest sound leaked out of the headphones, a pulsating rhythm. "I doubt he can hear it."

"It's his favourite tape," snapped Julien. He was rather proud of his idea of using Cinn's songs to attempt to lure him back into his body. "He plays it all the time."

Noir picked up the cassette tape case—*Doolittle* by the Pixies. Well worn, the plastic surface bore countless scratches. The intriguing artwork featured a bizarre monkey with a halo floating on his head, sitting on a concrete step.

Giving Julien a look you'd give to a child you were humouring, Noir said, "I don't doubt. Any sign of movement yet?"

"Absolutely none." Julien had never seen a human body so still; he often hovered his ear above Cinn's mouth to see if he was actually breathing, even though his heart-rate monitor reassured him he was still alive. He spent most of his time in Cinn's room, closely scrutinising him for the twitches they'd seen the two times they'd watched him shadowslip, to no avail. This time was different. Julien knew it in every bone in his body.

Noir made a humming noise.

Through gritted teeth, Julien said, "He's been like this for five days now. There must be something else we can try. I know that records of shadowslippers are limited, but there must be *some* helpful information out there!"

"Yes. There is some relevant information." Noir's solemn, lined face crinkled. "This is how a lot of them end, I'm afraid."

"What?"

"How shadowslippers die," Noir said, so matter-of-factly Julien's hand itched to punch him. "A large majority of recorded cases end with their body entering this stasis." Noir waved his hand toward Cinn's body. "This coma-like state, with their consciousness remaining stuck in the shadowrealm. Often, their bodies eventually give up. One shadowslipper, after extensive electric-shock treatment, opened their eyes again, but had lost most of their brain function."

Julien blinked at Noir as shock gripped him. Then he let his mouth gape open as icy fury shot through his veins. "*Excusez-moi?* Your plan is to wait for him to become a vegetable?"

Sighing, Noir removed a pipe and tin from his pocket, made to light it. Julien scowled it right back into his pocket again.

"I'm only preparing you for the worst-case scenario."

"Well, if you've got nothing actually helpful to offer, you may as well leave," Julien spat, throwing himself back down in the bedside armchair, pointedly staring at Cinn.

As Noir moved towards the door, it swung open. Darcy had finally arrived.

Once she'd clicked the door shut behind Noir, Julien snapped, "You're late." Then, after a wash of guilt, mumbled, "Sorry."

Darcy ignored it, just like she'd done every other time Julien had let his stress colour his tone. "I had to pop home for some bits. I've brought you dinner." She threw him something sandwich-shaped, wrapped in tinfoil.

Julien forced himself to smile at her. "Thanks. Still no sign of our cat?"

"Nope."

They hadn't seen the 'cat' again since its brief appearance at the attack. Although Julien was starting to think he may have imagined it, the result of adrenaline and heartbreak.

Darcy dropped her voice low and soft. "You know Elliot is right about it likely not being Béatrice, right?"

"*Oui,*" he snapped. "Of course." A lie—as soon as his sister's name had come out of Cinn's mouth, his brain latched on to the idea, dug its claws in deep. After months of grief, worry and wondering about her death, he'd take demon-cat Béatrice over no Béatrice at all.

Hopefully she didn't bite.

"In other news, Noir just told me that Cinn will likely waste away and die," Julien announced, in a monotonous voice that he'd curated to not show any of the turbulent emotion threatening to spill out of him at the news.

Darcy's lips pursed together in a thin line, seeming unsurprised. "So our limited literature maintains. He discussed this with me here the other day, when you and Elliot went to grab coffee. I did tell him not to share that information with you, though."

"What? Why?"

"Because you're already an absolute mess," she snapped. "And it didn't seem very helpful."

"Actually, it's *very* helpful."

Darcy stilled.

"It's very helpful, because it's solidified our next plan of action."

Their gazes collided, and so began their silent battle of wills. Julien unflinchingly stared into Darcy's dismayed eyes—for she knew what was about to come out of his mouth.

"I'm going to try to shadowslip again. To try to find him. Save him."

"No," Darcy said. "Absolutely not. Not after last time. I thought I'd lost you."

He'd known she'd say that—his next words slid off Julien's tongue. "I'm doing it, Darce, with or without you."

"Good luck getting hold of the Mortalisfade elixir without me."

"I didn't need luck. I only needed the key to your basement, which was hanging on your kitchen wall."

Darcy's jaw hit the floor. "You didn't," she whispered, horror-struck. Then, far louder: "Julien, what is this madness? What exactly do you think you're going to achieve? Apart from risking your life?"

"Hear me out." Julien paced the limited floor space of the small room. "For one, we do it here, in the hospital this time. Then, if anything does go wrong, help will be on hand, *oui*?"

"Great. I can't wait to explain to the doctors that you're seizing and frothing at the mouth as a product of your own stupidity." She had that stubborn pout on her face now, arms crossed like an angry schoolteacher.

"Next, we have a far better chance of success this time, because we have the ultimate magnet item."

"We… do?" Darcy's nose wrinkled, and Julien raised his eyebrows, then gave one smug nod toward Cinn's unconscious body. "You're joking. You want to use a live human as a magnet item? Is that even a thing?"

"Well, we're about to find out."

Darcy shook her head. "There's no way Elliot will agree to this."

"He already did. Yesterday morning. In your basement."

"Wha—?" Shaking her head even more violently, she continued, "No, Julien. No, no, and no! You're not doing this!"

Closing the space between them, Julien gently grasped both of her arms. "I have to, Darce," he whispered. Darcy closed her eyes, and he brought her slight frame to his chest. "I couldn't save them. *Mère*. Béatrice."

"Jul—"

"Shh. I've heard it all from you before. I know you mean well, *ma chérie*. But your kind words will do nothing to change how I feel."

For a moment, Julien was back *there*, the place where his *mère* died, with the church collapsing around them because of his failure to control his channelling. His legs were heavy with the weight of his mother's head on his lap as he screamed and sobbed. Then, Béatrice reached him, dragging one leg limp behind her, her face covered in dust, wearing that expression he would only ever interpret as, *what have you done?*

"I would do exactly the same for you or Elliot," he said into Darcy's hair.

She pulled back to burn her fierce gaze into Julien's. "Of course you would," she said. "That doesn't make it a good idea."

"Please help me," Julien begged, taking both of her cheeks in his palms. "Help me try once, and if it doesn't work, I won't ask again."

He'd won—Darcy's eyes melted into green puddles. "Fine," she relented. "But I'm in charge."

Julien kissed her forehead. "When are you ever not?"

Breaking apart, they simultaneously turned to study Cinn, the steady beep of his heart monitor the only sound—his Walkman had finished the cassette.

"We're coming for you," Julien said, watching the subtle shift of the blankets as they rose and fell with Cinn's shallow breathing. "We're coming for you."

Thirty-Four

CINN

His trousers are muddy.

His trousers are muddy, and he needs to clean them. *Needs* to clean them.

His mum will be so mad if she sees them like this. She only washed them the other day.

So he'll just scoop some water into his hand and wipe them. That'll do the trick.

Fluffy ducks quack cheerfully at him as he does so, the last thing he hears before the water rushes in, silencing the world above.

This is the part where he panics, right? This is the part where he splashes and screams and chokes and drowns. But not this time, for Cinn is sinking, sinking, sinking. Sinking far deeper than the river in the park would ever be.

Cinn doesn't try to suck in air. He doesn't need it as he lets himself sink down, watching the sun's weak light get dimmer and dimmer until there's only a murky blackness.

A punch to his chest, and Cinn is no longer in the dark. He's back at Feltham Young Offenders, in the shower room, fully clothed but sopping wet from the water that's jetting down on him. He stares down at his soaked shoes, wondering how on earth he'll dry them, as another punch comes, to his stomach this time.

There's three of them. He knows this without looking up. The usual three that hadn't left him alone, that first month at Feltham, before he'd joined the Spiders and become cocooned in their web of protection.

He doubles over in side-splitting agony, falling into a defensive ball on the floor. Then the kicks begin, followed by the slurs. Ones about him being a sissy. One about his mother, and who she likes to fuck. One about what they'll do to him, if he dares to report them to the warden.

This isn't what happened! A tiny part of him cries. Because they'd only kicked him a few times before Tyler had burst in to save him, tipped off by a mate. He's yet to make an appearance this time, and Cinn's body continues to be battered by a torrent of unrelenting, vicious blows.

It stops.

He lifts his head slightly.

Stretches out his bruised arms to assess the damage.

Confusion strikes him, because now he's staring at his hand and the tiny scar is missing from his thumb. The one he'd got week one at Feltham, from being under pressure to chop too quickly in the prison's kitchen.

He uncurls himself fully, stands up, blinks twice—he's now in the small garden of one of his many foster families. A blue bike lays sprawled on the ground, being claimed by weeds.

Then, he knows the day. It's the day of his arrest. His first arrest.

Because he's standing by the shed, the shed where they made him hide all the cash they'd nicked, and the gate is swinging open, two male police officers bursting through it.

They made me do it, he'll say to them much later, in the interview room. *They said they'd burn my house down.* It won't matter. Not with his previous minor offences. Not with the amount of cash in that shed.

The cash. He needs to get rid of it. Spinning, he darts into the shed and slams the door behind him. When he turns however, he's not in the damp, cramped space stuffed full of paint tins filled with forged bank notes. He's in the office at Rosewood Parlour, standing by the safe.

Now there are two different police officers with him. Two different officers, and the two men Richter had sent to accompany him, and him, heart pounding, knowing he's about to shadowslip. He reaches for the headphones around his neck that aren't there, then digs his fingernails into his hands.

It'll be futile, of course. He'll slip, then bring back the man with the scarred face, the one that'll slaughter all of them.

Blood on his hands.

Mud on his trousers.

Mud on his trousers, that he needs to clean.

Thirty-Five

JULIEN

"Alright, let's get this show on the road." Julien turned to Darcy. "Luminaquartz birch bark?"

"Check. I ground it at home," said Darcy, holding up a bag of powder. "Ink?"

"Check." Elliot wiggled the dark bottle.

"Last minute change of heart?" Darcy asked hopefully, and Julien shook his head.

Outside of the hospital room window, a full moon peered curiously down at the array of items now scattered across Cinn's hospital bed. It was past eleven and Julien's favourite nurse had just finished her final round of the evening, bringing apple juice for all three of them.

Prior preparations complete, Julien began the final steps. He gently manoeuvred Cinn upright to tug down his hospital gown. His heavy body didn't stir, and his head lolled lifelessly to one side. With the utmost care, Julien placed him back down onto the pillow, brushing his brown curls from his forehead. Next, he whipped off his own shirt, throwing it down onto the floor.

In a different setting, either he or Elliot would have made some sort of joke, but the sombre atmosphere didn't allow for it.

Julien settled back into the armchair and Elliot groaned as he knelt on the floor with the ink. His body was still recovering from the umbraphage attack, where he'd become moteblown in his efforts to dissipate the monster that had grabbed Cinn. Julien tortured himself for the thousandth time with the memory of the umbraphage going directly for Cinn, as if it had a personal vendetta against him. If only Julien had moved that little bit quicker...

Elliot's face was expressionless as he propped open the book to copy from, before using the aethraven ink to decorate Julien's stomach and chest with the circle of now-familiar runes.

"Cover as much of my body with it as possible," Julien said to Darcy, who was busy making the paste that would bind him to Cinn, their magnet item. "Every inch of skin that isn't inked."

The paste felt odd against his skin, the texture rough. "That'll have to do." Darcy finished off with one long swipe of the stuff against his ribcage. "We're out."

The three of them paused for a few beats, frozen with the knowledge they were at the edge of the precipice, and not wanting to jump. Julien fractured the tableau by moving to Cinn's bedside and pulling back the blankets with one quick flourish.

Ever so carefully, he climbed in beside Cinn. His body was pleasantly warm. It should be, for the amount of extra blankets Julien had put on him. As his arm slid around him, a shred of guilt gnawed at him. If Cinn could see him now, he'd likely shake with fury at Julien manhandling his semi-naked body, pressing it to his own. "Sorry," he whispered into Cinn's ear. "I have to."

Inhaling deeply, he savoured the citrusy scent of Cinn's hair, as it tickled his face. After all, this could be the last time he ever held Cinn. Even *if* he succeeded in bringing Cinn's consciousness back, he'd still have broken the fragile thing they'd had blooming between them. He'd still look into Cinn's eyes and see the anger, the hurt, the betrayal.

But at least his eyes would be open. At least he'd be alive.

And maybe, after a long time, Julien could earn Cinn's trust again. They could be friends at least, surely.

Yes, this could be the very last time he held Cinn, so Julien clutched him so tightly that there wasn't a fraction of an inch between Julien's chest and Cinn's back, the paste sticking and sealing them together. Binding them.

"Remember what we agreed?" Julien's gaze darted between Darcy and Elliot.

Elliot snorted, then ran an exasperated hand through his wild curls. "We didn't agree to your stupid plan where we pretend we found you like this and had nothing to do with it."

"Well, your funeral then, when Eleanor comes for you. At least if I do die, she'll have to be at least partially nice to you."

"*Julien!*" Darcy glared at him. "We definitely agreed we'd stop with the dying jokes."

Julien flashed her a sheepish smile. "Let's have the poison, then."

Face a controlled mask, Darcy slowly brought out the small vial of Mortalisfade from her satchel. Inside the flask, the thick indigo liquid subtly swirled, even though Darcy held it still. Wiggling the stopper free, she pulled out of her pocket an oral syringe.

"We went for ten millilitres last time, with Elliot. The most I'm willing to give you today, factoring in your reduced body mass, is eight," she announced, voice authoritative, holding the vial and syringe close to her chest.

"Whatever you say, boss," Julien said, causing Elliot to cackle.

Darcy scowled as she stepped towards him, inserting the syringe into the liquid and drawing up the precise amount.

Wrapping his arms tightly around Cinn, Julien pressed a palm against his chest, wishing he could rip the heart monitor off to feel the beat of his pulse against his fingers. He settled for tracing his fingers over the lyric Cinn had inked against a rib—*go your own way*—in artful calligraphy.

Elliot slid into the armchair. "See you on the other side," he said, as Darcy's hand hovered an inch from Julien's open mouth. His expression was light, but Elliot's steady voice held the slightest edge of fear. "Go get him."

Once Julien had squeezed his eyes shut, Darcy squirted the dose right into the back of his mouth. He tasted the deep, earthy bitterness regardless. He swallowed.

Every attempt he or Elliot had ever made to shadowslip using Darcy's home-brewed Mortalisfade had failed.

Too low doses had done nothing but send them drifting into a deep, dreamless sleep.

Too high doses had abruptly knocked them out cold, then stopped their hearts, forcing Darcy to revive them with her box of tricks.

"Come on," Julien whispered into Cinn's hair. This time would be different. This time *had to* be different. "I can't lose you, *mon chéri*. I *won't* lose you."

As his thoughts lost form, slipping out of his reach with increasing fluidity, Julien focused only on the steady beat of Cinn's breath, and the feel of his warm skin on his.

Thirty-Six

CINN

C inn was trapped.

Trapped in an endless cycle of his worst memories, warped into worse versions of themselves, like a ride at the fair that never stopped spinning, making you dizzier, and dizzier and dizzier.

Friday the thirteenth of July, the day the social worker had come to collect him. In reality, his mum had sunk to the carpet and sobbed, but his cruel mind had his mother laughing maniacally to herself.

The day Tyler ended up in an ambulance after an overdose was a favourite on the list of replays. He'd been seamlessly transported to the hospital and treated, but in this personal hell, Cinn had to watch him die again and again, paramedics failing to save him.

Back to Rosewood Parlour, *again*, but this time, it's Benny and Sarah who end up a bloody mess on the floor, and this time, it's the knife in Cinn's hands that puts them there.

And then, the blackness again. Nothingness. Nothing but an impenetrable void stretching into eternity.

That was, until he saw *him*. Julien. A tiny speck of light that floated towards him, getting infinitesimally bigger until it became human-shaped. Julien walked on the black nothingness as if it were tangible stepping stones, seeming to be aiming right for him.

Julien! he tried to call out, even though he had no control of his petrified vocal cords.

Walking towards him in a loose fitting white shirt he'd never seen him wear before, Julien's grey eyes looked right through him, unsmiling.

Julien! He tried desperately again. *Julien! Julien!*

Something slightly dislodged in his throat; a strangled sound emanated.

Julien! Julien! Julien!

He tried and tried again to force the name onto his lips, but every strained half syllable was a shard of glass against his throat, tearing and ripping the soft flesh in searing waves of pain that escalated into a dissonance of anguish. Soon, he found himself choking on the metallic taste of his own blood, the hot liquid molten agony.

But Julien was so close! Touching distance, if Cinn could only move. Eyebrows pinched, face turning this way and that, Julien appeared lost. Lost in the darkness.

Julien! Cinn attempted one more time, as Julien passed straight by him.

Blood poured out of his mouth now, he could feel it dripping down his chin, even though he had no access to his other senses.

Please! he shouted, in his mind now, relenting his futile efforts for Julien to hear him. *Let me go. Let me go.*

Who he was asking this of, he had no idea.

All he knew was that his mind couldn't survive this much longer. Wouldn't survive.

And so, on he screamed.

Thirty-Seven

JULIEN

Julien glanced down, dazed, to find himself dressed in a loose-fitting white shirt that billowed at the sleeves. He plucked at the material before casting his eyes across his surroundings.

There was no mistaking it: he was in Cinn's red city, in all its dusky twilight glory.

Here was the cracked asphalt, red hazy mist, the crawling scarlet ivy over every surface. Derelict buildings, some of which were mere piles of concrete. To his left, it appeared like someone had attempted to build a makeshift shelter out of salvaged metal sheets and tattered fabric. The structure seemed precarious, with mismatched pieces held together by improvised ties and ropes. Faded graffiti adorned the makeshift walls, tags left by artists long since gone.

Across the road were the strange, streamlined cars Cinn had described, all curves. They looked fast, he'd give them that. None of them would be a patch on Maz, of course.

Half-ripped billboards filled the sky, advertising products or people Julien couldn't place.

However, this wasn't quite *Cinn's* red city, was it? Because that had turned out to be London, and this *wasn't* London. Julien knew this for sure, because he was in Paris. Far across the horizon, the Eiffel Tower's steel structure still stood, but twisted, warped, sagging down towards the ground on its right side. An eerie red hue was emanating from the colossal vines of the invasive red ivy that choked almost every beam of it.

This was the City of Lights no more.

After another second spent gazing at the iconic monument that he'd always openly joked about hating, but now felt rather sorry for, his head snapped up to seek another element of Cinn's red city that had always intrigued him. Sure enough, he found the disturbing fractured moon Cinn had described. For a moment, he stared at it—the artist in him itching to capture the strange, unsettling sight.

Forcing himself to walk on, he understood why the Beksiński paintings in his old bedroom had reminded Cinn so much of here. This place dripped with surrealism. *Oozed* with it. Julien half expected to melt into the ground as he travelled, or turn the corner to find a giant skull with spider demons crawling out of it.

An almighty crashing sound in the distance had his head snapping up. Colossal plumes of dark smoke billowed across the skyline.

Then, the ground began to shake.

Heart thumping, adrenaline surging, Julien turned in the opposite direction and ran.

Footsteps pounding on the volatile surface, Julien pushed his body to the absolute limit, forcing his muscles to carry him faster and faster, until his thighs ached and begged for mercy. His chest tightened painfully as he struggled to inhale.

He pressed on, regardless. He'd always been the master of his own body—the years of intense physical training during his youth had proved that to him.

Why did it feel like he was running out of time?

One wrong step away from the world crumbling around him?

A hair's breadth away from death?

Something prickled down his spine. An icy prickle. There was an umbraphage behind him. *Close* behind him. Julien was certain of it.

Not glancing behind him even for a millisecond, he continued to press his body into the punishing pace. He tuned everything out—the growing hiss of his pursuer, the agony in his legs, and the sound of his blood rushing through his ears—to focus only on his next step.

A tiny blur of dark flitted across his vision, zipping left, then right. A… collection of *shadowmotes*? He'd never seen them before. It was bizarre to sight them but not *feel* them the way he felt all the others. Regardless, he stretched out his arm to them, as if he were a child chasing a butterfly. He followed them down a narrow Parisian street, which opened into the wide thoroughfare of Champs-Élysées. A giant double-decker tour bus, red ivy invading every smashed window, brushed up against him as he sprinted towards the Arc de Triomphe, the motes a pace or two ahead of him. The arch's once majestic facade was now marred by mighty cracks, chunks of stone missing from its structure.

A sudden thought consumed him: the knowledge that he *had* to reach the arch at any cost.

And so he continued, using his last reserves of energy to catapult himself down the ruined avenue, debris and ivy threatening to trip him at every step. Finally, he was there, in the deep shadow of the monument. Reaching his predetermined destination, he turned to face the umbraphage.

It wasn't there.

After a moment of blinking through shock and confusion, the ground disappeared from under him. There wasn't a prelude, neither a tremor nor shake, but the cobblestone beneath him fell away, sending him plummeting into an abyss.

Then he was freefalling downwards, white shirt billowing out around him like a parachute.

He should, of course, be terrified—the scientific part of his brain told him he was about to break every bone in his body. Conversely, he felt little to nothing as he plunged downwards.

A handful of seconds, a minute, longer? Time became irrelevant as cool air whipped his cheeks.

Initially a speck in the distance, the bottom became steadily larger as it filled his vision with dark brown hues. When Julien reached the ground, his chest hit the firm surface with a tremendous thud, but he did not experience the agonisingly rib-shattering, body-destroying impact that he should have.

Dusting himself off, his eyes slowly adjusted to the extremely dim light, his murky brown surroundings eventually somewhat revealing themselves to him.

An expansive cavern of sorts, rocky walls circling him on all sides. His unsteady panting echoed off the walls, his lungs still feeling the effects of being pushed to their limits above.

And there he was.

A mere handful of metres away.

A gasp escaped Julien, loud in the silence of the cave, and his hand flew to his mouth before he urged his body forward to close the distance between himself and Cinn.

Encased horizontally in a rib-like cage made of black. The texture and glossy shine of it reminded him of an umbraphage's inky tendrils. Indeed, as he stepped closer, the bars of Cinn's jail writhed with life. Through the gaps, his body was just visible. Naked, laying on his back on a slab of grey stone. Very much as still as the body that Julien currently cradled in his arms, back in the hospital, a place that felt aeons away.

There was something attached to Cinn's skin, several *somethings*, all across the side of him. The more he looked, the more he saw—a row of tiny wormlike creatures wiggling fluidly, stretching from his neck to his feet. As if sensing Julien's presence, one lifted a head, turned to Julien and hissed, revealing rows of miniscule sharp teeth before it burrowed into Cinn's side again.

Julien stepped even closer towards the cage. *What the fuck are they doing to you?*

His hand reached out to hover an inch from one black curve.

He wouldn't be able to touch it. To be able to simply snap it off. Of course he wouldn't.

But he had to try.

Excruciating pain shot through him, originating with the tips of his fingers where the black material burned him. He blew on fingers that were already blistering, biting the inside of his cheek to distract him from the agony.

From behind the cage, darkness deepened and twisted into a boundless shape, rising up like a black phoenix ascending from hell, wing-like protrusions spreading wide across the expanse of the cavern.

OURS NOW

Julien staggered back before holding his ground. The sudden revelation that these creatures could communicate wasn't lost on him, despite the limited processing time.

The raspy voice, emanating from the core of the being, thundered again:

POWERFUL

HE BELONGS TO SHADOW

"No! You can't have him. He belongs to us," Julien shouted, half of his mind chastising himself for entertaining the idea of reasoning with an umbraphage.

A ripple cascaded through the shape of the creature, then part of it bulged out, lunging towards Cinn's body as if about to devour its prey.

Julien had no time to think about what came next.

This was it. The moment his body had been waiting for, and the moment his mind most feared.

Closing his eyes, he gave in, finally relenting after all these years. He reached for the motes that were always within his grasp, no matter where he was. Not lumenmotes: there was far too little light down here for them to be of use. Not windmotes, though there was plenty of air. No, Julien sought out another type of mote. The ones that were always waiting for him. The ones that nobody else could feel. The ones that he'd never allowed himself the opportunity to learn to control after they'd killed his mother.

The nameless motes.

The illicit motes.

The motes that made him feel like a god, with all the power and destruction that brought with it.

They came to him, as quick as light, ready to be commanded, so eager to serve.

A feeling of euphoria submerged Julien, wrapping him in a bubble that numbed his senses to the world around him.

A drink of water after being parched in the desert.

A long-awaited sunrise after an endless night.

That first gasp after being held underwater.

Stepping out of the shadows and into the sunlight.

Power coursing through him, he aimed the motes straight at the umbraphage, which made a harrowing screeching sound, as it flapped its formless shadowy contours this way and that.

Its dark shape threw itself at Julien, but his motes were there in nanoseconds, protecting him without him consciously channelling them to do so, their pure whiteness forming an impenetrable barrier. The umbraphage flew backwards as if electrocuted. Its booming voice seemed to annunciate scraps of syllables that were too garbled to make meaning of.

With each fresh pummel of Julien's motes, the umbraphage's skin—if it could be described as that—started to peel off. Inky layer after inky layer floated in the air before breaking apart into black confetti. Smaller and smaller the creature became, until its harrowing scream quietened to a pathetic broken whimper.

Then there was only silence.

Silence, and Julien, and *Cinn*.

The cage was gone, and so were the worms, although they'd gifted Cinn's flesh with a line of circular bite marks. Still Cinn slept on, and Julien's heart lurched—because he was all out of ideas, of energy. His small stockpile of hope dwindled as his throat constricted, and he blinked back hot tears. The plan had been simple—come here, find Cinn. He had no roadmap for how to actually revive him.

Joining Cinn on the rock slab, he perched on the edge of it, looking down at him. "Wake up, Sleeping Beauty," he whispered into the silence of the cavern, brushing a thumb over Cinn's forehead before tracing the outline of his face all the way to his lips.

Should he attempt to wake him up with a kiss?

The fairytale would be all well and good, up to the moment Cinn woke up and punched him. He laughed, a tiny hollow sound that echoed through the space, and the shake of his body caused two teardrops to fall on Cinn's cheek.

Who was he kidding? Cinn wasn't going to wake up. Julien would either remain trapped here forever, or have to go back and face telling everyone Cinn loved he'd failed and Cinn would die.

"I'm sorry." Julien ran his fingers through Cinn's curls. "I'm so sorry I couldn't save you. I tried. And I'm sorry for Tyler. God, I'm so sorry, Cinn. I've never regretted anything more in my life. I know it's my own stupid fault. I wish I was normal. I wish I could have treated you how you deserved from the beginning."

Julien pressed a kiss to Cinn's forehead, before continuing to caress his cheeks.

"Now you'll never know how special you are. Because you are. So special, to everyone, especially to me. And the more I realised it, the more I acted stupidly. I wish I'd told you. I should have, a thousand times, until you believed it."

He interlaced their fingers, bringing Cinn's hand to his lips.

Then the miracle occurred: the slightest flutter of Cinn's dark eyelashes.

The tiniest stir of his body, shoulders rolling backwards.

The quietest groan from his lips.

When his eyes cracked open, Julien wrapped his arm around his back to pull him upright. "Cinn," he half choked out, as he pressed his palm to Cinn's chest, watching every precious dazed blink of Cinn's eyelids as he took in their surroundings.

"Julien? Why the fuck are you crying?" Cinn's voice was croaky and hoarse, as if unused for a hundred years. His expression morphed into one of tender concern as he reached up to cup Julien's face, swiping away a tear. "Why are you here? Why are *we* here? *How* are you here?"

"Don't worry about that now. Are you alright? Are you hurt?" Julien's hand slid up to grip the back of Cinn's head, rubbing a thumb in slow circles.

"I..." Cinn's eyes fell shut for a moment as a shudder racked through his body. He scraped his teeth across his bottom lip. "Are you real? I don't know if you're real. I've been trapped in this horrible endless cycle of different versions of reality. My memories..."

"I'm real," Julien said on an unsteady exhale. "I'm real, I promise."

Cinn's hand pulled the collar of Julien's shirt to reveal his bare chest. "Your locket is missing," he said, with panicked suspicion.

Yeah, and this isn't even my shirt, and you're buck naked. The clothing rules in this place seem pretty loose.

"It's back at the hospital. Where we're all waiting for you to wake up."

"This is just another trick," Cinn said, alarmed panic creeping into his voice, as he clutched at Julien's shirt, holding it tightly. "You're about to kill me. You've done that twice already. Kill me, or just leave me here alone forever." His face crumpled in desperate fear, making Julien want to do anything in his power to make Cinn okay, to absorb his terror for himself.

Julien pressed his forehead against Cinn's. "I'm not going to leave you. Ever. Not even if we have to live in this cave for the remainder of our days."

A weak chuckle.

"We'll eat maggots and grow our own weeds."

Cinn's mouth twitched upwards; he felt it under his fingertips.

"Darcy will be so impressed when we tell her."

"Julien," Cinn whispered, before crushing their lips together in a kiss so fierce, it was a collision of stars, an igniting of a wildfire of passion that bloomed blindingly bright. Julien savoured each press of Cinn's mouth, each firm glide of his tongue, searing them into his memory, lest this be the last kiss he ever received.

"Cinn," he protested weakly, pulling back. It seemed highly probable Cinn had some sort of memory loss, forgetting that he currently hated him.

An exhale of breath. "I'm just checking that you're really real." Cinn tangled his hand in Julien's hair and tugged as if to test its legitimacy.

"And how's that going for you?"

"Pretty well. There's no way anything could imitate the way you kiss me."

Julien stilled. "Which is?"

"Like you need me like air. Like you'll never let me go. Like I'm everything."

"You are, *mon amour*, you are."

Cinn blinked at him, wide-eyed and fawn-like, a tiny smile blossoming on his lips. Julien ran his thumb over it. He swallowed before pressing a kiss to Cinn's forehead. "Let's get out of here." *Let's get out of here so I can make you smile like that every day.*

"I can't just choose to leave. I've never been able to."

"That umbraphage seemed to think you were Mr. Almighty Powerful."

At that moment, a tiny humming noise popped into existence. A shadowmote landed on Cinn's nose.

"It's you!" Cinn declared, going cross-eyed.

"There's no way in hell you recognise one specific mote, Cinn."

Cinn slid off the rock, landing with a soft thud. He held his palm upright, and soon there was a writhing ball of shadowmotes floating above it. With his other hand, he reached out and tugged Julien towards him. A soft blow of air later, Cinn had scattered his shadowmotes, who quickly multiplied and started circling them, enclosing them in the eye of a tornado.

"Are you... channelling them?"

Cinn shrugged. "They kinda do their own thing. I'm cool with it."

As the shadowmotes picked up their pace, Julien reached for his own motes, if only to feel their power one more time. Instantly at his fingertips ready to be commanded, their bright white light illuminated the cavern.

"Woah!" Cinn almost stumbled back in shock, but Julien steadied him. "That's new."

With a flick of his wrist, Julien sent the motes spinning into Cinn's shadow vortex. Merging together, the dark and light motes danced between each other, humming. Cinn slid his arm around Julien's waist, and Julien tugged him closer and closer, pressing Cinn's warm body against his until his head rested on his shoulder. The volume of the noise surged to a near deafening cacophony as the motes formed an increasingly tight whirlwind.

They clutched each other like they never wanted to let go. Like they were holding a piece of themselves. Flickering flames in a hearth, merging as one. Two puzzle pieces, slotting seamlessly together. Two wings of a bird. Two hands, bound in prayer. Two halves of a whole.

One shadow, and one light.

Thirty-Eight

CINN

Bright lights. *So bright.*

Cinn brought one aching arm up, draping it across his eyes. Sadly, he was defenceless against the irritating loud beeping of the machinery that promised he was alive.

His first act was to tear out the numerous wires and tubes that were burrowed into him while Elliot tried to restrain his arms and Darcy shouted for a doctor. Julien, lying bare chested on the bed next to him, had simply stared at him, frozen still aside from his slow blinks.

As soon as Cinn was functional, the multiple rounds of him demanding his discharge began—from Cinn only, as Julien, Elliot and Darcy traitorously seemed to want to keep him there for as long as possible—and he was signed off to be discharged after one more night of observation. His sudden, rapid recovery astounded the doctors, and Noir, who'd dropped in to see him later that day.

And so, Cinn was released into the cool, quiet evening, the hospital doors a more than welcome sight.

After a single step, he stumbled to a halt, frozen stone still, processing what he could see.

Almost every inch of tarmac, pavement, and brick wall was plastered in a layer of... *trash*? No, the paper turning Auri into a red sea, was too uniform. Cinn bent his aching body down to snatch one from the ground.

The Arcane Purifiers's mark, printed in a stark crimson, took up most of the space. The colour choice accentuated the impression of violence that the sharp slashing lines through the central circle alluded to. Underneath the symbol, a lone sentence in a harsh scrawl: *Ignorance will lead to certain peril.*

Someone scoffed. Cinn dragged his eyes away from the ominous warning to find Elliot scowling.

"If the gendarmerie get ordered to clean up this mess, I'm rioting."

Darcy slowly turned her head, slack-jawed. "There must be thousands."

Julien kicked the ground with his boot, uplifting several pieces of paper, sending them flying off in the breeze. "All they've achieved is to piss everyone off even more. Pathetic."

For a fleeting moment, Darcy opened her mouth, then a glance at Cinn had her snapping it shut again. "Let's get you home."

Julien pursed his lips. "Wait here and I'll bring Maz up to you."

Cinn laughed in Julien's face.

"Wow. Pardon me. You literally almost died," Julien snapped.

"So did you, by the sound of it, you fucking idiot," Cinn snapped right back. He still couldn't quite believe Julien had played Russian roulette with the Mortalisfade again.

"Stop, or I'll bang your heads together," Darcy threatened.

The walk to the car was silent after that.

Then, with the smooth grace Cinn had come to expect from Maz and Julien, they were sliding out of the car park and soon cresting the top of the steep hill that overlooked Auri.

"Stop," Cinn suddenly declared, fairly dramatically and surprising himself. "Sorry. I mean, please could we stop for a second? I feel like I need some fresh air before the drive home."

Julien glanced at the other two in the rear-view mirror, likely sharing his concern for their still-crazed patient. Then he nodded, pulling over into a lay-by.

Leading the way, Cinn jumped over a fence to access a sweeping field, enjoying the stretch of his muscles that had been still for too long. Cinn threw himself down on the bank of long dewy grass, with Julien soon joining him, followed by Darcy and Elliot sandwiching them in between.

Although there was a chill in the air, there was no wind, only a profound sense of stillness, as if all of nature and all of Auri below them had come to a pause.

The dusky twilight view was breathtaking. He'd already been here for what felt like a lifetime now, but he still felt freshly awestruck every time he was in its presence. His eye drifted across the horizon, absorbing the towering spires of St. Caelum's, reaching up to touch the starry sky.

Just across from it was the grand building of Aurelia Library, where he'd been spending a shocking amount of free time. Yes, *him*, Cinn Saunders, *choosing* to be in a library. Cinn could read Noir's stupid texts far easier now, with Julien's motecraft overlay making the words stop dancing around the page. Plus, he couldn't deny it was cosy in there.

Next he studied the domed glasshouse, the Solstice Atrium, where apparently only the *very important people* of the consortium were allowed in for *very important meetings*. And if he squinted, he could even see the vague outline of Curio Café Collective, although half of it was hidden behind a large tree. Every drink he purchased from there was slowly turning him into a coffee snob. Soon he'd be joining Julien in throwing his Nescafé supply onto a bonfire.

All in all, Auri felt increasingly like... *home*.

Julien lit a single cigarette, and for a while they passed it between all four of them, blowing the smoke towards the glittering lights.

Something in Julien's partially unzipped rucksack caught his eye.

A bundle of soft, olive-green material.

He reached into the bag, snatched it out, and pulled it onto his head where it belonged, all without looking Julien's way.

The slightest catch of Julien's breath, whisper soft.

Wordlessly, Cinn inched his hand closer to Julien's, until he could hook his pinky finger around Julien's own. Julien didn't react, not until the slight up-curve of his lips as he squeezed around Cinn's finger, before sliding their palms together to entwine Cinn's entire hand with his.

Cinn exhaled an unsteady breath, wanting more than anything to throw his head on Julien's shoulder. He and Julien had a long, long road ahead, starting with a lengthy conversation. Julien had tried to have it with him in the hospital last night—Elliot and Darcy had left to find some sort of nurse come apple-juice witch, and a whole barrage of words had poured like a waterfall out of Julien. A ramble of an apology that bordered on insane, words of self-deprecation that Cinn wanted to shove back into his mouth.

"Julien," he'd said, and Julien had instantly stopped, pausing in his anxious pacing to look at him. "Not now." And then, after Julien's crestfallen face had just about broken his damned heart, he added in a far softer tone, "But later."

In the weeks spent ignoring him, Cinn discovered from Bradley—and then Tyler, under duress—the exact circumstances that had led to Julien's outrageously inappropriate boundary crossing. Cinn hadn't completely forgiven Julien; they were a way off that. He knew he could, though. And he hoped he could get through to his crazy, broken mess of a boy. Maybe slot a few of his pieces back into place. So he squeezed Julien's hand as tight as he could, enjoying the sight of relief and elation dancing across Julien's face.

"So... what now, team?" Elliot said after a stretching silence, to Darcy's laughter.

Where to begin?

A murderous locket, shrouded in treachery.

An ugly cat made of shadows on the loose, which may or may not be a reincarnation of a dead sister.

A community of moteblessed at war, divided into factions.

A world being increasingly threatened by the enigmatic umbraphage.

Just a handful of months ago, none of this would have had anything to do with Cinn. Really, he should be chopping vegetables at Rosewood Parlour right now, preparing for the evening sitting.

But should he actually? Cinn looked to Julien, then to Darcy, and Elliot. No. He was right where he belonged. And although their challenges felt insurmountable at present, that was just it. They were *their* challenges to face. Together.

Darcy was the first to speak. "Well, for starters, how about a nice cup of tea?"

salted Cinn's Dark Chocolate Chunk AWESOMELY DELICIOUS Cookies

300g cups all-purpose flour
1/2 teaspoon baking soda
1/2 teaspoon salt
12 tablespoons unsalted butter, melted
225g ~~200g~~ brown sugar
100g white sugar
1 large egg
1 large egg yolk
2.5 ~~2~~ teaspoons vanilla extract
220g dark chocolate chopped ⟶ ~~some big,~~ ~~some small~~
coarse sea salt for sprinkling

Julien said he
preferred larger
chunks

Cinn, when did Julien
become the authority on
cookies? — Darcy

Elliot, of course.
He says sorry.

Acknowledgements

Lucie - My French expert extraordinaire - thank you for all your fantastic translations!

Asa - Thank you so much for reading this book at the speed of light! Your comments were all incredibly helpful and motivational.

W.H - Thank you for providing me with endless guidance, enthusiasm, and, most importantly, gossip. Sorry there wasn't as much glasses-wearing-action in this one. I'll do better next time.

Dorian - Thank you so much for your helpful feedback!

Angela - Your suggestions on the final draft helped to make the book shine! Thank you!

And lastly, thank **YOU** for reading this book! If you enjoyed it, please consider leaving a rating/review on Amazon. Reviews are incredibly helpful for independent authors.

ALSO BY TJ ROSE
Monsters within Men

An MM Post-Apocalyptic Romance

London, 2053. One of the last remaining civilisations in the world.

A decade on from the first wave of human-flesh-craving monsters that wiped out most of society, Noah finds himself stepping up to lead Squad E, part of London's East Regiment, fighting back against the creatures that threaten mankind. But between battling monsters, struggling with grief, and his rivalry with another lieutenant, Noah is sinking, fast. The last thing he needs is a young, weak conscript with an attitude problem to add to his issues. Especially when he can't seem to get him out of his head.

Zeke, Squad E's newest recruit, would rather do anything else than be conscripted into the dwindling military force battling to save humanity. But when his research assistant job abruptly ends after his boss is arrested under mysterious circumstances, he must learn to embrace his new life as a soldier. But perhaps his attractive commanding officer—whom he is forbidden from dating—might offer the silver lining he never knew he wanted?

As the crisis escalates, London's time begins to run out. Food shortages, riots, and secrets buried by leadership all push the city towards its boiling point. The ten members of Squad E, along with their faithful dog, Wolf, must band together if they're going to make it out of this alive.

Scan the QR code to view online:

About the Author

TJ Rose is steadily turning her wild imagination into alternate universes, one happily-ever-after at a time.

By day, she weaves action-packed queer romances packed with vivid worlds and characters who dance between sugar, spice, and pure chaos. By night, she's either plotting doomsday scenarios or binging horror movies—sometimes simultaneously.

When not writing or daydreaming, you'll find her wandering through the British wilderness, coffee in hand, sunlight optional but strongly preferred.

Follow her on social media & sign up to her newsletter to stay up to date!